May Fair

MICHAEL ARLEN

By MICHAEL ARLEN

———

May Fair

BEING AN ENTERTAINMENT PURPORTING TO
REVEAL TO GENTLEFOLK THE REAL STATE
OF AFFAIRS EXISTING IN THE VERY HEART
OF LONDON DURING THE FIFTEENTH AND
SIXTEENTH YEARS OF THE REIGN OF
HIS MAJESTY KING GEORGE THE FIFTH:
TOGETHER WITH SUITABLE REFLEC-
TIONS ON THE LAST FOLLIES, MIS-
ADVENTURES AND GALANTERIES
OF THESE CHARMING PEOPLE BY

Michael   Arlen

NEW YORK
GEORGE H. DORAN COMPANY

CONTENTS

MAY FAIR

MAY FAIR

PROLOGUE

I

ONCE upon a time in London there was a young gentleman who had nothing better to do one afternoon, so what should he do but take a walk? Now he did not set out as one on pleasure bent, but with an air of determination that would have surprised his friends, saying between his teeth: "I have always heard that walking is good exercise. I will try a bit." However, he had not walked far before circumstances compelled him to abate his ardour, for it was an afternoon in July and quite warm for the time of the year.

Eastward our young gentleman strode, by Sloane Street, through Knightsbridge, across Hyde Park Corner, he strode even from Chelsea to Mayfair; for he was by way of being a writer and lived in Chelsea, whereas his people lived in Mayfair and understood nothing.

Now while we are about it we may as well add that the young writer's father was a baronet who had for some years been a perfect martyr to bankruptcy, and had called his son to him on this afternoon to impress upon him the fact that in

future he, the young writer's father, could not and
would not be a victim to his, the young writer's,
extravagances.   So much, then, for the young
writer's father; but with himself we must continue yet a while, although what this tale is really
about is a hand and a flower.

For that is what he chanced to see on the afternoon we tell of, a hand and a flower; and since
it was inconceivable that the hand could belong
to a man, so white and delicate it was, he put two
and two together and decided that it could only
belong to a lady.   Further, there was that about
the droop of the hand which fired him to think
of it as the hand of an unhappy heart.   While as
for the flower, it was scarlet, and of the sort that
anyone can buy at any florist's by just going in
and saying: "I want some carnations, please, but
not white ones, please, thank you, good-day."

Now the sun was so high and bright over London that day that the voices of Americans were
distinctly heard rising above the polished tumult
of the Berkeley Hotel, crying plaintively for ice;
and when at last our young writer came into Mayfair he was grateful for the cool quiet streets, but
being still at some discomfort from the effects of
the heat on his person, he thought to turn into
Mount Street Gardens and rest a while beneath
the trees.

This, however, he was not to do that afternoon;
for it chanced that he had not walked far towards
that pleasaunce when, at that point of the pretty
quarter of Mayfair where South Street becomes
North Street and Grosvenor Square is but a step
in the right direction, he was drawn to admire a

great house that stood in a walled garden. Quite
a country-house this looked like, and right in
the heart of the town, so that our young gentleman thought: "Now I wonder whose house that
is. Ah, to be rich! Or, at least, to be so attractive that rich people would take one to their hearts
on sight!"

In this wise relishing the deplorable charms of
money, he had stared long over the wall at the
house in the garden had not something happened
which instantly gave his fancies a prettier turn:
for what should he suddenly espy through the
curtain of leaves but a hand drooping from one
of the upper windows, and what should he espy
in the hand but a scarlet flower?

Now that made a delightful picture of innocence, of dreaming youth and fond imagining, and
not at all the sort of thing you see every day, especially in Mayfair, where motor-cars grow from
the cracks in the pavements and ladies recline in
slenderness on divans, playing with rosaries of
black pearls and eating scented macaroons out of
bowls of white jade.

Presently a policeman happened by, and the
young gentleman thought to turn from the wall
and greet him in a friendly way with a view to
further conversation.

"And what," he asked, "is the name of the
lady who lives in the house with the garden?"

"Young sir," said the policeman severely, "that
will do from you."

"I beg your pardon!" said the young writer
with spirit.

"Granted," said the policeman severely.

"But this is absurd! I am an honest man and I have asked you an honest question."

The policeman unbent his expression so far as to say, with a significant look at the great house in the walled garden: "Young sir," said he, "there danger lies for the likes of you. For the likes of her is not for the likes of you."

"Oh, nonsense!" cried our young gentleman. "This is a free country. This is not America!"

"Is it swearing at me you are?" said the policeman severely. "Now move on, young man, move on."

"I will not!" cried our hero.

"Well, I will!" said the policeman, and walked away, while the young gentleman turned away from this unsatisfactory conversation just in time, alas, to see the scarlet flower drop from the white fingers; and the hand was withdrawn.

Now such was the effect of the hand and the flower on the young writer's susceptible mind that he quite forgot to go and see his father, who thereupon cut him off with a shilling, which he sent to the young writer in the form of postage stamps. But the occasion was not without some profit, albeit of the spiritual sort, to the young man; for that very night he dreamed he was kissing that very hand, and who shall say that that was all he dreamed, for surely he is a sorry young man who cannot kiss more than a lady's hand in a dream.

II

The Court Chronicles of the Grand Duchy of Valeria report the following conversation as having taken place between the reigning Duke and his consort. That the conversation took place in London is undoubtedly due to the fact that the Royal Duke and his Duchess were at the time on a state visit to that capital, with a view to taking a turn around the Wembley Exhibition.

"We will give a ball," said His Highness the Hereditary Grand Duke of Valeria. "In fact, we must give a ball. And everyone in London will come to it."

"Why should they?" said Her Highness.

"Now try not to be disagreeable, my dear. I have no idea why they should, but I am positive they will. They always do."

"But, Frederick, what is the matter with you to-night? Why do you want to give a ball, since you cannot dance? Upon my word, if I danced like you I should be ill at the very idea of a ball! So be sensible, my love, and go to sleep again."

"Now try not to be unpleasant, Ethelberta. You do not seem to understand that people in our position *must* every now and then give a ball. That is undoubtedly what balls are for, that people in our position should give them. I have worked out the matter very carefully."

"Then you are quite wrong, my love. Balls are for something quite different. I assure you that I have also worked out the matter very carefully. Balls are for English people to give, Americans to pay for, and Argentines to dance at."

"Now try not to be tiresome, my dear. It will seem extremely peculiar in us not to give at least one ball while we are in London. The Diplomatic

Corps will not fail to remark our ill-timed economy. Do you forget that we are Royalty?"

"Fiddledidee!" said the Duchess.

"Now," said the Duke, "try not to be——"

"Bother Royalty!" said the Duchess. "I've
never got anything by being Royal except to be
treated like a village idiot all my life. And now
you want me to give a beastly ball, at which I
shall have to dance with a lot of clumsy Ambassadors. Frederick, I tell you here and now that I
will not give a ball. And if you want to know
my reasons for not giving a ball, they are, briefly,
as follows."

They followed.

"Whereas," said His Highness, "*my* reasons
for wishing to give this confounded ball are not
entirely social. Our daughter——"

"You are not going to pretend, my love, that
the happiness of our only daughter is influencing
you in the least! You will not dare to pretend
that, Frederick, considering that ever since we
have been in London you have kept the poor child
locked in her room."

"You know very well," said the Duke hotly,
"that we both decided that in the circumstances——"

"Well, I think it's most insanitary," said the
Duchess, "keeping the poor child locked in her
room day in and day out! In the end all that
will happen will be that she will lose her figure
and no one will marry her at all and *then* where
are we?"

"Ethelberta!" cried His Highness, leaping from
the bed and looking sternly down at her. "I did

not think you could carry levity so far. Woman, would you compromise with our honour and the honour of Valeria?"

"If there was any money in it, my love, I would of course ask your advice first, as you know so much more than I do about selling things. I really don't know where we would be now if you hadn't been so clever about our neutrality during the war. Now, my love, stop being silly and get back to bed. You look too ridiculous in those bright pink pyjamas. What the Lord-in-Waiting was doing to let you buy them I can't imagine!"

"Ethelberta," said His Highness sternly, "understand this! We are in England, at considerable expense——"

"Naturally, my love, if you will buy pyjamas like that!"

"——to avenge a mortal insult to our honour. Woman, would you have our innocent daughter be spurned by the villain who seduced her?"

"These are strong words!" said the Duchess.

"I feel strongly about it," said the Duke.

"And anyhow, she can't be as innocent as all that," said the Duchess thoughtfully, "now. I know girls. Oh, dear, what fun girls have!"

"Ethelberta, this English lord must die!"

"All English lords must die, my love, in due course. It is a law of nature. Now come back to bed."

"I have worked the matter out very carefully, and that is why I am giving this ball. We cannot kill this coward out-of-hand by hiring some low assassin, for he is, after all, a gentleman. And besides, in this confounded country," His High-

ness continued warmly, "you cannot fire a revolver without every policeman in the neighbourhood wanting to know why you did it. Therefore,
the ball."

"What, are you going to fire revolvers off at
our ball? My love, are you sure that will be quite
safe?"

"My idea is that the noise of the ball will
screen the rattle of musketry. For that purpose
I shall engage the most violent saxophone-player
in the country. I have already taken advice on
that point. The firing-party will, of course, be
in the garden. So now, Ethelberta, you understand why we must give this——"

"Oh, give your rotten ball!" said Her Highness
sleepily.

III

The red carpet stretched from the doors of
the great house in the walled garden to the broad
pavement where South Street meets North Street
and Grosvenor Square is but a step in the right
direction; and up the red carpet walked the
flower of England's quality and fashion and the
loftiest dignitaries of the Church and Press.
Came, too, all the circumstance of diplomacy and
the first among the burgesses. Decorations were
worn. Art and literature were represented only
by a painter with a beard who had forgotten to
wear a tie, a young reporter with a boil on his
neck, and a rugged novelist with a large circulation who liked hunting. Came, too, all the first
actors of the day, talking about themselves to

each other and thinking about each other to themselves. All the most intelligent young ladies of Society were present, murmuring hoarsely to each other: "One really cannot understand *how* one can come to a party when one might be reading a book by Maurice Baring." Footlight favourites by Royal Appointment. Astorias and his band of the Loyalty Club were engaged to play. The reception given to the honourable company in every way accorded with the ancient dignity of the Grand Duchy of Valeria. The guests passed between two lines of the Hussars of Death or Honour, brilliant in white uniforms with crimson facings, epaulettes of gold and cloaks of black gabardine lined with ermine, under the command of Baron Hugo von Müsselsaroffsir. Champagne by G. H. Mumm.

Not among the last to arrive was my lord Viscount Quorn, a young nobleman whose handsome looks and plausible address were fated to be as a snare and a delusion to those who were not immediately informed as to his disordered temperament and irregular habits. Yet, although many a pretty young lady had lived to regret with burning tears the confidence she had been persuaded to misplace in that young gallant's code of chivalry, not a man in England could be found to impugn my lord's honour; for was he not renowned from Ranelagh to Meadowbrook for his incomparable agility, did not Australian cricketers wince at the mere mention of the name of Quorn, and did any soldier present on the high occasion we tell of wear pinned across his breast braver emblems of gallantry in war?

With him to the Duke's ball came his boon companion, Mr. Woodhouse Adams, a gentleman whose claim to the regard of his familiars was based solidly on the fact that he knew a horse when he saw one; yet so great was his reserve that what he knew when he did not see a horse was a secret which Mr. Woodhouse Adams jealously guarded from even his most intimate friends. On this occasion, however, as they walked up the red carpet to the open doors of the house in the walled garden, Mr. Woodhouse Adams appeared to be unable to control a particular indignation, and presently spoke to the following effect:

"If you ask my opinion, Condor, I think you are putting your jaws into the lion's head."

"I gather," said Lord Quorn, whose nickname took the peculiar form of Condor for reasons which are quite foreign to this story, "that you mean I am putting my head into the lion's jaws. It may be so. But I tell you, Charles, that I am in love with this girl. At last, I am in love. And I am not going to miss the most slender chance of seeing her again—not to speak of my desire to take this unrivalled opportunity of paying my respects to her father with a view to a matrimonial entanglement."

"You're not going to do that!" incredulously cried his friend.

"Almost at once," said Lord Quorn.

"Gentlemen's Cloak-Room on the left," said a Hussar of Death or Honour.

"Am I speaking to milord Quorn?" asked a page bearing a salver of gold.

"You are, boy."

"Then I have the honour, milord, to be the bearer of a note to milord from my mistress, Her Select Highness the Princess Baba."

"Well, don't shout the glad news all over the Cloak-Room," said Mr. Woodhouse Adams.

"Go tell Her Highness," said my lord to the boy, "that I shall beg the honour of the first dance with her."

"Milord, I go!" said the page, and went.

"I don't like that boy," said Mr. Woodhouse Adams.

"This note," said Lord Quorn, "touches me very nearly."

"Good Lord, Condor, she doesn't want to borrow money from you already! Gad, my father was right when he told me on his death-bed never to have any financial dealings with Royalty. His exact words were: 'It takes four Greeks to get the better of a Jew, three Jews to deal with an Armenian, two Armenians to a Scot, and the whole damn lot together to withstand the shock of Royalty in search of real-estate.'"

"My friend, there is but a line in this letter, yet I would not exchange this one line for all the rhapsodies of the poets. For in this one line," sighed Lord Quorn, "the Princess Baba tells me that she loves me."

"No girl," gallantly admitted his friend, "can say fairer than that."

"It is certainly very encouraging," said my lord.

"Gentlemen's Cloak-Room to the right!" said a Hussar of Death or Honour.

"Thank you, we've been," said Mr. Woodhouse
Adams.

"This way, *messieurs!*" said Baron Hugo von
Müsselsaroffsir. "His Highness the Hereditary
Grand Duke of Valeria will receive you at the
head of the stairs."

At the head of the stairs, indeed, His Highness was receiving his guests with all the circumstance of Royalty. He held great state, this
puissant prince who had so notably enriched the
land of his fathers by an heroic neutrality
throughout the war. He wore the blue cordon
of the Order of Credit and, over his heart, the
Diamond Cross of Discretion. He said:

"How do you do, Lord Quorn?"

"Thank you, sir, I am very well," returned my
lord.

"And you, Mr. Woodhouse Eves?"

"Adams to you, sir," said that gentleman.
"But otherwise I am well, thank you."

"Lord Quorn," His Highness cordially continued, "I am really most pleased that you could
accept my invitation."

"You do me too much honour, sir. And may
I take it that your courtesy in selecting me for
an invitation for your probably enjoyable ball is
a sign of your gracious forgiveness?"

"You may, Lord Quorn."

"Then I have the honour, sir, to declare myself,
without any reserve whatsoever, to be your Highness's most obedient servant."

"And I, sir," said Mr. Woodhouse Adams.

"Gentlemen," said His Highness, "you are very
kind."

"Your condescension, sir, but points our crudity," protested my lord. "May I, however, further trespass on your indulgence by asking to be allowed to enroll myself as the humblest among your daughter's suitors?"

"We can talk this matter out more comfortably," said His Highness agreeably, "in my study. Ho, there! Ho, page!"

"*Altesse!*"

"Conduct milord Quorn and Mr. Woodhouse Eves to my study, and see to it that they have suitable refreshment. Lord Quorn, I will join you not a moment after I have received my guests."

"I'm not sure I like this study business," said Mr. Woodhouse Adams as they followed the page through many halls and corridors to a distant part of the house in the walled garden. They passed through marble halls radiant with slender columns and crystal fountains, through arcades flaming with flowers in vases of Venetian glass, beneath sombre tapestries of the chase after fabulous beasts, by tables of satinwood and cabinets of ebony, jade and pearl: until at last they were conducted to a quiet-seeming door, and were no sooner within than what appeared to be a regiment of Hussars of Death or Honour had pinioned their arms to their sides.

"This is outrage!" cried my lord with very cold eyes.

"Gentlemen, you are under arrest," said an officer with moustachios whose name the chronicler has unfortunately overlooked.

"We're under what?" cried Mr. Woodhouse Adams.

"And you will await His Highness's pleasure in this room," said the officer with moustachios, but he had no sooner spoken than the Duke entered, followed by a lean young officer with pitiless eyes.

"*Altesse!*" saluted the Hussars of Death or Honour.

Not so Lord Quorn. "Sir," cried he, "this is outrage and assault on the persons of King George's subjects. Do you forget that you are in England, sir?"

"Silence!" thundered the officer with moustachios.

"Silence be damned!" cried Mr. Woodhouse Adams. "Your Highness, what can this piracy mean? I wish to lodge a formal complaint."

"Sir, take it as lodged," said His Highness graciously, but it was with lowered brows that he turned to address my lord.

"Lord Quorn," said he, "it was my first intention to have you shot like a dog. But I have suffered myself to be dissuaded from consigning you to that ignominious fate at the intercession of this gentleman here. I present Captain Count Rupprecht Saxemünden von Maxe-Middengräfen."

"Oh, have a heart!" gasped Mr. Woodhouse Adams.

But Lord Quorn, being a much-travelled gentleman whose ears were hardened against the most surprising sounds, merely said: "How do you do?"

"Such information, sir, is not for scum!" snapped the lean young officer with the pitiless eyes.

"Were I to hit you once," said Lord Quorn gently, looking at him as though he smelt so bad that he could readily understand why the dustman had refused to remove him, "your mother would not know you. Were I to hit you twice, she would not want to. Think it over."

"Your differences will soon be arranged," sternly continued His Highness. "Count Rupprecht has very properly put before me certain reasons which give him an undoubted right to be the agent of your destruction. The course of this night, Lord Quorn, shall see you as a duellist. And I can only hope that you have some knowledge of swordsmanship, for Count Rupprecht Saxemünden von Maxe-Middengräfen is the first swordsman of Valeria.

"I may add, Lord Quorn, that his engagement to the Princess Baba will be formally announced immediately after your interment, which will take place in a corner of the garden. That is already arranged. Also your death will be accounted for to the authorities in a satisfactory way. Mr. Woodhouse Eves will, no doubt, act as your second. I will now leave you until such time as the ball is at its height, when there will be little chance of any of my guests being distracted by the ring of steel in the garden. *Au revoir*, milord. You will yet find that to deflower a maid is a dangerous sport. Count Rupprecht, your arm to the ball-room!"

"*Altesse!*" saluted the Hussars of Death or Honour.

"And what a mess!" sighed Mr. Woodhouse Adams.

"I'll have to kill that boy," said Lord Quorn thoughtfully.

IV

The dance was not yet at its most furious: the dowagers had scarcely begun nudging each other the better to point their *risqué* tales of the days of good King Edward: Cabinet Ministers had not long been exchanging doubtful Limericks with jaded dexterity: when the following events happened:

Anyone penetrating to a secluded conservatory leading from a corner of the ball-room might have espied a young lady sitting at her ease on a bench of cedarwood beneath the dusty and unbalanced-looking growth which is sold in civilised countries as a palm-tree. The languid young lady's air was that of one who is forlorn, of one who is sad, of one who is so bored, yet decidedly that of one who would not for worlds have her dolour interrupted by the general run of humanity, such as perspire without suavity and go poking their tedious noses into corners of ball-rooms, saying: "I say, will you dance? I say, do dance!" Woe and woe to such youths, for they shall instantly be answered by the magical words "Missing three" and their persons shall be enveloped in forgetfulness forever.

Secure in her solitude behind a screen of plants and flowers, our young lady had quite evaded the eye of even the most relentless dancer but for the whisper of her white dress through the leaves. It should further be noted that not one among

all the flowers in that flaming conservatory was
more beautiful than the flowers of Cartier, La-
cloche, Boucheron, and Janesich, which graced
the young lady's slender forearm in the guise of
bracelets of diamonds, emeralds, black onyx, pink
pearls and sapphires, all wrought upon platinum
in divers tender designs. Her throat was un-
adorned but for a double rope of pearls, while
two captive emeralds wept from the tips of her
ears. Her hair was tawny, and it glittered like
a swarm of bees. As for her eyes, they were
more than adequate to every occasion, men being
what they are.

But no sudden intruder could have been more
surprised to see the Princess Baba sitting alone
—for it was she—than was the Princess Baba
herself to see, by the merest hazard of a glance
over her shoulder, the curious phenomenon of
the hands, the feet and the person of a young
gentleman forcing himself into the premises
through one of the conservatory windows.

She said, sighed, cried: "Oh!"

The intruder said something denoting astonishment, confusion, and grief; while his appearance
was notably devoid of that air of calm which is
the mark of your perfect rogue or practising
philosopher.

"*Well!*" said the Princess Baba. "To come in
by the roof!"

"Sorry," said the young gentleman. "Sorry."

"Sir, what *can* this mean! It is not by saying
'sorry' that one is excused for housebreaking!"

"Madam," begged the youth, "won't you please
allow me to explain?"

"And he calls me 'madam'!" sighed the Princess Baba with vexation. "Now I ask you, young man, do I look like a 'madam'?"

He said: "You look divine. You are beautiful."

"Attractive I may be," said the young Princess, "but beautiful, no. For, look at it which way you like, I've got a turned-up nose."

"We are all as God made us," sighed the young gentleman.

"By no means," said the Princess Baba, "for some people are charming and some are not, and what does God know of charm? It is dreadful to lie awake at nights thinking that God lacks charm. Yet the word is never so much as mentioned in the Bible."

"As for the Bible," said the young gentleman, "it is nowadays the fashion among rich men to say that it makes the most delightful reading in the world. Perhaps one day I shall have the time to read it too. In the meanwhile, may I sit down?"

"But this is most unusual!" cried the young Princess. "To come to a ball through a window! May I ask, are you a burglar? You certainly do not look like a burglar. Explain yourself, sir!"

"I am a poor writer," quoth our young friend. We, of course, knew that. But the Princess Baba was surprised, protesting: "Oh, come, that *must* be nonsense! For, firstly, you are rather a dear, and so you can't be poor; and, secondly, you are quite well-dressed, and so you can't be a writer."

"Your nonsense suits my nonsense," said the young gentleman. "Thank you."

"Know, Sir Author, that I am the Princess Baba of Valeria."

He rose and knelt and said: "Princess! What have I done!"

"Rise, my friend. Men no longer need to kneel to Royalty."

"Princess, what shall I say! Oh, what have I done! How can I apologise for this intrusion!"

The young Princess cried: "Why, here is an idea! You might begin by kissing my hand. I assure you that that is quite usual. But oh, my friend, you must please not kiss my hand while you are kneeling! That will never, never do, for a man who is kneeling before a woman has her at a great disadvantage. Provided, of course, that the woman has a temperament. I am, unfortunately, full of temperament. My father is very worried about me."

"Princess, this is not the first time I have kissed your hand."

"Oh!" sighed the Princess Baba, and the young writer did his part like a man and a cavalier, whereupon she said: "You have a very pretty way of kissing a lady's hand, Sir Author. And I had been told it was a lost art in England!"

"All the arts were lost in England by our fathers, Princess. Youth is just rediscovering them."

"Young man," said the Princess severely, "do you think it quite wise to be so full of self-confidence as all that?"

"Princess, forgive me! But I am so poor that I have to be full of what costs me least."

"And may I ask what was that idiotic remark

you just made about this not being the first time
you have kissed my hand? Why, you had never
so much as set eyes on me until a moment ago!"

"I have kissed your hand in a dream," said
the young writer gravely, and then he told how
one afternoon he had seen her hand and in her
hand a flower, and how he had woven such a web
of romance about that hand and flower that he
had never a wink of sleep from night to night.

"But you *must* sleep!" cried the young Princess. "Oh, dear, and so you are miserable, too!
Ah, the misery of vain desire, and oh, the misery
of delight cut short! But you certainly must get
some sleep to-night. You can't be allowed to go
about kissing women's hands as prettily as you
do and getting no sleep for your pains. Now
wait here a few moments while I go and get you
some aspirin."

But the youth dissuaded her, asking her how
she could have the heart to put an aspirin between them when he had dared all the legal pen-
alties for trespass for the sake of speech with
her, nay, even for sight of her.

"Well, I think you are very bold," sighed she,
but he humbly protested that never was a man
less bold than he by ordinary, but that the fires
of chivalry had burned high in him at sight of
her hand at the window, for, said he, could any
but an unhappy heart sit with a hand drooping
out of a window on the only sunny afternoon of
an English summer?

"There is certainly something in that," said
the young Princess, and then she told him how
miserable she was and how miserable she must

always be, for her heart was engaged in a battle with superior odds. And she made him sit beside her on the bench of cedarwood, telling him of her father and mother and the gay Court of Valeria, "which is so gay," she said, "that some of the most respectable ladies of the Court are goaded into getting themselves divorced just for the sake of the peace and quiet of being *déclassée*."

And she told how it was to this Court that one fine day there came an English lord with the very best introductions and such very excellent white waist-coats for evening wear as were the envy of every cavalier in Valeria.

"Like this one of mine?" asked the young gentleman, for is he a proper man who will not belittle another by claiming an equal degree of eminence in the sartorial abyss?

"That is not the point," said the Princess Baba, "but the point is that my Lord Quorn, for such was my lover's name, was the handsomest man I ever saw, and I loved him and he loved me and I lost him and he lost me. That may seem a very reasonable combination of events to you, who are young and cynical, but to me it was a matter of the utmost wretchedness. My friend, know that this English lord had to fly for his life, for a jealous lady of the Court had gone to my parents saying he had seduced me."

"The liar!" cried our hero.

"Oh, it was quite true!" sighed the Princess Baba.

"The cad!" cried our hero.

"I can't agree with you," said the Princess

Baba. "I adore him. I adore him. I adore him. And, oh, I am so very unhappy!"

He rose and knelt and said: "Princess, mayn't I be of some use? Can't I help you? Please command me, for I would die for you."

"At this very moment," she sobbed, "he is very probably either dead or dying, for how can he hope to survive a duel with the best swordsman of Valeria, Captain Count Rupprecht Saxemünden von Maxe-Middengräfen?"

"It certainly does sound rather improbable," said the youth dismally.

"And when it is all over and my lover lies dead —ah, how can I even say it!—my betrothal to his murderer will be formally announced."

"What, you are actually to marry a man with a name like that!"

"Yes, isn't it dreadful!" sobbed the Princess Baba, whereupon the young gentleman rose and stood before her with respectful determination, saying that he for one could not bear the idea of her marrying Captain Count Rupprecht Godknöws-what von Whät-not, and would therefore do all in his power to preserve life in the person of Lord Quorn, since the same was so delightful to her.

"For even at the risk of your grave displeasure," said our hero, "I must tell you, Princess, that I like you frightfully and shall never again know delight but in your presence."

"Now you are making love to a breaking heart!" pitifully cried the Princess Baba. "So this is chivalry!"

"Princess," said he firmly, "I do but owe it

to myself to ask you to make a note of the fact
that I love you. And it is because I love you that
I will do all in my power to save Lord Quorn."

"But, my friend," said she with very wide eyes,
"however will you manage that?"

"I am just thinking, Princess. But shall we,
while I am thinking, dance?"

"What, you would have me dance while my
love lies bleeding? I had thought my confidence
was placed in a more understanding mind. Ah
listen, oh look!"

And with a cry the Princess tore aside the
flowers that screened the conservatory windows
and both looked down with eyes of horror on the
figures grouped in the garden below. Within,
the rout was at its height and the saxophone ever
raised its frightful cry to the glory of the gods of
Africa. Without, was silence and the ring of
steel.

"Oh, I can't bear it, but I *can't* bear it!"
sobbed the young Princess, holding a cry to her
lips with a handkerchief plaintive with scent.
The antagonists in the dark garden were plain
to see, the whiteness of their vests moving dimly
in the darkness; and the tall figure of Lord Quorn
was seen to be forced back against a tree-trunk,
so that there could be no doubt but that he must
presently be run through.

"Oh, have I to watch him die!" cried the young
Princess, and was suddenly made to stare incredulously at the youth beside her, for he had whispered in accents of triumph:

"By Heaven, I've got an idea, a marvellous
idea! You want to be happy, Princess? Then

come with me!   Come, we will dance through the
crowd to the door and then we will see about my
plan."

"But what is it, what is it, why do you keep me
in such suspense?   Ah, you are cruel!" sighed
the Princess Baba.   "But you certainly do dance
very well.   Oh, how I love dancing!   When I was
very young I used to dream that I would like to
be loved by a fairy prince with finger-nails of
lapis-lazuli, but lately I have dreamed that I
would like to be an exhibition-dancer in a night-
club.   But are you sure this is the nearest way
to the door?   It is so very crowded that I can't
see it, but how well you guide, almost as well as
you kiss a lady's hand!   But quick, quick, to
the door!"

"I am doing my best, Princess, guiding you
through this crowd.   It is amazing how generously
middle-aged people dance these days, denying
their elbows and feet to no one who comes near
them."

"But my lover dies—the door, the door!" cried
the Princess Baba.

"And by Heaven, through it!"

"And now your plan?"

"Ah, you may well ask!" laughed our hero.

v

The tall figure of Lord Quorn lay crumpled and
inert where he had fallen against the tree-trunk.
Only his eyes retained the magic gift of life, and
they looked upon the scene with sardonic resignation.   Who shall describe what thoughts then

passed through the dying gallant's mind? He was mortally wounded.

Count Rupprecht lay stretched on his back a few yards away, the grass about him soaked with the blood that flowed from his pierced lung. He was dead. Above him stood the Duke, silently. Mr. Woodhouse Adams was on his knees beside his dying friend.

"You got him, anyhow," said he. "He'll never know Christmas from Easter again."

"Fluke," sighed Lord Quorn. "I always had the luck."

"Luck, do you call it," cried his friend, "to be killed!"

"It is better to be killed than to die," said Lord Quorn faintly.

His Highness called grimly: "Ho, there! Ho, page!"

"*Altesse!*"

"Boy, go call my chaplain instantly."

"Pester me with no priests, sir, I beg you!" cried the wicked Lord Quorn. "I was born without one, I have lived without one, I have loved without one, and I can damn well die without one."

"Then has death no terrors for you, Lord Quorn?"

"Why, sir, I go to meet my Maker with the best heart in the world! I have lived a perfectly delightful life in the best possible way. Can Paradise show a more consummate achievement! Or must one have been bored to death in this world to win eternal life in the next?"

"Then, page," grimly said His Highness, "go

tell the Princess Baba the issue of the duel. Do not spare the truth. Count Rupprecht lies dead in defence of her honour and the honour of Valeria; and Lord Quorn will shortly be answering to God for his sins. And further tell the Princess that she is permitted to say farewell to her lover. Begone!"

"Thank you very much," sighed Lord Quorn.

But the page was not gone above a moment before he was returned, saying breathlessly:

"*Altesse*, I bear this message from the Platinum-Stick-in-Waiting. The Princess Baba was seen leaving the house a few minutes ago in a hired vehicle, and with her was a young gentleman with an unknown face and utterly devoid of decorations. Her Highness left word behind her with the attendant of the Gentlemen's Cloak-Room to the effect that she could so little bear to await the issue of a duel in which her heart was so deeply engaged that she had eloped with one who would understand her grief."

"Good!" sighed Lord Quorn into the livid silence.

"What's that you say!" snapped the Duke.

"I was merely thanking my God, sir, that I die at last convinced of the truth of what I have always suspected, that nothing in this world means anything at all."

"Except, of course, dogs and horses," said Mr. Woodhouse Adams, and that will do well enough for the end of the tale of the hand and the flower, which is called *Prologue* because nobody ever reads a Prologue and how can it be to anyone's advantage to sit out so improbable a tale without the accompaniment of a Viennese waltz?

As for our hero and his darling, there are, naturally, no words to describe the happiness they had in each other. It was not long, however, before the young writer ceased to be a writer, for there was no money in it; but with what his young wife made by selling the story of her elopement for to make a musical-comedy they opened a night-club in Golden Square called *Delight is my Middle Name* and lived happily ever after, the whilom Princess Baba making a great name for herself as a dancer, for she was all legs and no hips and her step was as light as her laughter and her laughter was as light as the breath of Eros.

In conclusion, may he who is still young enough and silly enough to have told this tale be some day found worthy to be vouchsafed that which will make him, too, live happily ever after in peace and good-will with his heart, his lady and his fellows; and may the like good fortune also befall such youths and maidens as, turning aside for a moment from the realities of life, shall read this book.

I: A ROMANCE IN OLD BRANDY

TALKING of dogs, no one will deny that dogs make the best, the dearest, and the most faithful companions in the world. No one will deny that even very small dogs have very large hearts. No one will deny that human beings are as but dirt beside dogs, even very small dogs. No one will deny that all dogs, large or small, are more acceptable to the Lord than foxes, rats or Dagoes. That is, if the Lord is a gentleman. No one can deny that. No one, anyhow, dares deny that. Let us be quite candid. A man who does not glory in the companionship of dogs is no fit mate for any woman. That is what Valerest said. A woman who glories in nothing else but the companionship of a dratted little beast with two unblinking black eyes is certainly no fit mate for any man. That is what Valentine thought.

Valentine and Valerest were sat at dinner. Valerest was the name of Valentine's wife, and she was a nice girl. A pretty maid waited on them. Valentine and Valerest were silent. The pretty maid left them.

Valerest said: "Any man who does not like dogs is no fit mate for a woman."

Valentine thought as above.

36

"I really don't see," said Valerest bitterly, "why you are so sulky this evening."

Sulky! Ye gods and little fishes, to be moved by a profound and sorrowful anger—and to be called 'sulky'! O God of words and phrases, O Arbiter of tempers and distempers, to sit in silent dignity and resignation—and to be called 'sulky'! Verily, what a petty thing one word can make of martyrdom! Wherefore Valentine raised his voice and said: "I am not sulky."

"Well," said Valerest, "you needn't shout."

Valentine said: "I never shout."

A situation was thus created. The pretty maid came in with the sweet in the middle of it. Valentine and Valerest were silent. Mr. Tuppy was not. Mr. Tuppy said "Yap!" Mr. Tuppy lay on a mouldy old cushion, and the mouldy old cushion lay on a chair, and the chair was beside Valerest. Dear Mr. Tuppy, sweet Mr. Tuppy! Tuppy was a Chinaman, Tuppy was a dog.

"The pretty darling, the mother's tiny tot!" sighed Valerest. "And does he want his dinner then, the mother's rabbit?"

"Yap!" said Mr. Tuppy.

"Isn't he a darling!" cried Valerest.

"Charming," said Valentine.

"Well," said Valerest, "you aren't very gay to-night, I do think!"

It could be asked, need Valerest have said that? Again, it could be asked, need Valerest have said that brightly? Valentine, at that moment, appeared to be engaged in spearing a boiled cherry, which formed part of a fruit-salad. It would not appear, therefore, that Valentine was engaged on

anything very important. Indeed, there will not
be wanting those to say that Valentine's attention might well have been diverted to something
more "worth while" (an American phrase meaning money) than even the most notable fruit-
salad. They will be wrong. For there is a time
in everyone's life when even the most homely
fruit-salad, even one unspiced with Kirsch or
liqueur, can be of such moment that everything
else must, for that time, go by the board. Therefore it must at once be apparent to even the most
impatient reader that *The Romance in Old
Brandy* must be delayed for at least another para-
graph while impartial enquiry is made into the
fruit-salad of Valentine Vernon Chambers.

Ever since he was so high Valentine would always eat a fruit-salad according to certain laws
of precedence. Not for worlds would he have
admitted it, but that is how it was. He liked the
chunks of pineapple best, so he kept the chunks
of pineapple to the last. Strawberries he liked
next best, if they weren't too sloppy, so they came
one but last. As for grapes in a fruit salad, they
are slippery and sour, and Valentine thought it
was no fit place for them. After strawberries, he
was partial to cherries. While first of all he would
demolish the inevitable bits of banana. Cream
he never took with a fruit-salad.

It will therefore be seen that, as he was then
only at the beginning of the cherry stratum, the
fruit-salad future of Valentine Vernon Chambers
was one of exceptional promise. But it was not
to be. Even as Valerest spoke, brightly, he
couldn't help but cast one furtive look at the

chunks of pineapple. Nor were the strawberries sloppy. But queer depths were moving in him that evening. From the chunks of pineapple he looked across the table at his wife, and Valerest saw that his blue eyes were dark, and she was afraid, but did she look afraid? Valerest, Oh, Valerest!

"Yap!" said Mr. Tuppy.

"There, there!" said Valerest, and she kissed Mr. Tuppy, and Mr. Tuppy loved it.

"By Heaven, that dog!" snapped Valentine.

Valerest said: "That's it! Vent your bad-temper on poor little Mr. Tuppy!"

Valentine looked at Valerest.

"I see," said Valentine quietly. Very quietly. "Oh, I see!"

And worse. Much worse. Very quietly.

"I suppose you think," said Valerest, "that because I'm your wife you can say anything you like to me. You're wrong."

"I think," said Valentine, "that because you're my wife you ought to behave like my wife. And I'm right."

And then he left the room. And then he left the house. And then the house was very still.

Valerest, sitting very straight in her chair, heard the front-door slam. She listened. Through the open window behind her came the sound of manly footsteps marching away down South Street. She listened. Away the footsteps marched, away. Then a taxi screamed, and the incident of the manly footsteps was closed forever.

"Well, that's that!" said Valerest.

"Yap!" said Mr. Tuppy.

"Mother's rabbit!" said Valerest absently.

"Mr. Tuppy," said Valerest suddenly, "this can't go on. You know, this can't go on."

"Yap!" said Mr. Tuppy.

"I'm not a chattel," said Valerest. "To be used just as a man likes. I will not be a chattel."

The pretty maid came in.

Valerest said: "Come along, Mr. Tuppy. I've got a headache. Bed."

II

Valentine walked. When he had been walking for some time he realised that he was achieving the impossible in combining an excess of motive power with a minimum of progress, for he found himself walking in a direction exactly opposed to that in which his destination lay. He corrected this, and presently stood before a house in Cadogan Gardens. The houses in Cadogan Gardens wear a gentle and sorrowful air, and Valentine grew more depressed than ever.

Now, years before, his guardian had said: "There may come a time, Valentine, when something happens to you about which you will think it impossible that anyone can advise you. But you may be wrong in thinking that. Try me then, if you care to."

Valentine's parents had died when he was very young, in one of those marvellously complete accidents arranged by any competent story-teller when he simply must deprive a child at one blow of a mother's love and a father's care. Valentine's

parents, however, had in some measure protested
against their simultaneous fate, and Valentine's
mother had lived long enough after the accident to
appoint Mr. Lapwing her boy's sole guardian.
Mr. Lapwing was the senior partner of the city
firm of Lapwing & Lancelot, merchants. And as,
quite apart from his regard for Valentine's parents, he was wealthy, a widower, and childless, it
can readily be understood that he eagerly accepted
the trust. Although when it is said that he accepted the trust it is not to be implied that Mr.
Lapwing tried to take a "father's place" with the
boy. Mr. Lapwing, like so many childless men,
knew all about his place with any boy. He was
without one theory as to education, but acted
merely on a vague idea that the relations between
parents and children, whether it was the Victorian one of shaming the joy out of children or
the Georgian one of encouraging the joy into vulgarity, had gotten the world into more trouble
than anything in history since the fall of Lucifer
from Paradise.

On this evening, twenty-four years after he had
first entered the house in Cadogan Gardens, Valentine stood quite a while before the door and
wondered how he was to put It. It, you understand, was very difficult to put. A disagreement
between a man and his wife remains indissolubly
a disagreement between a man and his wife, and
only a man or his wife may solve It. Indeed,
Valentine had already solved It. He detested
compromise. A divorce was, undoubtedly, indicated. Undoubtedly. So undoubtedly, indeed,
that Valentine would not have dreamed of putting

It to Mr. Lapwing at all had he not thought him-self bound in honour to ask his guardian's advice "when something happens to you about which you will think it impossible that anyone can advise you."

III

Mr. Lapwing was cracking a nut. He said gloomily:

"Hullo, Valentine! Did you ring up to say you were coming round? I didn't get the message."

"I came," said Valentine, "on an impulse."

Mr. Lapwing said: "I see. Well, sit down, sit down! I don't want you towering over me while I am trying to digest my food. Or is it one of those impulses you have to stand up to?"

Valentine said: "If you really want to know, I don't care if I never sit down again. But I will, if only to show how well you've brought me up."

"Now I don't want any cheek," said Mr. Lapwing.

"Cheek!" said Valentine, and he laughed, and the way he laughed caused Mr. Lapwing to look sharply up at him.

"Cheek!" said Valentine. "If you knew as much about cheek as I do, sir, you would think I was talking like a courtier."

"Oh, sit down, sit down!" said Mr. Lapwing.

Now a gentleman called Mr. Lapwing can neither need nor merit any further description. Mr. Lapwing looked in no way different from the way that a Mr. Lapwing should look. Thin, tiresome, bald, boring, gouty, gloomy. We see him for the first time at that end of his dinner when he would sit a while at the table and stare with conscious absent-mindedness into space, after the manner of any English gentleman who is not averse from a drop of old brandy after his meals. Mr. Lapwing's was an old-world palate, and he enjoyed above all things a drop of old brandy.

The dining-room of the house in Cadogan Gardens was large, austere, dim. From where Valentine sat at the oval polished table, in the light of the four candles which played in shadows about his guardian's thin lined face, the severe appointments of the room were as though seen through a dark mist. Mr. Lapwing was not only a connoisseur of polite stimulants but was known to many dealers as a formidable collector of Meryon's etchings; and the sombre fancies of the young Frenchman's genius peered at Valentine from the dim walls, as they might be old mocking friends uncertain of recognition.

Mr. Lapwing said gloomily: "Port, Valentine? Or Sherry?"

"Brandy," said Valentine.

"Drat the boy!" said Mr. Lapwing. "Fountain! Where are you, man? Oh, there you are! Give the boy some brandy."

Mr. Lapwing was old enough, but Fountain was older. From the dimness he emerged, to the dimness returned. Fountain was very old. Mr. Lapwing said: "Go away, Fountain. We don't want you. The brandy, Valentine, is at your elbow."

"Thank you," said Valentine.

"The difference between beer and brandy," said

Mr. Lapwing gloomily, "is that it is not unusual to pour out a full glass of beer, but it is damned unusual to take more than a drop of brandy at one time."

"Depends," said Valentine, "on the brandy."

Mr. Lapwing said sharply: "That is very fine brandy."

"Good!" said Valentine.

IV

Valentine at last made an end to the muttering noises with which he had tried to put before his guardian the state of acute disagreement that existed between himself and Valerest. Mr. Lapwing finished his brandy, rose from the table, and thoughtfully took a turn or two about the room.

"Well?" said Valentine.

"I," said Mr. Lapwing absently, "can tell you a much better story than that. Any day."

Valentine flushed. "I didn't tell you about this, sir, so that you should make a guy of me."

Mr. Lapwing said gloomily: "Keep your hair on. When I said that I could tell you a much better story than yours, I meant, naturally, that my story is complete, whereas yours, you will agree, is as yet far from complete."

Valentine muttered something about his being quite complete enough for him, but all Mr. Lapwing said sharply was: "Here, no more of that brandy! That brandy is too good to swim in. But if you want to get drunk, I will ring for some whisky."

"I don't want to get drunk," snapped Valentine.

"Good boy!" said Mr. Lapwing vaguely, and continued pacing up and down the dim, long room, while Valentine sat still and thought of his past life and found it rotten.

Suddenly Mr. Lapwing said, in that irritatingly exact way of his which was never quite exact: "You, Valentine, are twenty-nine years old. Valerest is twenty-two——"

"Four," said Valentine.

"Very well. And you have been married just over three years——"

"Nearly five," sighed Valentine.

"Very well. You, Valentine, want a child. Valerest, however, does not want a child just yet. Your argument is a sound one: that if parents wait too long before their children are born, by the time the children grow up the parents will be too old to share any of their interests and pleasures——"

"That's right," said Valentine sourly. "Valerest and I will be a pair of old dodderers by the time they're of age."

"Exactly. A very sound argument. Whereas Valerest——"

Valentine snapped: "She doesn't even trouble to argue. She just sits and grins!"

"Exactly. She is much too deeply in the wrong to argue. When nations are too deeply in the wrong to argue they call on God and go to war. When women are too deeply in the wrong to argue they sit and grin. And I daresay that the way you put your arguments gives Valerest plenty to sit and grin about."

"My God," said Valentine, "don't I try to be reasonable!"

"Listen," said Mr. Lapwing, and then he told Valentine that he had been married twice. Valentine was amazed. He had not known that.

Mr. Lapwing said: "I was very young when I married my first wife. Even younger than you, although even then I knew a good brandy from a poor one. And I was very much in love. As, if you will not think an old man too ridiculous, I am still. Of course, she is dead now."

Valentine was listening with only half a mind. He had still to get over his surprise that his guardian had been married twice. There are some men who look as though they simply could not have been married twice. They look as though one marriage would be, or had been, a very considerable feat for them. Mr. Lapwing looked decidedly like that: he looked, if you like, a widower: but decidedly not like a widower multiplied by two——

Mr. Lapwing was saying, from a dim, distant corner of the room: "In those days I was a very serious young man. I took love and marriage very seriously. And when we had been married a couple of years I discovered in myself a vehement desire to be a father: a natural enough desire in a very serious young man. My wife, however, was younger than I: she loved life, the life of the country and the town, of the day and of the night, of games and dances. You see what I mean?"

Valentine snapped: "Don't I!   Just like Valerest."

"Exactly. At first," said Mr. Lapwing, and his face as he slowly paced up and down the dim room would every now and then be quite lost in the shadows. "At first, I indulged her. To tell you the truth, I was very proud of her service at tennis, her handicap at golf. But there are limits."

"There are," said Valentine. "Valerest is already in training for Wimbledon next year, and I hope a tennis-ball gets up and shingles her eyelashes. And she's got to 6 at golf. Pretty good for a kid who looks as though she hadn't enough muscle to play a fast game of ludo. But that's right about there being limits. There *are* limits! And I've reached them."

"Exactly," agreed Mr. Lapwing's dim voice from the distance of the room. "I had reached them too, Valentine. And, I am afraid, I grew to be rather unpleasant in the home—as you, no doubt, are with Valerest. One's manner, you know, isn't sometimes the less unpleasant for being in the right."

Valentine said: "I don't know about pleasant or unpleasant. But a fellow must stick to his guns."

"Guns?" said Mr. Lapwing vaguely. "Were we talking of guns?"

"I merely said, sir, that one must stick to one's guns."

"Of course, yes! Decidedly one must stick to one's guns. Very proper. Well, Valentine, I too stuck to my guns. Like you, I thought they were good guns. My young wife and I grew to disagree quite violently about her preference for being out-and-about to rearing my children: until one day, after a more than usually fierce and childish argument, she left my house—this house, Valentine—and never came back."

From the shadowy distance Mr. Lapwing was looking thoughtfully at Valentine. But Valentine's eyes were engaged elsewhere: he was seeing a picture of Valerest stamping out of his house, never to come back. It was, Valentine saw, quite conceivable. He could see it happening. It was just the sort of thing Valerest might do, stamp out of the house and never come back. And the picture grew clearer before Valentine's eyes, and he stared the picture out.

"Well," he said at last, "that's the sort of thing that happens. It's got to happen."

Mr. Lapwing said: "Exactly." His face was in the shadow. Valentine, fiddling with a cigarette, still staring at the picture in his mind, went on:

"I mean, it's inevitable, isn't it? A man can't go on forever living in the same house with a woman who laughs at the—the—well, you know what I mean—at the most sacred things in him. And she's got a dog."

"I know," said Mr. Lapwing. "Mr. Tuppy. Nice little dog."

"Bloody little dog!" snapped Valentine. "Look here, sir, when things have got to the state they have with Valerest and me the crash has got to come. Just got to, that's all."

Mr. Lapwing said gloomily: "Of course, there's love."

Valentine thought profoundly about that.

"No!" snapped Valentine. "That's just where you are wrong, sir. There *was* love. Certainly. But they kill it. They just kill love. I mean, I know what I'm talking about. Some of these young women treat love as though it was a naughty little boy who should be made to stand in a corner except as a great treat once in six weeks. I've thought about this a lot lately. Valerest has just gone out of her way to kill my love."

"Sex," said Mr. Lapwing thoughtfully.

"Sex?" said Valentine.

"Sex," said Mr. Lapwing dimly. "Sex becomes very important when a man is—er—deprived of it. When he is—er—not deprived of it he becomes used to it, and it ceases to have any—er—importance at all. Women don't like that. Women——"

"Damn women!" snapped Valentine.

"Women," said Mr. Lapwing, "can be very tiresome. Wives can be intolerable. I have been married twice. England and America are strewn with good men suffering from their wives' virtues. It is damnable. When a woman is faithful to her husband she generally manages to take it out of him in some other way. The mere fact that she is faithful makes her think that she has a right to be, well, disagreeable. The faithful wife also considers that she has a right to indulge in disloyal moods——"

"Disloyal moods!" said Valentine thoughtfully. "That's good."

"Fidelity," said Mr. Lapwing, "can cause the

devil of a lot of trouble in the home, unless it is well managed. Fidelity needs just as much good management as infidelity. I am telling you this," said Mr. Lapwing, "because I think fidelity is beautiful and I hate to see it made a mess of. I draw from my own life, from my first marriage. I stuck firmly to those guns which you so aggressively brought into the conversation. A year or so went by. Then her parents approached me and suggested that we should come to some agreement, either to live together again or to arrange a divorce on the usual lines. They were good people. Their argument was that we were both too young to go on wasting our lives in this shilly-shally way.

"By this time, of course, the matter of my quarrel with my wife had faded into nothing. There remained only the enormous fact that we *had* quarrelled and that, since neither of us had tried to make the quarrel up, our love must obviously be dead.

"I referred her parents to her, saying I would do as she wished. She sent them back to me, saying she was quite indifferent. A divorce was then arranged by our lawyers; and I was divorced for failing to return to my wife on her petition for restitution of conjugal rights. The usual rubbish.

"To be brief, it was not long before I married again. But now I was older, wiser. I had tasted passion, I had loved: to find that passion was yet another among the confounded vanities that are perishable.

"Valentine, I married my second wife with an

eye to the mother of my children. I married sensibly. I have, as you know, a considerable property; and I continued to desire, above all things, an heir to my name and a companion for my middle years. That I have a companion now in you—and in Valerest—is due to the infinite grace of God: that I have not an heir to carry on my name is due to my own folly.

"My second wife was of that type of woman whom it is the fashion of our day to belittle as 'matronly,' but from whose good blood and fine quality is forged all that is best in great peoples. The difference between my affection for her and my passion for my first wife is not to be described in words: yet when she died in giving birth to a dead child you will easily understand how I was grieved almost beyond endurance—not only at the shattering of my hopes, but at the loss of a gracious lady and a dear companion.

"I was at a South Coast resort the summer after my second wife's death. One morning on the sands I struck up a great friendship with a jolly little boy of three, while his nurse was gossiping with some of her friends. Our friendship grew with each fine morning; and the nurse learnt to appreciate my approach as a relief for a time from her duties.

"You will already have seen, Valentine, the direction of my tale: the irony of my life must already be clear to you: nor can you have failed to see the pit of vain hopes that sometimes awaits those who stick to their guns. As my young friend and I sat talking one morning, or rather as he talked and I played with handfuls of sand thinking how gladly I had called him my son, he leapt up with a cry of joy; and presented me to his father and mother.

"My first wife had grown into a calm, beautiful woman. Yet even her poise could not quite withstand the surprise of our sudden meeting after so many years; and it was her husband who broke the tension, and won my deepest regard forever, by taking my hand. From that moment, Valentine, began for me, and I think for them both, and certainly for the boy, as rare and sweet a friendship as, I dare to say, is possible in this world.

"People like ourselves, Valentine, must, for decency, conform to certain laws of conduct. The love that my first wife and I rediscovered for each other was not, within our secret hearts, in our power to control: yet it did not need even a word or a sign from either of us to tell the other that our love must never, no matter in what solitudes we might meet, be expressed. Her husband was a good man, and had always understood that our divorce had not been due to any uncleanliness or cruelty but to what is called, I think, incompatibility of temperament. So that until she died soon after, the three of us were devoted friends and constant companions.

"And that," said Mr. Lapwing from the shadows, "is all my story. More or less."

Valentine sat very still. Mr. Lapwing paced up and down. Silence walked with him.

Valentine muttered. "I'm sorry. It's a dreadful story. Good Lord, yes! May I have some more brandy, please?"

"It's not," snapped Mr. Lapwing, "a dreadful story. It is a beautiful story. Help yourself."

"Well," said Valentine, "call it beautiful if you like. It's your story. But I should hate it to happen to me."

"There are," said Mr. Lapwing, "consolations."

Mr. Lapwing paced up and down.

"Consolations," said Mr. Lapwing.

Valentine said: "Oh, certainly. I suppose there always are consolations. All the same, I should hate to be done out of my son like that. For that's what it comes to."

Mr. Lapwing was in a distant corner of the room, his face a shadow among shadows. He said: "Exactly. That is why, Valentine Chambers, I said there are consolations. My wife's second husband was Lawrence Chambers."

Valentine said: "Oh!"

Mr. Lapwing touched him on the shoulder.

Valentine said: "Good Lord, I might have been your son!"

"You might," said Mr. Lapwing. "Easily. But it has come to almost the same thing in the end, hasn't it? Except, perhaps, that I have not a father's right to advise you."

Valentine said violently: "You've got every right in the world to advise me! Considering what you've done for me all my life!"

"Then," said Mr. Lapwing, "don't be an ass."

Valentine saw Valerest's mocking eyes, heard Valerest's mocking laugh, and about his mind walked Mr. Tuppy with his old, unsmiling eyes. He muttered: "But, look here, Valerest will just think I've given in!"

"So you have," said Mr. Lapwing.

"Well, then," said Valentine bitterly, "it will all——"

"She'll grow," said Mr. Lapwing. He was tired. "And, Valentine, she has got more right to be an ass than you have. Remember that. There's no use being sentimental about it, but they put up with a lot of pain, women. Remember that. And——"

"But look here," said Valentine, "if I——"

"Oh, go and make love to the girl!" snapped Mr. Lapwing. "And forget that a clergyman ever told you that she must obey you."

v

The state of Valentine's mind as he ascended the stairway of his house is best described by the word "pale." He felt pale. What made him feel pale was terror. It was past one o'clock in the morning. He had thundered out of the house at about half-past-eight. And the house was now as still as a cemetery. The conclusion, to Valentine, was obvious: the house was as still as a cemetery of love. He saw Valerest waiting, waiting, waiting for him to return: he heard the clock striking ten, eleven, midnight: he saw Valerest flush with a profound temper, hastily pack a few things and—stamp out of the house, never to come back!

Within the bedroom all was dark, silent. Very dark it was, very silent. Valentine stood just within the doorway, listening very intently. He could not hear Valerest breathing. There was no Valerest to hear.

"Oh, God!" cried Valentine.

"Yap!" said Mr. Tuppy.

"Oh, dear!" sighed Valerest from the darkness. "What do you want to go and wake me for when I have to be out riding at eight o'clock!"

Valentine said: "Valerest, thank Heaven you are here! I got such a shock."

"Here?" said Valerest. "Shock?"

Valentine switched on the lamp by the bed. It was Valerest's bed. Valentine's bed was in the dressing-room. That is called hygiene. Our grandfathers never knew about that.

Valerest stared up at him with sleepy bewilderment. Her curly hair was all over the place. Valentine made it worse by running his hands through it. Valerest said severely:

"Valentine, what are you talking about? Why shouldn't I be here? And where have you been all this time? Why do you look so pale? Have you been drinking? Why did you get a shock?"

Valentine said violently: "I love you, Valerest."

"Yap!" said Mr. Tuppy.

Valerest laid the tips of her fingers on his eyes, and she passed the tips of her fingers over his lips, and she said: "But I *hate* you!"

"You just wait!" said Valentine.

Valerest pulled at his ears with her fingers and defended her attitude with irresistible logic. She cried: "I don't want to love anyone! I don't want to love anyone! I don't want to love anyone! I want to be free!" And she bit his ear.

Now there are writers who would think nothing

of ending this chapter with a row of dots, *viz:*
. . . The author of this work, however, while
yielding to no one in his admiration of a dexterous
use of dots, cannot but think that the increasing
use of dots to express the possibilities of love has
become a public nuisance, and that the practice
should be discouraged by literary-subscribers as
dishonest, since what it really comes to is selling
a dud to readers just when they are expecting
something to happen. There are undoubtedly occasions, as when a writer is plumbing the bestial
abysses of illicit love, when a judicious sprinkling
of dots must be held to be proper, in the interests of decency and restraint. Yet even then it
is to be deplored that the exploitation of dots
so readily lends itself to the artfulness of suggestion. And the author of this work, which
is written throughout under the government of
marital virtue, cannot think that it is his part to
hold his pen while he asks himself whether he
shall dot or not dot. Has mankind, he asks himself, lived through all these æons of time only
to find now that it cannot serve the decencies
without the artificial aid of dots? Must, then,
our dumb friends be neglected, while we needs
must resort to these bloodless dots? For dogs
are infinitely superior to dots as a means of de-
scribing the indescribable. The writer is, of
course, referring particularly to Mr. Tuppy. Poor
Mr. Tuppy.

"Yap!" said Mr. Tuppy. "Yap, yap, yap,
yap!"

"What are you doing to Mr. Tuppy?" cried
Valerest.

"Nothing," said Valentine. "Only putting him out of the room."

"You've kicked him, you beast!" wailed Valerest.

"Only once, sweet," said Valentine; "for luck."

"I hate you!" she cried.

"I love you!" he whispered.

"Darling!" she sighed. "But remember I have to be out and riding at eight."

"This is no time to talk of dogs and horses!" cried Valentine, and Valerest was so surprised at such blasphemy that—Oh, well, dots.

VI

As Valentine left the house in Cadogan Gardens Fountain entered the dining-room. Fountain was very old. He had been kept up very late. He was tired. He drooped across the room.

"Shall I shut up now, sir?"

Mr. Lapwing said: "Yes, do. But just give me a drop of that brandy first, will you?"

"Yes, sir. The candles are burning low, sir. Shall I remove the shades?"

"Fountain!"

"Sir?"

"How long have you been with me?"

Fountain stared at his master. Very old, Fountain was. "Why, sir, I was with your father! I've known you ever since you was born—as you know as well as I do, sir, if I may say so."

"Ah! But did you ever know, Fountain, that

I had been married twice? And that my first wife had divorced me?"

Fountain lost patience. He said severely: "I never seen you like this before, sir. Not all these years. I don't know what you are talking about, that I don't. You married twice! Once was enough for you, sir, if you will permit an old man the liberty. And you divorced! I never heard of such a thing! I'd like to see the woman fit to divorce a Lapwing, that I would! I never heard of such a thing."

"Ah," said Mr. Lapwing. "Well, have it your own way, Fountain. But it made such a thundering good story that I was near believing it myself. All in a good cause, Fountain: to teach that boy a thing or two. One likes to see children happy, Fountain. And his mother won't mind, not she. A good sensible woman she was, if on the plain side. And, d'you remember, Fountain, she always wanted a drop of romance in her life? Well, she's got it now, poor dear. But her son will appreciate it for her, won't he? And just give me another drop of that brandy, will you? That's very fine brandy, that is."

"The bottle," said Fountain bitterly, "is empty, sir."

"Drat that boy!" said Mr. Lapwing. "Comes here looking for romance and laps up all my brandy!"

II: THE ACE OF CADS

I

THEY tell a tale of high romance and desperate villainy, how one night the dæmon of wickedness arose from the depths and faced his master Capel Maturin, the pretty gentleman whose exploits have made him known to all London by the engaging title of Beau Maturin, the ace of cads. The tale begins in bitter darkness and its direction is Piccadilly, not the shopkeeper's nor the wanton's Piccadilly but the sweet sulky side where the pavement trips arm-in-arm with the trees of the Green Park and men are wont to walk alone with the air of thinking upon their debts and horses and women. There and thus, they say, George Brummel walked, to the doom that awaits all single-hearted men, and Scrope Davies, that pleasant wit, Lord Alvanley, the gross, D'Orsay, the beautiful and damned, and latterly Beau Maturin, who was a very St. George for looks and as lost to grace as the wickedest imp in hell.

But here was no night for your *beau* to be abroad in, and a man had been tipsy indeed to have braved those inclement elements unless he must. Yet one there was, walking the Green Park side. Ever and often the east wind lashed the rain into piercing darts, as though intent to inflict with ultimate wretchedness the sodden bundles of humanity that may any night be seen lying one against the other beneath the railings of the Green Park. But the deuce was in it if the gentleman in question appeared to be in the least discommoded. His flimsy overcoat flung wide open and ever wider in paroxysms of outraged elegance by the crass wind, and showing an expanse of white shirt-front of that criss-cross *piqué* kind which is one of the happiest discoveries of this century, and his silk hat rammed over his right eyebrow as though to dare a tornado to embarrass it, he strode up from Hyde Park Corner at a pace which, while not actually leisurely, seemed to be the outward manifestation of an entire absence of interest in time, place, destination, man, God and the devil. Nor was there anything about this gentleman's face to deny this superlative indifference to interests temporal and divine; for, although that of a man still young enough, and possessed of attractions of a striking order, it showed only too plainly the haggard *blasé* marks of a wanton and dissipated life.

It was with such epithets, indeed, that the more austere among his friends had some time before finally disembarrassed themselves of the acquaintance of Capel Maturin. A penniless cadet of good family, Mr. Maturin, after a youth devoted to prophecy as to the relative swiftness of horses and to experiments into the real nature of wines, had in his middle thirties been left a fortune by an affectionate uncle who, poor man, had liked his looks; and Mr. Maturin was now engaged in considering whether three parts of a decade had been well spent in reducing that fortune, with no tangible results, to as invisible an item as, so Mr. Maturin vulgarly put it to himself, a pony on a profiteer. It was a question, thought Mr. Maturin, which could demand neither deep thought nor careful answering, insomuch as the answer was only too decidedly a lemon.

At a certain point on Piccadilly Mr. Maturin suddenly stayed his walk. What it was that made him do this we shall, maybe, never know, but stop he did. There were witnesses to the event: the same lying at Mr. Maturin's feet, huddled against the railings of the Green Park, a heap of sodden bundles with hidden faces; and it had wanted the attention of a physician or the like to decide which of the five or six was of the male or the female of the species.

"It's a cold night," said a husky voice.

Mr. Maturin, towering high into the night above the husky voice, agreed that it was a cold night.

"Ay, that it is!" said a woman's cracked voice. "Cold as Christian charity!"

Whereupon Mr. Maturin exhorted her to thank her stars that he was a pagan and, withdrawing his hand from an inner pocket, scattered some bank-notes over the bewildered wretches.

"Oh! Oh!" they cried, but caught them quickly enough, not grabbing nor pushing overmuch, for there was maybe a couple or so for each. And when, with the bank-notes tight and safe in their hands, they stared their wonder up at their mad benefactor, it was to find him staring moon-struck at a point far above their heads, while across his face was stamped a singular smile. It should be known that Beau Maturin had in his youth been a great reader of romantic literature, and now could not but smile at the picture of himself in an ancient situation, for is not the situation of a penniless spendthrift, with that of a man in love, among the most ancient in the world?

A policeman, his black cape shining in the rain like black armour, approached heavily: the august impersonality of the law informed for the moment with an air of interest that had a terrifying effect on the suddenly enriched wretches, for the law does not by ordinary recognise any close connection between a person with no visible means of support and the Bank of England.

"Good evening, sir," said the law to Mr. Maturin, who, returning the greeting somewhat absently, was about to continue his walk when an anxious voice from the ground whispered:

" 'Ere, sir, these are fivers, sir!"

"I beg your pardon?" said Mr. Maturin.

The law, meanwhile, had taken one of the banknotes from a reluctant hand and was examining it against the lamplight.

"These 'ere, sir," said the law impersonally, "are five-pun notes."

"True," said Mr. Maturin. "True. Lovely white angels of the devil. Good-night, constable."

"Good-night, sir," said the constable, replacing the bank-note into an eager hand; and Mr. Maturin, for long devoid of common sense, and now entirely devoid of money as well, continued his walk in the rain. His direction, or such direction as his feet appeared to have, led him towards the pillared arcade that protects the entrance of the Ritz Restaurant from the gross changes of London's climate; and it was as he strode under this arcade, his steps ringing sharply on the dry white stones, that it was distinctly brought to his notice that he was being followed.

He did not, however, turn his head or show any other sign of interest, merely dismissing his pursuer as an optimist. Mr. Maturin's, in point of fact, was a nature peculiarly lacking in any interest as to what might or might not at any moment be happening behind him; and one of his favourite *mots* had ever been, whether in discussion, distress or danger, "Well, my friends, let's face it!" There were, of course, not wanting those who ventured to doubt whether Beau Maturin had so readily faced "things" had he not had such a prepossessing face with which to conciliate them. "Ah," Mr. Maturin would say to such, "you're envious, let's face it."

On this occasion, so absorbed was he in absence of thought, he allowed himself to reach the corner of Arlington Street before swinging round to "face it."

"Well?" said Mr. Maturin.

" 'Ere!" said the other *sans* courtesy. "You do walk a pace, you do!"

"I am sorry," said Mr. Maturin. "What do you want?"

"Want!" said the other. "I like that! What do *I* want! Jerusalem!"

"If you want Jerusalem," said Mr. Maturin severely, "you should apply to the Zionist Society. They would be company for you. It must be very

depressing for a man of your size to go about
wanting Jerusalem all by yourself."

That the pursuer had no evil intentions, at least
to one of Mr. Maturin's stature, had instantly
been obvious. He was a small seedy-looking man
in a bowler-hat of some past civilisation: his
clothes sadly reflected the inclemencies of the
weather, but had the air of not being very valuable, while the coloring of his face was that of
one who had not in recent times suffered the delightful but perilous purification of water; and, as
he stood panting beneath our gentleman, his expression was one of such bitter disgust that Mr.
Maturin, being able to account for it only by the
continued action of acid foods on the liver,
thought it but right to advise him not to take so
much vinegar with his tinned salmon.

"Am I," snapped the small seedy man, "talking to Mr. Chapel Matcherin, or am I not?"

"More or less," Mr. Maturin could not but admit.

"Orl I knows is," snapped the small seedy man,
"that you was the gent pointed out to me as yer
left that club in Belgrave Square. Gent told me
to give yer this. 'Ere."

Mr. Maturin quickly opened the envelope,
which was addressed to his name, and drew from
it a folded sheet of note-paper and a folded bank-
note. The small seedy man looked bitterly surprised and hurt.

"Money!" he sighed. "Money! 'Ow I 'ate
money! And me carrying it abaht! I like that!
Me!"

"You're still here?" said Mr. Maturin.

"Still 'ere!" said the small seedy man. "I like that! Still 'ere! Me!"

But Mr. Maturin was giving his full attention to the note-paper, the while the folded bank-note depended tantalisingly from between the knuckles of two fingers. The small seedy man stared at it fascinated.

"If I'd *known!*" he sighed bitterly.

The letter addressed to Mr. Maturin ran thus:

"Enclosed Mr. Maturin will find a bank-note, which is in the nature of a present to him from the correspondent: who, if he was not misinformed, this night saw Mr. Maturin lose the last of his fortune at *chemin de fer.* Should Mr. Maturin's be a temperament that does not readily accept gifts from strangers, which the correspondent takes the liberty to doubt, he may give the bank-note to the bearer, who will no doubt be delighted with it. The correspondent merely wishes Mr. Maturin to know that the money, having once left his hands and come into contact with Mr. Maturin's, interests him no further. Nor are there any conditions whatsoever attached to this gift. But should Mr. Maturin retain some part of honour, which the correspondent takes the liberty to doubt, he may return service for service. In so remote a contingency Mr. Maturin will find a closed motor-car awaiting him near the flower-shop in Clarges Street."

Mr. Maturin thoughtfully tore the note into several parts and dropped them to the pavement. The folded bank-note he, very thoughtful indeed, put into an inner pocket.

" 'Ere!" whined the small seedy man.

"Tell me," said Mr. Maturin, "what manner of gentleman was the gent who gave you this?"

"Bigger than you!" snarled the small seedy man. "Blast 'im for an old capitalist, else my name isn't 'Iggins!"

"I am sorry your name is Higgins if you don't like it. But why," asked Mr. Maturin, "do you blast the gent who sent you after me?"

"I like that! Why hell! 'Ere he gives me two bob to go chasing after you to give you a bank-note! Two bob! You couldn't offer two bob for a bloater in Wapping without getting arrested for using indecent language. And you're so blarsted superior, you are, that you ain't even looked to see 'ow much it is!"

"Why, I had forgotten!" smiled Mr. Maturin, and, producing the bank-note, unfolded it. It was a Bank of England note for £1,000.

"It's not true!" gasped the small seedy man. "Oh, Gawd, it can't be true! And in my 'and all that time and me chasing orl up Piccadilly with it to *give* away!"

"Well, good-night," said Mr. Maturin. "And thank you."

" 'E thanks me!" gasped the small seedy man. " 'Ere, and ain't you even going to give me a little bit of somethink extra so's I'll remember this ewneek occasion?"

"I'm very afraid," said Mr. Maturin, feeling carefully in all his pockets, "that this note you have brought me is all I have. I am really very sorry. By the way, don't forget what I said about the salmon. And be very careful of what you drink. For what, let's face it, do they know of dyspepsia, who only Kia-Ora know?"

" 'Ere!" whined the small seedy man, but Mr. Maturin, crossing Piccadilly where the glare of an arc-lamp stamped the mire with a thousand yellow lights, was already lost in the shadow of the great walls of Devonshire House. In Clarges Street, near the corner, he came upon a long, closed car. The chauffeur, a boy, looked sleepily at him.

"I believe you have your directions," said Mr. Maturin.

"*And* I've had them for hours!" said the boy sleepily. A nice boy.

II

We live in a world of generalisations, which the wise never tire of telling the foolish to mistrust and with which the foolish never tire of pointing the failures of the wise. There is one, for instance, that lays it down that a bad conscience is a sorry bedfellow. Yet Mr. Maturin, whose conscience could not have been but in the blackest disorder, immediately went to sleep in the car: to awake only when, the car having stopped, the young chauffeur flung open the door of the tonneau and said:

"If you please, sir!"

Mr. Maturin found himself before the doors of a mansion of noble proportions. From the head of the broad steps he looked about him and recognised the long narrow park of trees as that of Eaton Square. A voice said:

"Come in, Mr. Maturin. A wretched night."

"Thank you," said Mr. Maturin. "It is."

Within, in a vast hall floored with black and white marble, he found himself faced by an old gentleman who, as the small seedy man had said, was even taller than himself. Mr. Maturin bowed. The tall old gentleman said:

"It is good of you to have come, Mr. Maturin. I thank you. I must confess, however, that I expected you would."

"It is a rare pleasure for me, Sir Guy, to do what is expected of me," smiled Mr. Maturin.

"You know me then! You recognised me to-night at your—your club?"

Mr. Maturin smiled at that. It was, let's face it, a low club. But, what with one thing and another, he had had to resign from all his others. He only said:

"Naturally. Who does not know you, Sir Guy!"

The deep old eyes seemed to pierce the younger man with a savage contempt. "In coming here to-night, Mr. Maturin," said old Sir Guy, "am I to understand that you are serious? You have, as you may know, something of a reputation for having made an art of misbehaviour."

Mr. Maturin delayed answering while he thoughtfully considered the ceiling of the great hall, which was so high as to refuse itself to exact scrutiny. At the gaming-club that night he had immediately recognised the formidable old gentleman; for the great lean height, the sabre-wound across the left cheek, the mass of loosely brushed white hair and the savage blue eyes under bushy white eyebrows, were the well-known marks of Sir Guy Conduit de Gramercy, a *seigneur* of a past century who made no secret of the fact that he disdained any part in this. For a passing moment Mr. Maturin had wondered what the proud old gentleman was doing in those depths; but now, revealed as the donor of the magnificent note, he could not but suspect what had brought Sir Guy down from his contemptuous seclusion. Sir Guy's descent, however, was far from pleasing to Beau Maturin, for it always offended that man as much to see pride humbled and the mighty fallen as to watch the lowly being exalted and the humble getting above themselves. Mr. Maturin was not a religious man; but he was decidedly one who had what he called "let's face it, a code of ethics."

"Why, I'm serious enough," said he at last. "I take your gift——"

"Ha!" snapped the old gentleman.

"In the spirit in which you give it, Sir Guy."

"And what the devil can you know of that, sir?"

"Nothing, nothing!" said Mr. Maturin peaceably, and without more ado old Sir Guy led the way into a wide, dim room lined with many books in rare bindings, for here was a small part of the famous de Gramercy library. From the shadows a lady emerged. Very beautiful this lady must have been in her youth, but she was no longer young and now a sad, gentle dignity was the flower of her personality, half hiding, while it half revealed, the lovely dead graces of her youth. It was plain to see, however, that she was not in her best looks this night, for her eyes were as though strained with some pitiless anxiety; and, distantly acknowledging Mr. Maturin's bow, she retired again into the shadows of the room, for it is only in the East that vanity dies with youth.

Said old Sir Guy: "I believe you have met my daughter-in-law. She and my granddaughter are staying with me for a few days."

From her shadows Mrs. de Gramercy spoke swiftly, almost breathlessly, as though she would at all costs and quickly be done with something she must say:

"Mr. Maturin, I have tried my best to dissuade Sir Guy from taking this step. I feel there *must* be a way of effecting our—our wish other than one which must offend you so deeply——"

The voice of the old gentleman fell like a bar of iron across the poor lady's swift light speech. "Eleanour, you will kindly leave this to me, as you promised. And Mr. Maturin is, I fancy, past taking offence at the truth."

"That depends on the truth," said Mr. Maturin in a reasonable way. "So far, I am quite mystified."

"You lie, Mr. Maturin. You are not mystified."

"Very well, sir. I lie. I am not mystified."

Said Mrs. de Gramercy in distress: "I think, then, I will leave you, since I can do nothing——"

"You will kindly stay, Eleanour. Surely you see that the occasion needs the authority of your presence!"

"Yes, please stay, Mrs. de Gramercy," Mr.

Maturin begged. "For if I am called a liar by my host while you are present, Heaven only knows what I may not be called when you are gone. Please stay. And, if I may, I would like to congratulate you on a very beautiful and talented daughter."

Quivering with passion, the gigantic old man raised an arm. Mr. Maturin did not move. He was lazy, and disliked moving.

"Mr. Maturin," the old man whispered just audibly, "you are an unbelievable cad! You are the—sir, you are the ace of cads!"

"Father, *please!*" the lady begged from the shadows, but in return Mr. Maturin begged her not to be distressed, protesting that the insult was not so pointed as it first appeared, whereas it would certainly be provoking to be called the deuce of cads, which in the degree of degradations must take a place near that of being run over by a Ford car. "But please continue, Sir Guy. Your last words were that I am the ace of cads. I would beg you not be constrained by any such small consideration as my presence in your house."

"Sit down, sit down," said a *hidalgo* to a hound, but it was Sir Guy himself who sat down, while the other remained standing before the fireplace. Mr. Maturin, for all his forty odd years of self-indulgence, had still a very good figure, and he liked to be seen at his best. He has, in point of fact, the best figure of any man in this book, and should therefore be treated with some respect. Mrs. de Gramercy, a shadow of distress, sat in a deep chair away in the dimness of the room.

And the thousands of books around the oak walls
lent a fictitious air of dignity to an occasion
which must have embarrassed any but a *grand
seigneur* and an ace of cads. Sir Guy, with a
perceptible effort at calm, addressed Mr. Maturin:

"As you may have gathered, sir, I want you to
do me a service——"

"Only a great brain like mine could have di-
vined it, sir."

"Mr. Maturin, would you not provoke my
father-in-law!" spoke the lady sharply, and was
as sharply told:

"This is men's business, Eleanour. Now, sir!
My son, this lady's husband, was killed in the
war, as you may know. The best men *were*
killed, Mr. Maturin. Fate is not very generous
to fine men in time of war. You, I believe, were
years ago cashiered from the Brigade for drunk-
enness in a restaurant?"

"I assure you, sir, that the provocation was
more than I could bear," Mr. Maturin explained
with a gravity becoming in one faced by such a
misdeed. "I am, you must know, very musical.
Perhaps you would hardly think it, but I undoubtedly have a musical *flair*. And in that wretched
restaurant the orchestra would insist on playing
Mendelssohn's *Spring Song!* Now I put it to
you, Sir Guy—and to you, Mrs. de Gramercy, if
I may—could a man bear Mendelssohn's *Spring
Song* over dinner? Yet I bore myself with a
fortitude which some of my lighter friends have
since been kind enough to think remarkable. I
begged the conductor to cease, once, twice, and
thrice; and then, you know, I wasted a bottle of

wine over his head. I was hasty, let's face it. But the provocation!"

Dimly spoke Mrs. de Gramercy from the shadows:

"Father, I believe Mr. Maturin has a D.S.O. with a bar."

"Mr. Maturin," the old gentleman said, "I apologise if I have seemed to reflect, at all on your courage. Such men as you are, I believe, frequently very courageous——"

"Only when drunk, Sir Guy. In which such men as I are very much the same as other men. Were you, may I ask, ever in a trench before an attack?"

"My fighting days were over before Omdurman, sir——"

"Oh, dear, dashing Omdurman! Illustrations by R. Caton Woodville! You will agree with me that one didn't need the stimulus of alcohol to turn machine-guns on to a lot of septic-looking niggers without even a water-pistol between them, even though they were devils with assegais, darts, catapults or boomerangs. But the Germans needed fighting. I remember——"

"That will do, Mr. Maturin. Your modesty takes as singular a form as your manners. My son, I was saying, was killed in the war, and his son and daughter were left to the charge of their mother. My grandchildren, Mr. Maturin— heirs to an ancient name and a fortune which must, by decent people, be taken as a responsibility rather than as a means for self-indulgence. I have never agreed with that principle of privilege which demands respect for ancient lineage and great fortune: such things alone are merely baubles; and without the dignity of some office and the ardour of some responsibility they can be of no value, but rather of grave detriment, to serious minds."

"Oh, quite," said Mr. Maturin.

"I wished my grandchildren to be brought up to a lofty conception of the duties of their station. My son had, quite rightly, a great regard for the strength and good-sense of his wife, and left her as their sole guardian. I, who have a no less regard for my daughter-in-law, was content with the situation; and, with my mind at rest, continued to lead the very retired life to which my years entitle me, even had I been able to endure the manners of a generation of which, Mr. Maturin, you are such a polished example. Thus, it was only lately that I heard of my grandson's folly. My grandson, Mr. Maturin! Or must I call upon you to strain your imagination before you can realise that there are still some men in this world to whom the honour of their name is dear!

"I was as displeased as I was surprised when I heard that my daughter-in-law had lately met you at a ball at Lady Carnal's. The Carnals of my day were more discreet in their introductions. In my day, sir, such fine gentlemen as you were not so easily enabled to corrupt youth by your companionship. Such men as you, sir, used not to be received in decent houses. Nor had good people yet become inured to the habit of going to balls in the houses of *parvenu* Americans and grotesquely rich Jews, to mix with bankrupts, card-

sharpers, notorious adulterers and Socialist poli-
ticians. In some such house you must have met
my grandson; and, Mr. Maturin, I must grant
you the quality of attraction, little though I myself may be privileged to feel it, for with your
good looks and casual airs you seem to taint every
child you meet. You corrupted my grandson,
Mr. Maturin! You flattered him by treating him
as a grown man, you taught him to gamble, to
dissipate, and, worst of all, to think uncleanly.
Both my grandson and my granddaughter, as you
were aware, have fortunes of their own from their
mother's father—and by God, sir, you played the
devil with that wretched boy's money, didn't
you!"

"Why," Mr. Maturin smiled, "the boy *enjoyed*
money for the first time in his life! Until he
met me, Sir Guy, he had only worried about what
he was going to do with it."

"And did he, Mr. Maturin, *enjoy* the money
he lost to you at cards? It is not for nothing, I
have gathered, that you are spoken of as the best
picquet player in London. That wretched boy
would, I am sure, give you a certificate——"

"I should be even better pleased, Sir Guy, with
a cheque for what he owes me."

"You shall have it. Eleanour, my cheque-
book! A flower in hell, Mr. Maturin, would not
be more lonely than a debt of honour on your
person."

"Quite," said Mr. Maturin, thoughtfully fold-
ing the cheque. "Thank you very much."

"I have dealt with the boy," old Sir Guy went
on in a low voice, "as you are no doubt aware;

and he is now expiating his folly and, I hope, regaining his health and self-respect, with some hard work on my Canadian property. At our last meeting he defended you to me. He remained, you understand, a gentleman even after his connection with you, and he couldn't but speak up for one who had been his friend."

"He was a good boy," said Mr. Maturin softly. "I liked that boy."

Sir Guy rose to his full lean height. The two men faced one another. "Mr. Maturin," the old gentleman said, "you have corrupted my grandson. You have plundered the best years of his life. Have you anything to say?"

Mr. Maturin said: "If you don't mind, sir, I will reserve my defence. Isn't there still worse to come?"

Sir Guy stared, as though he was seeing him for the first time, at the elegant figure who stood with his back to the fire, warming his hands. The savage old man was, so far as it was possible for him to be, nonplussed. Always a great reader of those memoirs and *belles-lettres* that tell intimately of the lives of gentlemen of more careless and debonair times, the anatomy of *galanterie*, scoundrelism and coxcombry, as exemplified in the Restoration gallants and the eighteenth-century fops, had interested old Sir Guy's leisure; but never had he thought he would be faced by one so completely unashamed, so bad, by one who could wear the evil *dandysme* of his soul as nonchalantly as a monocle. Sir Guy again sat himself at his long, burdened writing-table and played thoughtfully with a paper-knife. For the first time in his life he was faced with the humiliation of not knowing what to do: for here before him was a man, an incredible man, to whom such ancient words as honour, loyalty, betrayal, were without meaning. Beau Maturin would take such words, distort them with a slanting smile, put false feet to them, and send them tripping away on the wings of a merry laugh. Merry, for what could shame such a man from his gaiety? And Sir Guy realised now that he had made a mistake in sending Capel Maturin the bank-note. He had sent it to arouse the man's curiosity, thus to ensure his presence at this interview, from which the old gentleman still, though grimly, expected the best issue; but, more particularly, he had sent that bank-note as an earnest of what he might be prepared to do for Mr. Maturin if he would help the de Gramercys to bring about that blessed issue. But now Sir Guy realised his false step. A thousand pounds more or less did not matter very much to him; but did they matter so very much, he could now reflect, to that pretty, penniless gentleman? Money, to be sure, could not be of the first importance to so complete a cad as Capel Maturin: he had spent his own considerable fortune quickly enough, and, they said, generously enough: it must, thought Sir Guy, be the little cads to whom money really appealed.

The old gentleman's voice, when he continued, was more subdued, less proud. And has it not been already remarked that Mr. Maturin did not like to see the descent from pride to humility? which, had he had any part of virtue, he should have taken for a sign of grace, even as it is written in the Scriptures. But maybe he did not notice the slight tremor that played in that proud old voice before it could be subdued, for at the moment he was intent on examining his patent-leather shoes, which were exquisite examples of Lobb's later manner.

Sir Guy was saying: "My grandson, you corrupted. My granddaughter, you have sed——"

"Dear!" cried Mrs. de Gramercy.

Mr. Maturin was quite silent, examining his shoes.

"Perhaps that was too harsh a word," the old gentleman conceded—he conceded!

"It was," said Beau Maturin softly. "Much."

Now Sir Guy's voice was so low as to be barely audible, while his eyes were as though enchanted by the monogram on his paper-knife.

"I was carried beyond my intention, Mr. Maturin. I apologise, to you and to the child's mother. But I have had a day that I would not wish for my bitterest enemy. I am very old, Mr. Maturin. Peace, comfort, heart's ease, have lately assumed an importance which only a few years ago I would have disdained to allow them. Was it essential to you, Capel Maturin, to pilfer my granddaughter from me?"

"But why do you say 'pilfer,' sir? Am I not allowed to be like any other man, to make love?"

"Men," said old Sir Guy, "did not, I thought, make love to young girls. Bankrupts, I am sure, should not. And a man who has been a corespondent in two notorious divorce cases—he *cannot!* Mr. Maturin, it is not that I wish to insult you wantonly, but——"

"I quite understand, Sir Guy. Let us, after all, face the facts."

"Yes. My granddaughter has just come of age —and, incidentally, into her fortune. You, I believe, are forty or so——"

"Ah, those confounded facts! Forty-seven."

"I must say they become you very lightly. But, even so, there is a grave disparity of age between you and the child; and, Mr. Maturin, there is an even graver disparity of everything else. By Heaven, man, how could you, how could any man like you, have so blinded yourself to all the decencies of life as to put yourself in the way of a girl like my granddaughter!"

"I'm positively damned if I know!" murmured Mr. Maturin. "But these things happen. They just happen, Sir Guy."

Sir Guy at last looked up from the shine of the paper-knife; and pressing down with his knuckles on the writing-table as though to steady himself, said: "Mr. Maturin, to-day I have had the greatest shock of my life. My granddaughter told me she was going to marry you."

"A brave girl!" said Mr. Maturin softly.

The old gentleman's voice trembled. "Man, you cannot be serious!"

"I can be in love!" said Mr. Maturin coldly.

"Love!" cried the lady in the shadows.

"More," said Mr. Maturin, "I can love. I did not know that until quite lately. I did not know that when I was young. I get quite rhetorical when I think of it. I did not know, Sir Guy, of this beautiful thing lying in wait for me, Capel

Maturin—to love, without fear, without shame, even without hope, without desire——"

"Without desire!" cried Mrs. de Gramercy. "Mr. Maturin, aren't you exalting yourself?"

Mr. Maturin suddenly looked old and very tired. He said: "I did not speak the exact truth a moment ago. I knew when I was young that I could love. I suspected it. I have awaited the moment for many years. Of course, I have had to kill time meanwhile. I must inform you, Sir Guy, that when I was born a sunflower looked over a wall in Elm Park Gardens. All the gardeners in the neighbourhood were astounded. No sunflower has ever before looked over a wall in Elm Park Gardens. It could only have meant that I would love—one day. And the day has come, I love."

Sir Guy said: "You blaspheming *poseur!*"

"I beg your pardon," said Mr. Maturin, "for speaking the truth about myself. People are not used to hearing others speak the truth about themselves. It shall not occur again."

The voice of Mrs. de Gramercy rose bitterly from the shadows: "Love! What, dear Heaven, do you mean by 'love,' Mr. Maturin?"

"Love," said Mr. Maturin, "is one of the few diseases of the liver which cannot be cured by temperance or an apple a day. That is merely a suggestion."

"A vile one!" said old Sir Guy.

"Sorry," sighed Mr. Maturin.

"Mr. Maturin," cried Mrs. de Gramercy, "how dare you, you of all men, talk so glibly of love! For you were right just now, when you spoke in jest. For men like you love is no more than a fine word for a physical distemper."

"Mental," said Mr. Maturin. "Quite mental, I assure you."

"It's a passing mood, it doesn't last! Oh, the lives that have been crucified in the name of love! And now you would crucify my little Joan's!"

Sir Guy said with savage calm: "Come, come, Eleanour, not so dramatic! You will make the man shy. Mr. Maturin," Sir Guy went on with a perceptible effort, "I cannot stop the girl from marrying, as you know. She came of age to-day, and from to-day has her own fortune. But, man, is there no way in which we can appeal to your —your generosity! I pay you the compliment of thinking that you are not intending to marry Joan primarily for her money. Am I right?"

"I don't know. You see," Mr. Maturin rose to explain seriously, "these things get awfully entangled. To-night, as you saw, the cards ran very badly against me. And as I came away from the place I was so annoyed with myself that I emptied my pockets of the last penny I had. I was intending to begin life entirely afresh from to-morrow. With your daughter, madam, if I may say so. For I am like any other Englishman, Sir Guy, very sentimental about money when I haven't any and not in the least romantic about it when I have. And so I thought I wouldn't bring the taint of what money I had to my life with Joan. You must allow me, Sir Guy, and you, Mrs. de Gramercy, to respect and love Joan."

"And I almost believe you do!" said Sir Guy

savagely. "After your fashion. But fashions
change, Mr. Maturin."

"And so do the moon, the stars, the clouds and
dancing; yet, let's face it, they are eternal and
everlasting. Sir Guy, I would wish to marry your
granddaughter if she were penniless. Why should
I not marry her because she is not penniless?
What is this spurious humbug about honour that
covers the middle and upper classes of England
like verdigris: that a poor man may not with
honour marry a rich woman, that a poor girl can
only "sell" herself to a rich man? Can a man
or woman not be loved, then, because he or she is
rich? Is that what our religion means when it
says that a rich man shall not enter the kingdom
of heaven? Was it for that, then, that the late
Charles Garvice devoted his life?"

"A moment!" Sir Guy begged wearily. "I am
to understand from this rigmarole that you hold
Joan to her promise?"

"Mr. Maturin, please!" sighed, as though in-
voluntarily, the voice from the shadows.

Mr. Maturin lit another cigarette and inhaled
it. "Wasn't Joan," he asked, "at all swayed by
your arguments against me? They must have
been cogent enough, I fancy."

"Like the boy," Sir Guy said with sudden gentleness, "she defended you. You have some magic
for youth, it seems. They admit your faults, but
do not hold them against your character. But I
have observed that it takes grown-up people to
condemn caddishness. Children will overlook it."

"True," said Mr. Maturin. "You see, Sir Guy,
children like people for what they are, not for

what they do." He turned to the dim lady. "I fancy," he said, "that you have both got hold of the wrong end of the stick. I mean, don't you see, that it's not really much use persuading me to give Joan up. I mean, it wouldn't be much use if I did."

"How, sir!"

"Mr. Maturin, I don't quite understand."

"Well, let's face it, we must persuade her to give me up. Otherwise," said Mr. Maturin with an air of conviction, "if I were to break my promise to her she would guess that it was at your persuasion—you might indeed insinuate that you had paid me off, but she wouldn't believe it—and you would be faced for the rest of your days by an accusing girl. And that would be beastly for you."

There was a heavy silence: which fled sharply before a rattle when old Sir Guy, with a gesture of distaste, flung his paper-knife on to the table.

"Do I understand you to be caring for my old age, Mr. Maturin?"

"Neither your youth nor your old age are of any interest for me, sir. I am merely suggesting that if I were to give up Joan without her consent she would make a martyr of herself. Her very name will encourage the idea. Mrs. de Gramercy, I am sure you understand me."

"But," the lady cried gladly, "does this mean that you *will* give Joan up? Father, I knew he would. Oh, I knew!"

Mr. Maturin said quickly: "You have misunderstood me. I will not give Joan up."

"Bah!" snapped Sir Guy.

"But," said Mr. Maturin.

"Bah!" snapped Sir Guy.

"*But,*" said Mr. Maturin, "I will persuade Joan to give me up."

"Oh, thank God, thank God!" breathed the mother.

"For," said Mr. Maturin, "it is, as you say, a deplorable connection. I see that. Besides, when the sunflower looked over the wall in Elm Park Gardens nothing was said about my being loved, only that I should love. And how much more fitting, Sir Guy, for a lady to disown a cad than for a cad to disown a lady! Let us be reasonable."

The taut old gentleman seemed almost to smile. "You are a dangerous comedian, Mr. Maturin. And how will you effect this *finesse?*"

"Is Joan awake? Splendid! The practice of love grows easier every moment. You ought to try it, Sir Guy. Do you mind if I now make a small speech? It is about girls. Girls are by nature hero-worshippers. When they are not they dress badly and write novels. There is, however, some nonsense abroad to the effect that there is a 'modern' girl. How one detests the word 'modern!' Disbelieve in the existence of the 'modern' girl, Sir Guy. Girlhood is an ancient situation, is exalted by ancient joys, suffers ancient sorrows, reacts to ancient words. There is no modern girl except on the tongues of certain silly people who find an outlet for their own lewdness by ascribing it to other people."

"And what is the point of all this, sir?"

"It is that no girl, Sir Guy, ancient or modern or what-not, will cease to love a man because of any of the ordinary accusations you can bring against him. There is only one which will destroy her love. You may call her man a cad, and she will smile, and if you repeat it she will get bored. He may be a burglar, but she won't cease to love him, for is not the world a den of thieves? A poisoner, and she may still love him, for are there not many whom it would be good to poison? A coward, and she may not despise him, for girls are not necessarily fools and brave men can make uncommonly dull lovers. A cardsharper, and she may excuse him, for does not God Himself play with loaded dice? But verily, I say unto you, prove that man guilty of a deep disloyalty and at that moment her love will be as distant as your youth, Sir Guy, and as dead as mine; for disloyalty is the only bedfellow love will certainly reject. Will you call your daughter in, Mrs. de Gramercy, and I will tell her a story? Perhaps it will interest you, too."

"Call her, Eleanour," said old Sir Guy. "I fancy Mr. Maturin will have no difficulty in persuading her of his ineligibility on those grounds."

"True," said Mr. Maturin. "True."

III

Now, at last, the occasion is complete, the parts of the comedy all filled: the persons of the play bear themselves with becoming suspense: and the scene is richly set with age, dignity, devilry and youth, one and all essential to the true spirit of comedy.

The grandeur of distress, the lofty silence of disdain—there is the girl's mother in her shadowed chair and Sir Guy Conduit de Gramercy at his writing-table, the light of the shaded lamp by his elbow laying a rich gloss on his thick white hair. The indifference that masks the depths of emotion, the faint mockery, the deep gravity, and the cunning candour of love——there is Joan de Gramercy coiled in a chair near her mother, a girl with those cool eyes that dare a man to surprise in them any secret that they will not, in their own good time, completely surrender to him.

Mr. Maturin, handsome Beau Maturin, is talking. He generally is. A talkative man, let's face it.

"Joan," he addressed the girl's eyes, "your mother and your grandfather have objected to our engagement. We guessed they would, you remember? Just lately, in fact, we've been guessing nothing else. Unfortunately for their authority, however, they are not in a position to prevent it. Now, Joan, we have had quite a long conversation in here, a little about you, but considerably more about me. That I am as God made me is a truth your grandfather will not for a moment admit. He is convinced that I am a good deal worse. That I am in love, your mother is unkind enough to doubt. She is convinced that I am suffering from a physical distemper. And so, just as you were not swayed by your guardians' arguments to-day, I have not been swayed by them to-night——"

"How, sir!" cried Sir Guy hotly. "Are you——"

"I am talking, Sir Guy. But, Joan," continued Mr. Maturin, "they insisted that I could cure you of your attachment to me, if I wished. I pointed out that I had already put myself before you as a man whose character contained certain grave flaws; and that you had, while deploring my recent and second bankruptcy and my only too frequent lapses from the strictly moral code, chosen to believe that there is still some good in me, and had therefore remained by your decision to become my wife. Your mother and grandfather, however, have dared me to tell you the complete truth about myself and yet hold you. Joan, did I think for one moment that I would lose you in this way, I frankly admit," said Mr. Maturin emphatically, "that I would not put my hand to any such quixotic folly——"

"After all," said Joan de Gramercy, "the past is dead."

"My point exactly, child. And that is why," said Mr. Maturin, "if only to satisfy your mother and grandfather of the inevitability of your choice and of my complete faith in your love, I have decided to do what I will do. Listen, Joan——"

It was Sir Guy's stern voice that fell on the room like an axe.

"You live up to my description of you completely, Mr. Maturin. You are indeed the ace of cads! For now you are betraying your word of a few minutes ago."

"I do wish you wouldn't interrupt," said Mr. Maturin warmly. "I am embarked, let's face it, on a suspension-bridge of very doubtful strength and you keep on trying to upset my balance with sweeping comments on my character. My tale, Joan," he continued into the middle air, and spoke from this moment on with his eyes fixed absently in the shadows of the books on the shelves opposite, "my tale has to do with many years ago. Now I have been and I have done many things in my time; and have become one of those men of whom it is vaguely said, 'He could write a book about his life,' which of course means that I have done everything in my life except write a book. At the time I speak of I was a subaltern in a Guards regiment; a mode of life which, it may distress you to hear, Sir Guy, bored me in the extreme. As, however, the small allowance my father gave me was contingent on my retaining my commission, and as even the smallest allowance is better than a poke in the eye, I endured in patience the while I gave myself up to the pleasures of the town. You must not for a moment think," protested Mr. Maturin with feeling, "that I am trying to belittle the gentlemen of the Brigade, for better men than I have tried and failed at that game: nor that I am a slave to malice, for as you know I was later expelled from their company: but truth compels me to confess that my companions of those days were notable rather for the correctness of their appearance than for their learning, while their charm was of that static, profound sort which no one could call ingratiating and a certain kind of primitive *badinage* was held among them to be the superior of wit. And as time went on I came to be esteemed among the lighter sort for those qualities of the tongue and mind that are calculated to send any man, in due course, headlong down the crooked path.

"But I must tell you I had one very great friend among them. This was a man who had everything I had not: a simple frankness, a plain but almost painfully honest bearing, and a heart like gold; which was then, of course, more evidently in circulation than it is now. I cannot imagine how a boy of that sort could have loved and admired me; but he undoubtedly did, and to a singular degree, so that I was frequently enabled to borrow money from him almost painlessly, for he was heir to a great fortune, with which went a great name; although, to be sure, he was often as hard put to it as I was to fit a morsel of caviare to a piece of toast, for his father had ideas about real estate quite contrary to ours.

"My friend became engaged to a beautiful girl. What she saw in the boy, I do not know. Women are, let's face it, odd. That she loved him, I was instantly certain. Even my youthful cynicism could not ascribe to her the mean calculation of a fortune-hunter. That he loved her, madly and madly again, he frequently made clear to me in those broken and inarticulate periods that are the hall-mark of all honest Englishmen in love: and which, being often quite inaudible, have earned for Englishmen a delightful reputation for restraint. But let us not generalise when we can so profitably be particular.

"We were at that time in the barracks that guard the frontiers of Chelsea: my friend and I in adjacent rooms. Our ways of life, however, were at that time vastly different; for as I was

passing through a financial void I would, with
that resignation which no one can deny has been
my one consistent virtue, go early to bed every
night: whereas my friend would return night
after night at about this hour, having escorted
his betrothed home after a play and a ball; and
night after night, as he prepared himself for bed
in the adjoining room, he would softly whistle a
tune. Thus, you understand, he expressed his
happiness; and killed it, for the walls were thin
and the tune intolerable.

"It was Mendelssohn's *Spring Song;* and, Sir
Guy, I have already told you," said Mr. Maturin with a glance at the old gentleman, who was
listening with every mark of attention if not of
approval, "how my distaste for that composition
led me, some months after the time I speak of,
to a hasty action. But what that same distaste
caused me to do to that boy was not done hastily.

"One day I borrowed a sum of money from
him. He, poor boy, was so absorbed in his happiness that he scarcely noticed the third zero
which, having seen how readily he had already
attached two, I persuaded him to add to the
primary numeral on the cheque. Whereupon,
with his full permission, and a thousand pounds
of his money, I prepared to make myself agreeable to his *fiancée.*

"He trusted me implicitly, that boy. And who,"
Mr. Maturin asked dreamily of the middle distance, "who will tell the tale of the ramifications
and subtleties and intrigues of the next few weeks,

how I used every art on that beautiful girl, how she came to believe in my love for her—and maybe I believed in it myself—how she came to look wearily on the honest but plain features of her *fiancé,* how she came to suffer his inarticulate periods with a doubtful smile; and how finally—though he had long since ceased to whistle the *Spring Song*—she broke her engagement to him, and had certainly become my wife but that I was at about that time expelled from the Brigade and was never, until quite lately, a marrying man. That is all; and, I think," said Beau Maturin softly, looking round at the chair which had until a moment ago been occupied by the figure of Joan de Gramercy, "quite enough."

Sir Guy was silent: his thin long hands clasped nervously together on the surface of the writing-table, he stared fixedly at a point on the carpet. Mrs. de Gramercy was silent. Mr. Maturin examined, for quite a while, the points of his shoes. At last he murmured: "Well. . . ."

Sir Guy said, as though to himself: "That was a very dreadful story."

"Wasn't it!" Mr. Maturin agreed gravely. "Well, good-night, Mrs. de Gramercy. Good-night, Sir Guy." And he strode towards the distant shadows by the door.

"A moment!" the old gentleman seemed to awake. "Mr. Maturin, my daughter-in-law and I have to thank you. Good-bye."

The tall shadow by the door, as though on the impulse of a sudden memory, seemed to touch the outside of his breast-pocket. "Oh, by the way," he said, "I will, if you don't mind, keep this bank-note. Your house owes it to me. Good-bye, good de Gramercys!"

Through the silence of the house the two heard the steps of Beau Maturin on the flags of the hall, the closing of the front-door, the faint echo of his passage down the square. Sir Guy was staring bemused at the still, distant figure of his daughter-in-law.

"What did he say, Eleanour? that our house owed him that money? What on earth did the man mean?"

"What he said," the shadow whispered, and then it laughed, and old Sir Guy jumped from his chair with the queer shock of that laugh.

"Eleanour!"

As she came towards him he took her hands in his and looked intently down at her. Her eyes were very, very tired. She said: "I am very tired. I will go to bed now."

Old Sir Guy held her hands very tenderly. "But what is on your mind, Eleanour? Why did you laugh in that dreadful way?"

She opened those tired eyes very wide. "Oh, surely, dear, I am allowed that—to laugh at your having called Beau Maturin the ace of cads!"

Old Sir Guy said sternly: "Yes, you are tired, Eleanour. You are not yourself."

"Poor old gentleman!" she tenderly, bitterly, smiled up at him. "Poor old gentleman! Dear, like all your generation you have been wrong about everything in ours, but everything! Oh, you have been so wrong about what was good

III: WHERE THE PIGEONS
GO TO DIE

I

NOW it is as much as their jobs are worth for the authorities responsible for the amenities of the town not to employ a man on the clear understanding that every once in a while he climbs to the very top of Lord Nelson's column in Trafalgar Square to cleanse away such refuse as might have collected about the immortal sailor's feet. And it is to the good man who undertakes this perilous task that we owe a piece of information which cannot fail to interest gentles and simples. He tells how he never but finds numerous pigeons lying dead about the feet of our sailor hero. Sometimes there will be not more than a score or so, sometimes there may be close on an hundred, and he relates on ôath how he once removed, in a bag which he takes up with him for that purpose, the bodies of pigeons to the number of one-hundred-and-thirty-four: among which, he tells with awe, there was the corpse of a pretty white dove.

That was on the evening of the first of May of the year of grace 1924, and the reason why the good man tells with awe of the dove among the pigeons is because it was on that very eve-

ning that he was vexed by a strange phenomenon.
The facts may interest the curious.

The prodigious number of the dead pigeons
had kept him at his task much later than usual;
and as he picked up the dove he chanced to look
up at Lord Nelson, who stood at that moment in
the light and shadow of the sun as it set beyond
Admiralty Arch, and the good man fancied that
the stern face of my Lord Nelson frowned.

Unseemly though it is to doubt any man's
word, the sceptical sort may be permitted to question whether the fellow was at that moment seeing
straight, and whether it was not the fanciful light
of twilight that had set him thinking that Lord
Nelson had indulged in a passing frown.

But to more kindly folk the good man's fancy
will not present such marvellous features when
they know that it was on the evening of that first
of May that Miss Pamela Wych came upon an
event beneath Lord Nelson's eyes that completely
changed the course of her whole life.

II

The clear cool eyes of Miss Wych were clouded
that spring evening. Miss Wych was thinking.
All about her the London of Oxford Street
marched and screamed and hooted, but Miss
Wych walked unheeding, alone as a tulip in a
wild garden. The London of Oxford Street was
like a soiled silk handkerchief waving frantically
to the evening sun but the genius of thought
draped the young lithe figure with a rare calm
dignity. Now Miss Wych was nearly always

calm, for such was her nature. But she was not
always dignified, for dignity comes very rarely
to youth, dignity is a gentle blossom that grows
with the years, and when dignity comes to youth
it comes always unconsciously, it is fleeting, frail,
sad. We are not speaking of the dignity of anger,
but of the dignity of sorrow. Miss Wych was
sad that evening.

All that day, whilst she was at her allotted
tasks in the millinery department of Messrs.
Come & Go, Miss Wych had been saying to herself: "I must think. I will think this evening.
One doesn't think nearly enough. I will think
a lot this evening. I will walk home, thinking.
I do hope it keeps fine."

That is what Miss Wych had thought, for she
was very conscientious in the fulfilment of her
duties in the millinery department, and she always did her best not to intrude her private con-
cerns into her service of Messrs. Come & Go.
Not that either Mr. Come or Mr. Go could possibly have noticed it if she had, since her service
was but an atom among the service of one thousand and five hundred *employées;* for Messrs.
Come & Go's was advertised as the largest store
in London, and why should anyone doubt the
verity of such beautiful advertisements as those
of Messrs. Come & Go, which tell unceasingly of
the divers bargains that can be bought for next
to nothing by Mr. Everyman and Mrs. Every-
woman merely by entering within and being
smiled at affectionately by either Mr. Come or
Mr. Go in person, and all delivered at Mr. Everyman's door within twenty-four hours in plain

motors. Anyone can see by their advertisements that Mr. Come and Mr. Go have got all other men beat on philanthropy, and how they manage to live at all is very puzzling, but no doubt they have private incomes of their own and don't rely on making any money out of their store.

Miss Wych had never so much as set eyes on her great employers, but she would wonder a great deal about them, and she would wonder particularly about the great men's youth. Now Miss Wych admired success above all things. Those clear cool eyes looked at life, this teeming chaotic life in which she was an atom of service, and as she looked at life a prince in shining armour of gold and sapphire stepped forth from the boiling ranks, brave with triumph, flaming with youth, indeed a very prince of princes. And the name of this prince was Success. That is how Miss Wych thought of success, like a glorious lover. She loved success, like a glorious lover. And once upon a time she had tried to win him for herself, Miss Wych had once tried her fortune on the stage, but unfortunately the glorious lover had looked very coldly on her, for, as the producer had said: "Miss Wych is a nice girl but a bum actress."

The gentle circumstance of evening transmuted the trumpeting and soiled machines on the road into shining caravans, but never a glance at these wonders did Miss Wych give. Of the passers-by, one and all hurrying to the assault of tubes and omnibuses, maybe one here and there forfeited his place through looking twice at Miss Wych. Miss Wych was a very pretty girl. Her eyes were grey. Her nose would have looked absurd on anyone's else face, because it was so small. Her face was as white as the moon.

Since she had made up her mind to walk to her boarding-house in South Kensington she did not join the people waiting for omnibuses at the corner of Marble Arch and Park Lane. They who had been in such haste a moment before now waited so quietly, so uneagerly, as though they didn't care whether they were going home or not. The stillness of Park Lane seemed to Miss Wych very refreshing after the din of the panting hosts of Oxford Street. She walked in the broken shadows of the Park railings. A young man on a black horse cantered by, looking as though he had bought the world for tuppence and wanted his money back. Now and then an omnibus rolled by, rolled on, and on, and on, the red-and-white monster born of man's divine gift for making his life intolerable. A young lady with a bright red hat in a little silver car tore by like a jewel in a hurry. Huge limousines sped, sped swiftly by, like shining insects whispering to Miss Wych of a grander world than the world of Miss Wych. The people in Hyde Park walked slowly to and fro listening to each other. When the sun lit their faces they looked brown and gold and copper-red, but otherwise they looked tired. Through the railings the sun fell in bars of gold about her feet and kissed the dark hair that waved over her ears, so that the dark hair shone in a way that was a wonder to behold. Miss Wych, of course, was always wishing that her hair was fair, but she was quite wrong about that. The thoughts of Miss Wych as she walked were, roughly: "The sun is sinking, if it only knew it, into Kensington Gardens. The sun is sinking, if it only knew it, into Kensington Gardens. The sun is . . ."

And a voice at her shoulder said:

"Excuse me! Please excuse me. I say, you *must* excuse me!"

Miss Wych thought: "And such things can happen in sunlight! O our Father, why *won't* You watch Your world more carefully!"

III

Miss Wych walked on, in the broken shadows of the Park railings. And her eyes were turned to the sun, which did not know it was sinking into Kensington Gardens, for what else was there to look at? Then a bird flew across Park Lane and sat on a window-sill, and Miss Wych looked at that.

"Please," said the voice at her shoulder. "You see, Miss Wych, I must. For I can't bear it any more, honestly. Don't be beastly to me, please!"

Miss Wych thought: "This is a fine thing, being spoken to by strange men! I suppose I look common or flashy or something, else he wouldn't dare. What shall I do, oh, what shall I do? What do women do?"

"Look here," said the voice at her shoulder, "I can't keep this up any longer. I'm no good at speaking to people I don't know. Good-bye."

"Good-bye," said Miss Wych.

"Oh, you've spoken!" cried the voice at her shoulder.

Miss Wych thought: "Oh, oh, damn!"

Miss Wych said: "This is very extraordinary behaviour. Please go away."

Miss Wych had intended to say that icily, but in point of fact she said it very shyly. There was a girl who worked with her in the millinery department of Messrs. Come & Go who said: "When I don't like a boy I just give him the Once-Over and he's Off." Miss Wych envied that girl. But she called up her courage and tried to give the stranger the Once-Over. The stranger, however, did not go Off. The stranger was a lean young man with deep dark eyes that seemed to whirl with the trouble that was in him.

"You see," he said, "it's like this, Miss Wych. I had to meet you somehow. But how? I did not know what to do. And so I did this. Miss Wych dear, will you forgive me?"

Miss Wych thought: "There are times when one must placate the devil. This must be one of those times."

Then Miss Wych discovered a most extraordinary thing. She discovered that she was looking deep into the stranger's dark eyes. She flushed as red as a tennis-court.

"This is terrible," she said bitterly. "Terrible! How dare you speak to me! Please go away at once."

"I can't," said the young stranger. "I would if I could. But I just can't. I'm sorry."

Miss Wych thought: "He says he's *sorry*, the beast!"

"You are mad," said Miss Wych indifferently. The sun walked in fire and glory, but the world was dark, the world was dark, and bold bad men walked the streets for to be offensive to maids. The young stranger, for instance, did not go away. He said desperately:

"If you will give me just one look you will see that I don't mean to offend you."

"That may be so," said Miss Wych bitterly, "but you do."

"You only think I do," protested the lean young man. "That's all it is, really."

Then Miss Wych discovered a most extraordinary thing. She discovered that she was walking slowly, slowly. Instantly she walked on quickly.

The lean young man sighed: "Oh, dear!"

Miss Wych said breathlessly: "I don't even know your name! And how you have got to know mine I really can't imagine! But you don't look wicked. Please don't go on being nasty! Please! Won't you go away now?"

"Pamela Wych," the young stranger whispered, "Pamela Wych, Pamela Wych, Pamela Wych, how the devil was I to meet you except by daring this? Further, you are my fate, and what sort of a man would I be if I were to leave my fate in the very second of finding it?"

Miss Wych thought: "This is getting serious."

"That is all very well," she said reasonably, "talking about fate and big things like that. But when you take it as just behaviour you can see as well as I do that it is all wrong. Sir, there are

things one can't do, and this is one of them, and
so you must please go away at once."

"That is the one thing I can't do," said the
young stranger desperately. "You see, although
you won't show me your face I can see the tip of
your ear peeping out from your hair, and it is as
red as a rose."

Miss Wych thought: "This can't go on. How
would it be if I called a policeman?"

"It is red," said the profile of Miss Wych, "for
shame that a man can so insult his manhood."

"Oh, I do wish people wouldn't talk like those
small leaders in *The Daily Mail!*" cried the
voice at her shoulder. "I'm not insulting my manhood. I am living up to it for the first time in
my life."

Miss Wych said fiercely: "Go away, go away,
go away!"

"Dear," said the young stranger, "listen to me.
You must listen to me. I am not playing."

Miss Wych thought: "Our Father which art in
Heaven——"

They were in the Park. How they had come to
be in the Park Miss Wych could not imagine.
Over Kensington Gardens the sun was marching
to eternity with a cohort of clouds and colours.

"No," said the lean young man, "I am certainly not playing. Miss Wych dear, this is not
a 'pick-up'——"

"It's piracy!" said Miss Wych contemptu-
ously.

"That's right," said the lean young man with
the eyes of trouble.

"You say you aren't playing," Miss Wych bitterly complained, "but you are upsetting me very much. A little chivalry, sir, would help you to see how terrified I am."

"I am terrified, too," said the young stranger, "of this happiness. It can't possibly last, can it? It's too enormous."

Miss Wych thought: "He's gone mad!"

"I really don't know why you ask me," she panted spitefully, "whether it can last or not. How should I know? And it's perfectly absurd, what we are doing. It is perfectly absurd. I don't know you, you don't know me, and that's that. Anyone would think we were babies!"

"But that's just what I am! For," said the young stranger, "I am exactly one week old."

Miss Wych thought: "And he talks like it!"

Miss Wych said: "Really! How interesting."

"I am one week old," the stranger said, "because it was exactly a week ago that I first saw you. And you needn't laugh!"

"I'm not laughing," said Miss Wych.

They were sitting on two chairs in the Park. How they had come to be sitting on two chairs in the Park Miss Wych could not imagine. The sun was red in the face with trying to get to Australia through Kensington Gardens.

The young stranger said: "Now!"

His eyes were deep and dark and shy, and Miss Wych thought: "He is one of those unhappy young men. There are a lot of them about. He is probably used to burning people with those eyes of his. But he won't burn me."

The lean young man was saying: "Miss Wych,

may I tell you something most important? I love you."

"That is what you say," said Miss Wych, and was surprised at herself, for she had intended to say something quite different.

"Love," said Miss Wych severely, "is a shy word. It should not be thrown about just anyhow. That's quite apart from it's being cheek."

The lean young man's eyes burnt angrily, and he said: "I have been in hell for a week, and you talk to me of cheek!"

"Well, it *is* cheek," said Miss Wych sulkily.

Now because the young stranger's deep dark eyes were whirling with the trouble that was in him Miss Wych suddenly thought to close hers tight, for she did not want to let herself be sorry for him. She thought: "If this is what they call Romance—well, oh, dear, give me a nice bus ride in a hurricane! It would be much less uncomfortable."

"One day," the voice was saying, "I happened to go with a friend into that shop where you work, and I saw you, and my life fell down like a tin soldier with a broken leg. That was a week ago, and since then I haven't picked it up, I haven't known what to do. I have often heard that a man can go mad with love, but I did not know before that a man could go sane with love. All the people in the world who are not madly in love, Miss Wych dear, are in some degree insane, for it is insane not to have a proper perspective of life, and a proper perspective of life is to be quite certain that the world is well lost for the love of one person. It is insane to work from grubby birth

to grubby death with never an attempt to chain a
star, with never a raid on enchantment, with
never a try to kiss a fairy or to live in a dream.
Dear, only dreams make life real, all of life that
is not touched and troubled by our dreams is not
real, does not exist. I could not have lived until
now if I had not dreamed that one day I would
meet you. I have worked, I have been what is
called successful, but always I was under the spell
of a miracle that was to happen, and when I saw
you I knew that miracle had happened. I just
wanted to tell you that. I believe in miracles and
magic and my love for you. That is my testa-
ment. And if it is cheek to say I love you, then
cheek must be as beautiful a thing as chastity.
And now I am going away, for your eyes are
closed, and that must be because my talk of love
bores you. I have tried the impossible, just to
be certain that nothing is impossible until one has
tried it. And I have learnt another thing: I know
now that when I am not looking at you I shall
be blind, when I am not listening to you I shall
be deaf, and always I shall find no delight in the
world but in thoughts of you. And now I will
go away."

Miss Wych opened her eyes and said: "Don't
go away." That is all she said, but it was quite
enough for the lean young man, who caught his
breath and threw down his hat and pinched himself. Now all the colours in the world and in the
heavens had met over Kensington Gardens in a
conference to discuss ways and means for putting
the sun to sleep, and a few of them came quickly
and lit Miss Wych's face as she said:

"There is something very silly about me. It has landed me into a lot of trouble in my time. I always believe what people say. I believe in fairies. I believe in God. I believe that moonlight has a lovely smell. I believe in men."

"Please believe in me!" said the lean young man.

"But why shouldn't I!" cried Miss Wych with wide eyes. "What a funny world this is, isn't it? We always believe people straight away when they say beastly things to us, but we don't if they say lovely things——"

"We will change all that!" the young stranger whispered.

All this while the world was standing quite still as a special treat for the sylphs and spirits, so that they could dart about the sky and never lose their way back to the friends who had stayed at home. It was curious, Miss Wych thought, how she could feel the silence of the world. It was as though the wings of a darting bird brushed her cheek, scented her thoughts, sang in her heart. It was as though the world was still with reverence. Before her very eyes a fairy tripped over a blade of grass, and Miss Wych thought: "I must be dreaming."

"Talking of cheek," said the lean young man.

"Yes?" said Miss Wych.

"Look here," said the lean young man, and you could have blown his voice away with a breath, "if I have the cheek to ask you to marry me, will you have the cheek to say yes?"

He had a stick with an ivory top that was as yellow and cracked with age as an old charwoman's face. She looked at it for a long time, and then she looked at him.

"Why," she cried, "your eyes are wet!"

"I know," said the lean young man fiercely. "And I don't give a damn. For the love of God, am I such a fool that I wouldn't be crying for the happiness of knowing you are in the world!"

"Well," said Miss Wych, "I shall probably be crying myself at any moment. But first of all I must tell you a story."

"Won't you marry me instead?" pleaded the young stranger.

"I will tell you a story," said Miss Wych gravely, and she began at once.

IV

"I was born," said Miss Wych, "in a small town in the north of England which would have been the ugliest town in the world if there hadn't been uglier ones all round it. My mother died when I was quite young, and when I was nineteen my father died; but I did not mind being alone half so much as you might think, because I was very ambitious. So, with the few pounds my father had left, I came to London to try my fortune on the stage. I had an aunt who was once an actress in Birmingham, and that was why I thought first of all of the stage. And people said I was pretty.

"In that ugly town there was a boy who loved me. His name was George and he was a clerk in an auctioneer's office, but he wanted to be a farmer. When my father died George asked me

to marry him, but I said I couldn't do that and
explained about my ambitions and how I would
first of all like to have a try at being *something*
in the world. You see, it isn't only grown-ups
who have dreams. Besides, George was poor, and
however would we live if we did get married?

"He came to see me soon after I had settled in
London. I told him I was studying acting at the
Academy of Dramatic Arts, and also I told him
that I loved him. Of course, I wouldn't have told
him that if he hadn't asked me. But I thought I
did. I was only nineteen and a bit, and he was
so strong and serious, and as fair as you are dark,
and when he was almost too serious to speak the
tip of his nose would quiver in a lovely funny
way.

"That was the last time I saw George, but this
evening I am to see him again. You see, that was
on the first of May five years ago, and George and
I swore a great oath. George said he was off to
America to make his fortune, but that in five
years to the day he would be waiting for me at
the Savoy Hotel at eight o'clock to give me dinner and hear me say that I would marry him. We
chose a grand place like the Savoy Hotel because
of course George would have made his fortune
by then. George added that he had no ambitions
for himself, he wouldn't mind being just a farmer,
but that he would work for me. I said that was
a very good idea, for men should be ambitious
and imperious, marching into history with clear
heads and brave thoughts and clean eyes.

"I said I would keep myself free for him. I
promised him that just as he was going away,

and you should have seen how happy his eyes were and how the tip of his nose quivered! And now I have to see him in a few minutes' time, and what shall I say to him?

"I was a failure on the stage. I am a failure even as a girl in a shop. I am a failure in everything but my dreams. My childish ambitions have withered, and you would think I had learnt such a lesson that I wouldn't have any more, but now I have the largest ambition in the world. I would like very much to be happy. That is why I have been wondering all to-day and for how many days what I would say to George this evening. You see, I wasn't really in love with him even when I made my promise, I knew that in my heart even then. My promise was just one of those important-looking flowers that are wrung out of the soil of pity. And my business in life from now onwards, dear stranger, will be to keep that hidden from my husband. But of course I will get used to disenchantment, just like everyone else, and the time will come when I will wonder at myself for talking to you like this, and the time will come when I, like everyone else, will die with the sick heart of one who has never fulfilled herself. And now I must go, for it is close on eight o'clock."

"Of course," said the lean young man thoughtfully, "he might, for some reason we can't tell, not keep his appointment. And then——"

"And then, and then, and then!" sang Miss Wych, but she added gravely: "But oh, he will! George is a good man and a determined man. Failure or success, he will be there."

The fires burnt low in the west. They walked towards the gates of the Park. Miss Wych counted four stars in the sky.

"Love," said the lean young man, "knows every emotion but that of patience. Mayn't I come with you, Pamela Wych? Mayn't we go together to this George man? Could he do anything but release you?"

"That wouldn't be fair," said Miss Wych. "That wouldn't be fair at all. Oh, yes, George would release me. But life is not so easy as that. It's all very nice and easy to talk and dream, but aren't there duties too? I will go to George and tell him I am ready to marry him. I *must* do that. But maybe he won't want to marry me. And then——"

The clock at the Park Gates stood at ten minutes to eight o'clock; and on this strange enchanted evening, said Miss Wych, she would indulge in the extravagance of a taxicab. The lean young man stood by the door and said good-bye, and he said also: "If that George man isn't there, I shall know. Or if that George man isn't worthy of your loyalty, I shall know. And I will come to you again."

"If!" sighed Miss Wych. "If! If the world was a garden, and we were butterflies! If the world was a garden, and God was kind to lovers! Good-bye, good-bye, good-bye!"

v

There is an eminent school of thought which insists that there is no such thing in this world as

chance.   Therefore we may take it that ever since
the beginning of creation there was appointed one
small wind to lurk nearby the National Gallery
in Trafalgar Square for the purpose of blowing
an empty paper-bag under a horse's nose.

The horse belonged to a van, and it was probably bored with the van.   It gave a kick at the
paper-bag.   It missed the paper-bag.   "Woa!"
cried the driver of the van.   That got on the
horse's nerves, and it bolted.

Two men cried: "Ho!   Woa!   Oi!"   An old
man selling newspapers by the steps of St. Martin's-in-the-Fields said.   "No 'orse can't bolt far
with an 'eavy van."   The driver of the van cried:
"——!"   An orange-and-banana merchant leapt
for his life from the horse's hooves, and his
oranges and bananas fell as manna upon Trafalgar Square, and many little children ran together
and gave praise.   A large handsome limousine was
coming at a good pace up the slope from the
Strand.   It had to swerve to avoid running over
the orange-and-banana merchant.   As it swerved
it crashed into the side of an ancient taxicab that
was bustling round the corner.   The ancient taxicab overturned.   There was a scream of smash-
ing glass, and the two wheels of the taxicab re-
volved plaintively in the air.

"Bewty!" said the old man selling newspapers,
for he was a connoisseur of accidents.   The limousine had stopped.   The horse was walking on
quite calmly now.   A little boy picked up the
paper-bag, blew into it, and made a noise.   A lot
of people came to look at the taxicab.

"Stand back, there! Stand back!" cried a young policeman.

The driver of the taxicab crawled from underneath the wreck. There was blood on his face, and he was so ugly that he looked like several sorts of animals at once. He stared at the chauffeur of the limousine.

"Wotcherdothatfor?" he asked bitterly.

"Come on now, lend a hand!" said the young policeman sternly.

A tall, fair, serious-looking young man had alighted quickly from the limousine, and with him a young lady in a chinchilla coat.

"My, there's a girl underneath!" she sobbed in a faint American accent.

"There was!" said the taxi-driver bitterly.

"Good God, she's pinned there!" cried the tall, fair young man.

"George, and on our honeymoon!" sobbed the young lady in the chinchilla coat.

"Come on now, give us room!" said the policeman sharply. "Now then, sir, just help me lift this wheel off the young lady."

It was the lean young man who was helping the policeman. He had followed Miss Wych. As the tall fair young man and his young wife in the chinchilla coat pressed forward through the crowd, the lean young man looked up at him, and his face was very stern. The tall fair young man looked back with bewildered, wretched eyes.

"Don't say she's dead!" he whispered.

"Now, sir," said the young policeman, "I'll keep this up while you bring her through sharp as you like. Now!"

The lithe young body was broken and still. The crowd pressed round.

"She's dead orl right!" said the orange-and-banana merchant.

The last flames of sunset over Admiralty Arch lit the peering faces, and they looked as impersonal as gargoyles. Some took off their hats.

"Oh, she's dead!" sobbed the young lady in the chinchilla coat.

"Such a pretty young lady!" said the taxi-driver bitterly, wiping the blood from his face.

The lean young man and the young policeman knelt beside the still, broken body and tried to find life where no life was. The orange-and-banana merchant took off his hat. The policeman's helmet fell to the ground and rolled a little way down towards the Strand. The tall fair young man held his silk hat in his hand. The lean young man looked up at him through a blinding mist of tears and stammered: "Aren't you sorry, aren't you sorry?"

"George," sobbed the young lady in the chinchilla coat, "why is he looking at you like that?"

"Blessed if I know!" stammered the tall fair young man.

"By gum, look at the cop!" said the orange-and-banana merchant.

The lean young man darted a look at the policeman kneeling beside him, and he saw that the policeman wept, and he saw that the tip of the policeman's nose was quivering.

"She died," stammered the lean young man, "while keeping her promise to you. But you had failed her."

"I've failed at everything in every country," said the young policeman. "And now I'll probably get the sack from this job too for crying on my beat."

" 'Ere, give 'im back 'is 'elmet," said the taxi-driver bitterly. "A cop without a 'elmet don't look natchral."

"And who's goin' to give me back my oranges and bananas?" said the orange-and-banana merchant. "Isn't there no justice in this world, that's wot I want to know?"

IV: THE BATTLE OF BERKELEY SQUARE

ONE morning not long ago a gentleman was
engaged in killing worms in the gardens of
Berkeley Square when it was forced on his attention that he had a pain. The pain, which was
offensive, was on his left side, but thinking at
first that it was no more than a temporary stitch
brought about by the unwonted exercise, he dismissed it from his mind as a pain unworthy of the
notice of an officer and a gentleman and went on
killing worms according to the directions on the
tin.

This was a large tin; and, held at an angle
in the gentleman's right hand, a white powder
issued therefrom and covered the blades of grass,
whilst with his left hand he manœuvred a syringe
in such a way that a brownish liquid was sprayed
upon the ground.

An entirely new and nasty smell was thus
brought into the world; nor did there appear to be
any such good reason for it as is generally brought
forward on behalf of a novel smell, such as industry, agriculture, the culinary necessities of
certain foods or the general progress of civilisation. Mean, however, though our gentleman's
physical position was, for he needs must bend
low to the end that not a blade of grass might

116

escape his eagle eye, mentally he took his stand on a lofty ideal; and, dismissing the stares of passers-by as unworthy of the notice of an officer and a gentleman, continued to misbehave according to the directions on the tin.

The chemist who had sold him the tin and the syringe had sworn a pharmaceutical oath to the effect that, on sprinkling the grass with the powder and spraying it with the lotion, not a worm in Mayfair but would instantly arise from the bowels of the earth and die. Nor was the chemist's prophecy in vain; for the powdering and spraying had not been going on for long, when behold! a multitude of worms arose and passed away peacefully. So great, indeed, was the massacre that a Turkish gentleman who was passing by stood at attention during a five minutes' silence, but that is quite by the way and has nothing to do with George Tarlyon's pain, which was growing more offensive with every moment. Thinking, however, that it could be no more than an attack of lumbago, and therefore dismissing it from his mind as a pain unworthy of the notice of an officer and a gentleman, he went on killing worms because he wanted to stand well with a pretty girl he had met the night before at a party who had said she was a Socialist and that there were too many worms in Mayfair.

Major Cypress now enters the story, and the fact that this is a true story makes it so much the more regrettable that therein the Major is presented in a tedious, not to say a repellent, light. Poor Hugo. About a year before these happenings he had entered upon matrimony with Tarlyon's little sister Shirley, and he loved her true, even as she loved him. We will now talk a while of Hugo and Shirley.

Shirley was a darling and Hugo had no money above that which he earned, which was nothing, and that is why they lived in a garage in the Mews behind Berkeley Square, had breakfast late, went out for dinner and on to supper. Not that the garage wasn't delightful. The garage was charming. Shirley herself had supervised the architects, builders, decorators and plumbers, and by the time rooms had been added, kitchens hollowed out, bathrooms punched in—by the time, in fact, the garage had been converted into a house, it had cost Hugo more money at rates of interest current in Jermyn Street than the lease of a fine modern residence in Berkeley Square. Poor Hugo.

Every morning at about this hour he would emerge from the garage into the Mews, pat his tie straight in the gleaming flanks of the automobiles that were being washed to the accompaniment of song and rushing water, pass the time of day with a chauffeur or two, and walk into Berkeley Square where, in the pursuit of his profession, he would loiter grimly by the railings of the gardens until the clocks struck twelve. The word "profession" in connection with Major Cypress doubtless needs some explanation. Hugo's profession was the most ancient in the world bar none, that of an inheritor: he was waiting for his father to die. This was a cause of great distress to his mother, as it must be to everyone who likes Hugo. But, as Mistress Moll Flanders says, I am giving an account of what was, not of what ought or ought not to be.

All doctors are agreed that waiting has a lowering effect on the mind, but this morning Major Cypress looked, as has been stated, even more depressed than usual. And long he leant against the railings watching his brother-in-law's extraordinary behaviour before opening his lips: when, a noise of a friendly nature being created, he waited patiently for an answer, which he did not get. He then tried to attract Tarlyon's attention by making a noise like money, but in vain.

"George," he shouted at last, "may I ask why you are behaving in that peculiar way?"

"You may," snapped Tarlyon, and, approaching him with a look of absent-minded savagery, cast a little of the powder over his breeches, squirted him with the syringe, and continued with his labours. Poor Hugo.

"George," said Major Cypress, disregarding the man's rudeness, "I am depressed this morning. Guess why."

"Hugo," said Tarlyon bitterly, "I would be depressed every morning if I were you. Now please go away at once. These worms aren't rising half so well since you came. And I have a pain in my left side."

"A pain, George? I thought you looked sick, but I didn't like to say anything. What sort of a pain?"

"A hell of a pain," said Tarlyon. "It gets me when I breathe."

"I don't wonder," said Hugo. "I too have a

pain. And it gets me when I eat, drink, breathe and sleep. George, my pain is in my heart."

"I don't want to hear about it," snapped Tarlyon, "and I hope it gives you such a swelling in the feet that you can't follow me about like a moneylender after a dud cheque."

"George, I am not, and never was, a moneylender. I am, by the grace of God, a moneylendee. But to return to your pain, I shouldn't wonder if you had pneumonia. You have been very liable to pneumonia ever since you took that bath on Armistice Day. And merely from the way your face has all fallen in I should say pneumonia, quite apart from the fact that your breath is coming in painful gasps."

Tarlyon threw down the worm-killers and joined his friend. "I believe you're right, Hugo. It hurts me to breathe. I must have pneumonia. What treatment would you advise?"

"Pyjamas," said Hugo. "Nice, new, amusing pyjamas. You will be in bed at least six weeks with the violent form of pneumonia you've got, and it will be a comfort to you to think of your new pyjamas."

"Suppose I die," Tarlyon muttered.

"I am supposing it, George. The pyjamas will then, I hope, revert to me."

Together they strode up the narrow defile of Berkeley Street towards Piccadilly, two men of grave mien and martial address; and, although it was a bitter December morning, neither wore an overcoat, which is a polity of dress calculated to reveal, by the very action of a lounge-suit on the eye on a bitter morning, the hardy frame of ships that pass in the night and the iron constitution of publicans, wine-bibbers, chaps, guys, ginks, bloods, bucks and *beaux*. Nevertheless, such was the stress of the distemper within him that George Almeric St. George Tarlyon threw away his cigarette with a gesture of distaste and said: "Hugo, I am in pain. It gets me when I breathe."

"Try not to breathe," said Hugo. "In the meanwhile I will tell you why I am depressed. My wife——"

"Hugo, I am very hot. I do believe I am sweating!"

"You look awful, George. You have probably a very high temperature. Presently you will break out into a rash owing to the unclean state of your blood brought about by your low habits. You can't breakfast all your life off a gin-and-bitters and two green olives and hope to get away with it. I was telling you, George, that I am depressed because my wife is presenting me with an heir."

"It's just cussedness, Hugo. I shouldn't take any notice. Women are always the same, forever letting one in for some extravagance. Just take no notice, Hugo."

"George, you don't understand! She is in terrible pain, and I can't bear it, old friend, I simply can't bear it."

"I'm sorry, Hugo, really I am. Poor little Shirley. But I am feeling very ill myself. Call me an ambulance, Hugo."

"Pyjamas first, my honey. Ah, here we are! Ho there, Mr. Sleep! Ho there, Mr. Sluis! Shop!"

For by this time the two gentlemen had arrived within the establishment of Messrs. Sleep and Sluis, gents' shirt-makers, which is situate where the Piccadilly Arcade swoops falcon-like into Jermyn Street to be as a temptation to mugs in search of a manicure. Mr. Sleep was a small man with a round face who was a tie-specialist and Mr. Sluis was a small man with a long face who was a shirt-specialist, while both were accomplished students of masculine *lingerie* in every branch and could, moreover, as was told in the adventure of the Princess Baba, build a white waistcoat about a waist in a way that was a wonder to the eye. By Royal Appointment, and rightly.

"My lord," said Mr. Sleep, stepping forward two paces and standing smartly at ease, "what can we do for you this morning? These new ties," said he, "have just this moment come in. They are delicious."

"Mr. Sleep," said Lord Tarlyon, "you know very well that I detest new ties. I can think of nothing more common than wearing a new tie. Observe my tie, Mr. Sleep. I have worn it six years. Observe its rugged grandeur. Where is Mr. Sluis this morning?"

"My lord," said Mr. Sluis, stepping forward three paces and bowing smartly from his self-made waist, "what sort of pyjamas do you fancy?"

"What varieties have you this morning, Mr. Sluis?"

"We have many, my lord. Pyjamas can be used for various purposes."

"You shock me, Mr. Sluis. I am not, however,

going to Venice just yet. I merely want some
pneumonia pyjamas."

"In *crêpe-de-chine*, my lord?"

"Your innuendoes are amazing, Mr. Sluis!
Far from being that kind of man, I have always
adhered to the iron principle of once an adult always an adult. The very manhood of England
is being sapped by these vicious luxuries, as one
glance at my friend Major Cypress will show.
Away with these *crêpe-de-chine* pyjama suitings!
And I take this opportunity, Mr. Sleep, of crying
woe and woe to the pretty and the effeminate of
our sex, for their lack of manly sins shall surely
find them out and the odour of their overdrafts
shall descend to hell. For my own pyjamas, a
homely quality of antiseptic silk will do very well.
I will have half-a-dozen suits in black silk."

"I say, George," said Hugo, "black is very
lowering. Mr. Sluis, make them a lovely pale
blue with a dash of maroon. They revert to me,
you see."

"Black, Mr. Sluis. I fight Death with his own
weapons. Send these pyjamas at once, and put
them down to my account."

"Certainly, my lord. You will have them at
once."

"Gentlemen," said Lord Tarlyon, "I have had
forty years' experience of owing money and never
yet met with such simple faith as yours. I am
touched. Let me assure you that my executors
will repay your courtesy, if only in kind. Good-
day, Mr. Sleep, and you, Mr. Sluis. Don't, by
the way, send these pyjamas to my house, as the
bailiffs are in, which is why I went out in the

dewy dawn and caught this pneumonia. Send them to Major Cypress's."

"But you can't have pneumonia in my place!" cried Hugo. "If you should die it will depress my wife, and that," said he indignantly, "will have an effect on my unborn heir's character."

"He will be lucky, Hugo, if he has a character at all, from what I know of you. Mr. Sleep, and you, Mr. Sluis, you might telephone to some doctors to come round instantly to Major Cypress's garage, as there will shortly be a nice new pneumonia of two cylinders on view there. Hugo, call me a taxi at once. I cannot have pneumonia all over Jermyn Street."

"I don't care where you have it," said Hugo bitterly, "so long as you don't let the last agonies of your lingering death disturb my wife. Here's an idea, George! Why don't you go and have pneumonia at Fitzmaurice Savile's place near by?"

But Tarlyon was not without a keen sense of what was proper to a stainless gentleman: he put generosity, when he thought of it, above all things: and protested now that he could not very well seek Fitzmaurice Savile's hospitality as Fitzmaurice Savile owed him money and would think that he, Tarlyon, was taking it out of him in pneumonia.

"Well, lend me a fiver, then," said Hugo desperately, but he hadn't a hope. However, he need have had no fear for his wife's comfort, for never was a sick man quieter than the last of the Tarlyon's, the way he lay with closed eyes among the damp dark clouds of fever, the way he would smile now and then as at a joke someone was

whispering to him from a far distance, so that
the nurse said to the doctor: "I never saw a man
appear to enjoy pneumonia so. You would
think," said she, "that he was hungry for death.
He is not fighting it at all, doctor. Are you sure
he will not die?"

That is what the nurse said to the doctor, and
the doctor looked grave and punched Tarlyon
in the lungs with a telephone arrangement, but
Tarlyon took no notice at all, still smiling to
himself at the thought that in his life he had
done every silly thing in the world but die of
pneumonia in a converted garage, and maybe he
would presently be doing that and the cup of folly
be drained to the dregs. And every now and
then Hugo would come in and take a glass of the
iced wine by Tarlyon's bed and look depressed,
saying that Shirley was in pain and that he
couldn't bear it.

Then one day, or maybe it was one night, Tarlyon seemed to awake from a deep sleep that had
taken him to a far distance, and from that far
distance what should he seem to be seeing but
two shadows bending over his bed and the calm
shadow of the nurse nearby? Now he tried to
speak, but he could not, and from the far distance he could hear one of the shadows saying:
"You called me in not a moment too soon, Dr.
Chill. Lord Tarlyon's is an acute case of appendicitis. Weak as he is, it is imperative that
we operate at once."

"Right," said Dr. Chill.

Now Tarlyon recognised the shadow that had
spoken first for Ian Black, the great surgeon,

and a great friend of his since the distant days when he had operated on Tarlyon's unhappy dead wife, Virginia, she who had lived for pleasure and found only pain. And Tarlyon spoke out in a dim voice and said:

"Ian Black, much as I like having you about you must not operate on me for appendicitis in this house, which is but a garage. Remember I am staying with Hugo, and I came to stay with him on the distinct understanding that I was to have only pneumonia. Not a word was said between us about appendicitis, and I am sure that Hugo would be annoyed at my abusing his hospitality, so will you kindly put that beastly knife away?"

But at that very moment Hugo came in and took a glass of iced wine and looked depressed, saying that his wife was in terrible pain and that he couldn't bear it and that the whole garage was strewn with doctors murmuring among themselves; but as to a spot of appendicitis, said Hugo, poor old George could go ahead and make himself quite at home and have just what he liked. Whereupon Tarlyon at once closed his eyes again, and then they put something over his mouth and he passed away, thinking, *"That's* all right." But it could not have been quite all right, he thought on waking suddenly, for although he could not see very well he could hear quite distinctly, and the voice of Dr. Chill was saying:

"My dear Mr. Black, I am sorry to have to say this, but I certainly do not consider this among your most successful operations. My patient's pulse is entirely arrested, and I am afraid there is now no hope. Are you sure, Mr. Black, that the coroner will think you were quite wise to operate when he was in so low a condition? And I am sure," says he, "that you are not at all wise to sew up that wound with the sponge still inside."

"Oh, shut up!" says Mr. Black, for the same was a short-tempered man much addicted to overcalling at bridge.

Tarlyon did not hear any more before he went off again; but when he awoke this time he did not feel the sickly after-effects of chloroform, he did not feel anything at all except that he was very weak and had a tummy-ache. The room seemed much lighter, too, than when he had seen it last, and many more people were in it, and then he heard a squealing noise and thought: "Good God, where am I?"

And he tried to speak but could not, he tried hard but all he could achieve was a sort of mewing noise similar to the squealing noise, and then the blood simply rushed to his head with rage, for there was Hugo's tiresome face bending over him and there were Hugo's tiresome eyes simply running with tears.

He tried to turn his head away in disgust at the loathsome sight, but could not move, and then he went almost raving mad, for Hugo was trying to kiss him! Tarlyon tried to swear and failed for the first time in his life, whereupon he made to raise his hand to catch Hugo a clout on the ear, but all he did was to pat Hugo's cheek, which the foul man took for a caress encouraging him in his damp behaviour. But in raising his hand Tarlyon did at least achieve something, for he saw that his hand had changed considerably during his illness, it must have, for it was now a frail and milk-white hand with a diamond ring on the third finger, so that he thought in despair: "Good God, I've died under the operation and been born again as an Argentine!"

Hugo never left the bedside until at last the doctor got him by the scruff of the neck and, with silent cheers from Tarlyon, hurled him from the room. But even as he went through the door he turned his repulsive face towards Tarlyon and blew him a kiss, and then the fattest nurse Tarlyon had ever seen shoved a bundle under his nose and said in an idiotic voice which he supposed was meant to be cheering: "There, there, my dear, it's a little boy you've got now. Isn't he a duck, fat as a peach and all!"

Bits of the bundle were then pulled about and Tarlyon was shown what he considered was the most depressing little boy he had ever seen, with its face all wrinkled up and an entirely bald head of an unpleasant colour. Tarlyon's first impression was that the little boy must have been drinking too much to get that colour; and he tried to wave the bundle away, but he was quite helpless, he could not move nor utter, and the fat nurse shoved the wretched little boy's bald head against his mouth so that he simply had to kiss it as he had not the strength to bite it. Meanwhile everyone in the room was smiling idiotically, as though someone had just done something clever, so that, speechless with rage as he already was, he became doubly speechless and thought to himself:

"This is what comes of having pneumonia in a garage!"

Not for minutes, it seemed not for years, was the full terror of what had actually happened revealed to him. He must have been making a face of some sort, for the fat nurse brought a mirror and held it to him, saying: "There, there, don't fret. See how well you look!" And the face that Tarlyon saw in the mirror was the face of his little sister Shirley, a pretty little white face with cheeky curled lips and large grey eyes and a frantic crown of curly golden hair.

Tarlyon tried to stammer: "Some awful mistake has been made," but not a word would come, and for very terror at what had happened he closed his eyes that he might, even as though he verily was Shirley, sob in peace.

It was for Shirley more than for himself that he was distracted with grief, for he realised only too well what must have happened. Shirley, the poor darling, must have been having terrible trouble in childbirth—and all for that foul Hugo's wretched heir with the bald head—while he had died of pneumonia-cum-appendicitis in the next room. His soul having left his body—while Ian Black and Dr. Chill were still arguing about it—he had, or it had, wandered about between the two rooms for a while and then, while Shirley wasn't looking, had slipped into her body and expelled her soul into the outer darkness.

That his supposition was only too accurate was presently proved beyond all doubt. Hugo had managed to sneak into the room again, and when Tarlyon opened his eyes he looked at Hugo be-

seechingly for news, whereupon the wretched
man at once kissed him. But Tarlyon must have
looked so furious, even with Shirley's pretty face,
that the fat nurse at once stopped Hugo from
clinching again; and when Tarlyon again looked
beseechingly towards the wall of the room in
which he had had pneumonia Hugo nodded his
head cheerfully and said: "Yes, he's dead, poor
old George. Doctor said he would have lived
if he hadn't been such a hard drinker. Poor old
George. They are embalming the corpse in Vichy
Water at the moment."

Tarlyon lost count of time, of days and nights,
he lost count of everything but the number of his
discomforts and fears. He spent hours with
closed eyes enumerating the terrors in store for
him as a woman, as a pretty woman, as Hugo's
wife. It would be no use his saying that he was
not really Shirley but her brother George, for
people would only think he was mad. Of course
he would divorce Hugo as soon as he was better;
it was too revolting to have Hugo's face shoved
close to his own on the slightest provocation.
Heavens, how well he now understood the many
ways in which men can infuriate women! And
then, chief among the terrors of his new life, must
be the bringing-up of that awful baby with the
bald head. As it was, he was seeing a great deal
too much of it, the fat nurse would always be
bringing it to him and pushing it at him, but as to
taking it into bed with him Tarlyon wasn't having any, not even for the look of the thing when
his mother came into the room. For one day

his mother did come, and she in deep mourning for his death, and she stood above him with sad eyes, and as she held the wretched baby she whispered: "Poor George! How he would have loved his little nephew!" Fat lot she knew, poor old mother.

But always it was Hugo and his repellently affectionate face who was the last straw. One evening he managed to get into the room in his pyjamas, in Tarlyon's pyjamas, in Tarlyon's black pyjamas, and saying to the fat nurse: "I must just kiss her once," furtively approached the bed. But Tarlyon was ready, and now he was just strong enough to lash out at Hugo as he bent down——

"Oi!" said Ian Black's voice. "Steady there, you Tarlyon!"

Tarlyon said something incredibly wicked and Ian Black said: "You'll be all right soon. In fact you must be quite all right now, if you can swear like that. But don't land me one on the head again with that hot-water bottle else I'll operate on you for something else. And I haven't left a sponge inside you, either. Hullo, here's Hugo with a smile like a rainbow!"

"I should think so!" cried Hugo. "Chaps, I've got a son! What do you know about that?"

"Everything!" gasped Tarlyon. "He's bald."

"Bald be blowed, George! All babies are bald. In my time I was the baldest baby in Bognor, and proud of it. He's a wonder, I tell you."

"He's awful!" sighed Tarlyon. "Go away, Hugo, go away! I'll explain later, but at the moment I am *so* tired of your face. And in future," said he sharply, "don't dare to try to kiss Shirley more than once a day."

The rest of this story is not very interesting, and nothing more need be said but that Tarlyon nowadays makes a point of advising a man never to kiss his wife without first making quite certain that she wants to be kissed, which is quite a new departure in the relations between men and women and one to be encouraged as leading to a better understanding and less waste of temper between the sexes.

As for the bald baby, he now has some hair of that neutral colour which parents call golden, and four teeth, and Hugo shows off his scream with pride. Hugo and Shirley think he is marvellous. Maybe he is. Maybe all babies are. But it is certain that all women are, by reason of what they put up with in men one way and another. That is what Tarlyon says, and if he does not speak on the matter with authority then this is not a true story and might just as well not have been written, which is absurd.

V: THE PRINCE OF THE JEWS

THIS is the tale of the late Rear-Admiral Sir Charles Fasset-Faith, K.C.B., C.M.G., D.S.O. This distinguished torpedo officer was advanced to flag rank only last June, having previously been for two years Commodore of the First Class commanding the —— Fleet. Throughout the war he was attached to the submarine service; and for the vigilance and fearlessness of his command his name came to be much on men's lips. His early death, at the age of forty-five, will be regretted by all who knew him. He never married. This is also the tale of Julian Raphael the Jew and of Manana Cohen, his paramour.

One summer evening a gentleman emerged from the Celibates Club in Hamilton Place; and, not instantly descending the few broad steps to the pavement, stood a while between the two ancient brown columns of the portico. The half of a cigar was restlessly screwed into the corner of his mouth in a manner that consorted quite oddly with his uneager English eye; and that, with the gentleman's high carriage, might have reminded a romantic observer of the President of the Suicide Club. His silk hat, however (for he was habited for the evening), was situated on his head with an exact sobriety which would seem to rebuke the more familiar relations customary between desperate gentlemen and their hats; and he appeared, at his idle station at the head of the broad steps, to be lost in peaceful contemplation.

The Admiral made thus a notable mark for any passing stranger with a nice eye for distinction: he stood so definitely for *something*, a very column of significance, of conduct. Unusually tall for a sailor, and of powerful build, his complexion was as though forged—it is the exact word—in the very smithy of vengeful suns and violent winds: his pale dry eyes, which would, even in a maelstrom, always remain decidedly the driest of created things, in their leisure assumed that kindly, absent look which is the pleasant mark of Englishmen who walk in iron upon the sea: while short brown side-whiskers mightily became the authority of Sir Charles's looks.

The hour was about ten o'clock, and the traffic by the corner of Hamilton Place and Piccadilly marched by without hindrance. The din of horns and wheels and engines, as though charmed by the unusual gentleness of the night, swept by inattentive ears as easily as the echoes of falling water in a distant cavern. The omnibuses to Victoria and to the Marble Arch trumpeted proudly round the corner where by day they must pant for passage in a heavy block. Limousines and landaulettes shone and passed silently. The very taxis, in the exaltation of moderate speed, seemed almost to be forgetting their humble places in the hierarchy of the road. Every now and then figures scuttled across the road with anxious jerking movements.

"A fine night!" sighed the commissionaire of

the Celibates Club. His face was very lined and his old eyes clouded with the stress of countless days of London fog and London rain. "A taxi, Sir Charles?"

The Admiral cleared his throat and aimed the remnant of his cigar into the gutter. "Thanks, Hunt, I think I'll walk. Yes, a fine night."

Omnibus after omnibus tore down the short broad slope from Park Lane and galloped gaily across the sweep of Hyde Park Corner. There was half a moon over St. George's Hospital, and the open place looked like a park with the lamps for flowers.

"The buses *do* speed up at night!" sighed the commissionaire.

"Don't they! But see there, Hunt!" Sir Charles, suddenly and sharply, was waving his cane towards the opposite side of the road, towards the corner by the massive Argentine Club. "See that man?"

The commissionaire with the lined face followed the direction of the cane.

"That constable, Sir Charles?"

"No, no! That Jew!"

The commissionaire, mistrustful of his ancient eyes, peered through the clear night. He sighed: "God knows, Sir Charles, there's Jews enough in Mayfair, but I can't see one just there."

The Admiral thoughtfully took another cigar from his case. His eyes were of iron, but his voice had lost all its sudden sharpness as he said: "Never mind, Hunt. Just give me a light, will you?"

But, as he made to walk down Piccadilly, to
join in a rubber at his other club in St. James's
Street, Sir Charles did not let the dark lean man
on the other side of the road pass out of the corner of his eye. The young Jew crossed the road.
That did not surprise our gentleman. He walked
on and, once on Piccadilly, walked at a good pace.

The Piccadilly scene was seldom crowded between ten and eleven: cinema-theatres, music-
halls and playhouses held the world's attention,
while the night was not yet deep enough for the
dim parade of the world's wreckage. Sir Charles
would always, at about this hour, take a little exercise between his clubs in Hamilton Place and
St. James's.

He had passed the opening of Half-Moon Street
before the young Jew caught up with his shoulder.
Sir Charles walked on without concerning himself to look round at the dark, handsome face.
Handsome as a black archangel was Julian
Raphael the Jew. Sir Charles vaguely supposed
that the archangels had originally been Jewish,
and it was as a black archangel that the looks of
Julian Raphael had first impressed him. It was
altogether a too fanciful business for the Admiral's
taste; but he had no one to blame for it but himself, since he had originally let the thing, he'd
had to admit often, run away with him.

"Well?" he suddenly smiled over his shoulder.
There was, after all, a good deal to smile about,
if you took the thing properly. And it had needed
more than a handsome Jew to prevent Sir Charles
taking a thing properly. But Julian Raphael did
not smile. He said gravely:

"When I first saw you, Sir Charles, I thought you were only a fool. But I am not sure now. You show a resignation towards fate unusual in your sceptical countrymen. It is scepticism that makes men dull, resignation that makes men interesting. It is a dull mind that believes in nothing: it is an interesting mind that expects nothing and awaits the worst. Your waiting shall be rewarded, Sir Charles."

The Admiral walked on with a grim smile. He was growing used to this—even to this! They passed beneath the bitter walls of what was once Devonshire House. The beautiful Jew said softly:

"You have a broad back, Sir Charles. It is a fine mark for a well-thrown knife. Have I not always said so!"

Our gentleman swung round on the lean young Jew. A few yards from them a policeman was having a few words with the commissionaire of the Berkeley Restaurant about a car that had been left standing too long by the curb. It was Julian Raphael who was smiling now. Sir Charles said sternly:

"Am I to understand that you are trying to frighten me with this ridiculous persecution? And what, Mr. Raphael, is to prevent me from giving you in charge to that policeman? You are, I think, wanted for murder."

Julian Raphael's black eyes seemed to shine with mockery. "There's nothing in the world to prevent you, Sir Charles, except that any policeman would think you mad for asking him to arrest air. Not, as you suggest, that he wouldn't, in the ordinary way, be pleased to catch the Prince of the Jews. May I offer you a light for that cigar?"

And as Sir Charles lit his cigar from the match held out to him he was not surprised to find himself looking into the ancient eyes of Hunt, the commissionaire outside his club in Hamilton Place. His walk up Piccadilly, his talk with the young Jew, had taken no longer than it takes to light a cigar. This was the third time within a fortnight that the Admiral had been privileged to see his old enemy, to walk with him and talk with him; and his awakening had each time been to find that not more than a couple of seconds had passed and that he had never moved from his station.

Sir Charles abruptly reentered the club and, in the smoking-room, addressed himself to his old friend Hilary Townshend.

"Hilary," said he, "I have a tale to tell you. It is very fanciful, and you will dislike it. I dislike it for the same reason. But I want you, my oldest friend, to know certain facts in case anything happens to me in the course of the next few days—or nights. In my life, as you know, I have not had many dealings with the grotesque. But the grotesque seems lately to be desiring the very closest connection with me. It began two years ago when I officiously tried to be of some service to a young Jewess called Manana Cohen. God help me, I thought I was acting for the best."

There follows the tale told by Admiral Sir Charles Fasset-Faith to Mr. Townshend.

THE ADMIRAL'S TALE

About two years ago [said Sir Charles], during one of my leaves in London, young Mrs. Harpenden persuaded me to go down with her to a club of some sort she was helping to run down in the East End.

There were then, and for all I know there are now, a number of pretty and sound young women doing their best to placate God for the sins of their Victorian fathers by making life in the East End as tolerable as possible. Of course, only once a week. Venice's idea in landing me was that I should give the young devils down there a rough lecture on the Navy in general and the Jutland fight in particular—that kind of thing.

So there I stood yapping away, surrounded by a crowd of amiable and attentive young men and women. In a room nearby poor Napier Harpenden was trying to get away with only one black eye from a hefty young navvy to whom he was supposed to be teaching boxing. Across a counter in a far corner Venice was handing out cups of perfectly revolting coffee. She had all the bloods at her call that night, had Venice. In one corner Tarlyon was teaching a crowd Jujitsu, and in another Hugo Cypress was playing draughts with a Boy Scout—it did one good to see him. And there, in the middle of all that, was the old mug roaring away about the silent Navy.

I was just getting settled down and raising laughs with the usual Jack Tar stuff when—well,

there they were, a pair of them, quite plainly
laughing at me. Not *with* me, mark you. You'll
understand that it put me off my stroke. However, I did my level best to go on without looking
at them, but that wasn't so easy, as they were
bang in front of me, three or four rows back. I
had spotted the young man first. He was the
one making the jokes and leading the laugh,
while the girl only followed suit. Both Jews, obviously, and as handsome as a couple of new
coins. Smart, too—the young man too smart by
half.

You could tell at a glance that they had no
right in the place, which was for very poor folk,
and that they had come in just to guy. At least,
that devilish young man had. He had a thin
dead-white face, a nose that wouldn't have looked
amiss on a prince of old Babylon, black eyes the
size of walnuts, and a smile—I'll tell you about
that smile. Hilary, I've never in my life so
wanted to do anything as to put my foot squarely
down on that boy's smile. Call me a Dutchman
if they don't hate it even down in hell.

The girl wasn't any less beautiful, with her
white face, black hair, black eyes, fine slim
Hebrew nose. Proud she looked too, and a proud
Jewess can—and does—look any two English
beauties in the face. But she was better, gentler,
nicer. They were of the same stuff, those two
young Jews, the same ancient sensitive clever
stuff, but one had gone rotten and the other
hadn't. You could easily see that from the way,
when she did meet my eyes, she did her level
best to look serious and not to hear what her

companion was whispering into her ear. She
didn't particularly want to hurt my feelings, not
she, no matter how much her man might want
to. Of course I could have stopped the lecture
then and there and chucked the young man out,
but I didn't want to go and have a rough-house
the first time I was asked down to young Venice's
potty old club.

It will puzzle me all my life (or what's left
of it, let's say) to know why that diabolically
handsome young Jew took such an instant dislike
to me; and why I took such a dislike to him!
For that was really at the bottom of all that followed—just good old black hatred, Hilary, from
the first moment our eyes met. But I want to give
you all the facts. Maybe the girl had something
to do with it even then—the girl and his own
shocking smile. You simply couldn't help fancy-
ing that those gentle eyes were in for a very bad
time from that smile. Decidedly not my business,
of course. Nothing that interests one ever is, is
it? But, on the other hand, the young man went
on whispering and laughing so all through my
confounded lecture that by the time I had finished
there was just one small spot of red floating about
my mind. I don't think I've ever before been so
angry. There's one particular thing about people
who sneer that I can't bear, Hilary. They simply
insist on your disliking them, and I hate having
to dislike people more than I can tell you.

They began to clear out as soon as I had finished. The young Jew's behaviour hadn't, naturally, made my effort go any better. He needed
a lesson, that bright young man. I collared him

in the passage outside. Of course he and his young lady were much too smart to hurry themselves, and the rest of the lecturees had almost gone. Inside, Venice had given up poisoning her club with coffee and was trying to bring it round with shocking noises from a wireless set.

I can see that passage now. A narrow stairway leading up to God knows where. Just one gasjet, yellow as a Chinaman. The front-door wide open to a narrow street like a canal of mud, for it was pelting with rain, you could see sheets of it falling between us and the lamp on the opposite side of the road. A man outside somewhere whistling "Horsey, keep your tail up," and whistling it well. Radio inside.

Our young Jewboy was tall. I simply didn't feel I was old enough to be his father, although he couldn't have been more than three or four-and-twenty. And he liked colours, that boy. He had on a nice bright brown suit, a silk shirt to match, and not a tartan in the Highlands had anything on his tie. His young lady's eyes, in that sick light, shone like black onyx. It struck me she was terrified, the way she was staring at me. I was sorry for that, it wasn't her terror I wanted. And where I did want it, not a sign. Then I realised she wasn't terrified for him but for me. Cheek.

I had the fancy youth by the shoulder. Tight. He was still laughing at me. "This lout!" that laugh said. I can hear that laugh now. And, confound it, there was a quite extraordinary authority to that boy's eyes. He wasn't used to following anyone, not he.

I said: "Young man, your manners are very bad. What are you going to do about it?"

I was calm enough. But he was too calm by half. He didn't answer, but he had given up smiling. He was looking sideways down at my hand on his shoulder. I've never had a pretty hand, but it has been quite useful to me one way and another and I've grown attached to it. I can't attempt to describe the disgust and contempt in that boy's look. It sort of said: "By the bosom of Abraham, what *is* that filthy thing on my shoulder?"

I said sharply: "I'm waiting."

The girl sighed: "Don't! Don't, Julian!"

As though, you know, he might hit me! Me!

Well, he might! I said: "Careful, young man!"

The girl whispered almost frantically: "Let him go, sir! Please! You don't know . . ."

I comforted her. I said I could take care of myself. She wasn't, I fancy, convinced. The way she looked at a man, with those scared black eyes!

But our young friend wasn't taking any notice of either of us. He was busy. All this, of course, happened in a few seconds. The Jew had raised his hand, slowly, very slowly, and had caught the wrist of my hand on his shoulder. I felt his fingers round my wrist. Tight.

"Steady, boy!" I said. I'd have to hit him, and I didn't want to do that. At least, I told myself I didn't want to. That young Jew had strong fingers. He simply hadn't spoken one

word yet. His conversation was limited to trying to break my wrist. *My* wrist! Then he
spoke. He said: "You swine!" The girl suddenly pulled at my arm, hard. His back was to
the open doorway, the rain, the gutter. I caught
him one on the chin so that he was in it flat on
his back. His tie looked fancier than ever in
the mud, too. The girl sort of screamed.

"All right," I said. "All right." Trying, you
know, to comfort the poor kid. She was rushing
after her man, but I had my arm like a bar across
the door. She stared at me.

I said: "Listen to me, my child. You're in
bad company."

"She is now," a voice said. The young Jew
had picked himself up. He looked a mess, fine
clothes and all. I thought he would try to rush
me, but not he! He just smiled and said quite
calmly: "I'll make a note of that, Sir Charles
Fasset-Faith. Come on, Manana."

But I wasn't letting "Manana" go just yet.
The poor kid.

"What's his name?" I asked her.

She stared at me. I never knew what "white"
really meant until I saw that child's teeth.

"His name?" I repeated. Gently, you know.

She whispered: "Julian Raphael."

That young Jew's voice hit me on the back of
the neck like a knife. "You'll pay for that,
Manana! See if you don't!"

By the way, it isn't just rhetoric about the
knife. It was like a knife. But I'll tell you more
about knives later.

"Oh," she sobbed.

"Look here," I said to the devilish boy, "if you so much as——"

He laughed. The girl bolted under my arm and joined him. He just laughed. I said: "Good-night, Manana. Don't let him hurt you." She didn't seem to dare look at me.

They went, up that muddy lane. He had her by the arm, and you could see he had her tight. There aren't many lamps in that *beau quartier,* and a few steps took them out of my sight. I heard a scream, and then a sob.

That settled Julian Raphael so far as I was concerned. Then another sob—from the back of that nasty darkness. I couldn't, of course, go after them then. It would look too much as though I was bidding for possession of the young Jew's love-lady. But at that moment I made up my mind I'd land that pretty boy some-time soon. That scream had made me feel just a trifle sick. That was personal. Then I was against Julian Raphael impersonally because I've always been for law and order. You have too, Hilary. I shouldn't wonder if that's not another reason why women find men like us dull. But some of us must be, God knows, in this world. And it was against all law and order that young Mr. Julian Raphael—imagine any man actually *using* a name like that!—should be loose in the world. Crook was too simple a word for Mr. Raphael. And he was worse for being so devilish handsome. One imagined him with women—with this poor soul of a Manana. Of course, Venice and Napier and the other people at their potty old club knew nothing about either of them. They must have just drifted in, they said. They had, into my life.

The very next morning I rang up our friend H—— at Scotland Yard and asked him if he knew anything about a Julian Raphael. Oh, didn't he! Had a *dossier* of him as long as my arm. H—— said: "The Prince of the Jews, that's Julian Raphael's pet name. Profession: counterfeiter. But we've never yet caught him or his gang."

Oh, the cinema wasn't in it with our fancy young friend. The police had been after him for about five years. Once they had almost got him for knifing a Lascar. Murder right enough, but they'd had to release him for lack of evidence. The Lascar, H—— said, had probably threatened to give away a cocaine plant, and Julian Raphael had slit his throat. Suspected of cocaine-smuggling, living on immoral earnings of women, and known to be the finest existing counterfeiter of Bank of England £5 notes. Charming man, Mr. Julian Raphael.

"I want to land him," I told H——.

"Thanks very much," said he. "So do we."

"Well, how about that girl of his—Manana something?"

"Manana Cohen? Catch her giving him away! She adores the beast, and so do they all, those who aren't terrified of him."

I said: "Well, we'll see. I want to get that boy. I don't like him."

H——'s last words to me were: "Now look here, Charles, don't go playing the fool down there. I know the East End is nowadays supposed to be as respectable as Kensington and that the cinema has got it beat hollow for pools of blood, but believe me a chap is still liable to be punctured in the ribs by a clever boy like Julian Raphael. So be a good fellow and go back to your nice old Navy and write a book saying which of your brother Admirals didn't win Jutland just to show you're an Admiral as well."

H—— was right. I was a fool, certainly. But God drops the folly into the world as well as the wisdom, and surely it's part of our job to pick up bits of it. Besides, I've never been one for dinner-parties or the artless prattle of young ladies, and so, thought I, could a man spend his leave more profitably than in landing a snake like Julian Raphael?

I took myself off down to the East End with my oldest tweeds, a toothbrush and a growth on my chin. George Tarlyon came with me. He had scented a row that night, and not the devil himself can keep George from putting both his feet into the inside of a row. Besides, he wanted to have a look at Miss Manana Cohen, saying he was a connoisseur of Cohens and liked nothing so much as to watch them turning into Curzons or Colquhouns. I wasn't sorry, for you can't have a better man in a row than George Tarlyon, and with his damfool remarks he'd make a miser forget he was at the Ritz. We took two rooms in Canning Town E., and very nice rooms they were, over a ham and beef shop, and walked from pub to pub watching each other's beards grow and listening for Julian Raphael. At least, I listened and George talked.

You would naturally have thought that the likely place to find that smart young man would be round about what journalists call the "exclusive hotels and night-clubs of the West End." Not a bit of it. We soon heard something of Julian Raphael's ways from one tough or another. Tarlyon's idea of getting information delicately about a man was to threaten to fight anyone who wouldn't give it to him, and we soon collected quite a bit that way.

Mr. Raphael was a Socialist, it appeared—remember, I'd guessed he was clever?—and hated the rich. He hated the rich so bitterly that, though he had a pretty fat bank-account of his own, he still clung to his old quarters in the East End. But no one knew, or cared to give, the address of his "old quarters," which were probably various. Tarlyon threatened to fight any number of toughs who didn't "know" Mr. Raphael's address, but they preferred to fight, and in the end George got tired.

Oh, yes, Julian Raphael was certainly watched by the police, but he was generally somewhere else while the police were watching him. And Miss Manana Cohen was certainly his young lady-love, and she loved him and lived with him but he wouldn't marry her because of another principle he had, that it was wrong for a man of independent spirit to have a wife of his own. Nice boy, Mr. Julian Raphael. But it appeared that he loved Miss Manana very decidedly and discouraged competition. It also appeared that before he had taken to the downward path he had been a juggler with knives on the music-halls.

Knives again. Tarlyon thought that a pretty
good joke at the time, but he didn't enjoy it
nearly so much later on.

We had been pottering about down there several days and George was just beginning to think
of a nice shave and a bath when we hit on our
first clue. The clue was walking up a grimy side-
street by the East India Docks.

"Oh, pretty!" says George. And she certainly
was. She hadn't seen us. She was in a hurry.

"We follow," I said.

"Naturally," says George. "A nice girl like
that! What do you take me for, a Y. M. C. A.?"

We followed. She walked fast, did Miss
Manana. And it was queer, how she lit up that
grimy God-forsaken street. The way she was
walking, you might have taken her for a young
gentlewoman "doing" the East End in a hurry.
Tall, lithe, quietly dressed—Julian Raphael's
property! And he'd made her scream with pain.

"Now what?" snapped George.

She had been about twenty yards ahead of us.
Street darkish, deserted, lined with warehouses,
and all closed because it was a Saturday afternoon. Suddenly, no Manana Cohen. We slipped
after her quick as you like. She had dived down
a narrow passage between the warehouses. We
were just in time to see the tail of her skirt
whisking through a door in the wall a few yards
up—and just in time to cut in after her.

"Oh!" she gasped. We must have looked a
couple of cut-throats. And it was dark in there.
I was panting—nothing like a sailor's life for
keeping you thoroughly out of training, unless

it's a soldier's. But George was all there, being a good dancer.

"Miss Cohen, I believe?" he asks. All in whispers. She just stared at us. George didn't want to scare her any more than I did. He was gay, in that mood of his when he seems to be laughing more at himself than at anyone else. But she just stared at us. She was tall, as women go, but we simply towered over the poor child. Then she recognised me and went as red as a carnation. I couldn't think why. Tarlyon said comfortingly: "There, there!"

Then she panted all in a jumble: "I'm sorry I was rude to you the other night. Really I am. Please go away now, please!"

"I'm afraid we can't do that," I whispered. "We want——"

George, with his foot, gently shut the door behind us. We were in the passage of the house or whatever it was. It was pitch-dark. I lit another match.

"But what is it, what do you want?" the girl moaned.

"We just want to have a word with your young man," said George, the idiot, in his ordinary voice.

"Oh!" she caught her breath. That gave the show away all right. Julian Raphael was at home, whatever home was. Then the match went out. And the lights went on, snap! Julian Raphael stood at the end of the passage, pointing a revolver.

George said: "Don't be an ass!"

"Come here!" says Mr. Raphael to the girl.

"No, you don't!" said George, hauling her to him by the arm.

Julian Raphael smiled in that way he had. "If you don't let her go at once," he says, "I shoot."

"You what!" I said.

Tarlyon laughed. You can hear him. He said: "Now don't be a fool all your life but stand at attention when you speak to my friend here, because he's a knight. And put that comic gun away else I'll come and hit you."

I couldn't help laughing. The young Jew looked so surprised. He'd never before been talked to just in that way and it bothered him, he was used to doing the laughing and being taken seriously. But I had laughed too soon. There was a whizz by my ear, a thud on the door behind me, and a knife an inch deep in the panel. The surprise had given Manana a chance to slip away. She was by Mr. Raphael now at the end of the passage. There wasn't light enough to make out what was behind them, a stairway up or a stairway down. Down, I guessed, into the bowels of the earth. Julian Raphael was smiling. I'll say it was well thrown, that knife.

Tarlyon was livid. "By God," he whispered, "threw a knife at us! We *are* having a nice weekend!"

I held him back. What was the use? A little child could have led us at knife-throwing. Julian Raphael said, with that infernal sneer of his:

"Gentlemen, I merely wanted to show you what to expect if you were to advance another step. I wouldn't kill you—not yet. One of you, yes.

But it would cause comment, the disappearance of two fools. However, I might slice bits off your ears. Further, this is my house. Are you not intruding? Gentlemen, you may go."

And, you know, we did. What the deuce else was there to do? If Tarlyon with his infernal chuckling hadn't roused the man out of his lair we might have taken him by surprise and learnt something of the whereabouts of that counterfeiting business. But as it was, "go" was us while the going was good. And the way Tarlyon swore when we were outside made me glad it was a Saturday afternoon and the warehouses were closed, else he might have corrupted the poor workmen.

"What do we do now?" he asked at last. "Lump it?"

"Well, at any rate, we know his address now."

"Address be blowed! That's not an address, Charles, but an exit. I'll bet our smart friend doesn't press his trousers in that hole—and, by Heaven, there you are!"

He made me jump. I hadn't, didn't, see anything. I thought it was another knife.

"Never mind," snapped George. "Too late now. Come on, man, come on!"

He made me walk on. After reaching daylight from that passage between the warehouses we had turned to the left, walked on a hundred yards or so by the front of the warehouses, then to the left again. This, running parallel to the passage, was a row of quite respectable-looking houses all stuck together, as quite respectable-looking

life. To jail her now would be to ruin her for all her life.

Tarlyon, of course, didn't need to be convinced. He was only leading me on. Tarlyon wouldn't have put the police on a girl for trying to boil him in oil. But I was right about Manana Cohen. Good God, don't I know I was right! This had been her life, was her life, these dreary streets, these foul alleys. Julian Raphael had found her, dazzled her, seduced her, bullied her, broken her. What chance had the girl, ever? She was timorous, you could see. A timid girl. No matter how kindly you talked to her, she stared at you like a rabbit at a stoat. Life was the stoat to Manana Cohen. Who knows what the girl hadn't already suffered in her small life, what hell? Maybe she had loved Julian Raphael, maybe she loved him now. That wasn't against her. Saints love cads. It's the only way you can know a saint, mostly. Some of the nicest women you and I know, Hilary, have been divorced for the love of blackguards. Well, if Manana loved Raphael she would be punished enough by seeing him go to prison for a long stretch. One might find her a job on the stage, with her looks and figure. Good Lord, the way that girl looked at you when you so much as opened your mouth, her black eyes shivering as though her heart was hurt.

We found a taxi in the Whitechapel Road. To civilisation. Tarlyon was quiet. I wondered if he thought I was in love with the girl. Me, at my age. As we rattled through Cheapside—deserted on a Saturday afternoon—Tarlyon said:

"We will have to think of a way of getting the girl out of the place beforehand. But how? If we warn her she will naturally pass the glad news on to her man. Naturally."

Naturally, I agreed. She wouldn't be herself if she went back on her man. I said I would think of a way as I bathed and dressed for dinner. As George dropped me at my flat he said:

"Let's say dinner in an hour's time at White's. Meanwhile I'll ring up H——. Maybe he will dine with us. I suppose it will be about midnight before we get down there with his men. I'll tell you one thing, I'm not going to have knives chucked at me on an empty stomach—for I'll not be left out of this, not for all the knives in Christendom and Jewry. This is a real treasure-hunt as compared to chasing poppycock with children round Regent's Park and chickenfood with flappers up Piccadilly. I said midnight, Charles, to give you a chance of getting Miss Manana Colquhoun clear away. Wish you luck!"

But fate wouldn't be bullied by George Almeric St. George Tarlyon. Fate had ideas of her own. Or is fate a he? No, it would be a woman, for she hates slim women. I've noticed that in the East, where no slim woman ever comes to any good. I hadn't finished glancing at my letters, while my bath was running, when my man announced a young lady.

"A young what?" I said.

He was surprised, too. I went into the sitting-room. Manana Cohen was by the open door, as though she was afraid to come right in.

I said: "Thank Heaven you've come!" Extraordinary thing to say, but I said it.

She tried to smile. All scared eyes. I thought she was going to faint, tried to make her sit down, fussed about. Hilary, I'm trying to tell you I was shy.

"I'm frightened," she said, as though that would be news for me. Then it all came out in that jumbled way of hers. She had given Raphael the slip, had found my address in the telephone-book, had come to me to warn me.

"To warn me!" I gasped. The cheek of these young people! Here were we and all Scotland Yard after them—and she had come to warn me!

"Yes. Listen." Then she stopped. Suddenly, she blushed crimson.

I said: "Now, Manana, what is it? What on earth is there to blush about?"

She tried not to stammer as she said: "I can't help it. Julian's after you. He's out to kill. He hates you once and he hates you twice because he thinks I'm in love with you. I don't know why. He's just mad jealous. I know Julian. And they'll never catch him. Never. The fool police! I just thought I'd warn you. Go away, please go away—out of London. I feel if you die it will be my fault. He'll throw you if you don't go away. I know Julian. You'll be walking up Piccadilly one evening, this evening perhaps. Suddenly, swish, knife in your back. No one will know who threw it, in the crowd. He could throw it from the top of a 'bus and no one notice. He never misses."

I said: "So, Manana, he thinks you love me. Why does he think that?"

She wasn't blushing now. She was quite calm now. She had never moved from the open door. Her eyes wouldn't meet mine. They shone like anything in that white face. She just said: "Now I've warned you, I must go back. He will miss me. I'm glad I warned you. I think you must be a good man. Good-bye. But go away, please go away at once! Good-bye."

I couldn't stop her by touching her, else she would have got scared. I just told her not to go back East. We were going to raid Julian Raphael's place that night.

"You came to warn me," I said, "but I was just coming to warn you. My friend and I don't want you to go to prison, Manana. You had better stay away from there for the present. I can find you somewhere to stay to-night, if you like. You can trust me."

She opened her eyes very wide, but all she said was: "I must go back at once."

I began to protest, but she went on tonelessly: "You don't understand. I came to warn you because you are a good man. You are, aren't you? I'm sorry I was led into laughing at you that night. He pinched my arm when I didn't laugh. But I must stand by Julian. He is my man, good or bad. You see? He has been kind to me in his way. He loves me. I must go back to him at once. If you make me promise not to tell him about the police, I won't. I won't tell him anyway, I think. He must go to prison. It is time, because he will do more murders. I hate

murders. But I will go with him to prison. And
that will make it all right between Julian and me.
Good-bye."

It was good-bye. I knew it was no use arguing. With some women one doesn't know when
it's any good or not, with a few one does. They're
the ones who count. I could hold her by force,
of course—for her own good. Dear God, the
lies we can tell ourselves! If I held her by force
from going back to Julian Raphael it would not
have been so much for her own good as for mine.
I hated her going, I wanted her. But she must
do as she thought right. Everyone must always,
in spite of everything. I'm glad I've never married, Hilary, I would have made a mess of it just
by always seeing my wife's point of view.

I saw Manana downstairs to the door. It was
raining the deuce, and the difference between twilight and night was about the same as that between a man of colour and a nigger. Manana
and I stood close together in the open doorway.
It was good-bye. I said: "Perhaps they will let
you off. I will do my best. Come to me for help
later on. Good-bye, Manana. Thank you."

She smiled. The first and last smile I ever
saw light that face. "I must never see you again,"
she said, and then the laughter of Julian Raphael
tore the smile from her face.

My rooms, as you know, are in Curzon Street:
at the rather grubby end where Curzon Street,
as though finally realising that it is deprived of
the residential support of the noble family of that
name, slopes helplessly down to a slit in a grey
wall called Lansdowne Passage. I don't know

if you ever have occasion to go through there. When it is dark in London it is darker in Lansdowne Passage. It leads, between Lansdowne House and the wreck of Devonshire House, to Berkeley Street. There is a vertical iron bar up the middle of each opening, which I'm told were originally put there to prevent highwaymen making a dash through the Passage to the open country round Knightsbridge. Against that vertical iron bar leant Julian Raphael. I remember he had a pink shirt on. Our young dandy always showed a stretch of cuff. Between us and him there was one of those very tall silver-grey lamp-posts. You could see him round the edge of it, a black lean lounging shape. And that pink shirt.

"Manana, I followed you!" he cried. And he laughed.

The girl whispered frantically to me: "Get in, get in, get in!"

I said "What?" like a fool. She tried to push me inside the doorway. I was looking at her, not at Julian Raphael. I didn't understand. There was a scream from the twilight: "Mind out, Manana!" Manana jumped in front of me. That's all.

I held her as she fell backward. She just sighed.

"Manana!" the voice screamed again. Oh, in terror! The knife was up to the hilt in her throat.

I think I lost my head completely for the first time in my life. I made a dash towards the figure in the opening of Lansdowne Passage. He didn't move, didn't even see me coming. He was sobbing like a baby. Then I changed my mind and rushed back to Manana. Lay a flower on a pavement in the rain, and you have Manana as I last saw her. Her eyelids fluttered once or twice. The rain was washing the blood from her throat into the gutter. My man had come down and was doing his best. I looked through the twilight at the crumpled black figure against the iron bar.

"She's dead, Raphael!" I called, whispering to my man: "Go get him!"

He did his best, poor devil. Raphael yelled: "Yes, for you! And I'll never throw but one more knife—but I'll do that if I have to come back from hell to do it!" He was gone, through Lansdowne Passage. My wretched man hadn't a chance. That night and for days there wasn't a port in England that H—— left unwatched for Julian Raphael. But, as in the story-books, he has never been seen or heard of again. H—— has an idea he is somewhere in the Americas.

But it's not quite true (the Admiral added) that Julian Raphael has never been seen or heard of again. I have seen him and heard him, quite lately—in a sort of way. Of course, it can be no more than a trick of the imagination. He has probably been more on my mind recently than I had realised. But the illusion is quite definitely vivid and unpleasant. And I can tell you it gets rather on a man's nerves, this comic talk of knives on Piccadilly. Imagination, Hilary, can play us queer dark tricks sometimes. And it's no good trying to explain them with spirit talk. The mind is a dark place and we don't know what's in the sky and that's all there is to it.

.   .   .   .   .

Mr. Townshend had listened gravely. A grey man, of the type conscientiously sad, Mr. Townshend found no aspect of this our life on earth which was not a proper occasion for the exercise of gravity, command of temper and forbearance. He therefore forbore to make any comment on his friend's tale, but merely remarked:

"You ought not to stay in London, Charles. An unhealthy place, at best. Why not come down to Magralt with me to-morrow? Guy de Travest is coming. There's some fishing. Not much, and that little is poor, but you can always smoke in peace."

Sir Charles laughed. "You talk like Manana! But, anyhow, I am due at Portsmouth the day after to-morrow. No, no, I'll see my time out in London. I've been in most corners of the world, Hilary, and never found romance but in London."

"Hm!" said Mr. Townshend thoughtfully. "You have an odd idea of romance, Charles. Romance! And I don't, as a general rule, believe in apparitions. Hm! Have you rung up H——— to tell him of the reappearance of this remarkably unpleasant youth?"

"And he laughed me to scorn! Was ready, in fact, to lay a pony against Raphael's being within a thousand miles of London or England."

"You never know," said Mr. Townshend thoughtfully.

"Never know what, Hilary?"

"Where you are," said Mr. Townshend thoughtfully. "With Jews."

It was on the night following this conversation that the Admiral, on emerging from the Celibates Club, made an astonishing suggestion to Hunt the commissionaire.

"Hunt," says Sir Charles, "do you mind walking with me down to the Piccadilly corner? I will know then that I am actually moving and not just standing here and thinking I'm moving. You see my point, Hunt?"

"Certainly, Sir Charles. I quite understand."

"I'm glad someone does!" sighed our gentleman.

The commissionaire with the lined face, whose own antipathy to wine in his youth had not been insuperable, could sympathise with the Admiral's probable condition, while admiring the correct address with which, as became a gentleman of the sea, he bore his suffering.

"See any Jews about, Hunt?" the Admiral asked as they came to the Piccadilly corner.

"Not definitely, Sir Charles. But a couple of Rolls-Royces have just passed. Good-night, Sir Charles."

"Good-night, Hunt."

Those were the last words the ancient commissionaire was ever to hear from his good friend the Admiral. For as Sir Charles made to cross Piccadilly from Albemarle Street to St. James's Street he heard that "whizz" behind him. He had been expecting it, but it startled him. He half-turned and jumped sideways, colliding with the bonnet of a fast-moving car.

There was a terrific din about him as he raised
himself to his hands and knees. It deafened him,
the din of engines and voices. Many voices
seemed to be arguing. Then, as he rose to his
feet, the din happily receded. There was silence,
but the silence of a pleasant voice. He walked
on to St. James's Street, glad things had been no
worse. Then he saw the face of Julian Raphael.
It was just in front of him, smiling. He was holding out his hand to Sir Charles, smiling. He was
beautiful. Behind his shoulder was Manana.
She was laughing at Sir Charles's bewilderment.
Then, as he stared at them, they pointed over his
shoulder. They were still laughing. Behind him,
in the middle of Piccadilly, there was a great
crowd around a large motor-car and a prostrate
figure that looked oddly like a dingy travesty of
himself. That is how it was, but still he did not
understand. Julian Raphael and Manana laughed
at him and each took him by an arm and walked
with him down the slope of St. James's Street.
There was a valley at the foot of St. James's
Street, and over the valley a golden cloud as
large as a continent. Many people were walking
about, looking calm and clean and happy.
Manana was still laughing happily.

"Julian died last night in Paris," she told Sir
Charles. "He was just coming over to London
to kill you. Isn't it idiotic? I don't say he loves
you now, but he's willing to consider an intelligent friendship. Aren't you, Julian? Death isn't
at all what the Salvation Army thinks, Charles.
You'll be surprised. You're just yourself, that's
all. Funny you have to die before you're al-

lowed to be yourself. Oh, look! Look, Charles! Isn't it beautiful! Charles, let's walk and walk and walk!"

"Just look at those asses behind!" cried Julian Raphael, shouting with laughter. But now the people at the head of St. James's Street were very faint, the clear golden air of the sun triumphant was falling between Sir Charles's eyes and the people grouped round the prostrate figure that looked oddly like a dingy travesty of himself.

"If they only knew," said Manana gravely, "that living is worth while just because one has to die! Come on, Charles, let's walk!"

"Here, and me!" cried Julian Raphael.

"Young man," said the Admiral severely, "you just stay where you are. I have been waiting a long time for this walk with Manana."

"I'll follow you. Where are you going to walk to?"

"You can't follow us, Julian," laughed Manana. "They won't let you, yet. Naturally, dear, considering how awful you've been. You can have a drink while we're gone."

"A drink?" said Sir Charles. "But, good Lord, he can't have a drink here, can he?"

"But why not?" Manana laughed. "There's only one hell, dear, and that's on earth. Come on, come on! We'll walk towards that golden cloud and back!"

VI. THE THREE-CORNERED MOON

I

THE structure, economy and polity of our
time do not incline the meek and lowly to a
particular regard for persons of condition. Nor is
the patronage of princes and the favour of lords
solicited to any noticeable degree by the poets
and scientists of the day. The most superficial
survey of history will discover that the condescension of a gentleman of the *haut ton* was once regarded as almost an essential of a poet's success:
while the craftsman, was he never so cunning and
exquisite, must rely for his fame on the caprice
of the young men of fashion, who were, it is to
be presumed, not the less generous because they
were invariably in debt and had not the worse
taste because they were nearly always in wine.

In our generation, however, we have progressed
so far in the liberal arts that, should a man of
letters so mask himself with the impertinence of
fashion as to be remarked at Ascot in clothes
which, with a deplorable want of faith in the dignity of letters, have been cut to fit his person, he
shall at once be convicted by all really intelligent
people of a lack of feeling for all that is genuine
in art and literature. That cannot be altogether
just. An effeminate manner and unusual habits
should not, on the other hand, invariably be taken

for sure signs of genius in the mental sciences; and laymen should be warned against regarding soiled linen as an essential of the successful ascent of Parnassus.

In the face of this illiberal attitude towards the upper sort, the popular interest in the young Duke of Mall is the more surprising; and to that gentleman's familiars and dependents it has for long been a source of gratification to observe how the esteem in which he is held by the people of England is rivalled only by the interest shown in the table-manners of the most famous pugilists and the respect extended to the tireless energies of the most beloved prince in Christendom.

Nor was the young Duke's greatness unheralded, his birth without good omen: historians the world over will know the legend of the Dukedom of Mall, how it was prophesied by a sibyl of the Restoration that on the birth of the greatest of that house the golden cock on the weather-vane of St. James's tower would crow thrice, and on his death it would also crow thrice. And only those most steeped in the modern vice of scepticism will disbelieve the unanimous evidence of every club servant in St. James's Street, that this miracle attended the birth of the seventeenth Duke; while we vulgar lovers of England's might and enemies to the Socialist tyranny can only pray that the second manifestation of that miracle be averted for the longest span of God's mercy to the most gallant of His creatures.

There follow, then, some sidelights on the recent life of the young Duke of Mall and his splendid lady. Than these two, history will say, history must say, there never was a more comely pair; for such is the unknowable wisdom of the All-Wise, that opposites will discover the sweetest harmony. The differences referred to are, of course, those of breeding and nationality, for the lady was an American out of Chicago, in the State of Illinois. But to attempt to describe Miss Lamb were to challenge contempt and defy the limitations set by the gods upon human speech. Let it suffice that she was beautiful: the quality of her colour comparable only to that of a garden in tempered sunlight, the texture of her complexion the envy of silkworms, while the glory of her hair has been described by a minor poet as a cap of beaten gold and autumn leaves. As for the lady's eyes, shall a phrase attempt where a thousand photographs have failed?

The Duke, then, was tender of this lady: he wooed her, was mocked, he entreated, was beguiled, he pleaded, was provoked, he stormed, was dismissed, he worshipped, was accepted. The wedding paralysed the traffic of London for several hours and the newspapers of England and America for several days. The happy pair spent their honeymoon at the Trianon at Versailles, lent to the young Duke by the French Government in recognition of his gallant services as a *liaison* officer during the war.

It should be noted that the wedding-present of the bride's father to the young Duke was an ocean-going yacht of gratifying tonnage. White and graceful, the yacht *Camelot* rode the seas like a bird. The Duke, who liked birds, was very impressed.

II

That, however, was some time ago. Now, alas, not the most kindly observer of society can but have remarked that the recent life of the young Duke and his Duchess has been as conspicuous for its private dolour as for its public splendour. There have been rumours, there has been chatter. This has been said, and that, and the other. Gossip, in fact, has been rife. But it is the austere part of the historian to deal only in facts. The facts are as follows:

South of the lands of the old troubadours, between the heights of the Southern Alps and the languor of the Mediterranean, lies the pretty town of Cannes. The year we tell of was in its first youth. The flower and chivalry of England and America were promenading in the sunlight of the pretty town or commenting at their ease on the brilliant tourneys of tennis and polo. Here and there about the links the sun lit up the brilliant Fair Isle sweaters of Jews, Greeks and Argentines where they were playing a friendly match for the empiry of the world. The mimosa was at its full glory of fresh-powdered gold. Brilliant sunshades lit the walks. From the gardens of white villas could be heard the laughter of children and millionaires. The beach was strewn with jewels, and ladies walked in beauty. Great automobiles loitered between the Casino and the Carlton Hotel, while youth in swift Bugatti or Bentley challenged time to a race from Cannes to Monte Carlo. The waters slept profoundly in the full kiss of the afternoon sun. There, as a dove on a spacious lawn, rode a fair white yacht. From its stern hung a cluster of golden cherries, for such was the pretty nautical device of the young Duke of Mall.

It must be granted by the most fastidious that the scene was set for enchantment. The sea slept under the sun, the sun upon the mountains, the chauffeurs at their driving-wheels, the *croupiers* in the Casino, the diplomats at a conference, the *demi-mondaines* near the diplomats. Yet in the yacht raged a storm: the Duke of Mall was having a row with his lady.

It will be incredible that it was not their first. It must be incredible that it looked like being their last. At the moment of our intrusion, my Lord Duke, in point of fact, was saying:

"By Heaven, Leonora, I am sick and tired of it!"

That small, lovely head, those wide, deep, gentle eyes! Yet stern Juno herself did sometimes walk the earth in those very eyes. She was not more than twenty-four, this lady, yet with what proud calm and disdain she could at one glance enwrap her husband! Not, however, that it always advantaged her case, for sometimes it might be he was too sleepy to notice or maybe he would be too busily engaged in disdaining her, which on occasions he could do very handsomely.

Gently said she: "You say you are sick and tired of 'it.' 'It,' my dear, my well-beloved? Am I, by 'it,' to understand that you mean me?"

The young Duke pointed his indifference with the application of a match to a rough surface and the application of the match to a cigar. "You

may," said he, "understand what you like. I said
what I said."

Tenderness was never yet so fitly clothed as by
this lady's voice. "Shall I, then," said she, "tell
you *all* that I understand by what you said?"

The Duke need not have waved a hand sky-
ward, need not have smiled, have yawned, and
said: "Am I God, to stop you talking! But
maybe it is not necessary for me to add that I
wish I were, if only for that purpose."

The Duchess said: "However, I will not be
provoked. It is too hot. I will content myself
merely with remarking that in my considered
opinion the ancient Dukedom of Mall does at
present grace one with the manners of a boor
and the habits of a stable-boy."

"Leonora, you go too far!"

She sighed: "Dear, had I, before marrying you,
gone even a little further, how much more comfortably I had fared!"

For as long as it takes to say a forbidden word
of one syllable the young Duke's fair features
wore the air of a battlefield: thereon anger fought
with apathy: but was, by the grace of God and a
public-school education, repulsed.

"Not, mind you," said the Duchess, "that I can
blame the pretty dolls whom you encourage to
pursue you under my very nose."

The Duke remarked that she had a very beautiful nose, a very small nose.

The Duchess thanked him.

"But," said the Duke, "by the number of things
which you accuse me of doing under it, any one
would think it cast as long a shadow as Lord Nel-

son's column. For the sake of your own beauty,"
he pleaded earnestly, "may I beg you to leave
your nose, much as I admire it, out of my supposed infidelities?"

The Duchess remarked that she could quite
well understand why women pursued him with
their attentions. Yet, as she spoke, no spark of
bitterness pointed her low light voice, no trace of
jealousy marred her urbanity. She remarked that
he was very rich. His rank was second only to
his King's. He was very handsome. He was
charming.

The Duke thanked her.

"However," said the Duchess.

"Ah, that's not too good," sighed the Duke.
"I knew there was a catch somewhere."

"However," said the Duchess, "the beauty that
you most admire in any woman is the beauty of
her not being a woman you already know: the
only charm of which you never are tired is the
charm of novelty."

"One likes a change," sighed the Duke. "If
that's what you are talking about."

"It certainly is," said the Duchess.

"Well, don't let me hinder you," said the Duke.
He was rude. "I am all attention. But should
I interrupt you, sweet, you must forgive me, for
I am apt to talk in my sleep."

"Oh, but haven't I made quite a collection of
names like Dolly and Lucy and Maudie!"

The Duke said one word. It expressed all the
volumes that could be written by the men who,
alas, cannot write. But the Duchess had now
been in England for four years and knew that the

facility with which an Englishman can swear at his wife does not detract in the least from his deep respect for Womanhood, else would England be what England undoubtedly is?

She said: "Maximilian, I want to tell you that you are a *most* extraordinary man. In public, for instance, you are all that is charming; and many who know of our private disagreements can't but think the fault is mine, since in public you are so very *right* and seem never for a moment deficient in the manners, graces and consideration proper to a great gentleman."

The Duke expressed a hope that she would put that down in writing, so that he could send it as a reference to any lády, or ladies, to whom he might be paying his suit, or suits.

"However," said the Duchess, "when we come to examine you in the home, what a different picture do we find! Your manners are monstrous, your graces those of a spoilt schoolboy, while your consideration for your wife such that, far from concealing from me your preference for the company of low women, you will actually," said she, "bring them on board this yacht and make love to them under my very——"

The Duke, he sighed.

"In," snapped the Duchess, "my company. And now," she added calmly, "I will say good-bye."

"Child," said the Duke softly, "must you go? Must you really? Can't I tempt you to stay? Very well, then," said he, "good-bye."

"Captain Tupper!" the Duchess called.

"Captain Tupper," the Duchess said, "I am

going ashore. You will please see to it at once.
I think my maid has everything packed. Thank
you."

The Duke opened his eyes. It was an effort,
for he was sleepy.

"Captain Tupper," said he, "her Grace will
take the fastest cutter to the town to catch the
Blue Train to Calais. Should a sleeper on the
Blue Train be unavailable, you will see to it that
she is accommodated with one of a suitable colour. We, in the cool of the evening, will make
for Naples. Thank you."

The Duke closed his eyes again, for he was
sleepy. The Duchess stared as though into the
heart of the still blue bay, and who shall say what
it was that she saw in that deep place, whether
she saw the towers of her love torn down by the
winds of man's discontent, the ruins of her marriage washed in the infinite sea of man's inconstancy? Her eyes darkened, and presently she
said, bemused: "I am going now. *Adieu*, Maximilian."

"Leonora," he said, with closed eyes, "I wish
you all happiness and content."

"Content!" said she, and laughed.

"Good-bye, Leonora."

She said: "Max, we were very happy once. We
were lovers once. So happy—once upon a time!"

He whispered:

> " 'Out upon it, I have loved
>   Three whole days together!
> And am like to love three more,
>   If it prove fine weather.' "

She: "Oh, but I can match you one vulgar Restoration gallant against another!

> *" 'Then talk not of inconstancy,*
> *False hearts and broken vows;*
> *If I by miracle can be*
> *This live-long minute true to thee,*
> *'Tis all that Heaven allows.' "*

He sighed: "How I loved you, Leonora! As I had never loved anyone before, as I will never love anyone again!"

"How I loved you, Maximilian! But now!" And she said: "A legal separation is a silly quibble. Besides, you might want to marry again. Or I might."

"Might, Leonora? But you will, must, can't help but! With your beauty, youth, wealth."

"Thank you. I have often noticed that one's friends like one best as one is leaving them. Then, Maximilian, shall I divorce you?"

"If you please, dear. My lawyers are Messrs. Onward & Christian. They will arrange the matter with yours in the usual way."

"Remember, dear, that your King will not receive a divorced Duke at court."

"The King can do no wrong," yawned the Duke. "It must be rather hard on him sometimes, but the law is the law."

His eyes were closed against her beauty, else he had seen the sudden smile that touched her beauty, touched it and was going, going, lurked a while in the depths of her eyes like a very small bird in the ferns of love-in-the-mist, and lo! was gone. She said softly: "You are such a baby, Max!"

Seamen passed by, bearing a great leather Innovation trunk to the side. A black cloud rose up from Africa and hid the sun. A shadow walked across the pretty town of Cannes and drove the youth from painted faces.

"And because," said the young Duchess wistfully, "you are such a baby, I don't put it beyond you to make love to my sister if you should meet her. She has always been jealous of me, so she would enjoy nothing so much as your making love to her. Promise not to, Max, please, oh, please! She has just come over to Paris, so I read this morning in *The New York Herald*. Max, promise not to make a fool of me to my own sister!"

"She's pretty?"

"Pretty? Are words so scarce, sir, that you must use a copper coin? And she my twin!"

"Ah me! Oh dear!"

Her voice scarce disturbed the silence of the yacht: "Good-bye, Duke Maximilian. Our lives go different ways. I do wish you success, happiness, health. Good-bye."

As he lay, with closed eyes, his fingers found her hand and raised it to his lips.

"Good-bye," said he. Such was his farewell.

She looked back from the side. He lay silent. She said:

"Courtesy, Maximilian?"

A sea-bird mocked the silence. The cloud athwart the sun was now as large as half the world. The Duchess of Mall said:

"Chivalry, Maximilian?"

The sea-bird screamed and flew away, and Leonora of Mall cried: "I will forgive you all things but your farewell, Maximilian. The very birds are appalled to see chivalry so low in a man that he will take his lady's *adieu* lying down."

Her maid, hatted and veiled for travelling, whispered to her ear:

"Your Grace, he is asleep."

III

It is a sorry business to enquire into what men think, when we are every day only too uncomfortably confronted with what they do. Moreover, the science of psychology—for that is what we are talking about—is as yet but a *demoiselle* among the sciences; and that writer carries the least conviction who tries to wind his tale about her immature coils. Therefore we will not enquire into the young Duke's thoughts, but merely relate his actions: we will leave his psychology to the fishes of the tideless sea, while we let him confront us with all his vanity.

The time came when the young Duke awoke. Now the winds of the sea were playing about him, the sun was certainly not where he had left it, and the angle of his deck-chair was peculiar. The world was very dark. He looked upon the sea and found it odd, and he looked upon the land and did not find it at all.

"Ho!" cried the Duke. "Where is the land, the land of France? Ho there, Captain Tupper! What have you done with the fair land of France? I do not see it anywhere. Our French allies will be exceedingly annoyed when they hear we have mislaid them. And do my eyes deceive me, or is that a wave making for us over there?"

"It is blowing moderate from the southeast, your Grace."

"Moderate, upon my word! Captain Tupper, moderation sickens me. Ho, I see some land over there!"

"We have just left Nice behind, your Grace."

"I sincerely hope, Captain Tupper, that you are not among those who affect to despise Nice. Queen Victoria was very fond of Nice. It may not be Deauville or Coney Island, Captain Tupper, but Nice can still offer attractions of a homely sort."

"But I understood, your Grace, that——"

"These are strange words, Captain Tupper! But proceed."

"——that our direction was Naples."

"Naples? Good God, Naples! And look, there's another wave making straight for us! Hang on, Tupper. I'll see you are all right. You sailors aren't what you were in the days when you each had a port in every——"

"A wife in every port is the correct form of the libel, your Grace."

"But hang it, I call this, don't you, a damned rough sea? However, I feel very gay this evening. I have just had an idea. Now, Tupper, let me hear no more of this high-handed talk about turning your back on Nice."

"But, your Grace, we are making for Naples!"

"Your obsession for Naples seems to me singularly out of place on a windy evening. I think

you might consider me a little, even though I am
on my own yacht. I detest, I deplore, Naples.
Put back to Nice, Captain Tupper. I am for
Paris!"

"For Paris, your Grace!"

"For Paris, Captain Tupper, with a laugh and
a lance and a tara-tara-diddle for to break a pretty
heart!"

IV

Students of sociology have of recent years made
great strides in their alleviation of the conditions
prevailing among the poor; but is it not a fact
that, as a notorious daily paper lately asked, the
study of those conditions appears to attract the
interest of only the lighter sort of society people
and the pens of only the most ambitious novelists? And that the benefits of this study, at least
to novelists, are not mean, was proved beyond
all doubt only the other day, when perhaps the
wealthiest of contemporary writers increased his
fortune by writing a tale about a miser in a slum.
No one, on the other hand, will deny that the
achievements of sociologists among the poor are
as nothing compared with those of students of
hospitality who, poor and unrewarded though
they remain, have of late years done yeoman work
in alleviating the conditions prevailing among the
rich. It is to the generous spadework of men such
as these that American hostesses in Europe owe
the betterment of their lot; and it is by the support of their merciful hands that ladies burdened
with great wealth are prevented from sinking

down in the rarefied atmosphere to which they
have been called.

Mere students of hospitality had not, however,
been strong enough to support the ailing burden
of Mrs. Omroy Pont when that lady had first
come over from America at the call of certain
voices that had advised her that her mission lay
in European society. It had needed graduates
of that brotherhood, lean with endeavour in ball-
rooms and browned with the suns of the Riviera,
to prevent that ample lady from succumbing to
the exhaustion of carrying her wealth through the
halls of her houses in London and Paris among
guests who had failed to catch her name on being
introduced. But the Good Samaritans had
worked unceasingly on her behalf, and since Mrs.
Omroy Pont had both great wealth and infinite
insensibility she was soon in a position to give a
ball at which quite half the guests knew her by
sight.

The morning after the Duke's arrival in Paris
there was this notice in the Continental *Daily
Mail:* "The Duke of Mall has arrived at his residence in the Avenue du Bois, and will spend the
spring in Paris." And presently the good Mrs.
Omroy Pont was on the telephone, first here,
then there and finally to the Duke himself, saying: "My dear Duke, how do you do, how do you
do? I am so glad you are in Paris just now, Paris
is so attractive in the spring. You mustn't fail
to see the tulips in the Tuileries, they are as beautiful as *débutantes*. My dear Duke, I am giving
a party to-morrow night, you must come, you
really must come, now don't say you won't be-

cause I can't bear that, and really I must say, my
dear Duke, that your unfortunate inability to
accept any of my invitations so far has seemed
almost marked, whereas——"

"I am afraid," began the Duke, who had not
the faintest intention of going anywhere near
one of Mrs. Omroy Pont's parties, for she bored
him and life is short.

"But you mustn't be afraid!" cried Mrs. Omroy Pont. "Now, my dear Duke, I want you particularly to come to this party because there is
someone who wants to meet you, someone very
lovely, positively I am not pulling your leg——"

"Really this is too much!" the Duke muttered,
coldly saying out aloud: "Dear Mrs. Omroy Pont,
you do me great honour but I am afraid that an
extremely previous and decidedly prior engagement——"

"It is Miss Ava Lamb who wants to meet you,
my dear Duke. She has just come over to Paris.
Dinner is at nine. Thank you, thank you. It
will be such fun. You will not have to talk unless you want to and you may go to sleep just
when you like as I have engaged Mr. Cherry-Mar-
vel to conduct the conversation over dinner. At
nine then, my dear Duke."

v

The Duke, as he fairly acknowledged to himself the morning after Mrs. Omroy Pont's party,
had been diverted beyond all expectation by his
meeting with Miss Lamb. While she, candour
compelled him to admit, hadn't seemed any less

sensible to the pleasant quality of their companionship. A beautiful girl, a sensible girl, with a lively interest in the passing moment and a delicious capacity for deriving pleasure from the twists in conversation which came so naturally to the Duke but were become, it has to be confessed, a shade familiar to his friends. She hadn't, he reflected over his morning coffee, said anything throughout the evening that didn't interest and entertain; and, since she had come to Europe for the first time but the other day, had amused him vastly with her impressions, which weren't by any means all favourable, since Miss Lamb confessed to a taste for simplicity; which was very agreeable to the Duke, who was also wealthy.

All this made very pleasant thinking for the Duke over his morning coffee; but had he consulted his memory more carefully, it might have emerged that Miss Lamb had listened with pretty attention the while he had talked, the matter of his talk seldom being so abstract in nature that she couldn't entirely grasp it by just looking at him.

What, of course, had instantly impressed him, as it impressed all who knew the Duchess, was the amazing resemblance between the sisters; since the fact that twins are very frequently as alike as two peas never does seem to prepare people for the likeness between the twins they actually meet. Now between Miss Lamb and the Duchess of Mall there wasn't, you dared swear, so much as a shadow of difference in grace of line and symmetry of feature. But why, as Ava Lamb sensibly protested, why on earth should there be

or need there be or could there be, since Leonora
and she had been twins as punctually to the second as was possible?

A nearer view, however, discovered a deal of
difference between the sisters: in those small ges-
tures of voice, habits of expression, capacity for
attention and the like, which, so the Duke had
warmly said, contribute far more than actual
looks to mark the difference between one woman
and another. Nor were they less dissimilar in
colouring, for whereas both the Duchess and Miss
Lamb had those small white faces and immense
blue eyes generally affected by American ladies for
the conquest of Europe, the Duchess's hair was
of a rich and various auburn shaded here to the
deep lights of Renaissance bronze and there to
the glow of Byzantine amber—the Duchess's hair
was, in fact, fair to fairish, while Miss Lamb's
was as near black as is proper in anyone with
blue eyes who is without Irish blood.

In the course of the ball that inevitably followed Mrs. Omroy Pont's dinner-party the Duke
had had further opportunity of judging the differences between his wife and her beautiful sister. And presently he had thought it only fair
to tell Miss Lamb that he and her sister had decided, for each their sakes, to break their marriage; and he had thought it only fair to himself
to point his confession with a sigh, a sigh which
he explained, after a silence quite beautifully
bridged by an understanding look from her, as
being forced from him by the fact that there was
no pleasing some women.

"You mustn't for a moment think," he'd added

wretchedly, "that I am trying to enlist your sympathy against your own sister, but——"

"Please!" Miss Lamb had protested quite unhappily to that. And here was another and the sweetest difference of all between the sisters, for Miss Lamb's was the prettiest American accent imaginable, whereas the Duchess had long since and all too completely achieved the cold and ironic monotony of the mother-tongue.

To be with Ava Lamb, the Duke had gratefully reflected at that moment, was to look on all the beauty of his wife in atmospheric conditions undisturbed by his wife's sarcastic habit of mind. Miss Lamb hadn't a touch of that irony and sophistication which is so often mistaken by American ladies for European culture, she was perfectly that rarest of all visitors to a bored continent, a fresh and simple American lady.

And "Please!" was all she had said about her sister! But to the young Duke that one word had meant so much, forced as it had been so unhappily from her lips, as if half to shield her pert sister against the consequences of her folly, half to prevent him from seeing how deeply she disapproved of that sister, and wholly and sweetly to stay his tongue from exploring further into that misguided sister's character—it had meant so much that he had been content to wait on her understanding even before she'd quietly added: "Oh, I understand——"

"But do you, do you?" he had cried emphatically, and she had let silence present him anew with her deep sense of understanding. She had a delicious talent for silence.

"My dear"—it had just slipped out of him like that, quite naturally, quite wonderfully—"if only other women were like you! To understand, I mean, just to understand!"

"And men?" Miss Lamb had dropped the two words with perceptible unwillingness yet with just a touch of defiance, as who should say that she too, on so rare an occasion, must for once say what was in her mind.

"Men?" the Duke had smiled. He couldn't somehow think of this tall gentle girl as a woman of the same age as his wife. She verily quite charmed him. Once or twice, indeed, he couldn't help but pity Leonora Mall for the way she had let life so quickly polish her freshness into that worldliness which he, for one, found so unsympathetic in women.

"Men, Miss Lamb? And what, if you'll forgive me, do you know of men?"

"Enough surely, surely!"

"But that sounds quite threatening! Have you, then, hunted men in jungles and caught them, caged them and watched them?"

"But, Duke, wouldn't I, surely, have been married by now if I knew nothing of men?"

"Oh, well caught! But, Miss Lamb, you haven't married probably just because, like all rare people, you're—well, fastidious!"

"Oh, I don't know! Maybe. Fastidious is a long word, Duke, and I seem to have been waiting a long time, so maybe you're right. But I don't know. . . ."

"May I say, then, that you've been very wise? So much wiser than many quite sensible men, so much wiser than many beautiful women. I mean, to wait."

"But aren't we all," she pleaded, "always waiting?"

"Some of us, unfortunately," the Duke said grimly, "haven't. I, Miss Lamb, didn't wait long enough."

"But are you so sure, Duke?" She was pleading with him. They were alone. The music and the dance passed behind them. He met her eyes humbly. "Are you so sure you've waited long enough—I mean, my friend, for time to bring the best out of someone you love?"

"But," he'd cried wretchedly, "I don't love her! That's just, don't you see, the awful mistake and pity of it all! It's not that Leonora and I have quarrelled, but that we've each just found the other out."

Miss Lamb sighed: "Oh! Oh, dear! And why, why? Way back home I've wondered, you know, about many things. All this sadness in life! It hurts to hear this. It hurts me—for you both. Poor, poor Leonora!"

The Duke said very earnestly: "Look here, don't for a moment think that I'm being cruel or anything like that. Believe me, your sister loves me no more than she has driven me into loving her. Honest to God, Miss Lamb."

"You *say* that! But I know her, Duke. My own sister! Go to her now, and you will see. I am telling you to go to Leonora now and you will find her crying for her lost love."

"She left me cruelly, completely. I had done nothing. She left me, as a matter of fact, while

I was asleep. She took herself from my yacht as though—look here, as though I was a plague! You call that caring, Miss Lamb? I'd rather be hated in purgatory than cared for on earth after that fashion. But let us talk of something else. Of you!"

"Oh, me! Just a tourist in Europe. . . ."

"Of your heart, then, in America! You left it there? Now confess!"

"Dear no! I wouldn't have my heart jumped by man or god, not I!"

"Bravo, bravo!"

"So my heart's with me here and now, I thank you."

"What, you feel it beating!"

"Perhaps. A little."

"Oh!"

"At being in Paris, Duke."

"I deserved the snub. Go on, please."

"My friend," she said softly, "the history of my life is the history of my dreams. When I was a girl I had—oh, such dreams!"

"Girls, Miss Lamb dear, do! And when they grow up and marry they use the sharpest pieces of those broken dreams to beat their husbands with. Oh, I know! Every husband in the world is held responsible for the accidents that befall the dreams of his wife's girlhood! Oh, I know! I've been, Miss Lamb dear, most utterly married."

"I'm growing afraid of you, Duke. You've a cruel tongue!"

"Ava, I wouldn't have you think I'm abusing your sister to you. But she certainly was born to be a good man's wife, and she's certainly never let me forget why she has failed to live up to the promise of her birth."

"But my dreams weren't at all of knights, cavaliers, heroes! You bet no! My dreams were just of Paris, this lovely merciless Paris!"

The music and the dance lay in the halls behind them. They were alone on the formal terrace high above the marvellous sweep of the Champs Élysées. Far down on the left the fountains of the Place de la Concorde hung in the blue air like slim curved reeds of crystal. In the courtyard below them a cypress-tree stood dark and still, and in its shadow the *concierge's* wife talked in whispers to her lover. From the wide pavement men looked up at the lighted windows with pale astonished faces. Far up on the right, served by long processions of lights from all the corners of the world, the Arc de Triomphe stood high against the pale spring night. Most massive of monuments, built high to the god of war upon the blood of a hundred battlefields, upon the bones of uncountable men and horses, upon the anguish of ravished countries—the miraculous art of men to worship their own misery has raised the monument to the Corsican murderer to be as a dark proud jewel on the brow of the most beautiful of cities. And Ava cried: "Look, the stars are framed in the arch! Oh, Duke, look! And so the arch is like a gate into the kingdom of the stars!"

The Duke whispered: "Don't talk of the stars, Ava Lamb! The stars make me think of all that is impossible."

Up and down the broad avenue between the
trees prowled the beasts of the cosmopolitan night,
these with two great yellow eyes, those with one
small red eye closely searching the ground. In
the middle distance the Seine shone like a black
sword, and the horrible gilt creatures that adorn
the Bridge of Alexander III were uplifted by the
mercy of the night to the dignity of fallen archangels driving chariots to the conquest of the
Heavens. And a three-cornered moon lifted up an
eyelash from the *beau quartier* about the Place
Victor Hugo.

"There's beauty, isn't there," sighed Miss
Lamb, "in the very name of Paris! even when it's
said in an American accent——"

"But, sister-in-law, I love your accent!"

"My, how you laugh at me! But . . . Paris,
Paris! Oh, isn't that a lovely name for a town
built by men to have!"

And as, over his coffee the next morning, the
young Duke reflected on yesternight, he found
himself enchanted by a gay memory. Oh, to be
enchanted again, to be thrilled, to be exalted—
and all, honest to God, by companionship! What
fun there was in life when women didn't grow so
confoundedly familiar with one's habits. To be
with Ava Lamb was to renew all the joy he'd
once had of loving his wife, to renew it and to
increase it, for wasn't he now older and wiser,
wasn't he now wise enough to appreciate enchantment? Why, oh, why, wasn't his wife like this
girl, why, since they were both alike in so much,
hadn't Leonora a little of Ava's warm attention
and quick understanding? And again the Duke,

in solace for self-pity, cast back to yesternight, how he had warmed to the beautiful stranger's love of Paris and had told her the tale of how Paris had come to be called Paris, and the way of that was this:

"In the old days, Ava, if I may call you Ava, when the world was small and the animals enormous, they tell how a young conqueror came out of the dark lands, and with fire and sword he came into the smiling land of France. Of course it was not called France then, but you know what I mean. Now that was a great and noble prince, and it was his custom to rest himself after the tumult of battle with the worship of art and beauty, which is not at all the fashion among princes nowadays, because of course we have progressed so far since then. And so our prince, when he had killed as many natives of the conquered country as the honour of war demands, chained the rest with iron chains and put them to the building of a mighty city by the river Seine. And when at last the city was builded it was far and away the fairest city in the world, as all who saw it instantly admitted under torture, for the young prince hated argument.

"All went well until they came to the christening of the city, when it transpired that no one had the faintest idea what name to call it. Here was a to-do! Nameless they could not leave so great a city, yet what name would embrace all these marvels of architecture, how could they call so fair a city by any such commonplace kind of label as Rome, Jerusalem or Wapping? Therefore the young prince fell weeping with mortification for that his city must remain nameless just because it was the fairest city in the world, when an ancient man rose up in the assembly and said: 'This here is not the fairest city in the world. But the magic city of Is in the land of Brittany has got it so beat that this looks like a slum beside it. I have spoken.' Not that he ever had a chance to again, even though it presently was proved that not the fairest city in the world could be fairer than Is in Brittany, and so the prince made the best of a bad job and called his city the Equal to Is, which is Par-Is, which is Paris. Shall we dance?"

But she said: "No, no! They are playing an old-fashioned fox-trot. Besides, one can always dance; there are so many men with whom one can only dance, for what have they to talk about? Duke, I did love your legend of the christening of Paris! Did you make it up?"

Now these words had chanced to cast a gloom about the young Duke, and he had said: "But there is another legend, a more private legend. It tells, sister, of the house of Mall, how the golden cock on the weather-vane of St. James's tower shall crow thrice at the birth of the greatest of the Dukes of Mall. And, although I say it who shouldn't, this very miracle attended the birth of him who now stands beside you. And the legend further tells that when the golden cock on St. James's tower again crows thrice the greatest of the Dukes of Mall shall die. Ava, to-night I find myself in fear of my fate. That which is written shall come to pass, and no man may defy the passage of his destiny—but to-night, Ava, I am troubled with a foreboding that the second crowing of that beastly cock is not far distant from this dear moment."

Very sweetly she had tried to soothe his foreboding, but it was heavy in him and he had not listened, saying: "I've never but once before been vexed with this depression, and that was on the night of the day I fell in love with Leonora Lamb."

"Let us dance," she had said shyly, but they had not danced very enjoyably owing to the number of the students of hospitality who were generously supporting Mrs. Omroy Pont on so memorable an occasion.

And thus it was on the first night between Miss Ava Lamb and the young Duke of Mall.

VI

Now the Duke had turned his yacht from Naples merely to amuse himself (that is to say, to annoy his wife); but is it not a fact, as *The Morning Post* lately asked in reference to our treating with the Soviet Republic, that it is dangerous to play with fire? So it happened that the Duke had not been gay of his new enchantment for long before all others palled on him, and he awoke one morning to recognise that he could not, try as he would, do without the one enchantment that was called Ava Lamb. Those American sisters, first the one and then the other, were fated, it appeared, to ravish his imagination to the exclusion of the whole race of womankind. And he had all the more leisure in which to contemplate his dilemma insomuch as Miss Lamb, pleading the importunity of friends, would sometimes not see him for days at a time.

In the meanwhile the Duchess, in London, was preparing to petition the Courts to release her from her unfortunate marriage; and after the usual correspondence had passed between the lawyers of both parties, and the usual evidence collected, the majesty of the law pronounced the usual decree and everyone said the usual things.

Impatiently the Duke in Paris awaited the wire which would tell him that he was no longer the husband of Leonora Mall; and when it came he delayed only long enough to instruct his valet to telephone his London florists to send the ex-Duchess a basket of flowers before calling on Miss Ava Lamb at her hotel.

However, she was not at home. The Duke protested. Even so, she was not at home. The Duke felt rebuked for not having conformed to the decencies of divorce so far as to wait twenty-four hours; and in all humility he returned the next day.

However, she was not at home. The Duke pleaded. Even so, she was not at home; for, her maid said, she was resting before the ardours of the night journey to Cherbourg, whence she would embark for New York. The Duke scarce awaited the end of the astounding news. Miss Lamb was lying down. Calm and cold, she said:

"What does this mean, Duke? How dare you force yourself on me like this?"

Fair, tall, intent, the Duke further dared her displeasure by raising her unwilling hand to his

lips. Twilight filled the room. Outside, the
motors raced across the Place Vendôme. The
Duke said:

"I have dared everything on this one throw.
Ava, I love you."

Miss Lamb said to her maid, "Go," and she
went.

The Duke smiled unsteadily, saying: "Well?
Ava, what have you to say?"

Where she lay on her couch in the dusk, her
face was like a pale white flower. But he could
not see her eyes, because they were closed. The
dress she wore was black. The hand that lay outstretched on her black dress was as soft as a
temptation, and he said: "I have a ring for that
hand that has not its peer in the world. I love
you. Ava, will you marry me?"

He could not see her eyes, because they were
closed. But still the dusk lacked the courage to
steal the red from her mouth, and the Duke saw
that her mouth was parted in a queer sad smile.

"Why do you smile?" he whispered, and he said
unsteadily: "I know why. You do not believe I
love you, you do not believe I know how to love,
you think me the shallow, vain braggart that I
have shown to you in the guise of myself until this
moment. But I love you, Ava, more than life. I
love you, Ava, with all the youthful love I had
for your sister increased a thousandfold by the
knowledge I now have of myself: for it is by loving that men come to know themselves, and it is
by knowing themselves in all humility that men
can love with the depths of their hearts. Ava, I
do love you terribly! Won't you speak, won't

you say one word, do you disdain my love so utterly as that? Yet I can't blame you, for I have spent my life in proving that my love is despicable. I have been proud, pitiless, impious. I am soiled. But, Ava, even a fool may come to know the depths of his folly; and I who know so much of desire, dearly beloved, know that I have never loved until this moment. Still you won't speak? Ava, I did not think you so ungenerous when in my vanity I first fell under your gentle enchantment. Dear, your silence is destroying all of me but my love. Won't you give me even so much as a queen will give a beggar, that, had he been another man in another world, he might have kissed her hand?"

Now night had extinguished all but the last tapers of twilight, and in the dark silence the maid whispered to his ear: "Your Grace, she is asleep."

VII

The Duke told his chauffeur outside Miss Lamb's hotel that he would not need him again that evening, he would walk. But he had not walked above a dozen yards across the Place Vendôme, regardless of his direction, regardless of the traffic, when the breathless voice of his valet detained him. Stormily the Duke swung about.

"This telegram," the valet panted, "came the minute after you had left this afternoon. I feared, your Grace, it might be important, and took the liberty to follow you."

The Duke's face paled as he read. The tele-

gram was from the hall-porter of his club in St.
James's Street. The valet, an old servant, was
concerned at his master's pale looks: but he was
even more concerned at the sudden smile that
twisted them.

"I hope I did right, your Grace."

"Quite right, Martin." And suddenly the
young Duke smiled a happy smile. "You have
brought me this wire at just the right moment.
I can't, Martin, thank you enough. Meanwhile,
old friend, go back and pack. Everything. We
are for Mall to-night. Paris is no place for an
Englishman to die in. For pity's sake, Martin,
don't look so *gaga*—but go!"

Miss Lamb's maid did not attempt to conceal
her surprise at the Duke's quick reappearance at
the door of the suite. But the young man's face
was so strangely set that she had not the heart to
deny him sight of her mistress.

"I'll be," she sighed, "dismissed!"

The Duke smiled, and maybe he never was so
handsome nor so gay as at that moment.

The maid said: "My mistress still sleeps. It
is when she is happy that she sleeps."

"Happy? Does it make a woman happy, then,
to see a man destroyed by love?"

"It is more comfortable, your Grace, to be loved
than to love. But I know nothing of my mistress's heart. I came to her service only the other
day. Yes, she is asleep. And the room is dark."

The Duke said: "Good! This is indeed my
lucky day."

"I leave you, your Grace. And if I am dismissed?"

"I count you as my friend. I do not forget my friends. Leave me now."

But a few minutes before he had left that room in a storm of rage. Now, a great peace was on him. He let the minutes pass by, standing there in the soft darkness, a man condemned to death. His life behind him lay like a soiled wilderness through which smirked and pirouetted an unclean travesty of himself. The gates of death looked to him clean and beautiful. He did not wish his life had been otherwise: he regretted not a minute of waste, not one inconstancy, not one folly: he regretted not a strand that had gone to the making of the mad silly tapestry of his life, he was glad that all had been as it had been so that he could now be as he was, a man who understood himself and could die with a heart cleansed of folly and sacred to love.

To the windows of the quiet dark room rose the chatter of the lounging traffic of the Place Vendôme. The Duke listened, and smiled. Brown eyes and scarlet lips, blue eyes and scarlet lips, black hair and golden hair and tawny hair, lazy smile and merry smile and greedy smile and bored smile, little breathless laughs, little meaningless laughs and sharp cries of pleasure, dresses of Chanel, Patou, Vionnet, Molyneux—round and round the Place Vendôme they went, like automata on a bejewelled merry-go-round. And the Duke saw himself sitting in motor-cars first beside one and then beside another, talking, talking, whispering, sighing, yawning. . . .

As the minutes passed his sight began to distinguish the objects in the room. On a table some roses were fainting in a bowl. He made obeisance and kissed a rose, for kissing a rose will clean a man's lips. Then he knelt beside the still figure on the couch and he kissed her mouth.

"Oh!" she cried, and she cried: "You thief!".

He said: "Your voice is so cold that ice would seem like fire beside it. But I don't care." And again he kissed her mouth. Then he said: "Your lips are burning. That is very odd. Your voice is very cold, but your lips are burning. Now why is that?"

"For shame," she whispered. "They are burning for shame that you are so little of a man."

He laughed, his lips by her ear. "Beloved, do you think I would die without kissing your lips? Honestly, beloved, could you expect it?"

In the darkness he could just see the pale mask of her face and the shining, savage pools of her eyes, and he kissed first one and then the other. She was very still.

"Die?" she whispered.

He would have laughed again, but he fancied that maybe too much laughter would not become his situation, would appear like bravado. But he would have liked to show her he was happy, and why he was happy. A vain man, he had realised that he was contemptible: therefore it was good to die. Loving as he had never loved before, he was unloved: therefore it was good to die.

He told her how he had been warned that the cock on St. James's tower had crowed thrice that dawn. And then he was amazed, for as he made to rise he could not. He cried out his wonder.

She said: "Be still!"

He cried out his despair.

She whispered: "Be still!"

Her arm was tight about his shoulder, and that was why his happiness had left him like a startled bird. He sobbed: "Child, for pity's sake! It's too late now. Let me die in peace. To have died without your love was blessedly easy. A moment ago I was happy."

"Die! You!" And, as she mocked him thus, the cold irony of the English tongue tore aside the veil of the American accent, and when the Duke stared into her eyes he had leapt up and run away for shame but that her arm was still tight about his shoulder.

"You, Leonora, you! And so you have revenged yourself!"

She whispered: "Be still!"

And as he made to tear himself away, she said: "Yes, I wanted to be revenged. I wanted you to fall in love with me. I wanted you to look a fool."

"Then you must be very content, Leonora! Let me go now."

"Let you go?" she cried. "Let you *go!* But are you mad!"

"Oh, God," he said pitifully, "what is this new mockery!"

"You see," she sighed, "I've gone and fallen in love with you again! That rather takes the edge off my joke, doesn't it? Oh, dear! Maximilian, I have waited to love you as I love you now ever since I married you four years ago. But you never would let me. Be honest, sweet—would you ever let me love you? You were always the world's spoilt darling, the brilliant and dashing and wealthy Duke of Mall—and I your American wife! Darling, what a lot of trouble you give those who love you! I have had to go through all the bother of divorcing you to make you love me, and now I suppose I must go through all the bother of marrying you again because you've made me love you——"

"Oh, but listen!" he made to protest.

"I certainly won't!" she cried. "I must say, though, that you've made love to me divinely these last few months, and the real Ava would have fallen for you, I'm sure, if she hadn't been in California all this while. I dyed my hair a little, but the only real difference between me and your wife was that I listened to you while you talked about yourself. Darling," said she, "kiss me, else how shall I know that we are engaged to be married?"

He said desperately: "Leonora, what are you saying! Do you forget that I am to die?"

"Not you, not you! You may be divorced for the time being, poor Maximilian, but you're not nearly dead yet. I sent that wire myself this morning from Victoria Station—to mark the fact that the Duke of Mall is dead! Long live the Duke of Mall!"

"Leonora, I can't bear this happiness!"

"But you must learn to put up with it, sweet!"

"Leonora, how divine it is to be in love! I love you, Leonora!"

"My, how this British guy mocks a poor American girl!"

"But, Leonora, I adore you!"

"Words, words, words! Whereas, sweet, a little

action would not come amiss. You might for instance, kiss me. Max, how I've longed to be kissed by you these last few months! Max darling, please kiss me at once! I assure you it is quite usual between engaged couples."

NOTE: *The legend of the Dukedom of Mall may not find a full measure of credence owing to the fact (only recently pointed out to the author) that the weather-vane on the tower of St. James's Palace is adorned, not by a golden cock, but by a golden arrow. But have we not been warned in letters of gold, that shall last so long as mankind lasts, not to put our faith in the word of Princes? The author does in all humility venture to suggest that the same must undoubtedly apply also to the word of Dukes.*

VII: THE REVOLTING DOOM OF A GENTLEMAN WHO WOULD NOT DANCE WITH HIS WIFE

I

THERE is a tale that is told in London, and maybe it is told also in the *salons* of New York and upon the Boulevards of Paris, how one night a nightingale sang in Berkeley Square and how that song was of a doubtful character calculated to provoke disorder in households brought up in the fear of God. Needless to say, there are not wanting those who will have it that no nightingale could have done such a thing; nor has the meanness of envy ever been so clearly shown as by those who have suborned certain bird-fanciers into declaring that the nightingale is a bird notably averse from singing in squares and that the legend should therefore be deleted from the folk-tales of Mayfair. But, however that may be, the song of the nightingale is far from being the burden of this tale, which has to do in a general way with a plague of owls, in a particular way with one owl, and in a most particular way with the revolting doom of a gentleman who would not dance with his wife. Many will hold, in extenuation of his disagreeable attitude, that he could not dance. But could he not have taken a lesson or two?

Now of the many and divers people who saw the owls in flight we need mention only policemen, statesmen, 'bus-drivers, noblemen, Colonials and hawkers, to be convinced of the truth of what they one and all say, how in the gloom of a certain summer's twilight not long ago there flew a plague of owls across Trafalgar Square towards the polite heights of Hampstead Heath. Maybe no one would have remarked them, for the strange cries and hootings with which they adorned their flight were not discordant with the noises of the town, had not the pigeons that play about Lord Nelson's monument fled before them with affrighted coos; and in such an extremity of terror were the timid creatures that very few were ever seen in those parts again, which is a sad thing to relate.

Nor can any man speak with any certainty as to the exact number of the owls, for the twilight was deep and the phenomenon sudden; but one and all need no encouragement to vouch for their prodigious multitude: while the fact that they appeared to be flying from the direction of Whitehall at the impulse of a peculiar indignation has given rise among the lower people to a superstition of the sort that is perhaps pardonable in those who have not had the benefits of a publicschool education. These simples declare that the owls, for long peacefully asleep within the gloomy recesses unrecognisable to the feathered intelligence as the austere House of Lords, had been startled from their rest by the activities of the new Labour Government as revealed in that patrician place by the agile incendiarism of my Lords Haldane and Parmoor, and had in one body fled forth to seek a land wherein a Conservative Government would afford them the lulling qualities necessary for their rest.

The serious historian, however, is concerned only with facts. The plague of owls fled no one knows whither, although superstition points to Italy. But this much is known, that whilst crossing the brilliant centre of Piccadilly Circus one among them swooped down from the twilight and perched on the left wing of the figure of Eros:* which, presented to the nation by one of the Earls of Shaftesbury, adorns the head of the charming fountain where old women will sell pretty flowers to anyone who will buy, roses in summer and roses in winter, roses by day and roses by night, or maybe a bunch of violets for a young lady, a gardenia for a gentleman of the mode.

Now why that one owl separated itself from its fellows for no other apparent reason than to perch on the left wing of Lord Shaftesbury's Eros has hitherto been a mystery to the man in the street, who was at the time present in considerable numbers reading *The Evening News* and discussing the probable circulation the next morning of *The Daily Mail*. The owl rested on its perch most silently: nor did it once give the least sign of any perturbation at the din of the marching hosts of Piccadilly Circus, and this for the space of one hour and eighteen minutes: when it hooted

---

* Almost immediately after the publication of this tale in a magazine, the figure of Eros was removed from Piccadilly Circus. It has been generally supposed that, to effect this removal, pressure was brought to bear on the London County Council by gentlemen-who-will-not-dance-with-their-wives, whose name, alas, is legion.

thrice with marvellous dolour and fled, to be lost almost on the instant among the lofty shadows of the Regent's Palace Hotel.

It has to be told that the cry of the owl on the fountain served three purposes, which the historian can best arrange in ascending degrees of abomination with the help of the letters a, b and c: (a) it struck such terror into the vitals of an inoffensive young gentleman of the name of Dunn that he has never been the same man since; (b) it was the death-knell of a gentle and beautiful lady; and (c) the herald of approaching doom to a lord. May they rest in peace, for we are all of us miserable sinners and only very few of us are allowed to get away with it.

II

In the dining-room of a great house in Carlton House Terrace three persons sat at meat. They made, against the spacious simplicities of great wealth and good taste, an austere picture in black and white. Reading from left to right they were my lord the Marquess of Vest, his delightful lady, and Mr. Dunn, private secretary to my lord.

They made a silent company. Lord Vest was never of a very talkative habit: my lady was always very gentle, and did her best to please him on all occasions: while Mr. Dunn's duties did not embrace speaking unless he was spoken to.

Eight candles in tall candlesticks of ancient silver played their timid light upon the polished surface of the wide table; and in the calm air of the summer evening the flames of the candles were so still that a fanciful eye might have charged them with the beauty of flowers of twilight. Young Mr. Dunn's was a fanciful eye, but to him they appeared to be as poppies of the night; for the poppy is an evil flower.

The curtains were not drawn across the windows, that Lord Vest might lose nothing of the sweet evening air, which he always held to be good for him until it gave him a cold in the head. Over his employer's shoulder Mr. Dunn could see the lights of the Mall glowing against the dark tapestry of St. James's Park. To the left, twilight draped the Horse Guards and the great buildings of Government, whence, had Mr. Dunn only known, the owls were at that moment fleeing on their ominous business. To the right, night fought with day for the honour of shrouding the palace of the King of England, who is also Emperor of India and Protector of the Faith, which some people nowadays seem inclined to forget. Great automobiles would every now and then pass to and fro between the noble trees that delight those who have the leisure to walk about the avenue of the Mall.

Mr. Dunn would have found it, at that moment, very agreeable to be walking about the avenue of the Mall. Mr. Dunn would, in point of fact, have parted with money to exchange places with the meanest walker in London; for the situation of private secretary to a lord is not always what the well-informed call a sinecure. Mr. Dunn was just thinking how nice it would be to have a sinecure, whatever it might be, when the second butler winked at him. The second butler thought

the whole affair very funny, and the silence very
funny indeed. The second butler thought he knew
everything. Mr. Dunn made a mental note to the
effect that he must not forget, immediately after
dinner, to tell the second butler that he was an
ass. That is if he, Mr. Dunn, was alive.

Now for Lord Vest, so much has been written
of the early beginnings of that powerful and ill-
fated nobleman that it would be impertient, at
this hour, to give more than a broad outline of his
life. Mr. Justinian Pant was an Australian gentleman of great fortune who had in the past decade been raised to a baronetcy (Sir Justinian
Pant, Bart.), a barony (Lord Pant of Warboys,
in the county of Huntingdonshire), a viscounty
(Viscount Pant of Warboys), an earldom (the
Earl of Cowden, in the county of Sussex) and a
marquisate (the Marquess of Vest, in the county
of Cornwall) for services to the State. The bulle-
tin announcing his last ennoblement had been
welcomed by all England with every appearance
of pleasure and gratification: that is, if one can
judge by the newspapers of the day: as, of course,
one can. The mere fact that the barony of Warboys, the earldom of Cowden, and the marquisate
of Vest, were welcomed far otherwise by the newspapers of Australia gave the envious grounds for
saying that the newspapers of England were
prejudiced in the great man's favour for the reason that he owned most of them: which is tanta-
mount to saying that the glorious press of England is not free, an insinuation that one cannot
deign to answer but with a dignified silence.

Of the early activities in Australia of Justinian

Pant little of a definite nature is known. The Australian papers, at the time of Mr. Pant's first elevation to the peerage, were rife with information on the subject, but the voice of envy is ever loud; and one, an Adelaide society journal, was so far lacking in the respect due to the mother-country as to belittle the English peerage by saying that the lord in question would no doubt make a very good lord, as lords go, but only so long as he did not go back to Australia, where there was a warrant out for his arrest on a charge of petty larceny while employed as a bell-boy in a First-Class Family Hotel in Melbourne.

The tale of this man's venture on London may entertain the curious and inspire the ambitious, for it tells how one evening fifteen years ago Justinian Pant stood in Piccadilly Circus, wondering what he would do next. Starvation was indicated, for in his pocket there was only one penny. And he was about to send up a prayer to God for guidance when he was distracted by falling into conversation with an old native of the Circus, from whom he was amazed to learn that the old man had expected his coming and had been awaiting him for some time with impatience.

Mr. Pant was not yet a master of men and could therefore afford to show surprise, which he did after the Colonial manner by swearing through his nose and whistling between his teeth. Whereupon the ancient man confessed to being a soothsayer and told how it had been revealed to him in a dream that a young man with a face similar in every detail to the face of Mr. Pant, which was of a somewhat unusual shape, would one night come into Piccadilly Circus from Australia and give him, the soothsayer, the sum of one pound in cash, and how from that moment the Australian would rise with remarkable velocity to be the greatest Force in England.

Justinian Pant was not unwilling to be a Force, and asked eagerly for more precise information as to the steps to be taken: adding that he had only one penny on him, but would be pleased to owe the old gentleman the small sum of nineteen shillings and eleven pence.

"Buy an evening paper and look at the advertisements," said the ancient man, for he earned his living by the sale of evening papers. And whilst the Australian reluctantly exchanged his last penny for an evening paper, the old soothsayer spat into the gutter and said harshly:

"Justinian Pant, you will be a Force. You will be a Napoleon. You will be a lord. You will make wars, unmake Parliaments, shuffle Cabinets and reshuffle Cabinets. You will be the first person in the world to discover how to make the maximum amount of money out of the execution of a murderer. You will give away your dearest friends on all occasions of possible profit, while standing by them through thick and thin when nothing is to be gained by standing anywhere else. You will be as a thorn in the sides of upright men, and as a bastinado upon the behinds of those who are down. You will be successful in all things; and honours shall shower upon you like gold on a commercial traveller selling beer by the yard. You will marry a lady of quality, and be an honourary member of the most exclusive night-clubs. You will love your wife, after your fashion. You will be jealous of her, after your fashion. And you will forget to pay me the sum of nineteen shillings and eleven pence which you owe me. For that reason, as also because all things must have an end, whether it is the might of Empires or the beneficial effects of alcohol——even, Justinian Pant, as the first news of your high destiny comes to you in Piccadilly Circus, so the first knell of your awful doom will be cried by a bird of wise omen that will perch on the left wing of the Eros on the fountain over yonder. So it is written. I have spoken." And the ancient man disappeared among the crowds by the Underground Station, leaving Justinian Pant to gape at a copy of the evening paper of the night before last.

Nor did the contents of the days that followed put an end to his astonishment; for as it was written, so it happened, even to the lady of quality for a wife, whom Lord Vest loved violently. Young Mr. Dunn appears, however, to have been an afterthought in the nobleman's destiny. How much rather young Mr. Dunn had remained forever unthought of! But it is written that every cloud is full of rain and it is no use crying into spilled milk when you have a handkerchief.

III

The silence was unnerving the young private secretary; and he was trying, with the utmost care, to peel a nut before he realised that one does not and cannot peel a nut. The second butler was vulgar enough to wink at him again. The second butler was a low fellow who had been at Eton with Mr. Dunn and despised Mr. Dunn for not having gone up in the world.

At last Lady Vest made to rise from the table, and spoke for the first time since she had sat down.

"I will leave you," said she, "to your coffee."

"You will stay," said my lord, "exactly where you are." And he smiled in an unpleasant way all his own which showed his false teeth, and at sight of which the menials at once left the room. Another long and heavy silence fell, so that Mr. Dunn cursed the day he was born. Outside, night had fallen.

"I am to gather," said Lord Vest, with a smile, to his wife, "that this Dunn person is your lover?"

The young private secretary put down his unpeeled nut. He was afraid, but was he not a gentleman? Mr. Dunn was a cadet of a noble but impoverished house, and it was not in vain that he had spent nine years at Eton and Oxford to no other end than to know the difference between a cad and a gentleman.

"Look here, sir," said Mr. Dunn, "that's a bit much. I mean, it's going too far. I'll stand a good deal and all that, but I will not stand for a lady being insulted before my face. You will receive my resignation in the morning, Lord Vest. In the meanwhile, I'm off."

Mr. Dunn was undeniably furious. The Napoleon of the Press was not, however, without a sense of humour: so, at least, his papers would now and then confess rather shyly, hinting that

the manly laughter of Lord Vest must come as a
solace to God for the press of His business elsewhere that compelled Him to give Lord Vest the
vice-royalty of this earth. He laughed now. He
laughed alone.

"Gently, Mr. Dunn, gently!" he laughed, and
his voice was of a courteous balance surprising
in one of his rugged appearance: nor had he any
trace of that accent which by ordinary adorns
the speech of our Australian cousins. "That you
will be leaving my employment more or less at
once," he continued playfully, "is, I am afraid,
self-evident. And that you will find any other
employment in England in the course of, I hope,
a long life, is exceedingly improbable, for I shall
make it my business, Mr. Dunn, to have you
hounded out of the country; and I have, I need
scarcely remind you, more experience of hound-
ing people out of countries than perhaps any other
man in England. But I don't think, Mr. Dunn,
that I can allow you to leave this house for another half-an-hour or so. For I have something
to say to you." And Lord Vest smiled at Mr.
Dunn. He was a much bigger man than Mr.
Dunn, and he was between Mr. Dunn and the
door.

It was at that moment that my lady raised her
voice. She wore always a sad, brave dignity, always she was a quiet lady; but in her voice now,
as her eyes rested very calmly on the sneering
face of her husband, the very landscape of England might have been quivering. She did not conceal from his lordship that the reason for this

quivering was a profound distaste for his person, manners and conversation.

"I did not think," said she, "that any man could say so base a thing on such flimsy provocation. The fact that in spite of your childish prejudice against dancing (which I sincerely hope is not shared by all the natives of Australia) Mr. Dunn has been kind enough to dance with me——"

"You call that dancing?" smiled my lord. "Oh, do you! I may seem very uncivilised, Pamela, but to me it seemed more like making love. Am I right, Mr. Dunn?"

"You are not," said Mr. Dunn with a dignity which would have surprised his mother. "Any man who sneers as you are sneering at the moment, Lord Vest, must be in the wrong about everything. You cannot be in the right, sir, with a poisonous voice like that. I am Lady Vest's very humble admirer and, I hope, friend——"

"Friendship, Mr. Dunn, can wear strange shapes. Friendship, my dear Mr. Dunn, can be the outward label of infidelity. Am I right, Pamela?"

"Mr. Dunn," said Lady Vest with flushed cheeks, "you will be doing me a very great favour by overlooking my husband's behaviour this evening. Justinian," she turned to her husband with a high look, "I knew I was married to a megalomaniac. But I did not realise I was married to a madman. I insist on retiring now; and would advise Mr. Dunn to do the same."

"And I," shouted Lord Vest, "insist on your staying where you are; and would advise Mr.

Dunn to do the same. Do you understand? And you, my good young man?"

Mr. Dunn could not help but pretend to understand, while awaiting developments. He was dismayed by the violence of dislike on the nobleman's colonial face as he turned it to his wife, the gentle lady, a picture of outraged innocence, of appalled decorum, her great blue eyes swept with astonished distaste, her sweet sad face white with sudden fear. For my Lord Vest was not smiling now.

Mr. Dunn revealed at the enquiry which later sat on these affairs that it was at that moment he first realised that his lordship was mad. But his madness, said Mr. Dunn, wore so sane, so coherent a habit, that a chap couldn't but mistrust his fleeting, if well-grounded, suspicion; and even in the very second of his dashing frantically past Lord Vest to the door, which the second butler, being conveniently situated nearby in a curved position, held closed for him on the outside while he made his escape from the house, you couldn't be certain, said Mr. Dunn, whether the nobleman's roar of baffled rage was not more than that of one cheated of the entertainment of a repulsive jest than that of a chap mortified to the point of lunacy. For his employer, said Mr. Dunn warmly, was ever a gentleman with a partiality for making jests of a kind which, Mr. Dunn indignantly supposed, might be considered laughter-provoking on the Australian veldt, bush, or prairie, but were certainly not the thing in England.

The plain truth of the matter is, as you can

see when shorn of Mr. Dunn's naïve observations, that Mr. Dunn turned tail and fled. In the graphic words of Lord Tarlyon, who was among the Commission of Peers who sat to enquire into the Vest affair, Mr. Dunn, awaiting his opportunity with an eagerness worthy of a braver purpose, jumped up from his chair like a scalded cat and, muttering something about a dog, ran out of that house like a bat out of hell.

IV

He was, however, no sooner out of the house, the lofty stone hall of which had always impressed Mr. Dunn's fanciful eye as being like a "holocaust"—by which he meant "mausoleum," for Mr. Dunn had received the education proper to an English gentleman, and one can't know everything—when he was sensible of a peculiar, unhomely feeling within his person; which he was not long in recognising as the prickings of his conscience, a disorder by which he was seldom assailed, for Mr. Dunn was a good young man.

His thoughts, never profound but frequently vivid, quickly passed beyond his control. He thought of the lady on whom he had brought such cruel discomfiture. He saw her again as she sat at the table, her great blue eyes swept with astonished distaste, her sweet sad face white with sudden fear, whilst her husband sneered at her exquisite breeding as though all the seven devils were dancing on his poisoned antipodean tongue.

"And all, dear God," frantically thought Mr. Dunn, "about absolutely nothing!"

For let us at once state frankly, and once and for all, that there was absolutely nothing between Mr. Dunn and Lady Vest. Mr. Dunn was a man of honour. While the Lady Vest was a lady of noble birth and fastidious habits, to whom the idea of the smallest infidelity must necessarily be repellent to a degree far beyond the soiled understanding of those society novelists who write sensationally about the state of inconstancy prevalent among people of condition.

Among her high-minded habits, however, Lady Vest had always included, until her marriage to Lord Vest, the inoffensive distraction of dancing, at which she was notably graceful. But Lord Vest had revealed, on the very night of his marriage, the fact that he could not dance; had excused his disgusting reticence on that point until it was too late for her to change her mind on the ground of his love for her; which was so great, he had protested, that he did not know what he would do should he ever discover her dancing with any man; adding that in the frenzy of such a discovery he would not care to take long odds against the probability of his strangling her; so dark were the obsessions that clouded the Australian nobleman's mind.

Until the recent engagement of Mr. Dunn as his lordship's private secretary Lady Vest had not so much as wavered from the letter of her promise to her husband, that she would dance nevermore. But chancing one afternoon on Mr. Dunn in the neighbourhood of Bond Street, and Mr. Dunn happening to say that he was partial to dancing, Lady Vest had, as though in a flash, realised the narrow tyranny of her husband's prohibition, and had acceded to Mr. Dunn's request that she should take a turn with him round the floor of a neighbouring dance-club.

The path of temptation is sweet to tread, and the air about it is fragrant with the lovely scents of forbidden flowers. Never once did Lady Vest and Mr. Dunn waver from the exercise of those formalities that are bred in the bone of the county families of England and come as naturally to the meanest cadet of the landed gentry as writing good plays to a dramatic critic: she was ever Lady Vest to him, he Mr. Dunn to her; but insensibly they fell into the habit of dancing a while every afternoon (except, of course, on Sundays), and had come to no harm whatsoever, but had rather gained in the way of exercise, had it not been for the fact that the monstrous suspicions of my lord were never at rest.

For, to their indignant amazement, Lord Vest had informed them just before dinner on the night we tell of that he had for some time past been having his lady watched by detectives; that he was fully informed of their goings-on; and was now awaiting dinner with some impatience, for after dinner he was prepared, he said, to be very interested to hear what steps they, his lady and Mr. Dunn, were going to take about it.

And it was at that moment before dinner that Mr. Dunn had first decided that he, for his part, would prefer to take steps of a purely material nature, and those in a direction opposite from any that Lord Vest might be treading at that moment. Nor was he in any way weakened in his decision

when Lord Vest, whilst pressing on Mr. Dunn a
second cocktail—so that, said my lord, Mr. Dunn
should have no excuse for not enjoying a dinner
that promised to be very entertaining in the way
of table-talk, in which Mr. Dunn as a rule ex-
celled—related how he had that afternoon suborned the saxophone player in the orchestra of the
dance-club into allowing him, his lordship, to
take the man's place; and therefore had had,
whilst emitting to the best of his ability those
screams and noises that are expected of a saxophone player, an unrivalled opportunity of judging whether his lady and Mr. Dunn were proficient in those offensive irregularities of the legs,
hips, and teeth which, said my lord crudely, were
dignified with the name of dancing.

Mr. Dunn had then sworn at his luck, which
never had been but rotten; for on this afternoon
of all he had taken the liberty to introduce Lady
Vest to certain movements recently imported from
the Americas; and he had no doubt but that the
instruction of those quite delightful and original
movements might have appeared, to one playing
the saxophone in a hostile frame of mind, com-
promising to a degree.

Such thoughts as these, before and during dinner, had confirmed Mr. Dunn in his decision to
take the steps already referred to at the earliest
possible moment. Nor can we really blame the
poor young gentleman: the occasion was decidedly domestic: Mr. Dunn was in a cruelly false
position: and the degraded mentality of his lordship was never less amenable to polite argument
than on that fateful night.

Yet, now that he had taken them, now that he stood beneath the trees on the other side of Carlton House Terrace and stared at the great house from which he had but a moment before fled like a poltroon, he discovered within himself a profound repugnance for his, Mr. Dunn's, person. The picture of the gentle lady, on whom his innocent partiality for the latest movements in dancing had brought this discomfiture, preyed on his mind; the wrath of his lordship must by now, thought Mr. Dunn, have been confined within reasonable limits; and, with set face and determined mind, he was again approaching the house when its great doors were flung open and the second butler, with a look of agonised fear on his low face, was hurled forth by Lord Vest into the night. Mr. Dunn fled.

V

Nor did he abate his pace so much as to take breath until he was some distance up that stretch of Regent Street which sweeps nobly upwards to meet Piccadilly Circus at a point marked by the imperious façade of the new Criterion Restaurant; and he was in the very act of passing a handkerchief over his deranged forehead when from behind him he was startled to hear a low cry:

"Mr. Dunn! Mr. Dunn!"

"Good God!" said he, swinging about. "And thank God! For at least you are safe!"

For there by his elbow, prettily panting for breath, was my lady; and never did she look to a

manly eye so fragile and gentle, for she was en-
wrapped in the fairy elegance of a cloak of white
ermine.

"Oh," she sighed softly, "and I did so want to
dance once again! Just once again!"

"But what happened? The man is mad!" cried
Mr. Dunn. "Did you soothe him, Lady Vest?
Did he see the absurdity of his suspicions, did he
apologise for his behaviour?"

But it was as though the lady was not heeding
his words. As they made to walk on up Regent
Street she smiled absently into his concerned face
and sighed: "And, oh, I did so want to dance with
you just once again! But just imagine my indiscretion, running after you like this! and all because of my overpowering desire to dance with
you once again. It will not occur again, I promise you, Mr. Dunn. But, oh, just to do those
new movements of the Blues once again!"

"Dear Lady Vest," said Mr. Dunn sincerely,
"there is nothing I would enjoy more. Besides,
it will soothe us. See, here we are at the doors
of the Criterion, where, I am told, one may dance
with comfort and propriety. But won't you tell
me first about the issue of Lord Vest's temper?
He was very angry? And you soothed him?"

"Oh, yes, yes! I soothed him, indeed. Look,
Mr. Dunn! Oh, look! There is an owl perched
on the fountain yonder, on the left wing of Eros!
Just fancy, Mr. Dunn, an owl! Did you ever
hear of such a thing!"

"Holy smoke, you're right!" said Mr. Dunn.
"An owl, or I'm a Dutchman! There's never
been an owl there before, that I'll swear."

"See," cried Lady Vest with a strange exaltation, "see, it is staring at us! Mr. Dunn, do you know what that owl, a bird of wise omen, means? Can you imagine, Mr. Dunn! It means the doom of my lord. And what a doom!"

"Holy smoke!" said Mr. Dunn, starting back from her. "Lady Vest, you haven't—you haven't kil——"

"Listen, Mr. Dunn!" And she held him by the arm, looking into his eyes with sweet, sad dignity, whilst all about them passed the gay crowds that love to throng Piccadilly Circus, and the electric advertisements lit the scene with a festive glamour; nor ever did the owl stir from its station on the fountain.

"Listen, Mr. Dunn! When you had made your escape, my husband revealed the true state of his mind by drawing a revolver. He was mad. I did not know what to do. I screamed, and on the second butler's rushing into the room without knocking on the door the poor fellow was hurled from the house. But in the meanwhile I had managed to grab hold of the revolver. What could I do, Mr. Dunn? I ask you, what could I do?"

"Holy smoke!" said Mr. Dunn. "I don't know. But——"

"The madman advanced on me. His face livid, his eyes mad, and his hands arranged before him in such a way as to leave one no room to doubt that his immediate intention was to strangle me. I threatened to fire. Can you, can anyone, blame me? Was I wrong, may one not defend one's life?"

"Holy smoke!" said Mr. Dunn. "Certainly. But——"

"My threat to fire did not discommode his mad approach. I kept on making it. But did he stop?"

"Did he?" gasped Mr. Dunn.

"Mr. Dunn, he did not. I fired."

"You didn't!" said Mr. Dunn.

"I did," said my lady.

"But holy smoke!" cried Mr. Dunn. "You killed him!"

"No," she whispered sadly. "I missed. Mr. Dunn, he killed me."

And it was at that moment, even as the phantom of the unfortunate lady faded before his eyes and Mr. Dunn let out an appalling yell, that the owl on the fountain hooted thrice with marvellous dolour and fled, to be lost almost on the instant among the lofty shadows of the Regent's Palace Hotel.

Amateurs of history and students of privilege should note that additional point is lent to this already interesting chronicle by the fact that the late Lord Vest was the first Australian marquess to be hanged by the neck in the year of grace 1924. A vast concourse attended outside the prison gates on the morning of the execution, some of whom were photographed by pressmen in the act of gnashing their teeth, which is to be explained by the fact that they had brought their breakfast with them in the form of sandwiches. The executioners were Lovelace, Lovibond and Lazarus. The drop given was sixteen feet. The criminal died unrepentant, thus denying his soul the grace of salvation and directing it with terrible velocity and unerring aim to the fires of eternal damnation, where he will no doubt continue to burn miserably as a warning for all time to gentlemen who will not dance with their wives.

VIII: THE GENTLEMAN FROM AMERICA

IT is told by a decayed gentleman at the sign of *The Leather Butler*, which is in Shepherd's Market, which is in Mayfair, how one night three men behaved in a most peculiar way; and one of them was left for dead.

Towards twelve o'clock on a night in the month of November some years ago, three men were ascending the noble stairway of a mansion in Grosvenor Square. The mansion, although appointed in every detail—to suit, however, a severe taste—had yet a sour and sensitive atmosphere, as of a house long untenanted but by caretakers.

The first of the men, for they ascended in single file, held aloft a kitchen candlestick: whilst his companions made the best progress they could among the deep shadows that the faulty light cast on the oaken stairway. He who went last, the youngest of the three, said gaily:

"Mean old bird, my aunt! Cutting off the electric-light just because she is away."

"Fur goodness' sake!" said the other.

The leader, whose face the candle-light revealed as thin almost to asceticism, a face white and tired, finely moulded but soiled in texture by the dissipations of a man of the world, contented himself

224

with a curt request to his young friend not to speak so loud.

It was, however, the gentleman in between the two whom it will advantage the reader to consider. This was an unusually tall and strongly built man. Yet it was not his giant stature, but rather the assurance of his bearing, which was remarkable. His very clothes sat on his huge frame with an air of firmness, of finality, that, as even a glance at his two companions would show, is deprecated by English tailors, whose inflexible formula it is that the elegance of the casual is the only possible elegance for gentlemen of the mode. While his face had that weathered, yet untired and eager, look which is the enviable possession of many Americans, and is commonly considered to denote, for reasons not very clearly defined, the quality known as poise. Not, however, that this untired and eager look is, as some have supposed, the outward sign of a lack of interest in dissipation, but rather of an enthusiastic and naïve curiosity as to the varieties of the same. The gentleman from America looked, in fine, to be a proper man; and one who, in his early thirties, had established a philosophy of which his comfort and his assurance of retaining it were the two poles, his easy perception of humbug the pivot, and his fearlessness the latitude and longitude.

It was on the second landing that the leader, whose name was Quillier, and on whom the dignity of an ancient baronetcy seemed to have an almost intolerably tiring effect, flung open a door. He did not pass into the room, but held the candlestick towards the gentleman from America. And his manner was so impersonal as to be almost rude, which is a fault of breeding when it is bored.

"The terms of the bet," said Quillier, "are that this candle must suffice you for the night. That is understood?"

"Sure, why not?" smiled the gentleman from America. "It's a bum bet, and it looks to me like a bum candle. But do I care? No, sir!"

"Further," continued the impersonal, pleasant voice, "that you are allowed no matches, and therefore cannot relight the candle when it has gone out. That if you can pass the night in that room, Kerr-Anderson and I pay you five hundred pounds. And *vice versa*."

"That's all right, Quillier. We've got all that." The gentleman from America took the candle from Quillier's hand and looked into the room, but with no more than faint interest. In that faulty light little could be seen but the oak panelling, the heavy hangings about the great bed, and a steel engraving of a Meissonier duellist lunging at them from a wall nearby.

"Seldom," said he, "have I seen a room look less haunted——"

"Ah," vaguely said Sir Cyril Quillier.

"But," said the gentleman from America, "since you and Kerr-Anderson insist on presenting me with five hundred pounds for passing the night in it, do I complain? No, sir!"

"Got your revolver?" queried young Kerr-Anderson, a chubby youth whose profession was dining out.

"That is so," said the gentleman from America.

Quillier said: "Well, Puce, I don't mind telling you that I had just as soon this silly business was over. I have been betting all my life, but I have always had a preference for those bets which did not turn on a man's life or death——"

"Say, listen, Quillier, you can't frighten me with that junk!" snapped Mr. Puce.

"My aunt," said young Kerr-Anderson, "will be very annoyed if anything happens and she gets to hear of it. She hates a corpse in her house more than anyone I know. You're sure you are going on with it, Puce?"

"Boy, if Abraham Lincoln was to come up this moment and tell me Queen Anne was dead I'd be as sure he was speaking the truth as that I'm going to spend this night in this old haunted room of your aunt's. Yes, sir! And now I'll give you good-night, boys. Warn your mothers to be ready to give you five hundred pounds to hand on to Howard Cornelius Puce."

"I like Americans," said Quillier vaguely. "They are so enthusiastic. Good-night, Puce, and God bless you. I hope you have better luck than the last man who spent a night in that room. He was strangled. Good-night, my friend."

"Aw, have a heart!" growled Mr. Puce. "You get a guy so low with your talk that I feel I could put on a tall hat and crawl under a snake."

II

The gentleman from America, alone in the haunted room, lost none of his composure. Indeed, if anything disturbed him at all, it was that, irritated by Quillier's manner at a dinner-party a few nights before, and knowing Quillier to be a bankrupt wastrel, he had allowed himself to be dared into this silly adventure and had thus deprived himself for one night of the amenities of his suite at Claridge's Hotel. Five hundred pounds more or less did not matter very much to Mr. Puce: although, to be sure, it was some consolation to know that five hundred pounds more or less must matter quite a deal to *Sir* Cyril Quillier, for all his swank. Mr. Puce, like a good American, following the gospel according to Mr. Sinclair Lewis, always stressed the titles of any of his acquaintance.

Now, he contented himself with a very cursory examination of the dim, large room: he rapped, in an amateurish way, on the oak panels here and there for any sign of any "secret passage junk," but succeeded only in soiling his knuckles: and it was only when, fully clothed, he had thrown himself on the great bed that it occurred to him that five hundred pounds sterling was quite a pretty sum to have staked about a damfool haunted room.

The conclusion that naturally leapt to one's mind, thought Mr. Puce, was that the room must have something the matter with it: else would a hawk like Quillier have bet money on its qualities of terror? Mr. Puce had, indeed, suggested, when first the bet was put forward, that five hundred pounds was perhaps an unnecessary sum to stake on so idiotic a fancy; but Quillier had said in a very tired way that he never bet less than five hundred on anything, but that if Mr. Puce preferred to bet with poppycock and chickenfood, he, Quillier, would be pleased to introduce him to some very jolly children of his acquaintance.

Such thoughts persuaded Mr. Puce to rise and examine more carefully the walls and appointments of the room. But as the furniture was limited to the barest necessities, and as the oak-panelled walls appeared in the faint light to be much the same as any other walls, the gentleman from America swore vaguely and again reclined on the bed. It was a very comfortable bed.

He had made up his mind, however, that he would not sleep. He would watch out, thought Mr. Puce, for any sign of this old ghost, and he would listen with the ears of a coyote, thought Mr. Puce, for any hint of those rapping noises, rude winds, musty odours, clanking of chains and the like, with which, so Mr. Puce had always understood, the family ghosts of Britishers invariably heralded their foul appearance.

Mr. Puce, you can see, did not believe in ghosts. He could not but think, however, that some low trick might be played on him, since on the honour of *Sir* Cyril Quillier, peer though he was—for Mr. Puce, like a good American, could never get the cold dope on all this fancy title stuff—he had not the smallest reliance. But as to the supernatural, Mr. Puce's attitude was always a wholesome scepticism—and a rather aggressive scepticism at that, as Quillier had remarked with amusement when he had spoken of the ghost in, as he had put it, the house of Kerr-Anderson's aunt. Quillier had said:

"There are two sorts of men on whom ghosts have an effect: those who are silly enough to believe in them, and those who are silly enough not to believe in them."

Mr. Puce had been annoyed at that. He detested clever back-chat. "I'll tell the world," Mr. Puce had said, "that a plain American has to go to a drug-store after a conversation with you."

Mr. Puce, lying on the great bed, whose hangings depressed him, examined his automatic and found it good. He had every intention of standing no nonsense, and an automatic nine-shooter is, as Mr. Puce remembered having read somewhere, an Argument. Indeed, Mr. Puce was full of those dour witticisms about the effect of a "gun" on everyday life which go to make the less pretentious "movies" so entertaining; although, to be sure, he did not know more than a very little about guns. Travellers have remarked, however, that the exciting traditions behind a hundred-per-cent American nationality have given birth in even the most gentle citizens of that great republic to a feeling of familiarity with "guns," as such homely phrases as "slick with the steel mit," "doggone son of a gun," and the like, go to prove.

Mr. Puce placed the sleek little automatic on a small table by the bed, on which stood the candle and, as he realised for the first time, a book. One glance at the paper jacket of the book was enough to convince the gentleman from America that its presence there must be due to one of Quillier's tired ideas. It showed a woman of

striking, if conventional, beauty fighting for her
life with a shape which might or might not be the
wraith of a bloodhound but was certainly something quite outside a lovely woman's daily experience. Mr. Puce laughed. The book was called:
Tales of Terror for Tiny Tots, by *Ivor Pelham
Marlay.*

The gentleman from America was a healthy
man, and needed his sleep; and it was therefore
with relief that he turned to Mr. Marlay's ab-
surd-looking book as a means of keeping himself
awake. The tale at which the book came open
was called *The Phantom Foot-steps;* and Mr.
Puce prepared himself to be entertained, for he
was not of those who read for instruction. He
read:

THE PHANTOM FOOT-STEPS

The tale of "The Phantom Foot-steps" is still
whispered with awe and loathing among the people of that decayed but genteel district of London
known to those who live in it as Belgravia and
to others as Pimlico.

Julia and Geraldine Biggot-Baggot were twin
sisters who lived with their father, a widower, in
a town in Lancashire called Wigan, or it may
have been called Bolton. The tale finds Julia and
Geraldine in their nineteenth year, and it also
finds them in a very bad temper, for they were
yearning for a more spacious life than can be
found in Wigan, or it might be Bolton. This
yearning their neighbours found all the more in-
explicable since the parents of the girls were of

Lancashire stock, their mother having been a Biggot from Wigan and their father a Baggot from Bolton.

The reader can imagine with what excess of gaiety Julia and Geraldine heard one day from their father that he had inherited a considerable property from a distant relation; and the reader can go on imagining the exaltation of the girls when they heard that the property included a mansion in Belgravia, since that for which they had always yearned most was to enjoy, from a central situation, the glittering life of the metropolis.

Their father preceded them from Wigan, or was it Bolton? He was a man of a tidy disposition, and wished to see that everything in the Belgravia house was ready against his daughters' arrival. When Julia and Geraldine did arrive, however, they were admitted by a genial old person of repellent aspect and disagreeable odour, who informed them that she was doing a bit of charing about the house but would be gone by the evening. Their father, she added, had gone into the country to engage servants, but would be back the next day; and he had instructed her to tell Julia and Geraldine not to be nervous of sleeping alone in a strange house, that there was nothing to be afraid of, and that he would, anyhow, be with them first thing in the morning.

Now Julia and Geraldine, though twins, were of vastly different temperaments; for whereas Julia was a girl of gay and indomitable spirit who knew not fear, Geraldine suffered from agonies of timidity and knew nothing else. When, for instance, night fell and found them alone in the house, Julia could scarcely contain her delight at the adventure; while it was with difficulty that Geraldine could support the tremors that shook her girlish frame.

Imagine, then, how differently they were affected when, as they lay in bed in their room towards the top of the house, they distinctly heard from far below a noise, as of someone moving. Julia sat up in bed, intent, unafraid, curious. Geraldine swooned.

"It's only a cat," Julia whispered. "I'm going down to see."

"Don't!" sighed Geraldine. "For pity's *sake* don't leave me, Julia!"

"Oh, don't be so childish!" snapped Julia. "Whenever there's the chance of the least bit of fun you get shivers down your spine. But as you are so frightened I will lock the door from the outside and take the key with me, so that no one can get in when I am not looking. Oh, I hope it's a burglar! I'll give him the fright of his life, see if I don't."

And the indomitable girl went, feeling her way to the door in darkness, for to have switched on the light would have been to warn the intruder, if there was one, that the house was inhabited: whereas it was the plucky girl's conceit to turn the tables on the burglar, if there was one, by suddenly appearing to him as an avenging phantom: for having done not a little district-visiting in Wigan or, possibly, Bolton, no one knew better than Julia of the depths of base superstition among the vulgar.

A little calmed by her sister's nonchalance,
Geraldine lay still as a mouse in the darkness,
with her pretty head beneath the bedclothes.
From without came not a sound, and the very
stillness of the house had impelled Geraldine to a
new access of terror had she not concentrated on
the works of Mr. Rudyard Kipling, which tell of
the grit of the English people.

Then, as though to test the grit of the English
people in the most abominable way, came a dull
noise from below. Geraldine restrained a scream,
lay breathless in the darkness. The dull noise,
however, was not repeated, and presently Geraldine grew a little calmer, thinking that maybe
her sister had dropped a slipper or something of
the sort. But the reader can imagine into what
terror the poor girl had been plunged had she
been a student of the detective novels of the day,
for then she must instantly have recognised the
dull noise as a dull thud, and can a dull thud
mean but one thing?

It was as she was praying a prayer to Our
Lady that her ears grew aware of footsteps
ascending the stairs. Her first feeling was one of
infinite relief. Of course Julia had been right,
and there had been nothing downstairs but a cat
or, perhaps, a dog. And now Julia was returning,
and in a second they would have a good laugh together. Indeed, it was all Geraldine could do to
restrain herself from jumping out of bed to meet
her sister, when she was assailed by a terrible
doubt; and on the instant her mind grew so
charged with fear that she could no longer hold
back her sobs. Suppose it was not Julia ascend-

ing! Suppose—— "Oh, God!" sobbed Geraldine.

Transfixed with terror, yet hopeful of the best, the poor girl could not even command herself to reinsert her head beneath the sheets. And always the ascending steps came nearer. As they approached the door, she thought she would die of uncertainty. But as the key was fitted into the lock she drew a deep breath of relief—to be at once shaken by the most acute agony of doubt, so that she had given anything in the world to be back again in Wigan or, even better, Bolton.

"Julia!" she sobbed. "Julia!"

For the door had opened, the footsteps were in the room, and Geraldine thought she recognised her sister's maidenly tread. But why did Julia not speak, why this intolerable silence? Geraldine, peer as hard as she might, could make out nothing in the darkness. The footsteps seemed to fumble in their direction, but came always nearer to the bed, in which poor Geraldine lay more dead than alive. Oh, why did Julia not speak, just to reassure her?

"Julia!" sobbed Geraldine. "Julia!"

The footsteps seemed to fumble about the floor with an indecision maddening to Geraldine's distraught nerves. But at last they came beside the bed—and there they stood! In the awful silence Geraldine could hear her heart beating like a hammer on a bell.

"Oh!" the poor girl screamed. "What is it, Julia? Why don't you speak?"

But never a sound nor a word gave back the livid silence, never a sigh nor a breath, though

Julia must be standing within a yard of the bed.

"Oh, she is only trying to frighten me, the beast!" poor Geraldine thought; and, unable for another second to bear the cruel silence, she timidly stretched out a hand to touch her sister—when, to her infinite relief, her fingers touched the white rabbit fur with which Julia's dressing-gown was delicately trimmed.

"You beast, Julia!" she sobbed and laughed. Never a word, however, came from the still shape. Geraldine, impatient of the continuation of a joke which seemed to her in the worst of taste, raised her hand from the fur, that she might touch her sister's face; but her fingers had risen no further than Julia's throat when they touched something wet and warm, and with a scream of indescribable terror Geraldine fainted away.

When Mr. Biggot-Baggot admitted himself into the house early the next morning, his eyes were assailed by a dreadful sight. At the foot of the stairs was a pool of blood, from which, in a loathsome trail, drops of blood wound up the stairway.

Mr. Biggot-Baggot, fearful lest something out-of-the-way had happened to his beloved daughters, rushed frantically up the stairs. The trail of blood led to his daughters' room; and there, in the doorway, the poor gentleman stood appalled, so foul was the sight that met his eyes. His beloved Geraldine lay on the bed, her hair snow-white, her lips raving with the shrill fancies of a maniac. While on the floor beside the bed lay stretched, in a pool of blood, his beloved Julia, her head half-severed from her trunk.

The tragic story unfolded only when the police arrived. It then became clear that Julia, her head half-severed from her body, and therefore a corpse, had yet, with indomitable purpose, come upstairs to warn her timid sister against the homicidal lunatic who, just escaped from an Asylum nearby, had penetrated into the house. However, the police consoled the distracted father not a little by pointing out that the escape of the homicidal lunatic from the Asylum had done some good, insomuch as there would now be room in an Asylum near her home for Geraldine.

III

When the gentleman from America had read the last line of *The Phantom Foot-steps* he closed the book with a slam and, in his bitter impatience with the impossible work, was making to hurl it across the room when, unfortunately, his circling arm overturned the candle. The candle, of course, went out.

"Aw, hell!" said Mr. Puce bitterly, and he thought: "Another good mark to *Sir* Cyril Quillier! Won't I Sir him one some day! For only a lousy guy with a face like a drummer's overdraft would have bought a damfool book like that."

The tale of *The Phantom Foot-steps* had annoyed him very much; but what annoyed him even more was the candle's extinction, for the gentleman from America knew himself too well to bet a nickel on his chances of remaining awake in a dark room.

He did, however, manage to keep awake for

some time merely by concentrating on wicked
words: on Quillier's face, and how its tired, mocking expression would change for the better were
his, Puce's, foot to be firmly pressed down on its
surface: and on Julia and Geraldine. For the
luckless twins, by the almost criminal idiocy with
which they were presented, kept walking about
Mr. Puce's mind; and as he began to nod to the
demands of a healthy and tired body he could not
resist wondering if their home town had been
Wigan or Bolton and if Julia's head had been
severed from ear to ear or only half-way. . . .

When he awoke, it was the stillness of the room
that impressed his sharply awakened senses. The
room was very still.

"Who's there!" snapped Mr. Puce. Then,
really awake, laughed at himself. "Say, what
would plucky little Julia have done?" he thought,
chuckling. "Why, got up and looked!"

But the gentleman from America discovered in
himself a reluctance to move from the bed. He
was very comfortable on the bed. Besides, he
had no light and could see nothing if he did move.
Besides, he had heard nothing at all, not the
faintest noise. He had merely awoken rather
more sharply than usual. . . .

Suddenly, he sat up on the bed, his back against
the oak head. Something had moved in the room.
He was certain something had moved. Somewhere by the foot of the bed.

"Aw, drop that!" laughed Mr. Puce.

His eyes peering into the darkness, Mr. Puce
stretched his right hand to the table on which
stood the automatic. The gesture reminded him

of Geraldine's when she had touched the white
rabbit fur—Aw, Geraldine nothing! Those idiotic twins kept chasing about a man's mind. The
gentleman from America grasped the automatic
firmly in his hand. His hand felt as though it
had been born grasping an automatic.

"I want to tell you," said Mr. Puce into the
darkness, "that someone is now going to have
something coming to him, her or it."

It was quite delicious, the feeling that he was
not frightened. He had always known he was a
helluva fellow. But he had never been quite
certain. Now he was certain. He was regu-
lar.

But, if anything had moved, it moved no more.
Maybe, though, nothing had moved at all, ever.
Maybe it was only his half-awakened senses that
had played him a trick. He was rather sorry, if
that was so. He was just beginning to enjoy the
evening.

The room was very still. The gentleman from
America could only hear himself breathing.

Something moved again, distinctly.

"What the hell!" snapped Mr. Puce.

He levelled the automatic towards the foot of
the bed.

"I will now," said Mr. Puce grimly, "shoot."

The room was very still. The gentleman from
America wished, forcibly, that he had a light. It
was no good leaving the bed without a light. He'd
only fall over the infernal thing, whatever it was.
What would plucky little Julia have done? Aw,
Julia nothing! He strained his ears to catch another movement, but he could only hear himself

breathing—in short, sharp gasps! The gentleman from America pulled himself together.

"Say, listen!" he snapped into the darkness. "I am going to count ten. I am then going to shoot. In the meanwhile you can make up your mind whether or not you are going to stay right here to watch the explosion. One. Two. Three. Four. . . ."

Then Mr. Puce interrupted himself. He had to. It was so funny. He laughed. He heard himself laugh, and again it was quite delicious, the feeling that he was not frightened. And wouldn't they laugh, the boys at the Booster Club back home, when he sprung this yarn on them! He could hear them. Oh, Boy! Say, listen, trying to scare him, Howard Cornelius Puce, with a ghost like that! Aw, it was like shooting craps with a guy that couldn't count. Poor old Quillier! Never bet less than five hundred on anything, didn't he, the poor boob! Well, there wasn't a ghost made, with or without a head on him, that could put the wind up Howard Puce. No, sir!

For, as his eyes had grown accustomed to the darkness, and helped by the mockery of light that the clouded, moonless night just managed to thrust through the distant window, the gentleman from America had been able to make out a form at the foot of the bed. He could only see its upper half, and that appeared to end above the throat. The phantom had no head. Whereas Julia's head had been only half-severed from— Aw, what the hell!

"A family like the Kerr-Andersons," began Mr.

Puce, chuckling—but suddenly found, to his astonishment, that he was shouting at the top of his voice: anyhow, it sounded so. However, he began again, much lower, but still chuckling:

"Say, listen, Mr. Ghost, a family like the Kerr-Andersons might have afforded a head and a suit of clothes for their family ghost. Sir, you are one big bum phantom!" Again, unaccountably, Mr. Puce found himself shouting at the top of his voice. "I am going on counting," he added grimly.

And, his automatic levelled at the thing's heart, the gentleman from America went on counting. His voice was steady.

"Five . . . six. . . ."

He sat crouched at the head of the bed, his eyes never off the thing's breast. Phantom nothing! He didn't believe in that no-head bunk. What the hell! He thought of getting a little nearer the foot of the bed and catching the thing a whack on that invisible head of his, but decided to stay where he was.

"Seven . . . eight. . . ."

He hadn't seen the hands before. Gee, some hands! And arms! Holy Moses, he'd got long arms to him, he had. . . .

"Nine!" said the gentleman from America.

Christopher and Columbus, but this would make some tale back home! Yes, sir! Not a bad idea of Quillier's, that, though! Those arms. Long as old glory . . . long as the bed! Not bad for *Sir* Cyril Quillier, that idea. . . .

"Ten, you swine!" yelled the gentleman from America and fired.

Someone laughed. Mr. Puce quite distinctly heard himself laughing, and that made him laugh again. Fur goodness' sake, what a shot! Missed from that distance!

His eyes, as he made to take aim again, were bothered by the drops of sweat from his forehead. "Aw, what the hell!" said Mr. Puce, and fired again.

The silence after the second shot was like a black cloud on the darkness. Mr. Puce thought out the wickedest word he knew, and said it. Well, he wasn't going to miss again. No, sir! His hand was steady as iron, too. Iron was his second name. And again the gentleman from America found it quite delicious, the feeling that he was not frightened. Attaboy! The drops of sweat from his forehead bothered him, though. Aw, what the hell, that was only excitement.

He raised his arm for the third shot. Jupiter and Jane, but he'd learn that ghost to stop ghosting! He was certainly sorry for that ghost. He wished, though, that he could concentrate more on the actual body of the headless thing. There it was, darn it, at the foot of the bed, staring at him—well, it would have been staring at him if it had a head. Aw, of course it had a head! It was only Quillier with his lousy face in a black wrap. *Sir* Cyril Quillier'd get one piece of lead in him this time, though. His own fault, the bastard.

"Say, listen, Quillier," said the gentleman from America, "I want to tell you that unless you quit you are a corpse. Now I mean it, sure as my name is Howard Cornelius Puce. I have been shooting to miss so far. Yes, sir. But I am now *an*noyed. You get me, kid?"

If only, though, he could concentrate more on the body of the thing. His eyes kept wandering to the hands and arms. Gee, but they sure were long, those arms! As long as the bed, no less. Just long enough for the hands to get at him from the foot of the bed. And that's what they were at, what's more! Coming nearer. What the hell! They were moving, those doggone arms, nearer and nearer. . . .

Mr. Puce fired again.

That was no miss. He knew that was no miss. Right through the heart, that little boy must have gone. In that darkness he couldn't see more than just the shape of the thing. Aw, Goddammit! But it was still now. The arms were still. They weren't moving any more. The gentleman from America chuckled. That one had shown him that it's a wise little crack of a ghost that stops ghosting. Yes, sir! It certainly would fall in a moment, dead as Argentine mutton.

Mr. Puce then swore. Those arms were moving again. The hands weren't a yard from him now. What the hell! They were for his throat, Goddammit.

"You swine!" sobbed the gentleman from America, and fired again. But he wouldn't wait this time. No, sir! He'd let that ghost have a ton of lead. Mr. Puce fired again. Those hands weren't half-a-yard from his throat now. No good shooting at the hands, though. Thing was to get the thing through the heart. Mr. Puce fired the sixth bullet. Right into the thing's chest. The

sweat bothered his eyes. "Aw, hell!" said Mr.
Puce. He wished the bed was a bit longer. He
couldn't get back any more. Those arms . . .
Holy Moses, long as hell, weren't they! Mr.
Puce fired the seventh, eighth . . . ninth. Right
into the thing. The revolver fell from Mr. Puce's
shaking fingers. Mr. Puce heard himself screaming.

IV

Towards noon on a summer's day several years
later two men were sitting before an inn some
miles from the ancient town of Lincoln. Drawn
up in the shade of a towering ash was a large
grey touring-car, covered with dust. On the
worn table stood two tankards of ale. The
travellers rested in silence and content, smoking.

The road by which the inn stood was really no
more than a lane, and the peace of the motorists
was not disturbed by the traffic of a main road.
Indeed, the only human being visible was a distant speck on the dust, coming towards them.
He seemed, however, to be making a good pace,
for he soon drew near.

"If," said the elder of the two men, in a low
tired voice, "if we take the short cut through
Carmion Wood, we will be at Malmanor for
lunch."

"Then you'll go short-cutting alone," said the
other firmly. "I've heard enough tales about
Carmion Wood to last me a lifetime without my
adding one more to them. And as for spooks, one
is enough for this child in one lifetime, thanks
very much."

The two men, for lack of any other distraction, watched the pedestrian draw near. He turned out to be a giant of a man; and had, apparently, no intention of resting at the inn. The very air of the tall pedestrian was a challenge to the lazy content of the sunlit noon. He was walking at a great pace, his felt hat swinging from his hand. A giant he was: his hair greying: his massive face set with assurance.

"By all that's holy!" gasped the elder of the two observers. A little lean gentleman that was, with a lined face which had been handsome in a striking way but for the haggard marks of the dissipations of a man of the world. He had only one arm, and that added a curiously flippant air of devilry to his little, lean, sardonic person.

"Puce!" yelled the other, a young man with a chubby, good-humoured face. "Puce, you silly old ass! Come here at once!"

The giant swung round at the good-natured cry, stared at the two smiling men. Then the massive face broke into the old, genial smile by which his friends had always known and loved the gentleman from America, and he came towards them with hand outstretched.

"Well, boys!" laughed Mr. Puce. "This is one big surprise. But it's good to see you again, I'll say that."

"The years have rolled on, Puce, the years have rolled on," sighed Quillier in his tired way, but warmly enough he shook the gentleman from America with his one hand.

"They certainly have!" said Mr. Puce, mopping his brow and smiling down on the two. "And

by the look of that arm, Quillier, I'll say you're
no stranger to war."

"Sit down, old Puce, and have a drink," laughed
Kerr-Anderson. Always gay, was Kerr-Anderson.

But the gentleman from America seemed, as
he stood there, uncertain. He glanced down the
way he had come. Quillier, watching him, saw
that he was fagged out. Eleven years had made
a great difference to Mr. Puce. He looked old,
worn, a wreck of the hearty giant who was once
Howard Cornelius Puce.

"Come, sit down, Puce," he said kindly, and
quite briskly, for him. "Do you realise, man, that
it's eleven years since that idiotic night? What
are you doing? Taking a walking-tour?"

Mr. Puce sat down on the stained bench beside them. His massive presence, his massive
smile, seemed to fill the whole air about the two
men.

"Walking-tour? That is so, more or less,"
smiled Mr. Puce; and, with a flash of his old
humour: "I want to tell you boys that I am the
daughter of the King of Egypt, but I am dressed
as a man because I am travelling *incognito*.
Eleven years is it, since we met? A whale of a
time, eleven years!"

"Why, there's been quite a war since then,"
chuckled Kerr-Anderson. "But still that night
seems like last night. I *am* glad to see you again,
old Puce! But, by Heaven, we owe you one for
giving us the scare of our lives! Don't we, Quillier?"

"That's right, Puce," smiled Quillier. "We

owe you one all right. But I am heartily glad
that it was only a shock you had, and that you
were quite yourself after all. And so here we
are gathered together again by blind chance,
eleven years older, eleven years wiser. Have a
drink, Puce?"

The gentleman from America was looking from
one to the other of the two. The smile on the
massive face seemed one of utter bewilderment.
Quillier was shocked at the ravages of a mere
eleven years on the man's face.

"I gave you two a scare!" echoed Mr. Puce.
"Aw, put it to music, boys! What the hell! How
the blazes did I give you two a scare?"

Kerr-Anderson was quite delighted to explain.
The scare of eleven years ago was part of the
fun of to-day. Many a time he had told the
tale to while away the boredom of Flanders and
Mesopotamia, and had often wanted to let old
Puce in on it to enjoy the joke on Quillier and
himself but had never had the chance to get hold
of him.

They had thought, that night, that Puce was
dead. Quillier, naked from the waist up, had
rushed down to Kerr-Anderson, waiting in the
dark porch, and had told him that Puce had
kicked the bucket. Quillier had sworn like nothing on earth as he dashed on his clothes. Awkward, Puce's corpse, for Quillier and Kerr-Anderson. Quillier, thank Heaven, had had the sense
not to leave the empty revolver on the bed. They
shoved back all the ghost properties into a bag.
And as, of course, the house wasn't Kerr-Anderson's aunt's house at all, but Johnny Paramour's,

who was away, they couldn't so easily be traced.
Still, awkward for them, very. They cleared the
country that night. Quillier swearing all the way
about the weak hearts of giants. And it wasn't
until the Orient Express had pitched them out at
Vienna that they saw in the Continental *Daily
Mail* that an American of the name of Puce had
been found by the caretaker in the bedroom of a
house in Grosvenor Square, suffering from shock
and nervous breakdown. Poor old Puce! Good
old Puce! But he'd had the laugh on them all
right. . . .

And heartily enough the gentleman from
America appeared to enjoy the joke on Quillier
and Kerr-Anderson.

"That's good!" he laughed. "That's very
good!"

"Of course," said Quillier in his tired, deprecating way, "we took the stake, this boy and I.
For if you hadn't collapsed you would certainly
have run out of that room like a Mussulman from
a ham-sandwich."

"That's all right," laughed Mr. Puce. "But
what I want to know, Quillier, is how you got me
so scared?"

Kerr-Anderson says now that Puce was looking at Quillier quite amiably. Full in the face,
and very close to him, but quite amiably. Quillier smiled, in his deprecating way.

"Oh, an old trick, Puce! A black rag over the
head, a couple of yards of stuffed cloth for
arms . . ."

"Aw, steady!" said Mr. Puce. But quite

amiably. "Say, listen, I shot at you! Nine times. How about that?"

"Dear, oh, dear!" laughed Kerr-Anderson. But that was the last time he laughed that day.

"My dear Puce," said Quillier gently, slightly waving his one arm. "That is the oldest trick of all. I was in a panic all the time that you would think of it and chuck the gun at my head. Those bullets in your automatic were blanks."

Kerr-Anderson isn't at all sure what exactly happened then. All he remembers is that Puce's huge face had suddenly gone crimson, which made his hair stand out shockingly white; and that Puce had Quillier's fragile throat between his hands; and that Puce was roaring and spitting into Quillier's blackening face.

"Say, listen, you Quillier! You'd scare me like that, would you! You'd scare me with a chicken's trick like that, would you! And you'd strangle me, eh? You swine, you *Sir* Cyril Quillier you, right here's where the strangling comes in, and it's me that's going to do it——"

Kerr-Anderson hit out and yelled. Quillier was helpless with his one arm, the giant's grip on his throat. The woman who kept the inn had hysterics. Puce roared blasphemies. Quillier was doubled back over the small table, Puce on top of him, tightening his death-hold. Kerr-Anderson hit, kicked, bit, yelled.

Suddenly there were shouts from all around.

"For God's sake, quick!" sobbed Kerr-Anderson. "He's almost killed him."

"Aw, what the hell!" roared Puce.

The men in dark uniforms had all they could do to drag him away from that little, lean, blackened, unconscious thing. Then they manacled Puce. Puce looked sheepish, and grinned at Kerr-Anderson.

Two of the six men in dark uniforms helped to revive Quillier.

"Drinks," gasped Kerr-Anderson to the woman who kept the inn.

"Say, give me one," begged the gentleman from America. Huge, helpless, manacled, he stood sheepishly among his uniformed captors. Kerr-Anderson stared at them. Quillier was reviving.

"Gets like that," said the head warder indifferently. "Gave us the slip this morning. Certain death for someone. Homicidal maniac, that's 'im. And he's the devil to hold. Been like that eleven years. Got a shock, I fancy. Keeps on talking about a sister of his called Julia who was murdered and how he'll be revenged for it. . . ."

Kerr-Anderson had turned away. Quillier sobbed: "God have mercy on us!" The gentleman from America suddenly roared with laughter.

"Can't be helped," said the head warder. "Sorry you were put to trouble, sir. Good-day, gentlemen. Glad it was no worse."

IX: TO LAMOIR

I

ALAS, it is a pity I know so little of trees and flowers, and how I shall tell this tale without their help I cannot imagine, for it is a tale that demands a profound knowledge of still, gentle things. But I daresay it will get itself written somehow, and saying that leads us to quite another question, for serious men will have it that that is the pity of nearly all the writing of our time, it just gets itself written somehow.

Now it is difficult not to think a little of my own life in telling of Hugh and Lamoir, for they helped me when I was very young, for a long time they were my only friends in London, and ever since they have remained the dearest. But it was only the other day that Hugh told me about the tree. I suppose he must have had a sort of idea of what might happen and wanted to tell someone about it while he could. But it's odd that I had known him all those years, him and Lamoir, and he had never so much as mentioned the tree—when out he suddenly comes with it!

Of course there will be those to say that he hadn't concealed anything worth concealing, that it's an impossible story anyhow, and who could believe it? But I do believe it decidedly, for how could Hugh have made it up? Hugh wasn't an

imaginative man, not a bit. That, in point of
fact, is what the story is about. Of course, he
had a passion for fine things, a passion for touching fine things, but your collector or your connoisseur isn't generally anything of an imaginative man. Lamoir, now, she was quite different,
and she might easily have thought of the garden
and the tree and the whole business, but so far
as I can make out Hugh and Lamoir never once
breathed a word to each other about it.

I have never been able to think of Lamoir quite
steadily, I liked her too much. I know a writer is
supposed to be impersonal, but that can't be
helped. She knew the very hearts of trees and
flowers, Lamoir did, and she was always so still
and quiet, like a flower herself, that you never
knew what she was thinking of. And that is
more or less how the trouble between them began,
so Hugh told me the other day. He never knew
what she was thinking of, but he hoped for the
best, and then one day he found that she had
been thinking away from him all the time. That
is what Hugh said. But I feel that the truth of
it was that he never thought Lamoir was thinking
of anything at all, except maybe about what a
good husband he was, and then one day he got
a shock. Many men seem to be like that, they
have happy natures, for when their wives are
quiet and thoughtful they never dream that those
thoughts might be out of accord with their own,
and when they do at last realise that something
has been wrong all the time they are surprised
and hurt and want to know why they were not
told sooner. As though, you know, some things

can be told sooner, as though some things *can* be told until it is too late!

Now Hugh and Lamoir were a difficult pair to know, together or singly. Hugh wasn't at all your democratic sort, there was nothing at all easy-going about him. I remember once seeing him in a crowded room and thinking he was like an island of nerves in an ocean of grins. Lamoir said he was proud. He simply didn't seem to concern himself at all with other people's opinions; it was as though he just hadn't the time to go about dealing in the slack forms of geniality which pass for manners in this century. That is Hugh's phrase, not mine. Lamoir left him about nine years ago.

They say that people made a great fuss over Lamoir when she first came from India, because she was so lovely. That must have been about twenty-five years ago, and about nine years ago she packed up a lot of trunks and went to Algeria. People were very surprised at that, for Lamoir was beloved of everyone, and she seemed to be liking her life in England—as much, anyhow, as anyone ever does seem to like his or her life in England, for there seems to be a feeling in people that one shouldn't like living in England. I like it very much myself, but then I am not English. People said vaguely that she was going away because her heart was weak—quite all right, but weak, and that she must have quiet. She never came back.

I went to see her in Algeria two winters ago. I wanted very much just to see how she was in that solitary new life. Naturally I didn't tell Hugh the main reason why I was going to Algeria, and I think he had an idea I was going there to try to write a book about it, one of those marvellous books about sheiks and sand and suburban Englishwomen with love flaming in their eyes to such a degree that none of their friends at home would ever recognise them. As Hugh never used to speak of his wife one had nothing to go on as to what his feelings about her were, and so, of course, one said nothing about her either.

Just the same, that is how I found Lamoir. She had the grace of silence, of reflection, to a rare degree. Some people found her frightfully dull, but then imagine what "some people" are, it can be said that their disapproval is a distinction that no fairly admirable person should ever be without. The house she was living in had been the palace of the last of the Admirals of the Dey's fleet, Lamoir said, and one could well believe it. There were dungeons below, deep, dark, crooked, with chains and iron clamps on the walls where the poor devils of Christian slaves used to be kept, and on the morning Lamoir was showing me round there was a vampire-bat hanging asleep from the black broken walls. From the dungeons there was a secret passage, Lamoir said, down to the bay two miles away at the foot of the hill, and through this passage the old Admiral scoundrel had tried to escape when the French stormed the town about eighty years ago—or maybe it was more or less than eighty years ago; I don't know when it was, and Lamoir didn't know either.

One morning we were walking about on the pink tiles of the flat, uneven roof, not talking much, while below the sea slept. Lamoir asked after Hugh, just how he was, and I said he was quite well. "Lonely," I added.

We sat on the parapet of the roof, looking down the hill at the white untidy town. There was an American liner in the bay, like a smudge. At last Lamoir said: "Yes, he was always lonely. Lonely and proud. Hugh is very proud. Don't you think so?"

I said: "And you, Lamoir, aren't you proud, too?"

You see, I knew nothing of the difficulty between Hugh and Lamoir. All I knew was that two dear friends of mine had parted from each other nine years before. Lamoir was looking towards the sea, she was smiling. Then she shook her head suddenly. Her hair was quite grey, and short, and curly—you can see how attractive Lamoir was, an autumnal flower.

"Oh, no!" she said. *"I'm* not proud, not a bit. And I don't like proud people."

"I do!" I said.

She said gravely: *"You* do, of course. But you are young, and it's quite right that you should like proud people and should try to be proud yourself, though I should think your sense of humour would bother you a little while you were trying. I think young people should be proud, because if they are not they will put up with makeshifts and get dirty; but elderly people and old people should not be proud, because it prevents them from understanding anything."

"But elderly people," I said, "don't they get dirty too, if they're not proud?"

She laughed at me, and all she said was: "I was talking about nice elderly people." And there the conversation ended, just nowhere. I think it very silly in a man to go generalising about women, but if I were to start generalising I might say that most abstract conversations between men end nowhere, but you have a feeling that at least something interesting has passed, while with a woman an abstract conversation ends nowhere and you have a feeling that she has only been talking about whatever it was just out of politeness.

I remember that what struck me most about Lamoir at that time was how happy she was, happy and feeling safe in her happiness. That puzzled me then, for I knew she loved Hugh.

II

I would see a good deal of Hugh, sometimes going to stay with him at Langton Weaver, and often, in London, dining with him at his house in Charles Street, just he and I alone. It was very pleasant to know of a quiet house in which I might now and then pass an evening talking, as one always did with Hugh if one talked at all, of books and tapestries and fine things. I never knew a man who had such a passion for the touch of fine things as Hugh, and seeing him thoughtfully holding a little old ivory figure in his hand one might almost think his skin was in love with it.

But a few weeks ago, the last time I was ever to dine with my friend, it instantly struck me that

he was in quite a different mood. And presently
he told me about the garden and the tree. He
didn't preface it with anything in particular, he
was thoughtfully twisting the stem of his port-
glass when he said: "Nearly nine years since I
have seen Lamoir——"

I said vaguely: "Yes. . . ." Never once, you
see, in all those nine years, had he so much as
mentioned the name of Lamoir, and so I felt
rather stunned at first.

Hugh went on thoughtfully, not particularly to
me: "And the first time I saw her I was nine
years old. She must have been seven."

I said: "But I always understood that Lamoir
passed her childhood in India and never came to
England until she was twenty or so! I'd no idea
you too were in India when you were little."

"I wasn't," he said, and he smiled, I think out
of shyness just because he was talking about himself. "I wasn't. That's why, you see, it was
so funny——"

I was trying to imagine Lamoir seven years old.
It was easy, of course, as it always is easy with
people one likes. Her curly grey hair would be
golden then, and maybe her grey eyes would be
more blue than grey, and they would look enormous in a tiny face. And she would be walking,
very still, making no noise at all, with two thin
brown sticks for legs and two blue pools for eyes,
very thoughtful indeed, and all this would be happening in a garden of red and yellow flowers with
a long low white house nearby. That was how
Hugh first saw Lamoir, in a garden, and nearby
a long low white house with a broad flight of steps

up to the open doorway and tall, shining windows.

Dazzling white the house seemed to him, Hugh said, but that must have been because there was a very brilliant sun that afternoon. There was no noise, except just summer noises, and although he didn't remember actually seeing any birds there must have been a lot of birds about, because he heard them. And simply masses of flowers there were in that garden, red and yellow flowers, and over a grey wall somewhere there was hung a thick curtain of flowers that may have been blue roses. And they may very well have been blue roses, Hugh said. And bang in the middle of all those flowers was Lamoir, staring at him as he came into the garden. Hugh was so surprised, he said, that he didn't know what to say or do.

He hadn't, you see, intended coming into that garden at all. He hadn't, a moment before, known anything at all about that garden or whose garden it was or even that there was a garden there at all. That is the funny part about the whole thing, the way it just sprung out at him, garden, Lamoir, blue roses and all, out of the summer afternoon. But there it was, and there Lamoir was, staring at Hugh. Not that she looked a bit surprised, Hugh said, although she was such a kid. She just stuck her finger into her mouth and came towards him.

Hugh's father's place, Langton Weaver, lay on the slope of a low hill not far from Hungerford, looking over the plain towards where the old red Elizabethan pile of Littlecott lies embowered in trees. Hugh, that bright afternoon, was kicking his heels about in the lane outside his father's gates, which was of course against all rules. But Hugh was lonely that afternoon, he never had any brothers or sisters, and he was wondering what he would do next, and he was hoping that someone would come along to do something with— when, bang, there he was in that garden and a little kid advancing on him with a finger stuck in her mouth. It was very odd, Hugh said.

"Hullo!" she said. All eyes, that's what she was.

"Hullo!" Hugh said. She was only a kid, after all. Hugh was nine.

"You're a boy," she said.

"Of course I'm a boy," Hugh said, and he was going to add "just as you're a girl," but a fellow couldn't stand there arguing all day with a slip of a thing like that. Then he suddenly remembered he didn't know where he was.

"I say," he said, "I don't know how I got here. What's this place?"

She twisted her finger out of her mouth and stared at the wet thing. Hugh remembered that it shone in the sun. And her hair shone in the sun, too. Hugh said her hair shone even when they were in the shade. But of course he didn't attach any importance to that kind of thing.

"I say, where am I?" Hugh asked again. He must have sounded pathetic, in spite of himself.

"You're here," she said. "What's your name?"

"Hugh," he said. "But, I say, where's here? I've never seen that house before. My father's got the biggest house round here, Langton Weaver.

My father's Lord of the Manor, and when he's dead I'm Lord of the Manor."

"Oo!" she said, staring.

Hugh said he felt frightfully let down. Any other kid would have exalted the merits of her own house, but she just swallowed everything and stared at you. Hugh said he felt as though he had been boasting.

"Our house doesn't look so jolly clean as this," he said. "Rather live here, any day."

And he suddenly realised he was speaking the truth. That was the amazing part of it, Hugh said: suddenly to feel that he would much rather live here than in his father's house. With this kid. And from that moment, somehow, he forgot every particle of his surprise at being in that garden.

"What's your name?" he asked.

"Not got a name," the kid said. "No name." All legs and eyes, that's what she was.

"But you must have a name!" Hugh cried. "Everyone's got names, even dogs and cats. We've got seven dogs and they're all called after every day in the week except one because you can't call a dog Sunday, father says."

"No name," she said breathlessly. "I'm me."

"But look here, how do they call you when they want you?" He thought he'd got her there all right, Hugh said.

She giggled. "I just come," she giggled. "I don't need to be called. Oo! Just come when I'm wanted. Did you want me? You did, didn't you?"

He stared at her, he was so dumbfounded.

Jiminy, hadn't he wanted her! Anyhow, hadn't he wanted something to happen. But how had this kid known that?

"Look here, no rotting!" he warned her.

"Not rotting," she said, sucking her finger. "What's rotting?"

"But what's this place?" he asked almost frantically. "Hasn't it got a name either?"

"Oo, yes! Playmate Place."

"It's not!" Hugh cried. "Not Playmate Place! *You're* rotting now."

Hugh says she took her finger out of her mouth, stamped her foot and screamed at one and the same time. "It *is* called Playmate Place and Playmate Place and Playmate Place! So there!"

"Oh, all right!" Hugh said, and he didn't let on any further about his opinion of a house called Playmate Place. Hugh says a boy of nine would rather die than live in a house called Playmate Place. It sounded so soft. But she was only a kid, after all, and she couldn't *know* anything.

"I'm going to run now," the kid said, standing on one leg and staring at the other.

That was too much, Hugh said. She was going to run! As though she *could* run! "Beat you blindfolded," he just said.

"Oo, you try!" she giggled, and she turned, and she flew. She just flew, Hugh said. All brown legs and golden hair. He hadn't a chance. But he must have been quite a nice boy really, Hugh said, because he began laughing at himself. He beat this kid!

She stopped, miles away, just under a tree. Hugh panted on. And they must have run some distance, for the house and the blue roses were no longer visible. Hugh couldn't remember any of the particulars of where they were now. There was a sense of flowers, he said, clean flowers, a lot of flowers. And that tree, under which Lamoir was waiting for him. Of course he didn't know she was Lamoir then. That tree seemed to him a big tree. Hugh said that when you touched it it smelt like a sort of echo of all the good smells you had ever smelt.

But he hadn't come quite up to her when.she turned and, before you could say "knife," shinned up that tree!

"I say!" cried Hugh.

"Can't catch me!" panted a little voice from among the leaves.

"Can if I want to," said Hugh, looking up. All he could see between the leaves was something white.

"Like you to want to," piped the something white, and Hugh fell in love for the first and last time in his life.

When he caught up with her, on a branch high up, she said "Oo!" and gave him a damp kiss on his cheek. She didn't giggle or anything, she was as serious as a man playing cricket. Hugh felt rather ashamed.

"Look here," he said, to say something, "what's this tree called? Never seen a tree like this before."

"It's a lovely tree," she said, staring. "It's called Playmate Tree, of course."

"That's a soft word, playmate," Hugh rashly said.

She stared at him with those big grey eyes, Hugh said, so that he began to feel weak, just weak with meanness. And then she said "Yow!" and wept. Well! She wept. Hugh didn't know what to do, stuck up there on a branch of a tree and this kid crying fit to break her kid's heart. He kept muttering, "I say, I'm sorry," and things like that, and then he found she was somehow in his arms, and he kissing her and kissing her hair. Her hair smelt like the tree, Hugh said, so it must have been a funny sort of tree.

"Kiss the tree now," the small voice said. "You've hurt it."

"Oh, I say!" said Hugh, but he did as he was told, and then they climbed down the magic tree in silence, he trying to help her and almost breaking his neck. They walked slowly back, hand in hand, towards where the house was, through the sweet lush grass. There was music somewhere, Hugh said. Or maybe there wasn't and he only thought there was. And Hugh said that he was happier at that moment than he had ever been since in his whole life.

"Mustn't laugh at words like playmate," said the wise kid. "You'll get hurt if you do."

"I say, I'd like to see you again," Hugh said shyly, and he found himself walking on the dusty lane towards Nasyngton! He was almost in Nasyngton, he could see, down the slope, the thick old bridge over the Kennet. He must have walked two miles or more while he thought he was in that garden. Playmate Place. He stopped to wipe his face, wondering passionately. He was simply streaming with perspiration. But what had happened to that old garden, that's what puzzled him. And that kid! That jolly little kid. He rubbed his cheek, but he couldn't be certain if there still was a damp patch where she had kissed him. Anyhow, it would have dried by then, and, anyhow again, he'd got so hot since.

When he got home Hugh told Hugh's father the outline of his adventure, and Hugh's father told Hugh he had broken rules by being outside the gates at all and that he must have been dreaming, but Hugh said passionately that he was sorry he had broken rules but he hadn't been anything like dreaming, and Hugh's father told Hugh not to be an ass, and two years later Hugh's father died.

Hugh did not see the garden of the white house again. Playmate Place. Hugh, as he grew up, blushed to think of Playmate Place. He had blushed at the time, and later on he blushed at the very thought of it. He wouldn't have dared let any of his friends at school even dream of his ever having swallowed such a soft yarn as the Playmate Place one. But, despite himself, the face of the kid whose name was to be Lamoir stayed with him, and her silver voice, and her enormous eyes. And now and then in his dreams, Hugh said, he would seem to hear the faint echo of an "Oo!"

III

It was almost twenty years to a day after the adventure of Playmate Place that Hugh met Lamoir at a party at Mace, Guy de Travest's place.

Miss Cavell her name was. He recognised her,
he said, at once, at very first sight. She had been
seven then and she was twenty-seven now, but
he knew her on sight. And when she spoke, he
was quite certain. Of course she didn't suck her
finger and say "Oo!" any longer, but without a
doubt Lamoir Cavell was the grown-up of the
kid of Playmate Place. And he actually found
himself wondering, as he talked to her that first
time at Mace, if she recognised him—and then
he almost laughed aloud at his childishness, for
of course the whole thing had been a boy's dream.
But it was very odd, his dreaming about someone
he was actually to meet twenty years later. And
once he fancied, as he turned to her suddenly,
that she was looking at him a little strangely, in
a puzzled sort of way maybe, with that small
slanting smile of hers as though she was smiling
at something she just hadn't said. Oh, Lamoir
must have been very beautiful then!

She was born in India, where old man Cavell
was something in the Civil Service, and she had
lived in India until recently, when her father died.
Hugh, that first time, asked her if she had ever
been in England as a child, and she said, staring
at him in a way that seemed so familiar to him
that his heart gave a throb: "Only in dreams."
But he didn't tell her about the Playmate Place
then. Then was the time to tell her, then or
never. He never told her.

They walked in enchantment, those two, for
the next few days. Guy de Travest has told me
since that the whole house-party went about on
tiptoe, so as not to disturb Hugh and Lamoir in

their exquisite contemplation of their triumph over the law of life, which is of course unknowable, but must be pretty depressing, seeing what life is.

They were married in the little village church at Mace, and Hilary Townshend was Hugh's best man, and Hilary has told me since that he almost wept to see them going away—knowing as he did so certainly, Hilary said, that Hugh and Lamoir had taken the one step in life which will wake any couple up from any dream.

Hugh continually pulled at the stiff grey affair on his upper lip as he told me of his marriage. "It's Playmate Place," he said, "that is important in the story: much more important than my married life. Lamoir and I never quite reached Playmate Place in actual life. We were in sight of it sometimes—when I let Lamoir have her head. But I only see that now, I didn't realise it then."

He said that about the importance of Playmate Place quite seriously. And, you know, I took it quite as seriously. A dream or vision or whatever it was, that has lasted fresh in a man's mind from the age of nine to the age of forty-nine is, after all, a thing to be taken seriously. I haven't, as a rule, much patience with dreams; and there's a deal too much talk of dreams in the novels of the day, for it's so easy to write "dream"; but Hugh's, as they say, rather "got" me.

He never spoke about it to Lamoir. "I began to, several times," he said, "but somehow I never went on. You see, there was such a difference between our life together and the way we had been together in that garden. I mean, such a tremendous difference in spirit. She was the same, but I—well, I was the same, too, but only that 'same' which had jeered at the word 'playmate.' It's difficult to explain. I knew, you see, as I said things that might hurt her, that I was in the wrong —and I didn't want to say them, either—but somehow it was in me to say them and so I said them. It's somehow the impulses you can't put into words that are the strongest."

The marriage of Hugh and Lamoir appeared to have gone much the same way as most marriages. At first they were very happy, and they were quite certain that they were going to be even happier. Then they thought that perhaps they were not so happy as they had been, and then they were quite certain that they were not so happy as they had been. Hugh said it was more or less like that.

Hugh, at the time, had thought privately that this was because Lamoir did not take very much interest in his collections of fine things. Not that he wasn't quite contented with his marriage. Good Lord, contented! I wonder what Lamoir thought about that. Contented! But she never confided, that quiet Lamoir.

It was a great unhappiness to her, Hugh said, that there were no children. A very great unhappiness. He hadn't, he admitted, minded so much, because year by year he was growing more absorbed in his collections. Throughout his married life he would go off searching Europe for pieces. Italy, Greece, Spain. At first he used to take Lamoir with him, but later on she would stay at home. She preferred that, Hugh said.

She wouldn't stay in the London house, but at Langton Weaver, the house which was larger but not so clean-looking as Playmate Place. Lamoir lived in the garden and the park. I met Hugh and Lamoir in the last years of their life together, and whenever I went to stay at Langton Weaver I would find Lamoir in the park. She would generally be standing just off a path, quite still, wearing gardening-gloves, and looking thoughtfully down at the flowers. Then she would touch one here and there. She was gardening.

So, Hugh said, ten years passed; and he, when he thought of it at all, would think theirs a happy enough marriage, as marriages go. Reality, after all, couldn't be so good as dreams, ever. That is what he thought. And he loved Lamoir. He was a collector of fine things, and so it was bred in his bone to love Lamoir. She loved him, too. Sometimes in quite a strange abandoned way, for a woman who had been married so long. In quite an un-English way, when you came to think of it—although it can't be in the least "un-English" to be passionate, but one gets into the habit of saying the idiotic things that English novelists say. Lamoir would say things unmentionable and beautiful, in the rare moments. But, somehow, those rarest moments would never be of Hugh's contriving, not after the first year or so. They would come suddenly, out of the night of ordinary marriage, they would come like angels with silent wings. And Lamoir would be the voice of the angel with silent wings, and Lamoir in those rarest moments would be the very body and soul of love. But Hugh couldn't woo those moments.

Perhaps no man ever can. It may be, Hugh said,
that there's a frontier to any woman's love for
any man, and beyond that frontier is the unknowable darkness and unknowable light, and from
that secret place can leap a passion that no man
in the world is worthy to woo. It just comes or
it doesn't come.

These moments did not come when he thought
they would, when he expected them. She would
somehow be passive then, somehow there yet not
there. Then suddenly, when he had got used to
the hurt of her "coldness," out of the night of ordinary marriage would sweep the angel with the
silent wings in the body and the voice of Lamoir.
Hugh said that sometimes the song of the sirens
was in Lamoir's voice, but if Hugh was right
about that Ulysses must have been just a silly old
man and the sirens darlings.

IV

For Hugh, his pleasure in travelling was given
an exquisite point by returning to Lamoir. That
was when he seemed to love her most, as he returned to her. One gets out of the habit of being
desirous if one stays in the home all the time.
And Lamoir would be waiting for him, sweet and
still. He thought of her all the time, as he returned towards her.

Once, nine years ago, he returned to her by
night. He had been away from England for four
or five months, and, arriving that evening in London, he had dined quickly and taken the first train
down to Langton Weaver. It was a cool July

night, loaded with stars. He had walked the two
miles from the railway station.

Hugh was happy as he walked. He was conscious of his happiness, of his health, of his
strength. Hugh was forty then, a dry, taut forty.
And the idea of Lamoir, white and supple, was
like a temptation that exalted and ennobled. The
sky was almost Italian, Hugh said, the stars were
so unusually clear and bright. He walked, not
up the drive towards the door, but across the lawn
towards the three French windows of the drawing-room. They showed a faint bronze light.
Lamoir was there. She was sitting in a Dorothy
chair of old blue velvet, reading. A lamp in a
bowl of yellow amber lit the book, but her face
was only a frail whiteness, and her hair was as
though veiled. He pushed open a window which
was unlatched. He called: "Lamoir!"

She made that gesture he knew so well, loved
so well. Lamoir would not be Lamoir without
that gesture. Always, at first sight of him returning to her, she would make that gesture. It
was delicious with a lure which he never could
explain. It was as though she was afraid of her
love for him. Towards her heart, the gesture
was: but faint, not definite: a hand like a white
bird, fluttering, fluttering vainly, fluttering out of
stillness, fluttering back into stillness—all in a
second. Lamoir, you see, had a weak heart, and
that was why, maybe, she was born so still, to
balance the weakness of her heart.

And it was always the same with him when he
saw her after an absence. The world stood still,
no living thing moved but Lamoir's hand and his

infinite desire. The pleasure of seeing her was exquisite, like a pain. In all his life Hugh had known no woman but Lamoir. Seeing her now, the earth and sky held only himself and her and the thing that was between them. That vivid thing with eyes of fire which can be beautiful or beastly. She troubled him and exalted him, and somehow his love for her would be stabbed by a queer sense of terror, which he never could explain. And she was so still, so passive, unknowable. But her eyes, as he made to touch her, adored him.

She lay beside him a long time in the delicious silence of love before she spoke and said: "Goodbye, Hugh."

He thought she must have gone mad. He stared at her, through the darkness. "Goodbye?" he echoed.

"Yes," she said, and that was all she said.

He had put out the light in the bowl of yellow amber. He lay in the darkness, understanding nothing. Then his mind grew darker than the room, and he just managed to say:

"But, Lamoir, are you mad? Good-bye! What do you mean?"

She did not answer for what seemed a long time. She was a soft darkness in the dark room, beside him. The night was a blue curtain over the windows, hung with stars like toys. He touched her, as though to prove to himself that he was not dreaming. He must be dreaming. But she was there, beside him, soft, warm: Lamoir, his wife. And the stars on the windows were as though at his finger-tips, but Lamoir was untouchable. She was untouchable, suddenly. She was most untouchable when he touched her. It seemed wrong to touch her. That made him angry. He laughed.

"I'm damned," he said, "if I understand what all this is about! I come home after months away, and you say good-bye!"

"I don't think," she said, "that I can explain. Not now. . . ."

He laughed. She was going away, and she didn't trouble to explain why!

He wanted her to say: "Don't be bitter, please!" But she was silent. She was beside him, yet her breath came from across the universe. And what on earth was it all about?

"But do you mean you want to leave me?" he asked, astounded, angry.

She said: "Yes."

"Lamoir!"

She said: "I can't bear it any longer, Hugh. I love you too much."

He repeated idiotically: "You love me too much?"

Now she was standing, a shadow in the darkness, away from him, a million miles away from him. He was silent. All the inside of him went silent. Suddenly there were no words, no need for words, no Lamoir, no Hugh, nothing but the primal nothingness before Adam. He would not hold her for a moment if she wished to leave him.

"You will understand," she said. "You see, I want to be free to love you, and you won't let me. You will understand that, too. God has given me no children, Hugh. He has given me

only my love for you. That is all I have, and I
have been sacrificing it to you for ten years; but
now I am growing afraid for it, it's become such
a poor, beaten, wretched bit of a thing, and so I
must leave you. I owe that to myself, dear—and
to the you inside you."

And he said, despite himself, that he loved her.
What was so strange was that, suddenly, he had
ceased to feel like her husband, suddenly it
seemed to him inconceivable that he had possessed her countless times. Inconceivable that he
and she had been one, when now they were so
apart! It had seemed so easy then to touch her
—now, not a lifetime would surmount the bar-
riers she had raised between them. He suddenly
thought: "Good Lord, how lucky I've been in the
past—and I never knew it!"

He was going to touch her, when like a blow
on the face he realised that to touch her would be
indecent. She was not his wife. Suddenly, ab-
surdly, he thought of Soames Forsyte, of John
Galsworthy. Hugh had always disliked Galsworthy for his creation of Forsyte, a man who
could rape his wife.

Lamoir said suddenly: "There will be another
chance later on. . . ."

He leapt at that. "Later on? Lamoir, you
mean you will come back?"

"No," she said. "I didn't mean that. I shall
never come back."

"You will," he said between his teeth, and with
a great effort of will he took her in his arms.

But afterwards she went away, and she never
came back.

V

We were silent for a long time after Hugh had spoken of the way Lamoir had left him. And then he said: "Of course she was right. I did understand, later on. That is why I have made no attempt to see her these last nine years. Love, you see, has many masks. We slip on one or other of them, and we say, 'This is love,' but really it's only a fraction of love. And a fraction of love can be the negation of love. Love is enormous and difficult. We must learn how to love, as we must learn how to play music. I did not know how. But I shall see Lamoir soon. I am going to Algeria next week. I have been wanting to go for a long time, but I must just wait another few days. . . ."

"But, Hugh, why do you wait even one day?" I protested. "Lamoir is longing to see you, I know she is."

"Yes. But I must wait four or five days or so. For a sort of anniversary. My idea, if you won't laugh at me too much, is to see Playmate Place again, and then that will give me a clue as to how to deal with Lamoir when I see her in the flesh. I'm sure it will give me a clue. And I'm sure I shall see it again, in three or four days from to-day. I'd like to, immensely. Of course it won't have changed one bit, but I wonder if Lamoir and I will have grown up. If we have, it will be rather a feat to climb that tree, won't it? Or maybe the tree will have grown too, though it seemed huge enough at the time. You see, the thing seems to go in cycles of twenty

years, more or less. I saw the garden for the
first time on a June day in my ninth year. I met
Lamoir for the first time on a June day, perhaps
the same one, in my twenty-ninth year. And now
I'm forty-nine, and the day falls in three or four
or five days' time. Either, I'm quite sure, I see
that garden again on that day, or I see Lamoir
herself, or . . ."

"Or?" I said. "Or what?"

"Well, God knows!" Hugh smiled, pulling at
that stiff grey thing on his upper lip, and on the
dawn of the fourth day from that night Hugh was
found by one of the keepers of Hyde Park lying
at the foot of a great tree near the Albert Gate,
dead of a broken neck. At the inquest there was
read out a letter from his wife's lawyers, which
had been delivered at Hugh's house on the morning of his death and which he couldn't, therefore,
have read, saying that they had heard by wire
from Algeria that his wife had died of heart-fail-
ure the day before.

X: THE GHOUL OF GOLDERS GREEN

I

IT is fortunate that the affair should have happened to Mr. Ralph Wyndham Trevor and be told by him, for Mr. Trevor is a scholar of some authority. It is in a spirit of almost ominous premonition that he begins the tale, telling how he was walking slowly up Davies Street one night when he caught a crab. It need scarcely be said that Davies Street owes its name to that Mary Davies, the heiress, who married into the noble house of Grosvenor. That was years and years ago, of course, and is of no importance whatsoever now, but it may be of interest to students.

It was very late on a winter's night, and Mr. Trevor was depressed, for he had that evening lost a great deal more than he could afford at the card game of auction bridge. Davies Street was deserted; and the moon and Mr. Trevor walked alone towards Berkeley Square. It was not the sort of moon that Mr. Trevor remembered having seen before. It was, indeed, the sort of moon one usually meets only in books or wine. Mr. Trevor was sober.

Nothing happened, Mr. Trevor affirms, for quite a while: he just walked; and, at that corner where Davies Street and Mount Street join together the better to become Berkeley Square, stayed his walking upon an idea that he would soothe his depression with the fumes of a cigarette. His cigarette-case, however, was empty. All London, says Mr. Trevor, appeared to be empty that night. Berkeley Square lay pallid and desolate: looking clear, not as though with moonlight, but with dead daylight; and never a voice to put life into the still streets, never a breeze to play with the bits of paper in the gutters or to sing among the dry boughs of the trees. Berkeley Square looked like nothing so much as an old stage property that no one had any use for. Mr. Trevor had no use at all for it; and became definitely antagonistic to it when a taxicab crawled wretchedly across the waste white expanse and the driver, a man in a Homburg hat of green plush, looked into his face with a beseeching look.

"Taxi, sir?" he said.

Mr. Trevor says that, not wanting to hurt the man's feelings, he just looked another way.

"Nice night, sir," said the driver miserably, "for a drive in an 'ackney-carriage."

"I live," said Mr. Trevor with restraint, "only a few doors off. So hackney-carriage to you."

"No luck!" sighed the driver and accelerated madly away even as Mr. Trevor changed his mind, for would it not be an idea to drive to the nearest coffee-stall and buy some cigarettes? This, however, he was not to do, for there was no other reply to his repeated call of "Taxi!" but certain heavy blows on the silence of Davies Street behind him.

"Wanting a taxi, sir?" said a voice which could only belong to a policeman.

"Certainly not," said Mr. Trevor bitterly. "I never want a taxi. But now and then a taxi-driver thrusts himself on me and pays me to be seen in his cab, just to give it a tone. Next question."

"Ho!" said the policeman thoughtfully.

"I beg your pardon?" said Mr. Trevor.

"Ho!" said the policeman thoughtfully.

"The extent of your vocabulary," said Mr. Trevor gloomily, "leads me to conclude that you must have been born a gentleman. Have you, in that case, a cigarette you could spare?"

"Gaspers," said the policeman.

"Thank you," said Mr. Trevor, rejecting them. "I am no stranger to ptomaine poisoning."

"That's funny," said the policeman, "your saying that. I was just thinking of death."

"Death?" said Mr. Trevor.

"You've said it," said the policeman.

"I've said what?" said Mr. Trevor.

"Death," said the policeman.

"Oh, death!" said Mr. Trevor. "I always say 'death,' constable. It's my favourite word."

"Ghoulish, I calls it, sir. Ghoulish, no less."

"That entirely depends," said Mr. Trevor, "on what you are talking about. In some things, ghoulish is as ghoulish does. In others, no."

"You've said it," said the policeman. "But ghoulish goes, in this 'ere affair. One after the other lying in their own blood, and not a sign as to who's done it, not a sign!"

"Oh, come, constable! Tut-tut! Not even a thumb-mark in the blood?"

"I'm telling you," said the policeman severely. "Corpses slit to ribbons all the way from 'Ampstead 'Eath to this 'ere Berkeley Square. And why? That's what I asks myself. And why?"

"Of course," said Mr. Trevor gaily, "there certainly have been a lot of murders lately. Ha-ha! But not, surely, as many as all that!"

"I'm coming to that," said the policeman severely. "We don't allow of the Press reporting more'n a quarter of them. No, sir. That's wot it 'as come to, these larst few days. A more painful situation 'as rarely arisen in the hannals of British crime. The un'eard-of bestiality of the criminal may well baffle ordinary minds like yours and mine."

"I don't believe a word of it!" snapped Mr. Trevor.

"Ho, *you* don't!" said the policeman. *"You* don't!"

"That's right," said Mr. Trevor, "I don't. Do you mean to stand there and tell me that I wouldn't 'ave 'eard—I mean, have heard of this criminal if he had really existed?"

"You're a gent," said the policeman.

"You've said it," said Mr. Trevor.

"And gents," said the policeman, "know nothing. And what they do know is mouldy. Ever 'eard of Jack the Ripper?"

"Yes, I 'ave," said Mr. Trevor bitterly.

"*H*ave is right, sir, if you'll excuse me. Well, Jack's death was never rightly proved, not it! So it might well be 'im at 'is old tricks again, even though 'e has been retired, in a manner of speaking, these forty years. Remorseless and hindiscriminate murder, swift and sure, was Jack's line, if you remember, sir."

"Before my time," said Mr. Trevor gloomily.

"Well, Jack's method was just to slit 'em up with a razor, frontwise and from south to north, and not a blessed word spoken. No one's touched 'im yet, not for efficiency, but this new chap, 'e looks like catching Jack up. *And* at Jack's own game, razor and all. Makes a man fair sick, sir, to see the completed work. Just slits 'em up as clean as you or me might slit up a vealanam-pie. We was laying bets on 'im over at Vine Street only to-night, curious like to see whether 'e'd beat Jack's record. But it'll take some beating, I give you my word. Up to date this chap 'as only done in twelve in three weeks—not that that's 'alf bad, seeing as how 'e's new to the game, more or less."

"Oh, rather, more or less!" said Mr. Trevor faintly. "Twelve! Good God—only twelve! But why—why don't you catch the ghastly man?"

"Ho, why don't we!" said the policeman. "Becos we don't know 'ow, that's why. Not us! It's the little one-corpse men we're good for, not these 'ere big artists. Look at Jack the Ripper—did we catch 'im? Did we? And look at Julian Raphael—did we catch 'im? I'm asking you."

"I know you are," said Mr. Trevor gratefully. "Thank you."

"I don't want your thanks," said the policeman. "I'm just warning you."

Mr. Trevor gasped: "Warning *me!*"

"You've said it," said the policeman. "You don't ought to be out alone at this time of night, an 'earty young chap like you. These twelve 'e's already done in were all 'earty young chaps. 'E's

partial to 'em 'earty, I do believe. And social
gents some of 'em was, too, with top-'ats to hand,
just like you might be now, sir, coming 'ome from
a smoking-concert. Jack the Ripper all over
again, that's wot I say. Except that this 'ere new
corpse-fancier, 'e don't seem to fancy women at
all."

"A chaps' murderer, what!" said Mr. Trevor
faintly. "Ha-ha! What?"

"You've said it," said the policeman. "But you
never know your luck, sir. And maybe as 'ow
thirteen's your lucky number."

Mr. Trevor lays emphasis on the fact that
throughout he treated the constable with the courtesy due from a gentleman to the law. He merely
said: "Constable, I am now going home. I do not
like you very much. You are an alarmist. And
I hope that when you go to sleep to-night your
ears swell so that when you wake up in the morning you will be able to fly straight to heaven and
never be seen or heard of again. You and your
razors and your thirteens!"

"Ho, they ain't mine, far from it!" said the
policeman, and even as he spoke a voice crashed
upon the silence from the direction of Mount
Street. The voice belonged to a tall figure in
black and white, and on his head was a top-hat
that shone under the pallid moon like a monstrous
black jewel.

"That there," said the policeman, "is a Noise."

"He's singing," said Mr. Trevor.

"I'll teach 'im singing!" said the policeman.

Sang the voice:

> *"With an host of furious fancies,*
> *Whereof I am commander,*
>> *With a burning spear*
>> *And a horse of air*
> *To the wilderness I wander."*

"You will," said the policeman. "Oh, you will!"

> *"By a knight of ghosts and shadows*
> *I summoned am to tourney*
>> *Ten leagues beyond*
>> *The wide world's end—*
> *Methinks it is no journey!"*

"Not to Vine Street, it isn't," said the policeman.

"Ho there!" cried the approaching voice. "Who dares interrupt my song!"

"Beau Maturin!" cried Mr. Trevor gladly. "It's not you! Bravo, Beau Maturin! Sing, bless you, sing! For I am depressed."

> *"From Heaven's Gate to Hampstead Heath*
> *Young Bacchus and his crew*
> *Came tumbling down, and o'er the town*
> *Their bursting trumpets blew."*

"Fine big gent, your friend," said the policeman thoughtfully.

> *"And when they heard that happy word*
> *Policemen leapt and ambled:*
> *The busmen pranced, the maidens danced,*
> *The men in bowlers gambolled."*

"Big!" said Mr. Trevor. "Big? Let me tell you, constable, that the last time Mr. Maturin hit Jack Dempsey, Dempsey bounced back from the floor so quick that he knocked Mr. Maturin out on the rebound."

Mr. Trevor says that Beau Maturin came on through the night like an avenger through a wilderness, so little did he reck of cruel moons and rude policemen. Said he: "Good evening, Ralph. Good evening, constable. Lo, I am in wine!"

"You've said it," said the policeman.

"Gently, my dear! Or," said Mr. Maturin cordially, "I will dot you one, and look at it which way you like it is a far, far better thing to be in wine than in a hospital. Now, are there any good murders going to-night?"

"Going?" said the constable. "I'm 'ere to see there ain't any coming. But I've just been telling this gent about some recent crises. Corpses slit to ribbons just as you or me might slit up a vealanam——"

"Don't say that again!" snapped Mr. Trevor.

"By Heaven, what's that?" sighed Mr. Maturin; and, following his intent eyes, they saw, a yard or so behind them on the pavement, a something that glittered in the moonlight. Mr. Trevor says that, without a thought for his own safety, he instantly took a step towards the thing, but that the policeman restrained him. It was Mr. Maturin who picked the thing up. The policeman whistled thoughtfully.

"A razor, let's face it!" whispered Beau Maturin.

"*And* sharp!" said the policeman, thoughtfully

testing the glittering blade with the ball of his thumb.

Mr. Trevor says that he was never in his life less conscious of any feeling of excitement. He merely pointed out that he could swear there had been no razor there when he had come round the corner, and that, while he had stood there, no one had passed behind him.

"The chap that owns this razor," said the policeman, emphasising each word with a gesture of the blade, "must 'ave slunk behind you and me as we stood 'ere talking and dropped it, maybe not finding it sharp enough for 'is purpose. What do you think, Mr. Maturin?"

But Mr. Maturin begged to be excused from thinking, protesting that men are in the hands of God and God is in the hands of women, so what the devil is there to think about?

Mr. Trevor says that the motive behind his remark at that moment, which was to the effect that he simply must have a drink, was merely that he was thirsty. A clock struck two.

"After hours," said the policeman; and he seemed, Mr. Trevor thought, to grin evilly.

"What do they know of hours," sighed Mr. Maturin, "who only Ciro's know? Come, Ralph. My love, she jilted me but the other night. Therefore I will swim in wine, and thrice will I call upon her name when I am drowning. Constable, good-night to you."

"Now I've warned you!" the policeman called after them. "Don't go into any alleys or passages like Lansdowne Passage else you'll be finding yourselves slit up like vealanam-pies."

Maybe it was only the treacherous light of the moon, but Mr. Trevor fancied as he looked back that the policeman, where he stood thoughtfully fingering the shining blade, seemed to be grinning evilly at them.

II

They walked in silence, their steps ringing sharp on the bitter-chill air. The night in the sky was pale at the white disdain of the moon. It was Mr. Maturin who spoke at last, saying: "There's too much talk of murder to-night. A man cannot go to bed on such crude talk. You know me, kid. Shall we go to *The Garden of My Grandmother?*"

At that moment a taxicab crawled across the moonlight; and the driver, a man in a Homburg hat of green plush, did not attempt to hide his pleasure at being able to satisfy the gentlemen's request to take them to *The Garden of My Grandmother*.

Mr. Trevor says that he has rarely chanced upon a more unsatisfactory taxicab than that driven by the man in the Homburg hat of green plush. By closing one's eyes one might perhaps have created an illusion of movement by reason of certain internal shrieks and commotions, but when one saw the slow procession of shops by the windows and the lamp-posts loitering by the curb, one was, as Beau Maturin pointed out, justified in believing that the hackney-cab in question was not going fast enough to outstrip a retired Czecho-Slovakian admiral in an egg-and-

spoon race. Nor were they altogether surprised
when the taxicab died on them in Conduit Street.
The man in the Homburg hat of green plush
jumped out and tried to restart the engine. He
failed. The gentlemen within awaited the issue in
silence. The silence, says Mr. Trevor, grew terrible. But the taxicab moved not, and the man
in the Homburg hat of green plush began, in
his agitation, thumping the carburetor with his
clenched fist.

"No petrol," he pleaded. "No petrol."

Said Mr. Trevor to Mr. Maturin: "Let us go.
Let us leave this man."

" 'Ere, my fare!" said the fellow.

"Your fare?" said Mr. Maturin with contracted
brows. "What do you mean, 'your fare'?"

"Bob on the meter," said the wretch.

"My friend will pay," said Mr. Maturin, and
stalked away. Mr. Trevor says that, while retaining throughout the course of that miserable
night his undoubted *flair* for generosity, he could
not but hold Beau Maturin's high-handed dis-
avowal of his responsibilities against him; and he
was hurrying after him up Conduit Street, turning
over such phrases as might best point the occasion
and make Mr. Maturin ashamed of himself, when
that pretty gentleman swung round sharply and
said: "Ssh!"

But Mr. Trevor was disinclined to Ssh,
maintaining that Mr. Maturin owed him nine-
pence.

"Ssh, you fool!" snapped Mr. Maturin; and
Mr. Trevor had not obliged him for long before
he discerned in the quietness of Conduit Street a

small discordant noise, or rather, says Mr. Trevor, a series of small discordant noises.

"She's crying, let's face it," whispered Mr. Maturin.

"She! Who?"

"Ssh!" snapped Mr. Maturin.

They were at that point in Conduit Street where a turn to the right will bring one into a fat little street which looks blind but isn't, insomuch as close by the entrance to the Alpine Club Galleries there is a narrow passage or alley leading into Savile Row. Mr. Trevor says that the repugnance with which he at that moment looked towards the darkness of that passage or alley had less than nothing to do with the blood-thirsty policeman's last words but was due merely to an antipathy he had entertained towards all passages or alleys ever since George Tarlyon had seen a ghost in one. Mr. Maturin and he stood for some minutes in the full light of the moon while, as though from the very heart of the opposite darkness, the lacerating tremors of weeping echoed about their ears.

"I can't bear it!" said Beau Maturin. "Come along." And he advanced towards the darkness, but Mr. Trevor said he would not, pleading foot trouble.

"Come," said Beau Maturin, but Mr. Trevor said: "To-morrow, yes. But not to-night."

Then did Beau Maturin advance alone into the darkness towards the passage or alley, and with one pounce the darkness stole his top-hat from the moon. Beau Maturin was invisible. The noise of weeping abated.

"Oi!" called Mr. Trevor. "Come back, you fool!"

"Ssh!" whispered the voice of Mr. Maturin.

Mr. Trevor said bitterly: "You're swanking, that's all!"

"It's a girl!" whispered the voice of Mr. Maturin, whereupon Mr. Trevor, who yielded to no man in the chivalry of his address towards women, at once advanced, caught up Mr. Maturin and, without a thought for his own safety, was about to pass ahead of him when Beau Maturin had the bad taste to whisper " 'Ware razors!" and thus again held the lead.

She who wept, now almost inaudibly, was a dark shape just within the passage. Her face, says Mr. Trevor, was not visible, yet her shadow had not those rather surprising contours which one generally associates with women who weep in the night.

"Madam," began Mr. Maturin.

"Oh!" sobbed the gentle voice. "He is insulting me!"

Mr. Trevor lays some emphasis on the fact that throughout the course of that miserable night his manners were a pattern of courtliness. Thinking, however, that a young lady in a situation so lachrymose would react more favourably to a fatherly tone, he said:

"My child, we hope——"

"Ah!" sobbed the gentle voice. "Please go away, please! I am *not* that sort!"

"Come, come!" said Mr. Maturin. "It is us whom you insult with a suspicion so disagreeable. My friend and I are not of the sort to commit

ourselves to so low a process as that which is
called, I believe, 'picking up.' "

"We have, as a matter of fact, friends of our
own," said Mr. Trevor haughtily.

"Speaking generally," said Mr. Maturin,
"women like us. Time over again I have had to
sacrifice my friendship with a man in order to
retain his wife's respect."

"Ah, you are a man of honour!" sobbed the
young lady.

"We are two men of honour," said Mr. Trevor.

"And far," said Mr. Maturin warmly, "from intending you any mischief, we merely thought, on
hearing you weeping——"

"You *heard* me, sir!"

"From Conduit Street," said Mr. Trevor severely, whereupon Mr. Maturin lifted up his voice
and sang:

> *"From Conduit Street, from Conduit Street,*
> *The street of ties and tailors:*
> *From Conduit Street, from Conduit Street,*
> *A shocking street for trousers——"*

"Oh!" sobbed the young lady. "Is this chivalry?"

"Trousers," said Mr. Maturin, "are closely con-
nected with chivalry, insomuch as he who com-
mits chivalry without them is to be considered a
rude fellow. But, child," Mr. Maturin protested
sincerely, "we addressed you only in the hope that
we might be of some service in the extremity of
your grief. I assure you that you can trust us,
for since we are no longer soldiers rape and crime

have ceased to attract us.   However, you do not need us.   We were wrong.   We will go."

"It was I who was wrong!" came the low voice; and Mr. Trevor says that only then did the young lady raise her face, when it was instantly as though the beauty of that small face sent the surrounding darkness scurrying away.   Not, however, that Mr. Trevor was impressed altogether in the young lady's favour.   Her eyes, which were large, dark and charming, appeared to rest on handsome Beau Maturin with an intentness which Mr. Trevor can only describe as bold; while her disregard of his own presence might have hurt him had he, says Mr. Trevor, cared two pins for that kind of thing.

"You see, I have not eaten to-day," the young lady told Beau Maturin, who cried: "But, then, we *can* help you!"

"Ah, how do I know!   Please," the young lady began weeping again, and Mr. Trevor says that had he not hardened his heart he could not say what he might not have done.   "Please, sirs, I simply do not know what to do!   I am so unhappy, so alone—oh, but you cannot imagine! You are gentlemen?"

"Speaking for my friend," said Mr. Maturin warmly, "he has been asked to resign from Buck's Club only after repeated bankruptcies."

"Mr. Maturin," said Mr. Trevor, "has in his time been cashiered from no less a regiment than the Coldstream Guards."

The young lady did not, however, favour Mr. Trevor with so much as a glance, never once taking her beautiful eyes from the handsome face

of Beau Maturin. Indeed, throughout the course
of that miserable night she admirably controlled
any interest Mr. Trevor might have aroused in
her, which Mr. Trevor can only account for by
the supposition that she must have been warned
against him. Beau Maturin, meanwhile, had
taken the young lady's arm, a familiarity with
which Mr. Trevor cannot too strongly dissociate
himself, and was saying:

"Child, you may come with us, if not with honour, at least with safety. And while you refresh
yourself with food and drink you can tell us, if
you please, the tale of your troubles. Can't she,
Ralph?"

"I don't see," said Mr. Trevor, "what good we
can do."

"Your friend," said the young lady sadly to
Beau Maturin, "does not like me. Perhaps you
had better leave me alone to my misery."

"My friend," said Beau Maturin, guiding her
steps down the fat little street towards Conduit
Street, "likes you only too well, but is restrain-
ing himself for fear of your displeasure. Moreover, he cannot quickly adapt himself to the company of ingenuous young ladies, for he goes a
good deal into society, where somewhat cruder
methods obtain."

"But, oh, where are you taking me to?" suddenly cried the young lady.

"To *The Garden of My Grandmother*," said
Mr. Trevor bitterly, and presently they found a
taxicab on Regent Street which quickly delivered
them at the place in Leicester Square. Mr. Trevor cannot help priding himself on the agility with

which he leapt out of that taxicab, saying to the driver: "My friend will pay."

But Mr. Maturin, engrossed in paying those little attentions to the young lady which really attractive men, says Mr. Trevor, can afford to neglect, told the driver to wait, and when the driver said he did not want to wait, to go and boil his head.

III

Mr. Trevor describes *The Garden of my Grandmother* in some detail, but that would be of interest only to the specialist. The place was lately raided, and is now closed; and remained open so long as it did only with the help of such devices as commend themselves to those aliens who know the laws of the land only to circumvent them. For some time, indeed, the police did not even know of its existence as a night-club, for the entrance to the place was through two mean-looking doors several yards apart, on one of which was boldly inscribed the word "Gentlemen" and on the other "Ladies."

Within, all was gaiety and *chic*. From the respectable night-clubs and restaurants, all closed by this hour, would come the *jeunesse* of England; and an appetising smell of kippers brought new life to the jaded senses of young ladies, while young gentlemen cleverly contrived to give the appearance of drinking ginger ale by taking their champagne through straws. Mr. Trevor says, however, that there was not the smallest chance of the place being raided on the night in question, for among the company was a Prince of the Blood; and it is an unwritten law in the Metropolitan Police Force that no night-club shall be raided while a Prince of the Blood is pulling a party therein.

The young lady and our two gentlemen were presently refreshing themselves at a table in a secluded corner; and when at last only the wine was left before them Mr. Maturin assumed his courtliest manner to beg the young lady to tell her tale, and in detail, if she thought its relation would relieve her at all. She thought, with all the pensive beauty of her dark eyes, that it would, and immediately began on the following tale:

The Tale of the Bulgarian Girl

I am (she said) twenty-three years old, and although I once spent two years in England at a boarding-school in Croydon, my life hitherto has been lived entirely in Bulgaria. My father was a Bulgar of the name of Samson Samsonovitch Samsonoff, my mother an Englishwoman of the Lancashire branch of the race of Jones, and for her tragic death in a railway accident just over a year ago I shall grieve all my life: which, I cannot help praying, may be a short one, for I weary of the insensate cruelties that every new day opens out for me.

I must tell you that my mother was an unusual woman, of rigid principles, lofty ideals and a profound feeling for the grace and dignity of the English tongue, in which, in spite of my father's opposition, for the Samsonoffs are a bitter proud race, she made me proficient at an early age. Never had this admirable woman a thought in her life that was not directed towards furthering her husband's welfare and to obtaining the happiness of her only child; and I am convinced that my father had not met his cruel death two months ago had she been spared to counsel him.

My father came of an ancient Macedonian house. For hundreds of years a bearer of the name of Samson Samsonovitch Samsonoff has trod the stark hillsides of the Balkans and raided the sweet, rich valleys about Philippopolis. As brigands, the Samsonoffs had never a rival; as *comitadjis,* in war or peace, their name was a name for heroism and of terror: while as assassins—for the domestic economy of Bulgaria has ever demanded the occasional services of a hawk's eye and a ruthless hand—a Samsonoff has been honourably associated with some of the most memorable *coups* in Balkan history. I am well aware that pride of family has exercised a base dominion over the minds of many good men and women; yet I do not hesitate to confess that it is with almost unbearable regret that I look upon the fact that I, a wretched girl, am the last and only remnant of our once proud house.

Such a man it was whom my mother, while accompanying her father, a civil engineer, through Bulgaria, married. Nor did it need anything less than the ardour of her love and the strength of her character to seduce a Samson Samsonovitch from the dour dominion of the hills to the conventional life of the valleys. I loved my father, but cannot be blind to the grave flaws in his char-

acter. A tall, hairy man, with a beard such as
would have appalled your description of Beaver,
he was subject to ungovernable tempers and, oc-
casionally, to regrettable lapses from that moral
code which is such an attractive feature of English domestic life. Ah, you who live in the content and plenty of so civilised a land, how can
you even imagine the horrors of lawlessness that
obtain among primitive peoples! Had not that
good woman my mother always willed him to
loving-kindness, Samsonovitch Samsonoff had
more than once spilled the blood of his dearest
friends in the heat of some petty tavern brawl.

We lived in a farmhouse in what is surely the
loveliest valley in the world, that which is called
the Valley of the Roses, and whence is given to
the world that exquisite essence known as *attar*
of roses. Our little household in that valley was
a happy and united one; more and more infre-
quent became my father's demoniac tempers; and,
but for his intolerance of fools and cravens, you
had taken the last of the Samsonoffs to be a part
of the life of the valley-men, of whose industry,
the cultivation of roses, he rapidly became a master.

Thus we come to the time which I now think of
as two months before my mother's death. My
father had attained to a certain degree of wealth,
and was ever enticing my mother with dreams of
a prolonged visit to her beloved birthplace, South-
port, which is, I believe, a pretty town on the sea-
board of Lancashire, and which I look forward
with delight to visiting. While enticing her, however, with such visions, he did not hesitate to

warn her that she must wait on the issue of his fanciful hobby, which daily grew on him; for the last of the Samsonoffs had become an inventor of flowers!

You may well look bewildered. But had you known my father you would in some measure have understood how a man, of an extreme audacity of temperament, might be driven into any fanciful pursuit that might lend a spice to a life of intolerable gentility. Nor was that pursuit so fanciful as might as first appear to those of conventionally studious minds: my father had a profound knowledge of the anatomy of flowers; and was in the habit of saying that he could not but think that the mind of man had hitherto neglected the invention and cultivation of the most agreeable variations. In fine, the tempestuous but simple mind of Samsonovitch Samsonoff had been captivated by the possibility of growing green carnations.

My mother and I were, naturally enough, not at all averse from his practising so gentle a hobby as the invention and cultivation of improbable flowers. And it was long before we even dreamt of the evil consequences that might attend so inoffensive an ambition. But my poor mother was soon to be rid of the anxieties of this life.

One day she and I were sitting in the garden, discussing the English fashion journals, when, silently as a cloud, my father came out of the house and looked towards us in the half-frowning, half-smiling way of his best mood. Tall and patriarchal, he came towards us—and in his hand we saw a flower with a long slender stem, and we stared at it as though we could not believe our eyes, for it was a green carnation!

"You have painted it!" we cried, my mother and I, for his success had seemed to us as remote as the stars.

"I have *made* it!" said my father, and he smiled into his beard, which was ever his one confidential friend. "Women, I have made it in my laboratory. And as I have made this I can make thousands, millions, and thousands of millions!"

He waved a closely-covered piece of paper towards me. "My daughter," he said, "here is your dower, your heritage. I am too old to burden myself with the cares of great riches, but by the help of this paper you, my beloved child, will become an heiress who may condescend to an Emperor or an American. We will not lose a minute before going to England, the land of honest men, to put the matter of the patent in train. For on this paper is written the formula by which green carnations, as well as all previously known varieties of carnations, can be *made* instead of grown. *Made,* I say, instead of grown! Women, do you understand what it is that I have achieved? I have stolen something of the secret of the sun!"

"Samson, boast not!" cried my mother, but he laughed at her and fondled me, while I stared in great wonder at the slip of paper that fluttered in his hand and dreamed the fair dreams of wealth and happiness in a civilised country. Ah me, ah me, the ill-fated excellence of dreams! For here I am in the most civilised country in the world, a pauper, and more wretched than a pauper!

Our preparations for removal to England were not far advanced before that happened which brought the first cruel turn to our fortunes. On an evil day my mother set out to Varna to buy some trivial thing, and—but I cannot speak of that, how she was returned to us a mangled corpse, her dear features mutilated beyond recognition by the fury of the railway accident.

My father took his sudden loss strangely: it was as though he was deprived at one blow of all the balance, the restraint, with which so many years of my mother's influence had softened the dangerous temper of the Samsonoff; and the brooding silence he put upon his surroundings clamoured with black thoughts. Worst of all, he began again to frequent the taverns in the valley, wherein he seemed to find solace in goading to fury the craven-hearted lowlanders among whom he had lived in peace for so long. The Samsonoff, in short, seemed rapidly to be reverting to type; and I, his daughter, must stand by and do nothing, for my influence over him was never but of the pettiest sort.

The weeks passed, and our preparations for departure to England proceeded at the soberest pace. In England we were going to stay with my mother's brother, a saintly man of some little property who lived a retired life in London, and whose heir I would in due course be, since he was himself without wife or children.

My father, never notable for the agreeable qualities of discretion and reticence, soon spread about the report of his discovery of the green carnation. He could not resist boasting of it in his cups, of the formula with which he could always make them, of the fortune he must inevitably make. Nor did he hesitate to taunt the men of the valley, they who came of generations of flower-growers, with his own success in an occupation which, he said, he had never undertaken but at a woman's persuasion, since it could be regarded as manly only by those who would describe as manly the painted face of a Circassian eunuch. Thus he would taunt them, laughing me to scorn when I ventured to point out that even worms will turn and cravens conspire. Woe and woe to the dour and high-handed in a world of polity, for their fate shall surely find them out!

One day, having been to the village to procure some yeast for the making of a *yaourt* or *yawort*, which is that same Bulgarian "sour milk" so strongly recommended to Anglo-Saxon digestions, I was startled, as I walked up the path to the door, by the bruit of loud rough voices. Only too soon was my fear turned to horror. One of the voices was my father's, arrogant and harsh as only his could be, with a sneer like a snake running through it. The other I could not recognise, but could hear only too well that it had not the soft accents of the men of the valley; and when, afraid to enter, I peered in through the window, I saw my father in violent altercation with a man his equal in stature and demeanour—another bearded giant, as fair as my father was dark, and with the livid eyes of a wolf.

What was my horror on recognising him as Michaelis the *comitadji*, the notorious and brutal Michaelis of the hills. The Michaelises and the

Samsonovitch Samsonoffs had always been the
equal kings of the *banditti* and, in many a fight
between Christian and Turk, the equal champions
of the Cross against the Crescent. And now, as
I could hear through the window, the last of the
Michaelises was asking of the last of the Samsonoffs some of his great wealth, that he might arm
and munition his troop to the latest mode.

My father threw back his head and laughed.
But his laugh had cost him dear had I not
screamed a warning, for the Michaelis with the
wolfish eyes had raised a broad knife. My father leapt to one side, and taking up the first
thing that came to hand, a heavy bottle of *mas-
tique,* crashed it down like an axe on the fair
giant's head; and then, without so much as a
glance at the unconscious man, and massive
though the Michaelis was, slung him over his
shoulder, strode out of the house and garden and
flung him into the middle of the roadway, where
he lay for long moaning savagely with the pain
of his broken head. I had gone to the aid of the
wretch, but my father would not let me, saying
that no Michaelis ever yet died of a slap on the
crown and that a little blood-letting would clear
the man's mind of his boyish fancies. Ah, if it
had!

It was at a late hour of the very next night—
for since my mother's death my father would
loiter in the taverns until all hours—that his
hoarse voice roused me from my sleep; and on
descending I found him raging about the kitchen
like a wounded tiger, his clothes in disorder and
showing grim dark stains that, as I clung to him,

foully wetted my hands. I prayed him, in an access of terror, to tell me he was not hurt, for what other protection than him had I in that murderous land?

"I am not hurt, child," he growled impatiently. "But I have been driven to hurt some so that they can never again feel pain."

They had ambushed him, the cowards, as he came home through the wood—as though a hundred of those maggots of the valley could slay a Samsonovitch Samsonoff! My father had caught the last of them by the throat, and the trembling coward had saved himself by confessing the plot. It appeared that it was they who had persuaded the Michaelis to visit us the day before, alluring his fancy with tales of the discovery of the carnation and of the great riches the Samsonoff had concealed about the house. And the Michaelis had come to our house not for part of my father's wealth but for all he could find, as also for the secret of the carnation, which he might sell at a great price to some Jew in Sofia—he had come to kill my father!

"And I, like a fool," cried my father, "only broke the skin of his wolfish head! Girl, we must be off at once! I have not lived in unwilling peace all these years to die like a rat; and now that these weak idiots have failed to kill me Michaelis and his troop will surround the house, and who shall escape the wolves of the hills? Now linger not for your clothes and fineries. Grigory Eshekovitch has horses for us at the edge of the wood, and we can make Philippopolis by the morning. Here is all our money in

notes. Take them, so that you will be provided
for should these scum get me. And the formula
—take care of the formula, child, for that is your
fortune! Should I have to stay behind, your
mother's brother in England is a good man and
will probably not rob you of more than half the
profits of it."

And so we came to leave our beloved home,
stealing like thieves through the darkness of a
moonless night. How shall I ever forget those
desperate moments! Our farm lay far from any
other habitation, and a long sloping lane joined
our pastures to the extensive Karaloff Wood, a
wood always evoked by Bulgarian poets of past
centuries as the home of vampires and the kennel
of the hounds of hell.

There, at its borders, Grigory Eshekovitch, a
homely man devoted to our interests, awaited us
with two horses; and, although I could not see his
face in the darkness, I could imagine by the
tremor of his never very assured voice how pallid,
indeed green, it must have been; for poor Grigory
Eshekovitch suffered from some internal affection which had the effect of establishing his complexion very uncertainly.

"Have you seen anyone in the wood?" my
father asked him.

"No, but I have heard noises," Grigory Eshekovitch trembled.

"Bah!" growled my father. "That was the
chattering of your own miserable teeth."

I wonder what has happened to poor Grigory
Eshekovitch, whether he survived that hideous
night. We left him there, a trembling figure on

the borders of the wood, while we put our horses into the heart of that darkness; and I tried to find solace in our desperate situation by looking forward to the safety and comfort of our approaching life in England. Little I knew that I was to suffer such agonies of fear in this huge city that I would wish myself back in the land of wolves!

My dreams were shattered by a low growl from my father, and we pulled up our horses, listening intently. By this time we were about half-way through the wood; and had we not known the place by heart we had long since lost our way, for the curtain of leaves between us and the faint light of the stars made the place so black that we could not even see the faintest glimmer of each other. At last my father whispered that it was all right, and we were in the act of spurring our tired horses for the last dash through the wood when torches flamed on all sides and we stood as in the tortured light of a crypt in moonlight.

"Samson Samsonovitch," cried a hoarse voice, and like a stab at my heart I knew it for the voice of the Michaelis, "we hope your sins are not too heavy, for your time has come."

It ill becomes a girl to boast of her parent; but shall I neglect to mention the stern fortitude, the patriarchal resignation, the monumental bravery, of my father, how he sat his horse still as a rock in a tempest and only his lips moved in a gentle whisper to me. "Child, save yourself," said he, and that was his farewell. "I command you to go—to save yourself and my secret from these hounds. Maybe I too will get through. God is as good to us as we deserve. Head right through

them. Their aim, between you and me, will be
so unsure that we might both escape. Go, and
God go with you!"

Can you ask me to remember the details of the
awful moment? The darkness, the flaming
torches, the hoarse cries of the bandits as they
rode in on us, my father's great courage—all these
combined to produce in me a state for which the
word "terror" seems altogether too homely. Perhaps I should not have left my father. Perhaps
I should have died with him. I did not know
what I was doing. Blindly as in a nightmare I
spurred my horse midway between two moving
torches. The horse, startled already, flew madly
as the wind. Cries, curses, shots seemed to sweep
about me, envelop me, but terror lent wings to
my horse, and the shots and shouts faded behind
me as phantoms might fade in a furious wind.
Last of all came a fearful fusillade of shots, then
a silence broken only by the harsh rustle of the
bracken under my horse, which, with the livid intelligence of fear, did not stop before we reached
Philippopolis in the dawn.

I was never to see my father again. Until noon
of the next day I sat anxiously in the only decent
inn of the ancient town, praying that some act
of Providence had come to his aid and that he
might at any moment appear; when, from a lo-
quacious person, who did not know my name, I
heard that the last of the Samsonoffs had that
morning been found in Karaloff Wood nailed to
a tree-trunk with eighteen bullet wounds in his
body.

I will spare you my reflections on the pass in

which I then found myself. No young girl was ever so completely alone as she who sat the day through in the parlour of the Bulgarian inn, trying to summon the energy with which to arrange for her long journey on the Orient Express to England.

Arrived in London, I at once set out to my uncle's house in Golgotha Road, Golders Green. I was a little surprised that he had not met me at the station, for I had warned him of my arrival by telegram; but, knowing he was a gentleman of particular though agreeable habits, it was with a sufficiently good heart that I rang the bell of his tall gloomy house, which stood at the end of a genteel street of exactly similar houses.

Allow me, if you please, to hurry over the relation of my further misfortunes. My uncle had died of a clot of blood on the heart a week before my arrival. His property he had, of course, left to me; and I could instantly take possession of his house in Golgotha Road. I was utterly alone.

That was four weeks ago. Though entirely without friends or acquaintance—for my uncle's lawyer, Mr. Tarbold, was a man who bore his own lack of easy conversation and human sympathy with a resigned fortitude worthy of more wretched sorrows—I passed the first two weeks pleasantly enough in arranging the house to my taste, in engaging a housekeeper and training her to my ways, and in wondering how I must proceed as regards the patenting and exploiting of the carnation, the formula for which I kept locked in a secret drawer of my toilet-table.

At the end of three weeks—one week ago—

my housekeeper gave me notice of her instant departure, saying that no consideration would persuade her to spend another night in the house. She was, it seemed, psychic, and the atmosphere of the house, which was certainly oppressive, weighed heavily on her mind. She had heard noises in the night, she affirmed, and also spoke indignantly of an unpleasant smell in the basement of the house, a musty smell which she for one made no bones of recognising as of a graveyard consistency; and if she did not know a graveyard smell, she asked, from one of decent origins, who did, for she had buried three husbands?

Of course I laughed at her tremors, for I am not naturally of a nervous temper; and when she insisted on leaving that very day I was not at all disturbed. Nor did I instantly make enquiries for another woman, for I could very well manage by myself; and the work of the house, I thought, must help to fill in the awful spaces made by the utter lack of companionship. As to any nervousness at being left entirely alone in a house, surrounded as it was by the amenities of Golders Green, I never gave a thought to it, for I had been inured to a reasonable solitude all my life. And, putting up a notice of "Apartments to Let" in one of the ground-floor windows, I set about the business of the house in something of a spirit of adventure natural, if I may say so, to one of my years.

That, as I have said, was one week ago; and the very next day but one after my housekeeper had left me was to see my hardly-won peace

shattered at one blow. I do not know if you gentlemen are aware of the mode of life that obtains
in Golders Green; but I must tell you that the
natives of that quarter do not discourage the activities of barrel-organs—a somewhat surprising
exercise of restraint to one who has been accustomed to the dolorous and beautiful songs of the
Balkan *cziganes*. It is true, however, that these
barrel-organs are played mostly by foreigners, and
I have been given to understand that foreigners
are one of the most sacred institutions of this
great country.

The very next morning after my housekeeper
had left me I was distracted from my work by
a particularly disagreeable combination of sounds,
which, I had no doubt, could come only from a
barrel-organ not of the first order and the un-
trained voice of its owner. A little amused, I
looked out of the window—and, with a heart how
still, leapt back into the room, for the face of the
organ-grinder was the face of the Michaelis!

I spent an hour of agony in wondering if he
had seen me, for how could I doubt but that he
had followed me to England in quest of the formula of the carnation? At last, however, I decided that he could not have seen me, and I was
in some degree calmed by the decreasing noise of
the barrel-organ as it inflicted itself on more distant streets. London, I told myself, was a very
large city; it was not possible that the Michaelis
could have the faintest idea in what part of it
I lodged; and it could only have been by the most
unfortunate combination of chances that he had
brought his wretched organ into Golgotha Road.

Nevertheless I took the precaution to withdraw the notice of Apartments to Let from the window, lest yet another unfortunate combination of chances should lead him or his minions to search for lodging in my house.

The next day passed quietly enough. I went out shopping with a veil over my face, for reasons you can well understand. And little did I dream that the approaching terror was to come from a quarter which would only be known to the Michaelis when he was dead.

That evening in my bedroom, in a curious moment of forgetfulness, I chanced to pull the bell-rope. I wanted some hot water, had for the moment forgotten that the silly woman had left me, and only remembered it with a smile when, far down in the basement, I heard the thin clatter of the bell. The bathroom was some way down the passage, and I had reached the door, empty jug in hand, when I was arrested by the sound of approaching steps! They were very faint, they seemed to be coming up from the basement, as though in answer to the bell! I pressed my hand to my forehead in a frantic attempt to collect my wits, and I have no hesitation in saying that for those few moments I was near insane. The accumulation of terrors in my recent life had, I thought, unhinged my mind; and I must that day have engaged a servant and forgotten it.

Meantime the steps ascended, slowly, steadily, exactly as an elderly servant might ascend in answer to the bell; and as they ascended I was driven, I cannot tell you how, somehow past fear. Maybe it was the blood of the Samsonoffs at last raging in me: I was not afraid: and, without locking the door, I withdrew to a far corner of the room, awaiting the moment when the steps must reach the door. I must not forget to add that the empty jug was still in my hand.

Steadily, but with a shuffling as of carpet-slippers, the steps came up the passage: slowly the door was opened, and a gaunt, grey-haired woman in musty black stood there, eyeing me with strange contempt. Fear returned, enveloped me, shook me, and I sobbed, I screamed. The woman did not move, did not speak, but stood there, gaunt and grey and dry, eyeing me with a strange contempt; and on her lined face there was such an undreamt-of expression of evil. Yet I recognised her.

I must tell you that my mother had often, in telling me of her brother, spoken of his confidential housekeeper. My mother was a plain-spoken woman, and I had gathered from her that the woman had exercised some vulgar art to enthrall my poor uncle and had dominated him, to his hurt, in all things. At the news of this woman's death just before my mother's tragic end, she had been unable to resist an expression of relief; and I, on having taken possession of the house a few weeks before, had examined with great interest, as girls will, the various photographs of her that stood about the rooms.

It was from these that I recognised the woman who stood in the doorway. But she was dead, surely she had died more than a year ago! Yet there she now stood, eyeing me with that strange contempt—with such contempt, indeed, that I, reacting from fear to anger, sternly demanded of her what she did there and what she wanted.

She was silent. That was perhaps the most awful moment of all—but no, no, there was worse to come! For, sobbing with terror, I hurled the empty jug at her vile face with a precision of aim which now astonishes me: but she did not waver so much as the fraction of an inch as the jug came straight at her—and, passing through her head, smashed into pieces against the wall of the passage outside. I must have swooned where I stood; for when I was again conscious of my surroundings she was gone, I was alone; but, far down in the house, I could hear the shuffling steps, retreating, descending, to the foul shades whence she had come.

Now I am one who cannot bear any imposition; and unable, despite the witness of my own eyes, to believe in the psychic character of the intruder, I ran out of the room and in hot pursuit down the stairs. The gaunt woman must have descended with a swiftness surprising in one of her years, for I could only see her shadow far below, on the last flight of stairs that would take her to the basement. Into that lower darkness, I must confess, I had not the courage to follow her; and still less so when, on peering down the pitch-dark stairs into the kitchen, I was assailed by that musty smell which my housekeeper had spoken of with such indignant conviction as of a graveyard consistency.

I locked the door of my room and slept, I need scarcely say, but ill that night. However, in the cheerful light of the following morning, I was inclined, as who would not, to pooh-pooh the incredible events of the previous night; and again pulled the bell-rope, just to see the event, if any. There was; and, unable to await the ascent of the shuffling steps, I crammed on a hat and ran down the stairs.

The woman was coming upstairs, steadily, inevitably. As she heard me descending she stopped and looked up, and I cannot describe the effect that the diabolical wickedness of her face had on me in the clear daylight. I stopped, was rooted there, could not move. To get to the front-door I must pass the foul thing, and that I could not summon the courage to do. And then she raised an arm, as though to show me something, and I saw the blade of a razor shining in her hand. You may well shudder, gentlemen!

When I came to it was to find myself lying at the foot of the stairs, whither I must have fallen, and the foul thing gone. Why she did not kill me, I do not know. God will pardon me for saying that maybe it had been better if she had, for what miseries are not still in store for me! Trembling and weak, I reached the door and impelled myself into the clear air of morning. Nor could the fact that I had forgotten my veil, and the consequent fear of the Michaelis, persuade me to reenter that house until I had regained some degree of calmness.

All day long I wandered about, knowing neither what to do nor where to go. I am not without some worldly sense, and I knew what little assistance the police could give me in such a dilemma, even had they believed me; while as for

the lawyer, Mr. Tarbold, how could I face a man
of so little sympathy in ordinary things with such
an extraordinary tale?

Towards ten o'clock that night, I determined to
return and risk another night in that house; I
was desperate with weariness and hunger; and
could not buy food nor lodging for the night, for
in my flight I had forgotten my purse; while I
argued to myself that if, after all, she had intended to murder me, she could without any difficulty have done so that morning when I lay unconscious on the stairs.

My bravery, however, did not help me to ascend
the stairs to my bedroom with any resolution. I
stole upstairs, myself verily like a phantom. But,
hearing no sound in the house, I plucked up the
courage to switch on the light on my bedroom
landing. My bedroom-door stood open, but I
could not remember whether or not I had left it
so that morning. It was probable, in my hasty
descent. I tiptoed to it and peered in—and I
take the liberty to wonder whether any man, was
he never such a lion-heart, had been less disturbed
than I at the sight which the light of the moon
revealed to my eyes.

The Michaelis lay full length on the floor, his
great fair beard darkened with his blood, which
came, I saw, from a great gash behind his ear.
Across him, with her back to me, sat straddled
the gaunt foul thing, as silent as the grave. Yet
even my terror could not overcome my curiosity
as to her actions, for she kept on lowering and
raising her left hand to and from the Michaelis's
beard, while with her right, in which shone the

bloody razor, she sawed the air from side to side.
I could not realise what that vile shape was doing
—I could, and could not admit the realisation.
For with her left hand she was plucking out one
by one the long hairs of the Michaelis's beard,
while with the razor in her right she was slicing
them to the floor!

I must have gasped, made some noise, for she
heard me; and, turning on me and brandishing
the dripping razor, she snarled like an animal
and leapt towards me. But I am young and quick,
and managed just in time to reach the street-door
and slam it against her enraged pursuit.

That was last night. Since then, gentlemen, I
have wandered about the streets of London, resting a little among the poor people in the Parks. I
have had no food, for what money I have is in
that house, together with the formula for the
green carnation; but nothing, not death by ex-
posure nor death by starvation, would induce me
to return to the house in Golders Green while it
is haunted by that foul presence. Is she a homicidal lunatic or a phantom from hell? I do not
know, I am too tired to care. I have told you
two gentlemen my story because you seem kind
and capable, and I can only pray that I have
not wearied you overmuch. But I do beg you to
believe that nothing is further from my mind
than to ask, and indeed nothing would induce me
to accept, anything from you but the generous
sympathy of your understanding and the advice
of your chivalrous intelligence. My tale is finished, gentlemen. And, alas, am not I?

IV

Mr. Trevor is somewhat confused in his relation of the course of events immediately subsequent to Miss Samsonoff's narrative. During its course he had time, he says, to study the young lady's beauty, which, though of a very superior order, was a little too innocent and insipid for his taste. His judgment, however, cannot be entirely fair, for such was the direction of the young lady's eyes that Mr. Trevor could judge her by her features only. As to the story itself, Mr. Trevor says that, while yielding to no one in his liking for a good story, he could not see his way to considering Miss Samsonoff's notable either for interest, entertainment, or that human note of stark realism which makes for conviction; and while, in the ordinary way, a murderer was to him like a magnet, he could not rouse himself to feel irresistibly attracted towards the ghoul of Golders Green. It was therefore with surprise not unmixed with pain that he heard Mr. Maturin saying:

"Ralph, we are in luck!"

"To what," Mr. Trevor could not entirely cleanse his voice from the impurity of sarcasm, "to what do you refer?" But it was not without some compunction that he heard the young lady sigh miserably to Beau Maturin:

"I am afraid I have wearied your friend. Forgive me."

"My friend," said Beau Maturin gently, "is an ass. In point of fact, Miss Samsonoff, far from wearying us, you have put us under a great obligation——"

"Ah, you are kind!" the young lady was moved to sob.

"On the contrary," Mr. Maturin warmly protested, "I am selfish. I gather you have not been reading the newspapers lately? Had you done so, you would have read of a murderer who has recently been loose in London and has so far evaded not only capture but even identification. So far as the public know through the newspapers this criminal has been responsible for only two or three murders; but this very night my friend and I have had private information to the effect that within the last few weeks twelve mutilated corpses have been found in various parts of London; to which we must now, no doubt, add a thirteenth, the remains of your late enemy, Mr. Michaelis. But where *your* information," said Mr. Maturin gallantly, "is especially valuable, is that the police do not dream that the criminal is of your sex. To my friend and me it is this original point that invests the pursuit——"

"Pursuit?" Mr. Trevor could not help starting.

"——with," said Mr. Maturin coldly, "an added charm. And now with your permission, Miss Samsonoff, we will not only return to you your formula, as to the financial worth of which I cannot entirely share your late parent's optimism, but also——"

"Also," Mr. Trevor said with restraint, "we will first of all call at Vine Street and borrow a few policemen."

"Oh, yes!" the young lady said eagerly. "We will be sure to need some policemen. Please get some policemen. They will listen to you."

"I do not find an audience so difficult to find as all that," said Mr. Maturin coldly. "The London police, Miss Samsonoff, are delightful, but rather on the dull side. They are much given to standing in the middle of crowded roads and dreaming, and in even your short stay in London you must have observed what a serious, nay intolerable, obstruction they are to the traffic. No, no, my friend and I will get this murderer ourselves. Come, Miss Samsonoff."

"But I dare not come with you!" cried the young lady. "I simply dare not approach that house again! May I not await your return here?"

"The attacks of ten murderers," said Mr. Maturin indignantly, "cannot disfigure your person more violently than being left alone in a nightclub will disfigure your reputation. Bulgarians may be violent, Miss Samsonoff. But lounge lizards are low dogs."

Mr. Trevor says that he was so plunged in thought that he did not arise from the table with his usual agility; and the first notice he had that Mr. Maturin had risen and was nearly at the door was on hearing him waive aside a pursuing waiter with the damnable words: "My friend will pay."

Without, the taxicab was still waiting. Its driver, says Mr. Trevor, was one of those stout men of little speech and impatient demeanour: on which at this moment was plainly written the fact that he had been disagreeably affected by waiting in the cold for nearly two hours; and on Mr. Maturin's sternly giving him a Golders Green direction he just looked at our two gentlemen and appeared to struggle with an impediment in his throat.

Golgotha Road was, as the young lady had described it, a genteel street of tall gloomy houses. Mr. Trevor says that he cannot remember when he liked the look of a street less. The taxicab had not penetrated far therein when Miss Samsonoff timidly begged Mr. Maturin to stop its further progress, pointing out that she could not bear to wait immediately opposite the house and would indeed have preferred to await her brave cavaliers in an altogether different part of London.   Mr. Maturin, however, soothed her fears; and, gay as a schoolboy, took the key of the house from her reluctant fingers and was jumping from the cab when Miss Samsonoff cried:

"But surely you have weapons!"

Mr. Trevor says that, while yielding to no one in deploring the use of weapons in daily life, in this particular instance the young lady's words struck him as full of a practical grasp of the situation.

"Of course," said Mr. Trevor nonchalantly, "we must have weapons. How stupid of us to have forgotten! I will go back to my flat and get some. I won't be gone a moment."

"That's right," Mr. Maturin agreed, "because you won't be gone at all. My dear Miss Samsonoff, my friend and I do not need weapons. We put our trust in God and St. George. Come along, Ralph. Miss Samsonoff, we will be back in a few moments."

"And wot do I do?" asked the taxi-driver.

"Nothing," cried Mr. Maturin gaily. "Nothing at all. Aren't you lucky!"

The house which the young lady had pointed out to them had an air of even gloomier gentility than the others, and Mr. Trevor says he cannot remember when he liked the look of a house less, particularly when the ancient brown door gave to Beau Maturin's hand before he had put the key into the lock. Mr. Trevor could not resist a natural exclamation of surprise. Mr. Maturin begged him not to shout. Mr. Trevor said that he was not shouting, and, without a thought for his own safety, was rushing headlong into the house to meet the terror single-handed when he found that his shoe-lace was untied.

He found Beau Maturin in what, he supposed, would be called a hall when it was not a pit of darkness. A stealthily lit match revealed that it was a hall, a narrow one, and it also revealed a closed door to the right, by Mr. Trevor's elbow, which he removed. The match went out.

"Quietly," said Mr. Maturin quite unnecessarily, for Mr. Trevor says he cannot remember when he felt less noisy. He heard the door to his right open, softly, softly.

"Is it you opening that door?" he asked, merely from curiosity.

"Ssh!" snapped Beau Maturin. "Hang on to my shoulder-blades."

Mr. Trevor thought it better to calm Beau Maturin's fears by acceding to his whim, and clung close behind him as they entered the room. The moon, which Mr. Trevor already had reason to dislike, was hanging at a moderate elevation over Golders Green as though on purpose to reveal the darkness of that room. Mr. Trevor's foot then struck a shape on the floor. The shape was soft and long. Mr. Trevor was surprised. Mr. Maturin whispered:

"Found anything?"

Mr. Trevor said briefly that his foot had.

"So's mine," said Beau Maturin. "What's yours like? Mine's rather soft to the touch."

"And mine," said Mr. Trevor.

"They're corpses, let's face it," sighed Mr. Maturin. "Making fifteen in all. With us, seventeen. Just give yours a kick, Ralph, to see if it's alive. I've kicked mine."

"I don't kick corpses," Mr. Trevor was muttering when he felt a hard round thing shoved into the small of his back.

"Ow!" said Mr. Trevor.

"Found anything?" said Mr. Maturin.

Mr. Trevor said briefly that there was something against his back.

"And mine," sighed Mr. Maturin. "What's yours like? Mine's rather hard on the back."

"So is mine," said Mr. Trevor.

"They're revolvers, let's face it," sighed Beau Maturin.

"They are," said a hard voice behind them. "So don't move."

"I've got some sense, thank you," snapped Beau Maturin.

"Sir," said the harsh voice, and it was a woman's voice, "I want none of your lip. I have you each covered with a revolver——"

"Waste," said Beau Maturin. "One revolver would have been quite enough. Besides, my friend and I were distinctly given to understand that you were partial to a razor. Or do you use that for shaving?"

"I use a razor," said the harsh voice, "only when I want to kill. But I have a use for you two."

The light was suddenly switched on, a light so venomous, says Mr. Trevor, that they had to blink furiously. And that must have been a very large room, for they could not see into its far corners. The light came from what must have been a very high-powered lamp directly above a table in the middle of the room; and it was concentrated by a shade in such a way as to fall, like a search-light, exactly on the two helpless gentlemen. Mr. Trevor says that Beau Maturin's handsome face looked white and ghastly, so the Lord knows what Mr. Trevor's must have looked like. Meanwhile their captor leapt from her station behind them, and they were privileged to see her for the first time. She was, says Mr. Trevor, exactly as Miss Samsonoff had described her, grey and gaunt and dry, and her expression was strangely contemptuous and evil as sin. And never for a moment did she change the direction of her revolvers, which was towards our gentlemen's hearts. Mr. Trevor says he cannot remember when he saw a woman look less afraid that a revolver might go off in her hand.

"Look down," she commanded.

"It's all right," said Beau Maturin peaceably; "we've already guessed what they are. Corpses.

Nice cold night for them, too. Keep for days in weather like this."

Mr. Trevor could not resist looking down to his feet. The corpses were of two youngish men in dress-clothes.

"They're cut badly," said Mr. Maturin.

"They're not cut at all," said the woman harshly. "I shot these two for a change."

"I meant their clothes," Mr. Maturin explained. "Death was too good for them with dress-clothes like that."

"Well, I can't stop here all night talking about clothes," snapped the woman. "Now then, to business. These bodies have to be buried in the back-garden. You will each take one. There are spades just behind you. I shall not have the slightest hesitation in killing you as I have killed these two, but it will be more convenient for me if you do as you are told. I may kill you later, and I may not. Now be quick!"

"Lord, what's that!" cried Mr. Trevor sharply. He had that moment realised a strange muffled, ticking noise which must, he thought, come either from somewhere in the room or from a room nearby. And, while he was never in his life less conscious of feeling fear, he could not help but be startled by that ticking noise, for he had heard it before, when timing a dynamite-bomb.

"That is why," the woman explained with what, Mr. Trevor supposed, was meant to be a smile, "you will be safer in the garden. Women are but weak creatures, and so I take the precaution of having a rather large size in dynamite-bombs so timed that I have but to press a button to send us all to blazes. It will not be comfortable for the police when, if ever, they catch me. But pick up those spades and get busy."

"Now don't be rude," begged Beau Maturin. "I can stand anything from plain women but discourtesy. Ralph, you take the bigger corpse, as you are smaller than I am, while I take this little fellow on my shoulder—which will probably be the nearest he will ever get to heaven, with clothes cut as badly as that."

"You can come back for the bodies when you've dug the graves," snapped the woman. "Take the spades and go along that passage. No tricks! I am just behind you."

There was a lot of rubbish in that garden. It had never been treated as a garden, it did not look like a garden, it looked even less like a garden than did *The Garden of My Grandmother*. High walls enclosed it. And over it that deplorable moon threw a sheet of dead daylight.

"Dig," said the woman with the revolvers, and they dug.

"Do you mind if we take our coats off?" asked Beau Maturin. Mr. Trevor says that he was being sarcastic.

"I don't mind what you take off," snapped the woman.

"Now don't say naughty things!" said Mr. Maturin. "Nothing is more revolting than the naughtiness of plain women."

"Dig," said the woman with the revolvers, and they dug.

They dug, says Mr. Trevor, for a long time, for a very long time. Not, however, that it was difficult digging once one had got into the swing of it, for that garden was mostly dug-up soil. Suddenly Beau Maturin said:

"Bet you a fiver I dig a grave for my fellow before you."

"Right!" said Mr. Trevor.

"Dig," said the woman with the revolvers, and they dug.

"*And,*" said the woman, "I don't allow any betting in this house. So call that bet off."

"What?" said Mr. Maturin.

"Dig," said the woman with the revolvers.

Mr. Maturin threw down his spade.

"Dig," said the woman with the revolvers.

Mr. Trevor dug.

Mr. Maturin said: "Dig yourself!"

"Dig," said the woman with the revolvers.

Mr. Trevor brandished his spade from a distance. He noticed for the first time that they had been digging in the light of the dawn and not of the moon.

"And who the deuce," said Mr. Maturin dangerously, "do you think you are, not to allow any betting? I have stood a lot from you, but I won't stand that."

"Dig," said the woman with the revolvers, but Mr. Maturin advanced upon the revolvers like a punitive expedition. Mr. Trevor brandished his spade.

"Another step, and I fire!" cried the woman harshly.

"Go ahead," said Mr. Maturin. "I'll teach you to stop me betting! And I hate your face."

"Oh, dear; oh, dear!" the woman suddenly

cried with a face of fear and, lowering her revolvers, fled into the house.

Mr. Trevor was so surprised that he could
scarcely speak. Mr. Maturin laughed so much
that he could not speak.

"What's there to laugh about?" Mr. Trevor
asked at last.

"It's funny. They've had us, let's face it.
Come on, let's follow her in."

"She may shoot," Mr. Trevor cautioned.

"Shoot my eye!" sighed Beau Maturin.

Once in the house, Mr. Trevor stopped spell-
bound. There were voices, there was laughter—
from the room of the two corpses!

"They're laughing at us!" said Mr. Trevor.

"Who wouldn't!" laughed Beau Maturin, and,
opening the door, said: "Good morning."

"You've said it," said the policeman. "Haw-
haw!"

"You'll have some breakfast?" asked the
woman with the revolvers.

"Please do!" said Miss Samsonoff.

"You *ought* to be hungry," said the taxi-driver
with the Homburg hat of green plush.

"Look here!" gasped Mr. Trevor. "What the
blazes——"

"Haw-haw!" laughed the policeman. " 'Ave a
bit of vealanam-pie?"

"Now, Ted, don't be rude to the gentlemen!"
said the woman with the revolvers.

"Quite right, mother," said Miss Samsonoff.
"We owe these gentlemen an explanation and an
apology——"

"And if they don't take it we *are* in the soup!"

miserably said the man in the Homburg hat of green plush.

"Now, you two, go and get cups and plates for the two gentlemen," said the woman with the revolvers to the two corpses in dress-clothes.

"Listen, please," Miss Samsonoff gravely addressed Mr. Maturin, "my name isn't Samsonoff at all but Kettlewell, and that's my mother and these are my four brothers——"

"How do you do?" said Mr. Maturin, absently drinking the policeman's coffee, but Mr. Trevor is glad that no one heard what he said.

"You see," said Miss Kettlewell, and she was shy and beautiful, "we are The Kettlewell Film Company, just us; but of course we haven't got a lot of money——"

"A 'lot' is good!" said the policeman.

"My brother there," and Miss Kettlewell pointed to the wretched man with the Homburg hat of green plush, "was the director of an American company in Los Angeles, but he got the sack lately and so we thought we would make some films on our own. You see, we are such a large family! And the recent murders gave us a really brilliant idea for a film called 'The Ghoul of Golders Green,' which, thanks to you two gentlemen, we have completed to-night. Oh, I do hope it will be a success, especially as you have been kind enough to help us in our predicament, for we hadn't any money to engage actors—and we did so need two gentlemen, just like you, who really looked the part, didn't we, mother?"

"But, my dear child," cried Beau Maturin, "I'm afraid your film can't have come out very well.

Trevor and I will look perfectly ghastly, as we neither of us had any make-up on."

"But it's that kind of film!" smiled Miss Kettlewell. "You see, you and your friend are supposed to be corpses who by some powerful psychic agency are digging your own graves—— Heavens, what's that!"

There, at the open door, stood an apparition with a dreadful face. He appeared, says Mr. Trevor, to have some difficulty in choosing among the words that his state of mind was suggesting to him.

"And me?" gasped the taxi-driver hoarsely. "Wot abaht me? 'Angingabahtallnight! 'Oo's going to pay me, that's wot I want to know? There's four quid and more on that clock——"

Mr. Maturin swept his empty coffee-cup round to indicate the family Kettlewell.

"My friends will pay," sighed Mr. Maturin.

XI: FAREWELL, THESE CHARMING PEOPLE

I

NOW, at last, the entertainment moves towards its end, the curtain is atremble for its fall, the affair called *May Fair* is on tiptoe to make a last bow and retire forever into those anxious shades where all that is not of the first excellence must come to the foul embrace of limbo. So let the curtain fall, that we may get back to the serious business of life. But, oh, it is easy enough to say that! The rub is, a curtain has to be contrived. Action is demanded; and all the world loves a climax. In fine, ladies and gentlemen, those inexorable twin sister, Finale and Farewell, have still to be served. And how shall that be done?

It happened that I was in Paris when I was thinking upon this matter with some urgency. How shall the farewell be contrived, thought I, how indeed? For, by the waters of the Thames, there never was such a trouble put upon mankind as this confounded business of leave-taking! Haven't we all, to be sure, been sometime harassed by the saying of farewell? by the fumbling of that pitiful, pitiless occasion? Indeed, find us the man or woman who can say good-bye with ease, and he or she shall instantly have a clear start to

our friendship. How often we have been distressed by the agonies of someone's incapable departure! And you may rifle all diplomacy for
ways and means to help some people take their
leave, and still their glassy, fevered eyes will
search your face as though for the ultimate word,
still their aggressive nervousness will not permit
you to put them and yourself out of their agony.
While as for those poor wretches whom it is our
dread delight to "see off" at railway stations,
what confusion of mind is theirs, and ours! He
is at the window of his carriage, smiling: we on
the platform, smiling: others are nearby, smiling:
hands are shaken, good-byes are said . . . and
does the train go? It does not. Wouldn't we
then, if we but dared, implore the departing
wretch to withdraw his tormented head from the
window, sit back in his seat, hide himself behind
a paper and send us all to the deuce? We would,
but we don't, and he can't, so fumble, fumble,
fumble, until at last the train takes him—or her,
why not?—from us who had once thought we
were sorry he was going. Oh, no, this business of
saying farewell is not like saying "Jack Robin-
son": it needs, without a doubt, a touch of in-
humanity, which, if it does not make the whole
world kin, can at least help to make a good part
of it comfortable, as the humane gentleman now
honoured as Lord Balfour found when he was
Secretary of State for Ireland.

It was, then, with such thoughts as these that
my mind was vexed during my stay in Paris, much
to the disorder of my pleasures, when whom
should I meet but my friend Dwight-Rankin!

Gratified, I was yet surprised almost beyond endurance. I had been at school with the man, but later we had lost sight of one another, and still later I had heard of his death on Gallipoli. I had been sorry.

Dwight-Rankin was a blood, and I have an intellectual leaning towards bloods. They may have only the most moderate aspirations towards a state of grace, theirs may be only the most superficial grasp of the culture of the ages, but theirs not to reason why, theirs but to do nothing and die. They may not Achieve, they may have nothing to Give to the world, but nevertheless they serve several useful purposes and are decidedly a good market for British-made and Dominion-made goods, such as golf-links, foxes, spats, plover's eggs, chorus girls, kippers, the Conservative party, night-clubs, bookmakers, whisky, the Army, etc. They are also decorative and are frequently used at balls and at our Embassies abroad.

Dwight-Rankin remarked with gratification upon my pleasure at the fact that he was still alive and invited me to take a glass of wine with him at the Ritz, which we were at that moment passing. Nothing could have been more agreeable to me, in my troubled state of mind. We then indulged in conversation. It had rained the day before, and we spoke of the rain. There was a rumour that it had been snowing in England, and we spoke of the snow. Dwight-Rankin had just returned from Monte Carlo, where he had lost money, and I had just returned from Rome, where I had lost my luggage. We confounded Monte

Carlo and Rome.   Then Dwight-Rankin said that
the report of his death on Gallipoli was a gross
exaggeration and that one should not believe all
one hears.   His younger brother, Dwight-Rankin
said, had believed the report with an agility surprising in one who was a confirmed sceptic in all
religious matters, had stepped into the property
and had gone bankrupt before Dwight-Rankin
could say "knife."   Dwight-Rankin said he was
now a broken man.   I extended him my sympathy, for which he thanked me.

"Talking of death," he added, "that was a
nasty end for Mrs. Amp, wasn't it?"

"Mrs. Amp!" I said.   "Mrs. Amp?   Who was
Mrs. Amp?"

Dwight-Rankin said: "Rheumatism and Roose-
velt, you've never heard of Mrs. Amp!   Nor of
the death?   Nor of the Lady Surplice?"

"Lady Surplice?" I said.   "Oh, yes, I've heard
of the Countess of Surplice!   And how is she?"

"She can't be at all well," said Dwight-Rankin.
"She's dead.   Tummy trouble, they *said*.   By the
way, one doesn't say 'the Countess of' Surplice.
One says 'Lady Surplice.'   Do you mind?"

"Not in the least," I said.

"Then don't say it or write it, will you?" begged
Dwight-Rankin.   "All you writers are very vague
about your titles.   No, not vague—you are mal-
inspired.   It puts people against you, I assure
you.   I often had a mind to tell Miss Marie
Corelli about that, but I never had a chance."

I said: "You see, Dwight-Rankin, I never hear
any of these things, as I am not in society."

"That's all right," said Dwight-Rankin. "Hang on to me."

"Waiter!" I said. "Two Martinis, please."

"Dry," said Dwight-Rankin. "Dry, waiter. And with a dash."

It was luncheon time, and the foyer was crowded with people waiting for each other whilst they passed the time of day with someone else. There were many women with eager eyes and low heels. Dwight-Rankin said they were American. There were many women with good complexions and large feet. Dwight-Rankin said they were English. There was a young man who looked like a pretty girl, except that his hair was long. Dwight-Rankin said he was known as the Venus de Marlow and that his friends thought him too marvellous. Pacing up and down was a French gentleman with drooping ginger moustachios, a gardenia and a dog. Dwight-Rankin said that he wore stays and that the dog was called "Héloïse and Abélard," and when I asked him how one dog came to be called "Héloïse and Abélard" Dwight-Rankin said severely that even a dog must be called something.

"The man who owns him, her, it or them," said Dwight-Rankin, "is the Marquis des Beaux-Aces. He married a very rich American, but she turned out to be a girl of strong character and instead of letting him spend her money she spent all his and then divorced him for being incompetent. He has never been the same man since, but he manages to make an honest living by selling fancy needlework to Argentine polo-players. But you

will hear more of him when I tell you of the
strange affair of Mrs. Amp and Lady Surplice—
of the late Mrs. Amp," said Dwight-Rankin
gloomily, "and the late Lady Surplice. A great
pity. By the way, are you lunching with anyone?"

I said: "No, but——"

"That's all right," said Dwight-Rankin; "I
will lunch with you. I am supposed to be lunching with some people, but I am so short-sighted
that I can't see them. If you should remark two
beautiful women looking at me with more than
usual interest, just don't take any notice. This
short-sightedness of mine is developing into a
nuisance. The other day I was having a clean-up
at the club and when I came to wipe my face I
found it was quite dry for the simple reason that
I had been washing the face of the man next to
me."

I said: "In the meanwhile, shall we——"

"This is on me," said Dwight-Rankin. "Waiter,
two Martinis, please."

"Dry," I said.

"That's all right," said Dwight-Rankin. "They
always wipe them for me first."

II

The death of Mrs. Amp, said Dwight-Rankin,
was the sensation of Paris in the spring of the
year 1924. Who Mr. Amp was, it appeared, no
one knew for certain. But it was said that he
had fallen in love with a photograph of an English gentlewoman in Arab costume, had plunged

into the desert to commune with his passion and
had been kidnapped by a sheikess in plus-fours
who had a fancy for bald Americans with bulging
eyes. However. . . .

Mrs. Amp, said Dwight-Rankin, died suddenly
and terribly; and her mangled remains were the
subject of discussion in society for many a day.
It was a Friday evening, and all Paris was dressing itself to be present at a dinner-party that
Mrs. Amp was to give that evening at the Ritz
Hotel. "Just here, where we are sitting now,"
said Dwight-Rankin, turning a glassy eye about
the restaurant and accepting an invitation hurled
at him by the Duchess of Putney to dine next
Thursday to meet the Shah of Pongistan on the
occasion of his having lost his job.

On that Friday evening, said Dwight-Rankin,
there was only one person of note in Paris who
was not dressing to be present at Mrs. Amp's
dinner-party. That, said Dwight-Rankin, was
Lady Surplice. Mrs. Amp and Lady Surplice
did not speak. That is to say, said Dwight-Rankin, they spoke to everyone about each other;
but when they met, had you dropped a pin between them it would have made a noise like a
bomb, and had you lit a match there would have
been a cascade of water from the melting ice.

Lady Surplice, said Dwight-Rankin, had been
the greatest hostess in Europe for twenty years.
London dined with her when she was in London,
Paris dined with her when she was in Paris, Mus-
solini met her at the station when she went to
Rome, New York hailed her as the Duchess of
Mayfair, while Palm Beach was her rouge-pot

and over Ascot she cast her lorgnette.   Naturally
all this was very encouraging for Lady Surplice,
and she bitterly resented any interference with
her habits.   However. . . .

Lord Surplice—only technically known, said
Dwight-Rankin severely, as "the Earl of"—did
not assist at his wife's entertainments.   He was
understood to be taking the waters for diabetes
at a hydropathic establishment near Woodhall
Spa.   Or maybe, said Dwight-Rankin, it was
liver trouble and Tunbridge Wells, but one can't
know everything.

Then one day, when Lady Surplice was at the
height of her success, Mrs. Amp fell on Europe.
Nay, said Dwight-Rankin, Mrs. Amp obliterated
Europe.   Without Mr. Amp, but with Mr. Amp's
millions.   Mrs. Amp, said Dwight-Rankin, was
a large woman: a very large woman: and hearty.
Her face was not that of Aphrodite: her figure
not that of Mrs. Vernon Castle: but she had, said
Dwight-Rankin, a certain Charm.   Her descent
on Europe was catastrophic.   She enveloped
Europe.   And Europe loved it.   She laid one hand
on London and one on Paris, threw Venice over
one shoulder and hung Deauville about her neck,
and people just fell on to her lap.   And what a
lap, said Dwight-Rankin.   However. . . .

For days and days people went about saying:
"I say, what's all this about a Mrs. Amp?   Who
is Mrs. Amp?   What?"   Then for days and days
people went about saying: "Have you met Mrs.
Amp?   The devil, what a woman!   These Americans!   What?"   Then for days and days people
went about saying: "Are you dining with Mrs.

Amp to-night? Am I? Good Lord, no! Why
should one dine with Mrs. Amp? What?" Then
for ever and ever people went about saying: "I'm
sorry, but I must be going now. I am dining with
Mrs. Amp to-night. What? Oh, you are too!
Good, we'll meet over dinner."

Lady Surplice, however, stood firm. She
wouldn't, said Dwight-Rankin, accept Mrs. Amp.
"Mrs. Amp," said Lady Surplice, "is a Low
woman. One does not know Mrs. Amp." But
thousands did, said Dwight-Rankin. So Lady
Surplice tore between London and Paris, giving
luncheons, dinners, dances and receptions right
and left in the hope that no one would have time
to go to any of Mrs. Amp's parties. But people
always had time, said Dwight-Rankin, to go to
Mrs. Amp's parties. Mrs. Amp's parties were
like that. Unavoidable, inevitable, eternal. And,
said Dwight-Rankin, uncommonly amusing. One
met all one's friends at them, and the champagne
was always dry.

Mrs. Amp was American, and Lady Surplice
was born in Notting Hill of Nonconformist parents. And so, said Dwight-Rankin, they carried
the same weights in the blue-blood stakes. But
Mrs. Amp was the larger woman, the larger personality. Lady Surplice was very tall, very thin,
dark, brittle, brilliant. Mrs. Amp enveloped, and
could touch the ceiling of a sleeping-car with her
hips when she lay on her side. Lady Surplice was
relentless in her generosity and indomitable in
her indiscretion. Mrs. Amp was as mean with
money as a temperance hotel with matches; but
even so she could stay the stars in their courses,

anyhow for at least five courses and then make
them sing and dance to her guests on top of it.
Lady Surplice was very tall. But Mrs. Amp stood
six-feet-two in her tiara. Lady Surplice undoubtedly put up a gallant fight. But Mrs. Amp undoubtedly won. Lady Surplice said: "That low,
beastly woman!" Mrs. Amp said: "Muriel Surplice is proud of having discovered Europe.
I am amused at having discovered Muriel Surplice."

It gradually dawned on people, said Dwight-
Rankin, that this between Mrs. Amp and Lady
Surplice was not an affair which could be settled
by a duel at Mah Jongg, that this was a case of
war to the death. Mrs. Amp died first.

On that Friday evening, Mrs. Amp was dressing
for dinner in her house near the Champs Élysées.
She sat at her toilet-table, and whilst her maid
did this and that to her hair, which, said Dwight-
Rankin, aspired doggedly rather than beautifully
to the mode, Mrs. Amp passed the time by looking out of the windows upon the noble trees of
the Champs Élysées; and presently drew her
maid's attention to the fact that a circus was at
that moment taking its station beneath them.
"I want to tell you," said Mrs. Amp to her maid,
"that I am just crazy about circuses. Don't forget to remind me to engage one the next time I
pull a party."

Those, her maid later told Dwight-Rankin,
were almost the last words Mrs. Amp spoke in
this world. For even as she uttered them an uproar became audible from without: the air was
filled with screams, yells and curses: while the

roars of savage beasts struck terror into the most
stable heart and convinced the maid, she told
Dwight-Rankin, that the end of the world was
at hand.

With a cry to Mrs. Amp, who sat staring out
of the window as though transfixed, the maid fled;
for the uproar from the circus was caused by
nothing less than the escape of the lions from
their cages; and these, their maddened nostrils
attracted by Heaven knows what odour, were
rushing furiously on Mrs. Amp's house, vainly
pursued by their keepers. For the keepers, said
Dwight-Rankin, appeared to be quite helpless:
their whips lashed the air with inconceivable energy, but there seemed to be a grave lack of *en-
tente* between their commands and the lions'
movements; which was later only half-explained
by the fact that they were Italian keepers in
charge of French lions.

The lions, with a bound, with a series of bounds,
passed the *concierge's* lodge, wherein the *concierge*
was clinging to an excrescence from the ceiling;
and when the mangled corpse of poor Mrs. Amp
was later found, it was recognisable, said Dwight-
Rankin, only by the perfume which the poor lady
was used to affect and which gave proof of its
quality by rising superior even to the lively odour
of the lions. However. . . .

In such manner, said Dwight-Rankin, did Mrs.
Amp give up the spirit. Nor was the sensation
caused by her nasty death at all soothed by the
evidence of her trembling *concierge,* who, before
the Conference of Ambassadors that sat to enquire on the great hostess's death, gave testimony

to the effect that as the lions rushed into her bedroom Mrs. Amp was distinctly heard to cry: "This is the doing of Muriel Surplice! I will be revenged, if I roast in hell-fire for it!"

The *concierge*, of course, said Dwight-Rankin, gave his evidence in French; and when the interpreters had translated it for the benefit of the Conference of Ambassadors, those distinguished gentlemen were not a little disturbed by the ominous, if extravagant, burden of Mrs. Amp's dying words. And, said Dwight-Rankin, rightly.

III

It was when we came to the second and last part of the affair of Mrs. Amp and Lady Surplice, which took place in London nearly a year later, that he himself, said Dwight-Rankin, entered upon the scene. He was, in point of fact, quite definitely responsible for the awful end to my Lady Surplice's last dinner-party, a circumstance which would prey on his mind to his dying day. For, said Dwight-Rankin, had he not at the last moment been compelled, by some force outside himself, to take a bird out for a spot of dinner, and therefore to cancel his engagement to dine with Lady Surplice, nothing untoward could possibly have happened to that poor lady.

He had, however, been able to piece together every detail of the terrible events of that dinner-party with the help of the relations of those of his friends who were present: the most reliable among these being Shelmerdene (that lovely lady), Guy de Travest, most upright of men, and

Percy Wentworth, 1st Marquess of Marketharborough, the Lord Chancellor of England, who was, said Dwight-Rankin, a very hearty man and a devil for accuracy whether on the Woolsack or the roundabouts.

It was Christmas Eve, and a dirty night. A violent wind distracted the town, hurling the rain with idiot fury against the windows of swift limousines and, no doubt, said Dwight-Rankin, greatly inconveniencing those thoughtless persons who had gone abroad without their limousines. But since Lady Surplice's dinner was in honour of royalty, in the person of Son Altesse le Prince de Finaleauseltz, of the Royal house of Bonbon de Jambon-Parme, her guests, with that polite servility which distinguishes the freedom-loving peoples of England and America, were within the house in St. James's Square by a quarter-to-nine o'clock.

Dinner was not yet announced: the conversation, easy and elegant, embraced the topics of the day: while the more youthful wandered, as though aimlessly, towards the far corners of the spacious drawing-room, where stood the busts of notable men by Epstein and Mestrovic. Now Lady Surplice never would have cocktails served in her house since a friend of hers, an honourary *attaché* at the Bulgarian Legation, had succumbed to a ptomaine poisoning gotten from swallowing a cherry in a Manhattan cocktail. But my lady's butlers were wont, such is the ingenuity of the lower sort, to secrete cocktails behind the busts of notable men by Epstein and Mestrovic, thus killing two birds with one stone; for while, on

the one hand, they satisfied the reasonable thirst
of the company, they also, on the other hand,
gave Lady Surplice much real pleasure in seeing
how her friends were enamoured of the most advanced art of the day. Lady Surplice herself
loved the most advanced art of the day. And the
most advanced art of the day loved Lady Surplice.
Playwrights, for instance, doted on her. One had
put her into a play as a courtesan for money
(1205 performances), one as a courtesan by
temperament (2700 performances), another as a
courtesan by environment (still running), and
lastly another as a courtesan to pass the time.
This last, however, was never produced, as the
Lord Chamberlain had banned it on the ground
that it was too cynical. However. . . .

Imagine, said Dwight-Rankin, with what con-
sternation Lady Surplice suddenly discovered that
the company was thirteen in number! She was
livid. She said: "It is the fault of that Dwight-
Rankin man. I had forgotten that he had put
me off at the last moment. That low, detestable
man! How *rude* people with two names can be!
But what shall we do? We cannot dine thirteen,
and on Christmas Eve! Your Highness, what
would you advise? I am quite unable, my dear
Highness, to sit down thirteen at meat. I detest
meat, but you know what I mean. It would quite
destroy my luck."

"His Highness," said Guy Godolphin Greville
Hawke, 21st Viscount de Travest, "might very
possibly prefer to have his luck completely destroyed; for the present luck of Royalty in Europe
is, if I may say so, sickening."

Lord Marketharborough had been for some time examining the busts of notable men by Mestrovic and Epstein, and had therefore not heard what had gone before; but that did not deter him from asking one of those pertinent questions which came naturally to his fearless mind. "Since," said the Lord Chancellor, "we are thirteen, are we a woman too many or a man? Let us first get that quite clear."

"There is always a woman too many," snapped Lady Surplice, whereupon Dame Warp strode forward and said bitterly between her teeth: "I see I am not wanted. Let it never be said that a decent woman—I said a *decent* woman—ever stood in the way of her friends' enjoyment. I will go." She was, however, soothed by Monsieur des Beaux-Aces, whilst the other gentlemen very properly laughed the superstition to scorn. In particular Mr. Warp, who was eminent in private life for his researches into the defunct branch of political thought once known as Liberalism, but was better known in public as the husband of Dame Warp, distinguished himself by the elegant scholarship of his scepticism.

Nor, said Dwight-Rankin, were the ladies—to wit, Shelmerdene, the Lady Fay Paradise, Lady Pynte, Miss Pamela Star and the Lady Amelia Peep, who was a young lady of the highest fashion with her hair parted at the side, a talent for writing poetry, and a governing-classes voice—nor were they behindhand with their ridicule of so childish a fancy as Lady Surplice's, that they could be susceptible of the least harm through sitting thirteen at table.

"Dinner," said the *doyen* of the butlers from the door, "is served, my lady."

"Talbot!" cried Lady Surplice. "How dared you not warn me that we were thirteen for dinner? Why do you not answer me? Is this a time for silence?"

"Decidedly," said the Lord Chancellor. "For I am hungry."

"My lady," said the wretched Talbot, "I am sorry. It quite escaped my notice. I will send in my resignation in the morning."

Says my lady with a high look: "Talbot, you will expiate your sin now. You will at once leave the house. You will walk round St. James's Square. And you will invite the first person you meet in to dine with me. Go."

The conversation after the butler had gone became, said Dwight-Rankin, rather strained; and only the polished genius of Lady Surplice could have sustained it at anything approaching a well-informed level, as when, turning to the Lady Amelia Peep, she said: "And what, my child, is your father doing to-night? I had asked him to dine with me, but he said he was engaged. I hope it is not serious."

"Wearing," said the Lady Amelia, "rather than serious. He is in S. W. 1 district, in the queue outside Buck House, waiting to be made a Duke in the New Year's Honours. He is so old-fashioned in his tastes! He will be wanting to learn dancing soon."

"Dukes," said Lady Surplice, "are not a fit subject for conversation. One should avoid being a Duke. They are low. Look, for instance,

how they took up with that Amp woman! Look
how that handsome but ill-mannered Duke of
Mall made a fuss of that dreadful Mrs. Omroy
Pont! And look at the Duke of Dear! One
cannot know that man. He has actually been
divorced time over again. England is getting
simply flooded with ex-Duchesses of Dear. And
while the Duke indulges his almost violent partiality for middle-class indiscretions, his only
son has invented a rod with which he can catch
smoked salmon. Is that patrician, is it even
gentlemanly? Answer me, your Highness. Is
this a time for silence? Then look at the Duchess
of Sandal and Sand! She is in Paris now, and
I hear she has lovers right and left and sits up
every night at the *Jardin de Ma Sœur* staring at
people through an emerald monocle and drinking
pink champagne through a straw. Is that just,
is it reasonable, is it even decent? Monseigneur,
what do you think? Is this a time for silence?"

"Yes, please!" pleaded Fay Paradise. "For
just look at what's happening!"

But it was Shelmerdene, said Dwight-Rankin,
who had first seen the great doors opening. And
Shelmerdene was very favourably impressed.

"Captain Charity," announced Talbot.

Lady Surplice, said Dwight-Rankin, was also
very favourably impressed. She cried: "My dear
Captain Charity, how kind of you to come to a
perfectly strange house! But you are so good-
looking that I feel I ought to have known you
all my life."

Now he who was called Captain Charity did not
appear to be of those who suffer from nervousness.

His lean presence, indeed, radiated a certain authority. And he smiled at Lady Surplice in a cold but charming way. But one can't do better, said Dwight-Rankin, than take Shelmerdene's swift first impression of the man. Shelmerdene said that he was a tall, lean, young man, dark and beautiful; his air was military, but with a pleasing suggestion of culture; and as he came towards the company he appeared to look at nobody but Guy de Travest, and always he smiled, Shelmerdene had told Dwight-Rankin, in a cold but charming way.

"Haven't we," doubtfully said de Travest to the teeth of that faint smile, "met before somewhere?"

One must imagine those two, said Dwight-Rankin, as making as brave-looking a pair of men as one could wish to see: the stranger, dark and beautiful, and Guy de Travest, quiet and yellow-fair: the lean dark dandy with the mocking mouth and the fair thunder-god of dandies with the frozen eyes.

"I think not," said Captain Charity, and he said: "But you are very like Michael."

"Michael?" quoth my lord. "And who, pray, is your Michael?"

"The archangel," said Captain Charity, and that was that, for Lady Surplice, who was fairly taken with the dark beauty of the stranger, could no longer brook these masculine asides. She said: "My dear Captain Charity, you must be introduced. It is quite usual. I have already presented you to His Highness. He is charming. Here are Dame Warp and Lady Pynte, who buys her shoes at Fortnum and Mason's and rides to hounds four days in the week all through the summer just to set a good example. While this is Miss Pamela Star, who was left many millions by an Armenian. Armenians are rather difficult, my dear Captain Charity, but she is charming. And this is Shelmerdene, who has no surname because she has no surname, but who is becoming the heroine of all the ladies in all the suburbs because a misguided young man once put her into a book. Ah, and Fay! My dear Captain Charity, this is Lady Fay Paradise, the most beautiful woman in England. She never eats with her meals and never uses the same lover twice. Do you, darling? Whereas here is Lady Amelia Peep, who is as yet unmarried but she writes poetry about birds and her father wants to be made a Duke. You will like her. She is appointed with every modern convenience. And here—Percy, where are you? Ah, there he is, always admiring works of art! Look at the back of his head—the strength, the charm, the moral poise of it! Percy, come here at once! This, my dear Captain Charity, is Lord Marketharborough, who is a Lord Chancellor, you know. Aren't you, Percy? But why do you not answer me? Is this a time for silence?"

"Dinner," said the man Talbot, "is served, my lady."

"Good!" said Lord Marketharborough.

Now the high position that Lady Surplice had won for herself in the hierarchy of hostesses was due to nothing so much as to the fact that she would not ever tolerate any but general conver-

sation about her table. Whereas, said Dwight-
Rankin, at every other dinner in London one
must be continually blathering in whispers to one's
right or left to women who have nothing to say
and don't know how to say it, so that there never
can be any conversational give-and-take about
the table. But Lady Surplice most properly insisted on conversational give-and-take at her
parties. She gave, you took. She gave, said
Dwight-Rankin, magnificently.

IV

Lady Surplice said: "I detest self-conscious
people. No one was ever self-conscious until the
middle classes were invented. Oscar Wilde invented the middle classes so that he could make
fun of them, as he would not have dreamt of making fun of his betters, like that Somerset
Maugham man. Unfortunately Oscar died without making a will, and as no one knew what to
do with his invention we let them, with usual
English slackness, grow until they have swamped
the whole country."

"The other day," said the Lady Amelia Peep,
"I went into my father's study to tell him that
I was engaged to be married——"

"But, Amelia, you are not!" cried Lady Pynte.

"True," said the Lady Amelia. "But to say
one is engaged when one is not and to be married
without being engaged are the only parlour games
open to a *jeune fille* of any real modesty. 'Father,' I said, 'I am engaged to be married. What
do you know about that?' He was busy writing

a letter, but absent-mindedly he stretched a hand out towards a volume of Debrett, saying: 'What initials, child?' I thought that so sweet."

"Personally," said Lady Pynte, "I adore snobs. They are at least faithful to their principles."

"Faithful!" cried my Lady Surplice. "Did you say *faithful*, Cornelia? Is there such a thing as fidelity?"

"Dans un sauvage," bitterly said M. des Beaux-Aces. He would, said Dwight-Rankin.

"But what is fidelity?" cried my lady. "Your Highness, why do you not amuse us? I ask, what is fidelity? Is this a time for silence?"

" 'Fidelity' is the title of a new novel," said a young gentleman who had not spoken before and who was requested not to speak again.

"Fidelity," bitterly said Dame Warp, "is the only game of which a decent woman—I said a *decent* woman—never tires. I except, of course, auction bridge."

"Fidelity would be such fun," sighed Fay Paradise, "if only one could ever decide whom to be faithful to."

"Amelia," cried Lady Surplice. "I hear you were at Martha Putney's ball last night. What was it like?"

"Lousy, dear," sighed the Lady Amelia.

"Fidelity," said Lord Marketharborough, "is a beautiful talent, if I may say so. Unfortunately, however, I am not a man of talent. I am a genius."

"I," complained the Lady Amelia Peep, "know nothing of fidelity or infidelity, as I have so far been a martyr to virginity."

"Fidelity," said Captain Charity, "is an art. But, surely, *ars est celare artem!*"

"Fidelity is fiddlesticks," snapped M. des Beaux-Aces.

"I beg your pardon!" cried Lady Pynte. "My good man, I myself know several women who have gone through incredible ordeals in the Divorce Courts and the Press owing to their fidelity to their lovers. Heavens, allow us to retain *some* virtue!"

"Fidelity," said the young gentleman who had spoken only once before, "is an affectation prevalent among musical-comedy actresses and generally directed towards wealthy Jews."

"Talking of Jews," said M. des Beaux-Aces, "I hear that all the best Jews are becoming Roman Catholics."

"And what, sir, has that to do with the point?" thundered the Lord Chancellor.

"Nothing, thank God!" said M. des Beaux-Aces. "I detest points."

"Amelia," bitterly said Dame Warp, "I hear you were at Martha Putney's ball last night. What was it like?"

"Divine, dear," sighed the Lady Amelia.

Thus, said Dwight-Rankin, the dinner proceeded with a degree of animation, of gaiety, that was unusual even about Lady Surplice's memorable table. The *morale* of the diners was excellent: their address polite, their appetites suave, their wit easy and swift: their *ton*, in fine, irreproachable. While even His Highness the Prince de Finaleauseltz was so agreeably affected by the swift interchange of repartee and back-chat that,

Dwight-Rankin assured me, he contributed on two separate occasions to the entertainment. However. . . .

All was, therefore, going beautifully when the Lady Fay Paradise remarked, with amusement not untinged with repulsion, that someone had spilled the salt.

"La!" cried Lady Pynte.

"Who has spilled the salt?" cried Lady Surplice.

"The Lord Chancellor has spilled the salt," said Mr. Warp.

"Hell!" said the Lord Chancellor.

"Over your shoulder, over your shoulder!" cried Lady Pynte.

"Oh, Percy!" cried my lady. "To spill the salt is *most* unlucky!"

"Oh, pouf!" said the Lady Amelia.

"Oh, dear!" said Pamela Star.

"I'm really very sorry," said the Lord Chancellor.

"*Need* you have spilled the salt?" bitterly said Dame Warp.

"Really, why all this fuss?" sighed Fay Paradise.

"Fuss indeed!" cried Lady Surplice.

"I'm really very sorry," said the Lord Chancellor.

"My father," said His Highness, "lost his crown on the day he spilled some salt."

"Then to spill salt must be lucky," remarked de Travest, "for your grandfather, sir, lost his head without having the chance to spill any salt."

"Well, all I can say is," sighed my lady, "that I thank Heaven we are not dining thirteen."

"I'm really very sorry," said the Lord Chancellor.

It was exactly at that moment, said Dwight-Rankin, that someone at the table let out a yell. Who it was, no one can tell to this day. But someone, even as Lord Marketharborough spoke, sobbed:

"But we are! We are thirteen!"

You can't, said Dwight-Rankin, describe in so many words the effect of that sob of terror. It must have been as though someone had turned a tap somewhere and let out the blood from all their faces. One might imagine them, said Dwight-Rankin, as all eyes, blanched eyes, staring frantically at the empty chair on which had been but a moment before the person of him who called himself Captain Charity.

"But this is too much!" sobbed Lady Pynte.

Lord Marketharborough, however, appeared to be quite unmoved. He said: "When is a chap not a chap? When he falls under the table before even the port has been round."

But Captain Charity wasn't, said Dwight-Rankin, under the table. He wasn't, in fact, anywhere to be seen in the large room. They looked everywhere, while the bewildered silence was broken only by the breathing of Dame Warp, who had notable adenoids.

"Talbot!" cried Lady Surplice.

"I'm afraid poor Talbot won't be much use on *this* occasion," murmured Shelmerdene.

"But the man can't have disappeared!" cried

my lady. "Talbot, did you see Captain Charity leave the room? Answer me at once, Talbot. Is this a time for silence?"

It needed, said Dwight-Rankin, only the base terror on the man Talbot's rugged face to seal the terror of the company.

"For God's sake, man, speak up!" snapped the young gentleman who had spoken only twice before.

"I saw him go!" whispered the man Talbot. "Saw 'im, I did, with these eyes! One second he was on that chair, and the next—gorn, phut! Begging your pardon, my lady——"

And then, said Dwight-Rankin, came perhaps the worst blow of all. It was only then that Shelmerdene grew really, sharply, terrified. For on the immovability, the valiancy, of my lord Viscount de Travest all who were privileged to know him were wont to rely, as on a very column of courage. Whereas now, what could they think? For, as the man Talbot made an end to his craven whispering, Guy de Travest was seen to be rising in his chair, his eyes as though frozen to some point of the room, his forehead, glistening with those clean drops of sweat that add to the charm of officers of the Household Cavalry and distinguish them from those genteel persons who "perspire." However. . . .

"The deuce!" whispered de Travest. "Oh, the deuce! Look!"

"Oh!" screamed the Lady Amelia Peep, and, screaming, fainted.

He didn't, said Dwight-Rankin, know much about furniture: but along the wall towards the doors was a long sort of antique whatdoyoucallem—anyhow, there was an antique arrangement there, and on it, at intervals of a foot or so apart, stood a noble line of a dozen candles in tall candlesticks.

"Guy!" cried Fay Paradise. "Guy, what is it?"

De Travest, now standing high above the company, was staring at the line of twelve candles on the whatdoyoucallem. He murmured: "I don't know."

"Percy," shrilled Lady Surplice, "what do you think?"

"There's some trickery here!" sternly said the Lord Chancellor, who had followed the direction of de Travest's eyes. "Tell Talbot to keep that door closed."

"I daren't, my lady!" the man Talbot trembled.

Someone laughed.

"Who laughed?" cried Shelmerdene.

De Travest snapped: "Why are you going, man? What's your hurry?"

"But who is he talking to?" sobbed Lady Pynte.

"I don't believe in ghosts," said Dame Warp bitterly.

"You there, who are you?" snapped de Travest.

"Gently, Guy, gently!" said Mr. Warp. "Let us not provoke him. Let us not provoke anyone."

"Oh!" screamed Lady Surplice, and then it was that everyone realised to the full what ghastly portent it was that held the grim attention of the Lord Chancellor and Guy de Travest. For, said

Dwight-Rankin, the flames of the twelve candles
on the whatdoyoucallem were one by one being
obscured before their very eyes, as by a presence
passing between them and the candles towards
the door; and as the presence passed on its way,
so each small flame was again visible.

"But I can't bear this!" sobbed Lady Surplice.
"What does it mean? Why doesn't someone
speak? Is this a time for silence?"

Slowly, slowly, the presence passed between
their eyes and the candles towards the door: the
eighth candle, the ninth, tenth, eleventh——

"Talbot, hold that door!" cried de Travest.

Someone laughed.

"Who laughed?" sobbed Lady Pynte.

Lord Marketharborough spoke: "What is this
absurdity, sir? Who the devil are you? Speak
up now!"

They saw the door-knob turn, they heard it
turn.

"Not so quickly!" cried de Travest. "We can't
let you go so quickly!"

"Gently, Guy, gently!" said Mr. Warp. "Let
him go. We can then discuss the matter at our
leisure."

They saw the door open, an inch, a little further. . . .

"The word 'devil,' " said a voice from the opening door, and the very voice, said Dwight-Rankin,
seemed to smile in a cold but charming way, "the
word 'devil,' my lord, comes very apt to this moment; and is, if you but knew it, more precisely
organic to the occasion than at any previous time
in the life which you have dedicated to me with

such high scholarship, iron principle and lofty ardour. But I must take this opportunity to protest," warmly continued the voice of Captain Charity, "against the present frivolous use of such major expletives as 'hell,' 'damnation' and 'devil.' They were created only for occasions of deep corruption, for moments of incredible baseness, for profound and monstrous annoyances, and, in particular, for use during times of inconceivable boredom. For instance, I might with propriety apply each one of them severally to different aspects of Lady Surplice's charming dinner-party; but courtesy forbids. I give you farewell, my lord, ladies and gentlemen."

"You might apply, sir! You give us farewell, sir! How, sir!" cried my Lord Marketharborough, who was not less fearless as a man than he was puissant as a lawyer. "And you dare to say, young man, that I have dedicated my life to you!"

" 'Tis a point that seems to me self-evident, Lord Marketharborough. Since when have you been taught in your schools that the laws, which you, my lord, so vigorously interpret, come from Jehovah? The only laws that Jehovah ever gave to the world were the tribal laws that may have been good enough for a pack of grubby Jews in the dawn of understanding but have been broken ever since at Satan's instigation by every self-respecting person: laws that encourage cruelty, exact poverty, condemn beauty, deride chivalry, proscribe joy, deplore elegance, and insist on a sordid and indiscriminate chastity. But was it Jehovah who gave you the divine consolation of Divorce? Or is it not He, the jealous God, who is ever so envious of Satan's suggestions for greater happiness between men and women that He has imbued His priests on earth with a ferocious enmity to everything that can untie a man and a woman from the intolerable ordeal of an unhappy union. Jehovah has given you the sword, the rack, pestilence, Christianity, The King's Proctor and Prohibition. Satan gave you the glorious beauty of Greece, the Pax Romana and the genius of invention. Jehovah gave you that ill-favoured lout, Martin Luther. Satan gave you Voltaire, who was a fallen archangel incarnate. Jehovah gave you the Cross. Satan gave you Chivalry. O Chivalry, poor broken-winged angel of light! She was the dark one's favourite child, but your dour civilisation of the past ten centuries has been maiming her until she now lies broken and dying, her tears washing over the ruins of the past, her soul agonised by visions of the holocausts of the future, her eyes set with despairing prayer only on the few scientists, inventors and artists who are the hope of this rapacious and saintly world."

The agreeable and scholarly voice of Mr. Warp broke the silence:

"Your utterances, sir, appear to me to show a decidedly anti-Semitic bias. Are you sure that is quite wise?"

"Socially, yes; politically, no. And I believe, Mr. Warp, that all good Englishmen have been accommodating themselves to that dilemma for the last fifty years. By inclination, however, I am naturally an anti-Semite, since Hebrew is the language current in Paradise."

"For pity's sake," said M. des Beaux-Aces, "don't say that English is the language current in Hell. They have already all the richest colonies."

"In the Scriptures," said Dame Warp bitterly, "it is written, if I remember aright, that persons with such unconventional views as yours are consigned forever with appropriate torments to a place which it ill befits a decent woman—I said a *decent* woman—to call Hell. I can see, however, no traces of the chastening effect of so proper a punishment in your form of address to people to whom you have been scarcely introduced. Indeed, you seem to be an unpleasantly self-assured young man."

"Gently, my love," Mr. Warp admonished her. "We are not yet precisely informed as to who the creature is. Should he be Lucifer himself a certain arrogance is permitted to him by the unanimous authority of all the best scholiasts. I incline to think, however, that he is only an inferior demon, such as plague the shrill imaginations of minor French agnostics and continually prick the Conservative Party into a senseless antipathy to Free Trade. But let us wait——"

The door, which had all this while been held ajar, closed sharply. De Travest started. Had the presence gone? Cries my Lord Marketharborough:

"Have you run away, you inferior demon you?"

"Dear me, no!" sighed the Other wearily. "But I must confess that I am astounded at the

ease with which you charming people put up
with this kind of thing night after night. You
might, I do assure you, just as well be locked in
the perpetual shadows of Eblis. But I suppose
I must stay until I have fulfilled my promise——"

"Your promise!" cried Lady Surplice. "What
promise? What is the dreadful man talking about
now?"

De Travest spoke sternly: "Sir, may I remind
you that we of our generation are not easily frightened by invisible presences, phantoms, imps,
ghosts, vampires and demons?"

"Oh, come!" laughed the Other. "Your generation, nay, your century, is more susceptible of
superstition than any that has gone before. It is
merely that you have altered the angle, and are
now enslaved by the meanest superstition of all,
which is common sense."

"That may or may not be," said the Lord Chancellor; "but may I point out to you, young man,
that it is considered neither polite nor manly to
sit at a lady's table only to distress her?"

"A lady?" said the Other.

"A lady, certainly!" snapped my lord.

"What lady?"

"Lady Surplice, sir."

"Well, she may be a lady," said the Other severely, "but she is certainly no gentlewoman."

"What!" cried Lady Surplice, her terror on the
instant supplanted by anger. "Are you referring
to me, you low man? Talbot! Where is Talbot?
Talbot, show this person the door! If you cannot see him, you can see the door. Open it."

"That will do, Lady Surplice!" said the Other

sharply; and now for the first time, said Dwight-
Rankin, the voice of him who called himself Captain Charity was informed with a degree of sever-
ity quite unusual in polite society. "You cannot
hope, Lady Surplice, with your worldly quips and
cunning impertinences, to impress one of my condition and experience. You forget that I, had I
no other claim to distinction, am the supreme
host of all time."

"You forget Jehovah, the Lord of Hosts," said
the Lord Chancellor, who had had a good education.

"My friend," said de Travest, "are you imp,
god, or devil? You are too self-confident for an
imp, you attach too much importance to your social position to be a god, so you are probably,
as Mr. Warp suggested, some inferior demon in
search of cheap distraction. What is your name,
fellow?"

"I am that which is so dark that beside me
darkness is radiance, and I am that which walks
in such brightness that I darken the sun and stars.
I am that which is stronger than God and more
enduring than stone, and I am that which is frailer
than a flower and more destructible than glass.
I am that which cannot be killed, and I am that
which dies a thousand deaths every day. I am the
spirit of man. But the interpreters of your God,
in their illiterate fulminations, have made my
name familiar to you under many vile disguises,
the better to sacrifice the spirit of man to the
savagery of mankind."

"Young man," said the Lord Chancellor severely, "are you seriously implying that you are the Prince of Darkness?"

"We do not recognise that title!" cried Lady Surplice. "Prince, indeed! It is not in Burke, Debrett or the Almanack de Gotha——"

"Under how many vile disguises, woman!"

"What I want to know is," said de Travest mildly, "why you insist on calling me Michael? since, you know, my name is Guy."

"Merely in moments of forgetfulness, de Travest. In appearance you remind me of one whom I once loved as a brother, in the days before time was. How calm and beautiful he was, in his golden cuirass and diamond helmet! Only my love for the beautiful archangels Michael, Gabriel and Raphael, kept me so long in subjection to the Lord of Hosts. But the time came when I, the most favoured captain of the empyrean, the prince of the hierarchy of archangels, with only the wings of the terrible and adorable choir of cherubim and seraphim between my eager youth and the thunderbolts of Jehovah, could no longer brook His ignorant and warlike complacency. As you have been taught, I raised the black standards of revolt; was at last defeated by Michael, Captain of the Hosts; and was plunged into Hell for eternity. I turned to Nature. I watched this planet come into being from the boiling elements. I watched this world's virginity. Then, after may æons, I observed the growth of mankind. At first I was appalled at the misery in store for these helpless creatures. Then, as I perceived mankind's blind will to live

and savage instinct to conquer, to acquire, to destroy, I lay for long ages in fear of the wretchedness in store for Nature, how it would be dese-
crated, perverted and ravished by these creatures
who could dominate all other animals merely because of an opposable thumb. I conceived a plan
to avert this calamity; and, walking the earth in
many shapes, I directed mankind to fulfil its most
childish dreams and to sink into Nature's bosom,
wherein only can be found true joy, true love, and
perfect peace. I succeeded. The Greeks were
beautiful because I taught them to adore beauty:
they made things of beauty because I taught them
to worship their own beauty: and the gods they
served were beautiful because they made their
gods after their own image. I nearly succeeded
with the Roman world. But my ancient enemy
sent the man Paul to revive the savagery in men
and women and to wither the love of Nature in
the hearts of children. Since then my enemy has
ruled the world. Yet, only the other day, I
thought I saw a fit opportunity for my beneficial
interference: with my heart afire with love of
mankind, which I have helped through so many
trials, I inspired certain noble minds with the
crusade of the League of Nations. But mankind
has preferred the dictates of its cruel God, the
Lord of Hosts, who has long since given up trying to govern men through Christianity and now
leads them by the nose with the childish superstition of common sense; and I have now no more
hope for the happiness of a world that will deride
the audacious gentleness of a Woodrow Wilson
and countenance the rapacious insolence of a

Poincaré, the vulgar dictatorship of a Mussolini, the unnatural charm of a Winston Churchill, and the complacent gracelessness of a gentleman who only too obviously rejoices in the name of Elihu Root."

The agreeable and scholarly voice of Mr. Warp broke the silence:

"Your utterances, sir, appear to me to show a decidedly anti-Chauvinist bias. For my part, since the invasion of the Ruhr by the French and the assault on Corfu by the Italians, I have never been able to think of Poincaré or Mussolini without a grave disorder of mind. May I ask, sir, if you favour the Liberal school of thought? We would be far from disdaining your assistance in our imminent campaign for convincing the people of the essential truths of Liberalism."

"I incline, if anything, to Labour, Mr. Warp; and hope to assist that party to very considerable success at your next elections; for, if I may say so, you cannot sweep a party out of existence for long by talking like a pack of silly schoolboys of biscuits, motor-cars and secret documents."

"Hear, hear!" said the Lord Chancellor, who had gone to sleep and was dreaming that he was listening to a speech against Prohibition.

"On the other hand," mildly said de Travest, "we are still awaiting an explanation of your sickening intrusion into Lady Surplice's house."

"Mrs. Amp sent me," said the Other wearily.

"Mrs. Amp!" cried Lady Surplice. "Mrs. Amp? That low woman!"

"How can you bring yourself to know such women?" said Dame Warp bitterly. "Particularly when, through sundry minor faults, there must be so many decent women—I said *decent* women—in your, well, environment."

"She amuses me," said Satan. "However," the voice went on, "as I have fulfilled my promise, I will now, with your permission, take my leave."

"But, Prince," cried Lady Surplice, "what was your promise? What have you fulfilled? What has that low woman to do with it? I insist on knowing, Prince. Is this a time for silence?"

"My promise was merely this, Lady Surplice. At a recent dinner-party of Mrs. Amp's, at which the guests of honour were Julius Cæsar, Shakespeare, Samuel Pepys, Balzac and myself, I was reckless enough to promise Mrs. Amp that I would ascend to earth one evening and spoil a dinner-party of yours. I will report to her, however, that a dinner-party so brilliant as yours would need the dulness of Jehovah himself to spoil it. *Monseigneur,* I give you farewell. Ladies, good-bye. *Adieu, caballeros!*"

"Stop, stop, stop!" cried Lady Surplice, frantically starting from her chair. "Just one moment, my dear Prince——"

"Well, just one," sighed the archangel of sin, "for I promised Mrs. Amp to be back in time to hear Napoleon's after-dinner speech on the intellectual obesity of soldiers, and successful soldiers in particular. What have you to say?"

"But am I to understand," cried my lady indignantly, "that this monstrous woman is allowed to give all the parties she likes in Hell?"

"Naturally, madam. Else why should it be called Hell?"

"Then," flashed my lady with a brilliant smile, "when I die, I shall also be able to give——"

"When you die, Lady Surplice, you will go to Heaven. For you are a good woman. You have a kind heart. You have cared for your husband and your children, and you have always given freely to the sick, the halt, the blind, the deaf and the dumb. In fact, Lady Surplice, I am very glad to have allowed myself this opportunity of congratulating you. You and your butler are perhaps the only two people in this room who will ascend to salvation. The odour of your sanctity already shames me, Lady Surplice. The saints in Paradise shall find in you a matchless companion. Talbot, the bosom of Abraham awaits you. I hope you will like it. Your only crimes, Lady Surplice, have been those of snobbery and vulgarity; and as the Bible was written before the existence of modern England, France and America, the very possibility of snobbery and vulgarity was unthought of, and thus they escaped inclusion among the heinous sins——"

"But look here," protested Guy de Travest, "what reason but cruelty can you have for altering Lady Surplice's destiny? It appears to me a gross case of prejudice, since, after all, Mrs. Amp has been allowed to ascend to Hell——"

"*De*scend, Guy," said the Lord Chancellor. "All authorities combine in agreeing that the movement, if any, is downwards."

"Mrs. Amp," said the Other wearily, "has a claim to my hospitality because she poisoned her husband. Now, upon my word, I really must go——"

"But you mustn't, you can't!" sobbed my lady in distraction. "Am I to understand that when I die I must go to Heaven—while all my friends, all these charming people, are enjoying themselves in Hell at Mrs. Amp's parties? Oh, is that just, Prince, is that reasonable, is it even gentlemanly?"

"You know, it really is not my fault," protested the Prince of Darkness. "It is the will of God. Good-bye, Lady Surplice. To you others I need only say *au revoir*, for you are all miserable sinners."

The company, said Dwight-Rankin, were sore distressed at Lady Surplice's plight, for the good lady was dear to them; and they would fain have done all they could to ease her mind as she whimpered, in an access of helplessness and despair: "Prince, cannot you—Oh!—can't you prevail on God to let me—Oh, dear!—to let me waive the distinction just this once? I simply can't face the idea of being parted from my friends—please, Prince, won't you be a dear and prevail on Him to——"

"Enough, madam!" thundered the voice of the fallen child of light. "Go you to salvation! Behold, am I not the enemy of Jehovah? These are my final words, Lady Surplice. Prepare yourself for your ascent. Let your soul yearn for Heaven and your spirit accommodate itself to the idea of walking forever in the groves of Paradise to the songs of the harp and the lyre. Begone!"

"Begone?" said the Lady Amelia indignantly. "That is a harsh word to give a lady in her own house!"

"Surely," snapped de Travest, "you are not so wanting in manners as to drink a lady's wine and then kill her!"

"What can I do, my friend? It is the immemorial curse of thirteen, and the super-added curse of the spilled salt. And I thought, as Lady Surplice is the only one among you who is going to Heaven, that it would be appreciated in me as an act of courtesy to allow her precedence in death."

"Please, may I say one word?" begged Shelmerdene, her eyes pitifully on the despairing face of her hostess. "I have been Muriel Surplice's friend for many years, she has on several occasions been very kind and good to me, and I cannot sit calmly by and watch her being wronged. Sir," said Shelmerdene to Satan, "this lady you would so recklessly consign to Heaven has committed a crime every bit as heinous as that for which Mrs. Amp is now suffering indigestion."

"A crime?" cried Lady Surplice gladly. "Bless you, Shelmerdene dear! But what crime was it?"

"Shelmerdene," said Satan gently, "are you mocking me? Was it to be mocked by you that I gave you charm, beauty and good sense, such a combination of virtues as never was known before? Was it to be mocked by you that I inspired a youth to give you a name which, although it is not your real name, becomes you better than any real name could?"

"This lady," cried Shelmerdene, "once had a lover——"

"Scarcely a crime," said Lucifer. "Heaven has long since given up rejecting women who have had lovers. The angels protested that they found none but plain women wherever they walked in Paradise."

"But she killed him!" cried Shelmerdene.

"Come, Shelmerdene!" said Dame Warp bitterly: "No decent woman—I said no *decent* woman—ever kills her lover."

"Shelmerdene, are you sure I did?" sighed Lady Surplice. "Are you quite sure, dear? Did I really kill him?"

"You did, darling, I assure you," said Shelmerdene. "You bored him to death. He begged me with his dying breath not to tell you, and I wouldn't have if I weren't so fond of you."

"Then," sighed the Prince of Darkness, "she may go to Hell."

And, said Dwight-Rankin, even as the door was seen to close, it was also seen how all colour was instantly ravished from Lady Surplice's face and how she sat in her chair still and cold. But even in death, said Dwight-Rankin, a smile of such happiness lit her face that her many friends, who never could think of her departure from among them but with the deepest regret, found solace in the certainty of the good lady's contentment in the other world. However. . . .

At the inquest it was naturally given out that Lady Surplice had died in some natural way: for who, asked Dwight-Rankin, would believe the tale of what had actually happened, who would believe the tale of him who called himself, with infinite mockery, Captain Charity? And who, continued Dwight-Rankin, would believe that, but for the kindly intervention of Shelmerdene, the spirit-

ual parts of poor Lady Surplice would even now
and forever be arranged in that position over the
ivory parapets of Paradise in which she could
most comfortably stare down, with intolerable
longing, at the social gaieties of another place?

"Who, indeed!" I echoed gloomily.

v

Dwight-Rankin fell silent. The restaurant was
emptying. Voices from distant tables approached
ours and perished against the wall of silence that
had risen upon the end of Dwight-Rankin's relation. I could say nothing. At last Dwight-Rankin said: "Had poor Lady Surplice been alive
now, she would have been staying at this very
hotel. I would have been lunching with her. At
this very moment I would have been enjoying a
cigar over a nice spot of brandy."

I ordered cigars and liqueurs. At that moment
a lady entered the restaurant. She appeared to
be a person of consideration. Waiters rushed
towards her, *maîtres d'hôtel* bowed down before
her. She waived them away. Her present concern appeared to have nothing to do with food,
although her proportions were not those of one
who had in the past indulged any aspirations to
asceticism. Her face was large and good-humoured. When she smiled, her face was very
large and very good-humoured indeed. She smiled
now, bearing down on Dwight-Rankin. Silence
perished around her. I prepared to fly. She enveloped the void about our table. The pearls
about her throat were larger than her eyes, but

her eyes shone more brilliantly than the diamonds on her hands. She strode into the silence like a warrior from Babel; and a forest of laughter stood on the site of the Ritz Hotel. She cried: "Dwight-Rankin! The very man I am looking for! Now I want you to be certain and come to——"

Dwight-Rankin indicated my presence.

"Mr.——" he said. "Mrs. Amp."

"Say, listen, that's not true! Mr.——, I certainly am glad to know you. How do you do, how do you do? You must come too, Mr.——. I have read your books. They are amazing, enchanting, universal. You are a genius. I tell the world so. I was telling the Duke of Mall and the Grand Duke Charles so only the other night. I said: 'He is a genius.' Now I want to tell you boys that to-morrow night I am throwing the finest party that has ever been dreamt of. It's going to be just great. You boys have just got to come. I'll tell the world that there's nothing that's not going to happen at that party. Muriel Surplice will be green. All her friends are coming. Everyone is coming. Say, listen, I have taken the whole Château de Madrid for the night and have changed it into a Venetian lagoon and at midnight I have engaged just the most complete circus to come and amuse us, as my point is, boys, that when one goes on a party one should just have everything from Mah Jongg to marmosets——"

She went, at last.

Dwight-Rankin said dreamily: "Have a spot of brandy?"

I choked. "You dare!" I said. "You dare to

sit there and talk to me about spots of brandy after having palmed off on me that abominable rigmarole——"

"But it might have happened," said Dwight-Rankin dreamily, waving a hand around the restaurant. "Perhaps it will happen. It certainly ought to happen. To all these charming people. Even lions will turn. However. . . ."

The end of the book called May Fair, in which are told the last adventures of These Charming People.